Excursions
with the Chief

SEAN SIVERLY

PAGE PUBLISHING, INC.
New York, NY

First originally published by Page Publishing, Inc. 2018

ISBN 978-1-64350-538-1 (Paperback)
ISBN 978-1-64350-539-8 (Digital)

Printed in the United States of America

It is good to have an end to journey toward; but it is the journey that matters in the end.

—Ursula K. Le Guin

Never go on trips with anyone you do not love.

—Ernest Hemingway

I've been to Paradise, but I've never been to me.

—Charlene

There is something beautiful to find when ...

"Dammit. Scratch that."

There is nothing more beautiful to be found when ...

"Geez. Scratch that too. Why is this so difficult?"

When one seeks this trove of not only visual but complete sensory delights, they will discover that there is nothing more beautiful to be found on this Earth, nothing that can compare to such an experience. Upon departure, it's certain that a feeling of longing will envelope the traveler. They can return home and resume normal life, but the almost spiritual pull and undeniable mystique of this haven for the soul will certainly remain with them; filling their dreams for years to come ... or until they return to begin their next adventure.

"Finally. Let me read this back ..."

"*Really?* What the hell did I just ...? It sounds completely fake. What kind of a ...? Who truly says this shit: "a feeling of longing will envelope the traveler?" or "almost spiritual pull and undeniable mystique"?

"Jesus. This sounds like a forced art critique. This sucks. I give up. I can't write this damn thing."

"I need a break. Better yet—I need a drink."

My focus was shot. I closed my notebook and stood up from the desk. I didn't have a deadline to meet per se, but my publisher did want to see *something* of worth in the next few days. So far, I had a hell of a lot of pomp and zero circumstance to give him. I needed to step away from this and loosen up. I thought about the drink. That sounded quite good and probably just the thing to get me over this hurdle.

My hotel room was dark. I'd drawn the heavy curtains closed to help isolate me and my thoughts. I peeked through the drapes. I was struck harshly by a sharp beam of sunlight. What the hell time was it, anyway? I looked at my watch. It had stopped. I'd turned the small clock in the room around where I couldn't see it. I walked to the nightstand and spun the clock. The time showed 4:35 p.m. *Perfect,* I thought. It seemed just the right time to grab a bite to eat and that drink—then get back to work.

I picked up my notebook and left my room.

I made my way to the hotel restaurant, found a table, and ordered food. I ordered a sandwich called the San Franciscan: grilled ham and an exotic cheese blend on sourdough bread.

As I waited for my early dinner to arrive, I read through what I'd written. It still sounded ridiculous. The words just weren't right, but that was what I did—I wrote ludicrous statements about places to entice people to go and see them. I was a salesman for locales and landmarks. I made them sound outlandish and wonderful, whether they were or not.

I'd been to all the places I'd written about, and although I'd enjoyed most of them, some needed to be embellished and their aesthetic recreated. In short: they were lame, and I found them a waste of time. Yet what I'd said about them made them *the* place to be. I was a part-time liar. Then again—what writer isn't?

My food arrived, and the waiter asked if there was anything else he could get me.

"Yes," I said. "I was wondering what 'adult beverage' specials you have going at the moment."

"Well, sir," he said, "the bar doesn't officially start serving alcohol until 6:00 p.m. I'm sorry about the inconvenience."

I looked at the clock. "No, that's okay," I said. "I can wait forty-five minutes."

The waiter smiled. He began to walk away, but stopped and spoke, "Sir, if you don't want to wait till six, there are a few local pubs only steps away from the hotel."

"Thank you for the info," I said. "I may swing out to one of them."

"Do you need anything else right now?" he asked.

I thought for a second. "Yes," I said. "The check—and a to-go box."

I'd decided to hit one of the locals near the hotel. I took my food back to my room and put it in the refrigerator. I contemplated leaving my notebook behind. *No,* I thought. *Take it ... you just never know.*

I walked outside and into the dry heat of the city. I was in Sacramento, California—in August. It was hotter than hell. I'd traveled here from Crater Lake in Oregon. It was mild and a bit chilly there with a little snow remaining from winter. Suffice it to say, the climate change was immense.

I was happy to be in Sacramento. I could say I was happy to have been to Crater Lake as well. It was indeed awe-inspiring, but it was now giving me fits. *Forget it.* I didn't want to focus on where I was or where I'd been. I wanted to focus on where I was *going:* to the bar—to get a drink.

There were a few places along the block but none that truly struck me. I don't know why I was being so particular. I just wanted a drink. Maybe it was my *artistic temperament?* I was still so hung up on the *overly visionary* attempts at my article, I couldn't help but wonder if this was guiding my search for a watering hole. I kept going; however, I thought about returning to the hotel.

Just as I was about to turn around, I spied a little place. It was quite literally a hole in the wall. The front door was propped open, and the entryway was pushed back farther than the others along the same façade. It was the only establishment with no windows, and the structure wasn't much wider than the doorway itself.

From the street, it looked dark inside. However, there was a ruddy glow that softly floated deep toward the back of the entryway. Above the door frame was a small, worn, hammered brass plaque that simply read "Tavern." No overstatement there. No fanfare, pomp, or pretense, and above all, no bullshit. I found my place!

I strolled into the Tavern and was surprised at how large it was inside. *Surely, there must be a lot of mirrors or something to create such an illusion of space,* I thought. There was nothing of the sort. It was truly a nice, open area—very misleading.

There were a few people in random spots, enjoying drinks and talking quietly. There was a red-felt pool table along the wall opposite the bar. A sign above read "No Betting, No Fighting, and No Six-Ball." Since I'd never heard of a game called *Six-Ball,* I was under the impression that the six-ball itself was missing.

I took a seat at the bar next to a couple of other people; however, I was not here to mingle or socialize, I was here to order a drink and—at least for a little while—not think too hard. I was hoping that the drink would help bring me back to a reality that was a little less forced and fake.

I scanned the fare and decided what I was having. Strong but refreshing was of the utmost importance. I waved the bartender over.

"Can I get a tall scotch and soda?" I asked.

The bartender raised an eyebrow. "How tall do you want it?" he asked.

"Two and a half shots of scotch and eight ounces of Perrier over ice," I said. "*That* tall."

The bartender gave me a half-grin and shook his head. He showed me a highball glass.

"So you want one of these then?" he asked.

"Yes. That's it," I said.

I looked around the bar again. I checked out the patrons and admired the decor. Everything was a dark red wood and highly glossed. The lighting was typical of a bar of this ilk. It was dimly illuminated by the soft lights in the ceiling—a stark contrast to the bright, track-style lights beaming down over the bar itself.

I traced circles with my fingers on the bar top. The bartender gave me a look. He didn't seem too happy that I was smearing the fine polish on the wood.

I watched as the bartender worked. He pulled a bottle of Famous Grouse Scotch from the shelf and poured two and half perfect shots over the cracked ice in the glass. He finished off the tall libation with effervescent mineral water, garnished it with a lime wedge, and served it up.

I raised my glass to the bartender and thanked him. He nodded.

I took a quick sip from the glass and was hit with the cool, strong, perfectly blended bite of the drink. It was wonderful.

I watched the beads of condensation slowly glide down the side of the glass. I tried to go back to my work—or at least to the *idea* of it. The gentle trickle of the sweat on the glass made me think of tropical rain on a window. I took another drink. *Damn, this is good!*

As I sat contemplating what I was going to do next, I heard a gruff, husky, and somewhat belligerent voice at the end of the bar. I didn't look in the direction of the voice.

"Hey! *Churchill!*" the brash voice shouted. "Why did you serve me this old cup of piss, you Limey bastard?"

The bartender walked toward the voice.

"Dammit, *Chief,* I told you to stop calling me that," he said. "I'm not freakin' British, and I didn't serve you a cup of piss. You've been drinking the same beer for an hour. It's just warm—and you ordered the worst suds I have on tap."

The voice shouted again. "Say what you will, but I've been around. I know bad beer from piss—and *this* is piss!"

"If you keep this up, Chief, you're going to run off my regulars," the bartender said.

"What 'regulars?' I am your fucking regular!"

"Language, Chief. *Language.* You can be here as long you want—as long as *you're civil,* okay? Otherwise, it's the old *heave-ho.*"

This bar must have been a haven to this loud, boisterous cuss. As soon as the bartender offered the choice of "pipe down—or pack up," the voice changed, becoming compliant and apologetic.

I called the bartender over to get the skinny.

"Who is that guy?" I asked.

"Oh, that's the Chief," the bartender said. "He's been coming here for a while. He's just a crazy old man with a lot of bullshit stories to tell."

"Why do you call him *Chief*? Was he in the navy, or a fireman or something?"

"Not that I know of. He just told me and everyone else in here to call him that, so we do."

"Why does he call you 'Churchill'?"

The bartender pointed to a dark corner of the bar. There was an obscured Union Jack flag hanging on a wall next to some old British World War II posters. I had to squint to notice them.

"That's why," he said.

"How does anyone even see that?" I asked.

"I don't know, but the Chief—he sees damn near everything."

"Does it bug you that he calls you that?"

"Nah, it ain't my name, but I do smoke Winstons—go figure."

I finally looked over at the Chief. What I saw was a burly man, slightly hunched on the bar and staring at his "cup of piss." I detected a rugged look. He was world-weary but not worn out. His hair was close-cropped on the sides and back, a thick tuft of white, wavy curls on top. It was a classic look: pure 1940s and absolutely rebellious.

He was wearing a light button-down shirt with the sleeves rolled to the elbow. His trousers were dark brown, and his shoes were worn black leather—they must've had a million miles on them.

He looked dignified but slightly disheveled. If anything, I found him interesting. The bartender made him seem even more so. I wanted to chat with him. However, as a rule, I never approached strangers, especially drunk, old men.

As I took another drink of my warming, slightly weakening drink, the old man started toward me. It looked like I was going to talk to him anyway, whether I'd actually wanted to or not.

His figure became more intimidating the closer he got. He seemed large when he was sitting down, but this man was foreboding standing up. He was tall, solid, and strong-looking but drooping in the midsection where most men his age would. He smelled of alcohol—but not *booze* alcohol. It was as if he'd raided the men's grooming section of the local drugstore and sampled every bottle on the shelf.

The old man—the Chief—took a seat next to me at bar. He didn't say a word, nor did he look at me at first. I tried to shrink away, but I couldn't. I wasn't sure what to do. I had wanted to engage in conversation with him before, but that was from afar. He was here now, and I felt uncomfortable.

"Chief, go easy on my customer," Churchill warned. "This is a new guy. I don't want you running him off. He's a scotch drinker."

"I won't hurt him too bad," the Chief said. "I just want to find out what he's heard from the boys overseas."

I was confused. I had no idea what he meant by that statement. Apparently, Churchill did. He chuckled and winked at me. He spied my glass nearly empty and made me another drink.

I finally looked at the Chief. I got a better view of him. He didn't seem *quite* as rugged and brash as I'd thought. I was still slightly intimidated, though.

"Sir, let me buy you a drink," I said. "Something that's not 'piss.'"

The Chief slapped the bar top.

"That'll do just fine," he said. "Churchill, give me a glass of your best ale and put on this lad's tab. Hope you brought your checkbook, son."

I smiled. I didn't know if he was serious or not—about anything. I wanted to ask this man a question, but I didn't know where to start. I was not adept at initiating conversation of any sort. Mine was a life of writing and very little talking.

Churchill served us our drinks, and I held mine up in a toast. The Chief did the same. This was our icebreaker.

"Cheers!" we said as we clinked our glasses together. The Chief swilled down half his beer and slammed the thick glass mug on the table.

"That's much better!" the Chief bellowed. "Top me off, Churchill."

Churchill filled the mug but left a little foam head at the top. This aggravated the Chief slightly.

"See that, kid?" he whispered. "That son of a bitch tried to stiff me on the beer."

"Actually, sir, he's stiffing me," I said half-joking.

"Damn it, you're right!"

The Chief called for Churchill. He then proceeded to embarrass the hell out of me.

"Churchill," he said. "My friend is picking up this tab and paying your bills so you can keep this dive open, and you do this to him?"

"What did I do now, Chief?" Churchill asked.

"Consider this glass to be a woman," he said, tapping on the mug. "She needs to be filled completely—to her apex. Instead, you just slip a little head in. What's the matter with you?"

"That's quite all right," I said, my face reddening.

"Oh, no—it is not all right, son," the Chief claimed. "You know, I think Churchill is trying to say we're a couple of *bandits*."

"What does that mean?"

"Ol' Churchill is trying to ease the tip in. Oh, that limey—he can be such a bugger."

By now, I was flushed beyond belief; my face stinging from humiliation.

"Oh my God ..." I said.

"Don't worry, man," Churchill said. "This is just what he does."

I took a long gulp from my freshly made scotch and soda. I'd just come to this bar to relax and put a hammer to my writer's block. Now I was dealing with—and picking up the tab for—a cantankerous, loud old man, watching his interplay with an American nicknamed Churchill, all while discovering a possible case of my own latent homosexuality. I probably needed to get back to my room and back to work. That wasn't going to happen just yet.

"Well, since you're buying me drinks," the Chief said. "Perhaps you ought to tell me your name, right?"

I chuckled nervously and said, "My name is Louis DeCarlo." I held out my hand for the Chief to shake.

"DeCarlo, eh? That sounds *Eye-tal-yan*," the Chief noted. "You know what they say about Italians, right?"

"I've heard some things," I said, dreading what he might say next.

"Well then, you know. I'm not going to burden you with known facts."

Thank you so much, I said to myself.

"Louis, eh? So do they call you Louie?" the Chief inquired.

"No. No one's called me that," I said.

"Well, they do now—or at least I do," the Chief said. "Louie, welcome to Churchill's Scourge of London Tavern. My home until I get thrown out."

The Chief grabbed my hand and shook it firmly.

"You live here?" I asked.

"Only between eleven a.m. to close," Churchill said. "The rest of the time, he doesn't really exist."

It must've been an inside joke between these two men, but I thought that was a terrible thing to say.

"Where do you hail from, Louie?" the Chief asked. "What port of call do you drop anchor?"

"I'm from Atlanta, Georgia, originally," I said. "But I grew up in Southern California. I live in Valdosta, Georgia, now."

"Ah, so you're Southern all around. *Is it true what they say about Dixie?*"

"Is what true?"

"*Does the sun really shine all the time?* You know, magnolias, possums—all that?"

"I guess. I haven't … Is that a real song?"

"You should know it—it's by one of your countrymen: Mr. Dino Crocetti."

"I'm not familiar with that name."

"Sure you are, he hung out and drank with Mr. Francis Sinatra and the rest of those bums."

"Oh, you mean *Dean Martin?*" I asked.

Churchill chimed in. "You know, kid—he'll do this to you all night," he said. "You buy him drinks and he'll mess with your head."

13

Churchill looked at the Chief and back to me and said, "He should've been a broad. Ain't that right, Chief? You would've made a fine broad."

The Chief scowled at Churchill. "No, I would've made a fine *lesbian*," he said. "I like pussy too much to be a *regular* broad."

The Chief spied my notebook. "So what's your line, son?" he asked. "What do you do to keep yourself busy and keep your country moving?"

"I'm a writer. I write 'travelogues,'" I said. "I talk about things to see and do at certain places, while instilling an air of adventure and romance to them."

"Do you write for *Condé Nast* or something?" the Chief asked.

"No. I'm freelance. I've only been doing it for a short time," I said.

"Are you any good?"

"I don't know. I've never met anyone who's read one of my articles."

"Are you planning on writing about *Churchill's* Tavern and all the adventure and romance that abounds here?"

I laughed at his comment. "No, but what's in this notebook is why I'm here," I said.

"Well, son, why not give me a try?" the Chief offered. "I've seen a lot, and I'm a damned tough sell. If you can woo me with your words, then you're a hell of a writer. Let's see what you've got."

I opened the notebook to the page I'd been working on. I felt apprehensive about showing a perfect stranger what I'd written—worse because it was something I was struggling with. Then I thought, *Perfect strangers read my words all the time. It's how I make my living. Yes, but you don't get to see their reaction. True, but they can't be anywhere near as obnoxious as this guy.*

The Chief read the lines. It was taking him quite a while to get through them. He grumbled a little and took a sip of his beer. He cleared his throat and continued reading.

When he finally set the notebook down, he closed it hard. I felt as if the slamming of the cover was akin to slamming the coffin lid on my career. I was scared to hear what he had to say.

"Not bad," he said. "It's a bit chimerical and over-romanticized but not bad."

I smiled and breathed a quick sigh of relief.

"Where is this place?" the Chief asked.

"Crater Lake," I said.

"Crater Lake? *Oregon?*"

"The very same."

"Well, son, this is good stuff, but it ain't about Crater Lake," he stated. "You write this kind of fluff and polish about places like Seychelles, or Bora Bora—not some old volcano filled with frigid water in Oregon."

"And that's my problem," I said. "This is what I do. And lately, I just don't believe in what I'm writing."

"You're an artist, Louie," the Chief said. "You make it all up to make it look good. You're not supposed to fall in love with it. You leave that to the people you're trying to bullshit."

I was taken aback by what the Chief said. It was crass but made perfect sense.

"I've been around, son, and I've seen a lot," the Chief shared. "I know why you're struggling with your work."

"*Why?*" I asked, excitedly. I was hoping to hear some great wisdom that would instantly solve my dilemma.

"Because, Louie, you're struggling with *yourself,*" he said. "You're talking about places you've gone but haven't really *explored*. It's all pretty pictures and five-dollar words, but there's no *soul* to it."

I sipped my drink. *Goddammit*, he was right. I felt transparent. This crotchety old boozer saw right through me. He knew me completely, while I didn't even have a clue as to why he was called Chief.

I began to think, I could go to sleep tonight, wake up tomorrow, and start over. I'd take the Chief's advice and try to put some "soul" into my article. I could do a better job from now on. I could do a lot of things. I just couldn't leave this place—not yet. I had to know more.

The Chief had secrets and I wanted him to reveal them to me. I wanted to know where he'd been, what he'd seen, and the things he'd done. I wanted to know everything about him, just as he knew everything about me.

"Chief, could you tell me some of the places you've been?" I asked.

"It's not where I've been, Louie," he said. "It's what I've *experienced*. That's the difference between us. You've *been* places. I've *embraced* them."

Churchill drew the Chief another beer, made me another scotch and soda, and pulled himself a half mug of suds. He looked at us with great intent.

"I can't wait to hear this," he said with a laugh. "Now I get to find out how full of shit you really are Chief."

"I ain't full of anything but love, compassion, and beer," the Chief said. "I've got a few tales to tell. Where do you want me to start?"

"Where's the first place you remember going?" I asked.

"Cuba," the Chief said. "That's the first place I ever went."

"Damn!" I said. "When was this?"

The Chief didn't hesitate. "Nineteen forty," he said. "It was the place to be. Goddammit, I loved it there."

"What did you do there?" I asked.

"Everything, Louie," he claimed. "It was a beautiful island with the most amazing people. They'd gone through a lot of shit. They were ready to relax. They made that place a paradise."

The Chief continued to talk about the wonders of Cuba. The more he talked, the more I could feel I was there. I could smell the salt air on the beach and see the teal waters extend and change to deep blue. I could hear the palm fronds as they waved gently in the wind. I was suddenly in Old Havana, drinking rum with a few local friends; each of us on the lookout for Ernest Hemingway. *Pilar* had been spotted sailing nearby. The fishing was good today! Certainly "Papa" would be coming ashore soon to join us for drinks.

"Cuba was where I lost my virginity," the Chief said. "Oh, yes ... to a beautiful young *jeva*. Her name was Mariposa De Las Flores—*Butterfly of the Flowers*."

Churchill and I watched in awe as the Chief told us about his deflowering by the Butterfly of the Flowers. His face changed. He did not smile. However, the ruggedness of his skin softened, and his eyes gleamed. He looked younger—and by *younger*, I mean he looked like he was eighteen again.

"Gentlemen, this woman gave me my manhood," the Chief said dreamily. "I could spend my whole life saying the words but never truly thank her enough. To make love to a beauty such as her—only a few can claim that they have. I was one of them. *I was the first.*

"She had skin so soft—brown like gingerbread. It smelled and tasted just as spicy and sweet. And her hair? You could wrap yourself up and get lost in it. It was a web of wonder and magnificence: black as night and just as mysterious. Flowing and shimmering like the most majestic waterfall.

"Her eyes were clear and green, like a hidden garden pond. Looking into them was looking straight into heaven. You could see your destiny in those eyes. Her lips were full and always parted. They were sultry and soft. When she kissed me, I felt she could pull the soul right out of my body. Such passion—such intensity."

I couldn't speak for Churchill, but I myself had fallen in love with this girl.

The Chief was not done telling us about his beautiful Mariposa.

"I remember the first time we made love," he said. "We found ourselves a secluded spot on a beach. I know that sounds cliché, but that's where it happened.

"It was a beautiful night. The sky was filled with stars, and there was no moon out to obscure them. The waves were breaking softly in the distance, and the palm fronds were lightly tapping out a rhythm in the breeze. These sounds were creating a sonata for us. It was impossible to ignore the signals this night had given us.

"We fell into each other's arms and onto the sand. We kissed like lovers and the concerto played on. The music was getting louder as our desires got stronger."

The Chief took a long drink of his beer and resumed his story.

"I undressed her slowly," he said. "She was as delicate as her name. She was a gift from God Himself. To make haste in this moment was to commit a most unforgivable sin.

"When I first saw her naked body, I wept. How could I—some young punk kid from Chicago be blessed with such a glorious treasure? I didn't deserve her, but she was truly mine and here for me to love.

"My eyes adored her body—so perfect and divine. Her breasts were full, round, and irresistible. When I touched them ... oh, gentlemen ... I dare not speak of the sensations they invoked. Those are between me, her, and the Lord God."

The Chief suddenly stopped talking. He closed his eyes tight and breathed deep. He looked as if he was about cry. It would certainly be justified if he had.

"Where was I?" he asked. "Oh, yes ... in Cuba ... and with *mi hermosa Mariposa ...*"

The Chief stopped again. Churchill and I still sat awestruck, but he was done with his story. We wanted to hear more, but there was no more—at least not that he would share. He'd been with this girl sixty-six years ago. I swear he could *still* feel her wrapped around him.

This was one of the most beautiful stories I'd ever heard—*and it was real.* There was no way he could make it up, not with all the passion and emotion he'd conveyed in retelling it. This was what I wanted to be able to do.

I wanted to not only convince people of what I was saying, but make them feel it as well—as if they were there and in the moment. It was only a great storyteller who could instill such feeling and realism into their words. The Chief did it. I wanted him to teach me how.

The Chief and I sat quietly and drank. I drained the last of mine, while the Chief slowly nursed his as if he'd never get another.

The Chief stared into the mirror behind the bar. The age in his face had returned. He was no longer young, and the man looking back at him was tired and heartbroken.

"Chief, could you tell me about some of the other places you've been?" I asked.

"Not today, Louie," he said coldly. "Those are different stories for different times."

I could tell the Chief was not here. His body was on the barstool next to me, but his mind, heart, and soul were still in Cuba, and he was still making love to his beloved Mariposa.

Churchill asked me if I was ready for another drink.

"I'll have what the Chief's drinking," I said.

"This is my top shelf ale," Churchill claimed. "It's the Chief's favorite."

"Really?" I asked. "Then why do you serve him the 'piss'?"

"Because the 'piss' is what he orders. He's broke and can't afford the good stuff. I don't mind serving him. I just have to keep it on the cheap when he can't pay his tab."

"Don't worry about that. I've got his tab tonight."

Churchill smiled. "Nope, Lou," he said. "I've got this tonight."

I thanked Churchill for grabbing the check. I wasn't sure what the rest of the night held for any of us, but I did know I wanted to stay in this bar for as long as possible. I could say that there was some divine, magic force that drew me into this place earlier, but that would be a lie. What drew me in was the simplicity of it all. The unassuming nature of what I saw from the street. I had no idea that I'd be entering such a complex world. A world that was full of great drinks, interesting people, and incredible life lessons.

I looked at the Chief. I felt sad that once I left this bar, I'd never see him again. I wanted to mine his wisdom and hear more of his adventures. His step back to Cuba was overwhelming. This man had seen so much, and I wanted to hear about it. More than anything, I wanted to know how to be like him. I wanted him to impart his knowledge on me and help me create lush landscapes with my words.

"Chief, I want to thank you for sharing your beautiful story," I said. "I've never heard anything like it before. I only wish I could deliver such passion and truth into what I tell others."

The Chief looked at me. "You can," he said. "You just need to find what's missing."

"How do I do that?" I asked.

"By *going beyond.* By forgetting what you're *told* to do and doing what you know is right."

"How do I 'go beyond'?"

The Chief turned to me. "A lot of people travel to see sights or art or hear music," he said. "Hell, some people travel the world just to sample food. Now those people might be satisfied with a meal, a museum, or a mausoleum, but they're not *seekers.* Seekers need to know more. Seekers go beyond. They become a part of where they are. They immerse themselves in the culture, get to know the people. That's the only way you can experience a place and all it encompasses."

The Chief was right, and I knew it. He'd said it himself: what I did was good, but it was "bullshit." I didn't want to be a bullshitter anymore. I wanted to be a "seeker." I wanted to "go beyond."

"Louie, when you leave this place tonight, I hope you'll remember the things I've said," the Chief implored.

"I will. Most definitely," I said. "You've opened my eyes and my mind. I'm going to truly be a *seeker*—and not just a *speaker.*"

"Of course you could leave here and tell everyone you spent half a night with some drunk-ass old roustabout," the Chief said. "That sounds pretty good too. And it ain't a lie!"

I laughed at the Chief's assessment of himself. Earlier in the evening, this man scared me, but now I was seeing a different person. I found myself wanting to be like him the more time I spent in his company.

"Where do you go from here, me boy?" the Chief asked.

"Home for a couple of weeks," I said. "Then off to a new place and a new story."

"Well, I'll be right here," the Chief said sadly. "Maybe not in this same spot, but in this same bar. Ol' Churchill and I trading jabs. Him calling me a damn liar and me calling him a no-good, crumpet-stuffing son of a bitch."

I looked at the Chief. "You know Churchill's not really British, right?" I said.

"Yeah, I know," he said. "But if I didn't fuck with him about it, I'd have nothing to say to him except *thanks*. Where's the fun in that?"

I smiled and shook my head. Churchill asked if we were getting another round. The Chief drained his beer, and suddenly, I felt one more was in order for us. Churchill pulled two more ales, and the Chief and I drank them.

"I wish I didn't have to leave," I said to the Chief. "It's been great chatting with you and hearing your stories."

"I only told you one," he said. "And it was just about screwing on the beach."

"That cheapens the romance a bit, don't you think?"

"I'm an old man. Romance ain't what it used to be. And that was a long damn time ago. Hell, I don't even think I can fuck anymore."

"That's a terrible thought to have."

"It's worse when it's a reality. So far it isn't. At least I don't think so."

"Maybe you need a date?"

"That's rich, Louie. A date! Do you see any date-worthy trim in this place?"

"Here? No. You ought to go out and find a woman."

"Kid, I'm eighty-four fucking years old. Courting a dame at my age is tough on the *everything*. I can't even get a hooker. If I did, she'd probably pay me to keep my withered old tallywhacker away from her!"

I didn't know if I was supposed to laugh, cry, or stay quiet about the Chief's comments. They were funny but sad as well. It was difficult to listen to him talk this way after he'd painted such a beautiful scene of his virility and desire as a young man. I watched him take a drink. The look on his face epitomized heartbreak. I couldn't help but wonder if by telling the story of Mariposa, he may be longing not only for her but for everything else he felt he could never have again. I could feel tears welling in my eyes.

The Chief lightly drummed his fingers on the bar top.

"Goddammit!" he said loudly. "You're right, Louie. I need to get out of this place—just for a day."

"I'm sure Churchill will save your seat," I commented.

"He has to," he said. "I'm the only reason this place stays open."

The Chief laughed. "Yes, son, I need to get out and see something. *Do something*," he said. "I'm telling you how to get yourself together and here I am falling apart."

I wanted to help the Chief. Perhaps I could take him somewhere? I tried to think of something—some way to ask the Chief if he would be interested in my company for a day outside of the Tavern.

Then it happened: I was struck by the proverbial bolt out of the blue.

"Chief, I have an idea—a proposition, actually," I said. "It's probably going to sound just as weird to hear as it will be for me to say."

"You've got my ear, Louie," he responded.

"Why don't you come with me?" I offered.

"Where?"

"Why don't you leave with me when I go home?"

"What? To Valdosta? What am I going to do in Valdosta, Georgia?"

"That's not what I mean."

"Spill it kid. Put your words to good use."

"Travel with me. Let's go on some *adventures*. Let's be *seekers*."

The Chief looked at me like I was crazy.

"You want to drag my grizzled old ass all over the place?" he asked. "Where the hell are we gonna go and how will we get there?"

"I've got a rental car," I said. "I don't need to be anywhere for the next two weeks. We can leave tomorrow."

"I don't get it. Why don't you just drive me around town or something?"

"I thought about that. But I think we need to do more. I think something like this would do us both a world of good."

"Maybe you're right, kid, but I'm hell to deal with."

"Any worse than you were earlier? I can handle that."

The Chief laughed hard and smacked his hand on the bar. The thud of his palm on the bar top resonated throughout the room. Everyone jumped at the sound.

"Well, I don't know where you came up with this idea, but I like it," he said. "It's a damn fine idea. You've brought a little warmth to this old, dark heart, Louie."

Churchill drew two more ales and set them on the bar.

"I have to tell you, I can't take you to Cuba," I said, as I continued formulating my idea.

"Nobody's going to Cuba these days," the Chief said. "That pinko Castro ruined it for us all."

I nodded contemplatively.

"So where are we going, kid?" the Chief inquired. "This is a damn big country. We can't just drive to random places."

"That's the tough part," I said. "We need to find a way to pick our locales. It has to be a simple method. Something we can agree on."

"Well, think, Louie. Your brain is probably better at problem-solving than mine is."

I couldn't think of anything that made sense. I didn't know what I was doing now. The whole idea was starting to sound and seem ridiculous. Maybe I needed to forget it all, return my rental, and fly home as I'd planned. No. I really wanted to do this—crazy as it was. I know the Chief wanted to as well.

"Did you come up with anything yet?" he asked.

"No. Nothing that makes sense or is easy," I lamented.

I looked around. I scanned the bottles of booze along the wall behind the bar. The bolt from the blue hit me a second time.

"I've got it!" I exclaimed. "The booze will give us the answer."

"It always does," the Chief commented. "How's it work for this?"

"Pick a bottle," I said. "The first letter of its name will help us narrow things down."

"Easy enough," the Chief said. He pointed at a bottle. "Evan Williams—he's our man."

"That worked better than I thought," I said, surprised. "So how do we do this? Do we go with the first name or last?"

"Mr. Williams's name in this case is both a proper name and a brand. We're addressing him here by brand, which would be Mr. Williams's Christian name—so first letter."

I smiled uneasily. "Chief, are you sure *E* is good?" I asked.

"It's what we agreed on," he stated. "As per the terms of the game."

"Yeah, but it seems so …" I paused. "Well … *E.*"

"And this is where our adventure begins."

"What do you mean?"

"You're worried about a letter. This is the first challenge. You overcome it by simply finding places that begin with *E*. From there, we face everything else to come."

"Sounds reasonable."

"It is. You can't begin to learn about something if your first inclination is to change it before you even start. There's plenty of places that begin with *E*, Louie. We'll be fine."

Locales were bouncing in my head: Europe, England, Ecuador, etc. However, we were traveling by car; our destinations needed to be within a day's drive of each other. I began to wonder, how exciting is that really going to be? If I was having writer's block here, I'm sure I'd have it in Enid, Oklahoma, as well.

I ordered two more beers. The Chief and I proceeded to tell Churchill of our plans.

"You mean you're going to take this belligerent old fossil off my hands for a while?" Churchill joked. "You can't be serious. Who am I going to threaten to kick out of here?"

"It's true," I said. "We decided we both needed the trip."

"Where are you going to?"

"Points on the map that begin with *E*."

"How did you decide on that?"

"Blame Evan Williams."

"Do you have any idea what you're in for, Lou? The Chief can be a real bastard."

The Chief chimed in. "Only to you Churchill," he said. "Louie's all right in my book. We'll get on fine."

Churchill laughed and shook his head. "Best of luck to you both," he said. "You guys are absolutely nuts, but I think it's a grand idea."

"We'll send you postcards from where we stop," I said.

"Yeah, and we'll tell you all about the great bars we're drinking in," the Chief opined.

"I'm sure you can get a cup of piss at any one of them, Chief," Churchill retorted.

"When are you boys shoving off on this excursion?" Churchill asked.

"We're planning on leaving tomorrow," I said.

"That's … soon!"

"It is, but it makes sense. Why prolong it?"

"How you going?"

"I-80 East until I get tired and we find a town that starts with *E*."

"Like I said, you guys are absolutely nuts."

I wasn't sure how this cockamamie journey was going to go. I didn't even know if the Chief had a change of clothes handy. I'd just met the man a few hours ago, and here I was spiriting him away on a semirandom jaunt across the country.

For as far-fetched as it all seemed, this was going to be a trip for the ages; I just knew it. I don't know if it was going to help me become a poet of the travelogue, but I did know it was going to make me a better person. That was more important than anything.

"Chief, I have a couple of questions," I said.

"Ask away," he replied.

"Do you have everything you need to travel?"

"I do. And if I don't have it, I can get it on the way. That's one question. What's the other?"

"Do you have a place to stay for the night?"

Churchill spoke up. "Lou, I've got him tonight. You just worry about yourself."

"Thank you, Chur …" I paused. "What is your name, really?"

"It's Arthur," he said.

I told the Chief I was leaving for the night. When I saw his face, the youthful look he had earlier had returned enough to be noticeable.

"You seem happy I'm leaving, Chief," I said with a laugh.

"No, Louie," he said. "I'm happy I'm getting a chance to get back out there. I'm happy to be leaving *with* you."

"Speaking of that, what time should we leave in the morning?"

"I'll be ready to shove off at *oh-five-hundred.*"

"Not me."

"You're correct, Louie. You'll be ready at *oh-four-thirty.* We *leave* at oh-five-hundred."

I left the Tavern and made my way back to the hotel. As I walked through the streets of Sacramento—notebook in hand—I thought about the last few hours and how just walking into that doorway changed me forever. What I'd written earlier, those lines that had given me such hassle, were now a memory. The stress and worry they'd caused me was no longer valid. I wished I could fill this notebook with everything I'd seen and heard tonight. Those tales and talks could easily create a story like no other. Unfortunately, they were not mine to tell. Come tomorrow, I would begin writing my own new chapters, telling my own glorious tales. I couldn't wait to begin this journey.

I got to my room, gathered my things from the desk, and packed my clothes. I set my alarm for 4:00 a.m. I was not an early riser, but I figured I'd need to get used to the Chief's strange body clock. Early morning on the West Coast is just *morning* in the East and Midwest. Perhaps the Chief was still on Central Time? Maybe it was because of his upbringing or being in the military or something? Regardless of what it was, I was now subject to it and needed to train myself to endure it.

I did one final sweep of my room. I was set to go. I would call the car rental company somewhere on the road and get my time extended. I like this car. I'm going to love driving it to God knows where that begins with *E*. I'll need to cancel my plane ticket. My publisher is going to be pissed. The company paid for the ticket. I'll pay him back. Whatever the cost, it's a mere pittance compared to the wealth I was about to receive. I'll call him from the road as well. Hell, he may even dig this wild expedition idea I'd come up with. He may tell me to stay out there and …

When my alarm went off, it scared the holy hell out of me. It had the most incessant beep that pierced my eardrums. I'd fallen asleep in the lounge chair by the desk. All the lights in the room were still on, and their brightness only added to my dilemma. I felt like a bat in the sunshine. I was flapping aimlessly about in blinding light, while searching for a sound that was playing detriment to my equilibrium—and my sanity.

I found the alarm and shut it off. I looked at the menacing red digital numerals. They shouted at me silently: 4:02 a.m. The numbers seemed to throb—as did my head.

I knew I was not a morning person; however, this was not morning—this was still last night. Maybe once we got on the road and started hitting our spots, the Chief might ease up on the early-to-rise bullshit. I highly doubt it. It was a good thought, though.

I got in the shower. It was too early to think clearly; all I knew was that we had no plans other than to drive to a letter.

The first place I thought of was Elko, Nevada. Elko was about six hours from Sacramento. It wasn't a marathon distance, but it was a good starting point. We would leave here at five and depending on traffic factors and the like, we'd get into Elko sometime close to noon. It seemed perfect to me.

I dropped off my key and paid for the room. The clerk was bleary-eyed and seemed half out of it. I bade him good morning and goodbye. He nodded haphazardly and flashed a smile that looked like he had to work hard for it. Thirty minutes ago, I was akin to his condition. It was almost five in the morning, and I was starting to feel good.

I drove to the Tavern. I went past it twice. On my third attempt, I spied the Chief and Churchill standing on the curb outside the door.

I pulled along the curbside and got out to help the Chief put his things into the car.

"Louie, I'm proud to see to up and at 'em so early," he commented.

"It wasn't easy," I said. "I'm not used to rising before the sun."

Churchill sympathized. "Me either, Lou," he said. "It's too damn early for regular humans to be up."

I looked at the Chief's luggage. He had a medium-sized plaid zipper suitcase. It looked like it was from the 1960s. It was covered in stickers and different kinds of tape. The tape had been sliced from where he'd cut it to open the bag. In addition to all the tape, he had three varied elastic straps wrapped around the outside.

"Chief, would you like me to put your bag in the car?" I asked.

"Can you handle such a task, Louie?" he inquired. "It's a top-secret job. Only the best can do it."

I nodded and said, "I'm up for it. I've got a clearance."

Churchill heard my comment and said, "Yeah, you two are going to be okay on this trip."

I put the Chief's suitcase in the trunk. It was so light, I wondered what he had—or didn't have in it.

The Chief was already in the car. I didn't even notice him getting in. He opened the door and told me to "hurry on." I was a little surprised by his haste. He told me to give Churchill a "wet one" for him so we could get on the road.

I shook Churchill's hand and thanked him again for everything.

"You're a good guy, Lou," Churchill said. "Take care of that old man, okay?"

"I will," I said. "He's in good hands."

"I'm gonna miss him. He's been a pain in my ass for a long time."

"I'll take over for you. I don't have enough pains in my ass. I can spare another."

Churchill laughed and said, "Well, he's a big one!"

"Well, if what I saw last night was any indicator …" I said.

"That was mild," Churchill claimed. "You're gonna see some things!"

"I'm looking forward to it."

"Where you headed first, Lou?"

"I'm thinking Elko, Nevada. It's about six hours from here. It's a good start."

"What are you planning to do in these places—if you don't mind me asking?"

"I don't know yet. We'll play it as we go, I suppose."

"I'm sure the Chief has a plan already. He just won't tell you about it until the last second. Then he'll change it and piss you off."

"Ah! And this is where our adventure begins."

The Chief yelled out, "Damn it, Louie, kiss that gin jockey goodbye and let's get to it! Time to kick 'er in the ass!"

"His master's voice, eh?" I said.

"I guess!" Churchill replied.

"Well, this *is* goodbye, my friend. We'll write you from the road."

"You better."

The Chief waved to Churchill. He motioned him down. I don't know what they said, but Churchill laughed. The Chief rolled up his window and put his hands on the dash.

"Louie, let's get on our way," the Chief said. "Let us venture eastbound—toward the rising sun."

I didn't say a word. I put the car in gear, pulled from the curb and headed down the surface street towards Interstate 80. Churchill remained on the sidewalk. His figure got smaller and smaller as he faded into the darkness. It was not quite 5:00 a.m. We were off to an early start and on our way to Elko.

The early light of dawn was painting the sky with a beautiful panorama of colors. The clouds in the distance captured the vivid hues. It looked as if the red-orange tints of desert mesas were floating above the horizon. The scene was surreal.

We had traveled for nearly an hour and were making our way up into the Sierra Nevada Mountains. We were close to Donner Pass.

"You hungry, Louie?" the Chief asked.

"No, are you? We could stop for breakfast," I said.

"It was a question asked in jest."

"I don't understand."

"You know about the Donner Party, right?"

I was suddenly struck dumb. I got the joke now.

"Yes, Chief, I am familiar with the story," I said.

"I was obviously being facetious," the Chief noted.

"And very much in *poor taste* as well!"

"See, Louie. You're quicker than you think."

The Chief looked out the window, and I could tell he was feeling a vibe with where we were. He pointed at the peaks and spied the winding roads below the summits. He talked quietly to himself as if he were recollecting.

"This is beautiful country," I commented.

"That it is, Louie," he replied. "There's nowhere else like it on Earth."

"I've only been to this part of California once before. I was too young to remember it."

"I used to live up this way: Truckee, to be exact. My siblings and I used to go trout fishing in the Truckee River during the summer. That was before we got split up."

"Split up?" I asked. "What happened?"

"Life happened, kid," the Chief said mournfully. "*Life happened.*"

I didn't ask any more about it. I was beginning to feel I was playing havoc with the Chief's emotions. One minute I've brought him up, the next I've dragged him down.

"I'm sorry if I've upset you," I said.

"You didn't upset me—everything else did," he said.

"Can't let that shit bother me anymore, though. It was a long time ago. It's sad to say they're all gone."

I wanted to ask who or what was all gone. I didn't have to. The Chief shared the answer freely.

"The bad times, that is. They're all gone," he said. "My brothers and sisters are, for the most part, still with us."

"That's a good thing," I said.

"It is. I don't get to see them, but I know they're okay. Can't ask for more than that."

"I used to go fishing with my dad and my uncle when we vacationed in Michigan," I said. "Just a lake and small boat stuff. I loved it. I haven't been for years."

"It's one of the more joyous pastimes God has blessed us with," the Chief said with a smile. "It's the best way to get out with nature, be the hunter that you were meant to be, but without the killing—unless, of course, you're going to eat what you catch."

"Maybe we could get in some fishing at one of our stops?" I suggested.

The Chief looked sad again. He shook his head and said, "No, Louie, that's one activity I've relegated to my past and *my* past alone. I want to keep those memories as they are.

"Not to be an old jerk but when I think of fishing, I want to think of me being young and with my brothers and sisters and no one else."

"Fair enough, Chief. I understand completely," I said. I was lying. I truly wished I understood.

"All right, we've been driving for almost two hours and we don't know where we're going yet," the Chief stated. "Did you think of where we'll be stopping first on this ride?"

"I have," I said. "Our first stop is Elko, Nevada. Not too far from here."

"Elko, eh? I haven't been there for years, and I mean it's been goddamned *decades*. I don't think the freakin' railroad was even built then!"

We both laughed. It made me think about this journey on a broader scale. He'd been to Elko, but it was a while ago. I'd never been there. How many of the places we'd choose to stop would be like that? We were blindly picking locations along an indeterminate route. The only known factor was that wherever we landed began with an *E*. What about when we reached these destinations? What would we do there? Was there a plan for something? I had nothing in mind, but I had a feeling the Chief did—he just wasn't talking yet. I knew why I was doing this. I knew why the Chief was along for the ride. I just hoped that when this trip was over, the results we'd anticipated are the ones we'd receive. The only way to answer these queries was to get to where we were going and let things unfold.

We were in Nevada and had just passed Reno. I was ready to stop and stretch my legs. I was thirsty but not hungry enough to eat.

The Chief had said nothing about food or drink since his comment on Donner Pass.

"Chief, what say we stop for a bit," I suggested.

"That sounds okay to me," he said. "I need to piss."

I hadn't thought about that, but the mention of it caused my bladder to suddenly fill.

"Do you want to get some breakfast?" I asked.

"No. I just need a summer sausage or something," the Chief said. "No big meals just yet."

We pulled into a gas station and I decided to top off the car as well. The Chief went into the store to use the facilities. Once I was done with the fill-up, I went in as well. I grabbed a couple of colas and a candy bar for myself. I spied the snack meats section and got a Fat Freddie sausage for the Chief. I didn't know what he drank besides beer. I waited until he came out of the can so I could ask him.

"I'm getting a couple of drinks," I said. "What would you like?"

"I want a ginger ale," he said. "Something good and snappy."

I grabbed a couple of bottles of ginger ale and took everything to the counter to pay.

The Chief kept wandering around the small aisles of the store. He picked up every souvenir, knickknack, and piece of junk they had. He shook all the Reno snow globes and moved the magnets. He laughed at the lame sentiments on the shot glasses and scoffed at the "fake" scenes on the postcards. The clerk kept watching, just waiting for him to steal something.

"Is that yer grandpa?" the clerk asked snidely.

"No. But he is with me," I said.

"Well, he better not steal anything. That stuff costs money."

"He won't steal anything. Just chill. He's just browsing the wares."

The clerk wasn't convinced. I figured the best thing to do was finish this transaction, take my leak, and get us out of here. I gave the Chief the bag. He took it and I went to the restroom. When I came out, the Chief was gone. I panicked slightly.

"Yo, where'd that old dude go?" I asked.

"He's outside," the clerk said. "I think he stole something."

"I doubt it, man. Did your alarm go off?"

"No."

"Then it's all good. Have a nice day."

"Yeah …" The clerk mumbled something more, but I didn't stick around to listen.

I walked to the car. I saw the Chief sitting and eating the sausage I'd bought and drinking a ginger ale. He was looking at something and having a laugh about it. I peered into the passenger's side window but couldn't see what he had.

I got in the car and as soon as I sat down, the Chief pulled his arms in close like he was hiding something.

"I don't think I want to know, do I?" I asked.

"What? What don't you want to know?" he responded.

"Why, you look like the cat that ate the fucking canary. okay, what's in the bag that I *didn't* buy?"

"I don't know what you're talking about! I'm insulted!"

"What did you swipe? I know you hoofed something from the store. Let me see it."

"No. There's no *see* on all dry land."

"What the hell does that mean?!"

"It means your request cannot be granted. By the way, thank you for the sausage."

"You're welcome. Well. I hope whatever you stole was something cool or useful."

"I stole nothing, Louie. I *commandeered* it. There is a difference. And yes, both items fit the criteria of which you inquired."

"'Both items'? What the hell did you … *commandeer?*"

The Chief pulled out the ill-gotten items. He had stolen two postcards and two shot glasses. One of the postcards was a photo-collaged display of the Reno Arch. The other card had a photo of two burlesque girls—prostitutes, actually—with the caption "When You've Ended Things in Reno, Come See Us!" Obviously a crack about divorce.

"That's more than 'both,'" I said. "That's four items. *Two boths.*"

The Chief ignored me.

"I'm sending the arch postcard to Churchill," the Chief said.

"Why not the hookers?" I asked.

"Are you kidding me? I'm keeping the cheesecake for myself."

"Okay. Now the glasses."

The Chief showed me one shot glass. It was iridescent purple and had the Nevada State Flag on it. He kept the other one hidden.

"Let me see the other one," I said.

"Sorry, no see …" He began to repeat his quip about see on dry land. I cut him off.

"May I have a look at the other one?" I requested.

The Chief held up the glass. It was taupe colored and on one side was a donkey's head. The opposite side read, "I Lost My Ass in Reno." The joke was obvious, metaphoric, and literal—an ass was definitely missing. The Chief looked at the glass and started laughing like Fred Flintstone.

"You get it, don't you Louie?" he asked. "Isn't that a *mare's ass*? Pun intended!"

"I guess so," I said. "It is funny, but in a most juvenile way, don't you think?"

"Oh, come on, kid, lighten up! You're just pissed off because you couldn't be this clever."

"I'd be pissed off if I *was* that clever. I'd like to think my aspirations were higher."

"I was going to give you this glass, but now I'm not," the Chief said. He sounded like a bratty kid.

"I'll be okay," I replied.

"Are you sore at me for taking this stuff?" he asked.

"No. I don't care," I said. "You just can't make a habit of it, okay?"

"I can't promise anything. I'm a crazy old man in the desert. Things happen out here."

"They do, don't they? What say we go in the store and kill the clerk?" I suggested.

"Nah, let him live," the Chief said. "Some bastards weirder than us will come along later and blow his brains out anyway."

"Those guys will get the cash."

"There is no cash. That's why I took this stuff. I needed something to show for my crime spree."

I chuckled at the Chief's comment.

"You know you're sending Churchill a postcard from a place that's not on our list, right?" I said.

"I know, but what the hell," he said. "We said we'd get him one from the places we *stopped*. And we're stopped right now."

"That is very true—but only for the moment."

I started the car and looped around the store. We saw the clerk out back smoking a cigarette. The Chief flipped him the bird. He shouted some gibberish to him that sounded German as we peeled out and sped back toward I-80.

We were just under four hours from our first official destination. The Chief had already made the trip a lively one by committing petty larceny.

As we neared Elko, I was still wondering if the Chief truly had something planned for us when we got there. I'd been milling about it since we left Sacramento. It was time for me to find out what was going on—if anything.

"Chief, I've been wondering," I said. "What are we going to do when we get to the places we've chosen to visit?"

The Chief looked around the car. He seemed to be searching for something. I was hoping it wasn't the answer to my question. If it was, we were in trouble—it meant that he had no idea what the hell we were doing, either.

"Louie, me boy," he said. "I know exactly what we're going to do when we get to our destinations."

"Could you give me an idea as to what you have in mind?" I asked.

"I could, but that would spoil the surprise."

"I'm okay with you spoiling the surprise. I really am."

"You sound like you don't trust me."

"It's not that, it's just that I'd like to know *something* about what we're doing."

"When we get to Elko and settle in, I will tell you what you need to know."

"That doesn't help, you know?"

"I'm sure it doesn't, kid, but part of an adventure is not knowing what lies ahead."

"We've got that aspect covered pretty well."

"Louie. Trust me. High noon in Elko. Lunchtime. Then, you'll know."

I looked at the Chief. I wasn't overly concerned, but I didn't like being in the dark about things—especially things like this. I didn't know what I was doing. In all actuality, I was beginning to wonder what possessed me to come up with such a harebrained idea? I thought it was all about "finding my soul," but that notion seemed so far afield now it sounded ludicrous.

Elko, Nevada

We arrived in Elko. It was just past noon, and we drove through the city to find a place to eat. I hadn't thought about lodging just yet, but that was the next step after lunch. Fast food and other chain restaurant signs drifted outside the car's windows. We were searching out a place that was local, looked decent, and didn't advertise ten times a day on TV.

"What sounds good to you, Chief?" I asked.

"I'm in the mood for something with fish, or spicy—or both," he said.

We came upon a Basque restaurant. Such a place would fulfill both the Chief's lunch desires, as well as our mutual requirements for where we'd dine. We parked the car and went in to fill our bellies.

"I'd never eaten Basque cuisine before. Have you?" I asked the Chief.

"Yes. When I was in Spain," he said. "It's been some time, but you never forget food like this. You'll love it."

We took a table and ordered a couple of beers as we perused the fare.

The waiter returned and asked us our orders. We couldn't decide on a main dish. We heeded the waiter's suggestion of *pintxos:* a tapas-like platter that suited all our cravings. He left and returned with our starters: two bowls of soup and bread with lots of butter. The soup was delightful. It was thick with chorizo and ham and garbanzo beans, blended with shreds of cabbage, chopped onion, and carrots. It was spicy, and it made me sweat a little. I took a sip of my beer and a bite of bread.

"Hot soup?" the Chief asked. His concern was sprinkled with sarcasm.

"Little bit," I responded in kind.

"So what do you think so far?" the Chief wondered.

"I'm liking it," I said. "I hope the entrée is as good as the starter."

"It'll be good," the Chief assured me. "These Basque know how to cook."

Our pintxos arrived. There was a lot of food. The Chief took several of the haddock bites and placed them on his plate. I selected a variety of the toothpick-spiked snacks and put them on my plate. Everything was delicious. This was an excellent choice for our lunch.

I felt it was time the Chief drop the clandestine stuff and tell me his "plan"—if he even had one.

"Okay, we're here, it's high noon and it's lunchtime," I said. "It's time to reveal your plan, Chief."

The Chief pushed his pintxos around his plate. He was stalling. I began to feel like a fool. He didn't have a plan at all. I should've just driven him around Sacramento.

"You don't have a plan for us, do you?" I asked, somewhat aggravated.

"I do, Louie—I really do," the Chief claimed. "And part of it is happening right now."

"It is? I don't understand what you mean."

"What are we doing?"

"We're eating lunch and having a couple of beers. So what?"

"Think about that. Think about the importance of that."

"I'm not following."

"Eating and drinking are two basic necessities of survival, right?"

"Yes, but …"

"Do you think it's better to eat a meal, or drink a beer alone or with someone else?"

"With someone else, I guess."

"You enjoy having the company, right? It makes the whole situation better. The food tastes different, there's conversation, there's a fulfilling aspect to it all, right?"

"Yeah. I never thought about it like that."

"Louie, the basic things we do in life are enhanced when we share them with others. They're *even better* when we share them with one person in particular."

I was following him, but I was still confused.

"Can you elaborate?" I asked.

"Besides breathing, eating and drinking are the two things we do that keep us alive," the Chief explained. "They nourish us and in so many ways define who we are. The old cliché 'You are what you eat' is not a cliché at all when you get down to it. Same goes for drinking. We define each other by what types of drink we consume."

"I've never thought about it like that," I said.

"Most of us don't," he said. "We take those two life-sustaining acts for granted. Why do you think people eat terribly? They don't give a fuck. They just want to eat. I've always seen meals as a time to cherish the self and anyone you're sharing them with."

"Drinking too?"

"Oh yes, even more so. Drinking has become a social designator. Whether it's beer or water or a cola, we regard and label people by what they drink. You drink Gatorade? You're athletic. You drink wine? You're refined. You drink milk? You want calcium and vitamins. It's shit like that. We drink beer and scotch. *We're* drunks—but we know this!"

"So what you're saying is: you want to go to these places and eat and drink with me?"

"No, Louie, what I'm saying is I want to go to these places with you and I want *you to find someone to eat and drink with,"* the Chief declared. "I want you to find *a woman* to share meals and drinks with. I want you to find a woman who will see you for what you are—to *define* you, while in turn, you'll define her."

"That sounds complicated," I said. "Hell, Chief, it sounds damn near impossible."

"Impossible is part of adventure, Louie. If it was easy, everyone would be doing it. That's why only *some* people dare to take risks and grab the world by the balls."

What he said made sense, but I knew I was missing something. There was more to this than just finding someone to have a glorified date with. I hated the *bread-crumbing* the Chief was giving me. I had to have all the information. I asked the Chief to reiterate his criteria.

"Let me get this straight," I said. "You want me to find a woman to eat and drink with every day?"

"That's it. There's no guesswork," he said.

"A different woman for breakfast, lunch, and dinner? Then another for drinks at night?"

"If that's what it takes, yes. However, the whole idea is to find *one* woman. One whose company you crave so much you'll want to have these meals and drinks with her alone."

"This all sounds great, but how does it help me to find my soul and become a better writer?"

"It's all part of it. You'll learn as you go. Finding your soul is up to you. The right person by your side only enhances the journey."

"There has to be more than just eating and drinking," I said.

"There is," the Chief said. "There are three other factors as well."

"Are you going to tell me what they are?"

"I will, but not till later. Let's finish this wonderful meal. Call it our last as we are now."

I should have been addled by that statement, but oddly enough—it made sense.

After lunch, I found a nice hotel for us to stay. As I waited for the clerk, the Chief drifted off and began roaming the lobby. He talked to random people, no surprise most of them were female. He chatted them up and charmed them even more. I couldn't hear their conversations, but I could hear the women burst out with an occasional laugh. It was quite a scene. Watching the Chief work the room like he did made it hard to believe he felt he couldn't find a woman of his own. It was even harder to believe he was really eighty-four years old—he came across like a twentysomething.

"How long will you be staying, Mr. DeCarlo?" the clerk asked.

"Three nights," I said.

"How many rooms will you need?"

"Two. One for me and one for *Don Juan,* over there."

The clerk looked up and saw the Chief holding court.

"Interesting, gentleman, if I may say so," the clerk commented.

"That he is," I said.

I finished the paperwork and paid for the rooms. I called to the Chief and told him I was going to get our bags. He told me to hold off on the bags for a moment and waved me over to him.

"Chief, let me get our stuff in first, okay?" I said.

"No, Louie, come here," the Chief insisted. "I want you to meet someone."

I had a bad feeling about this but acquiesced. I walked over to see who the Chief wanted me to "meet."

"Louie, this is April," he said as he introduced me to his new "friend."

"Isn't she as beautiful as the month she was named for?" he asked.

April and I blushed simultaneously.

"Oh, stop that!" April said to the Chief. "You're such a crazy guy!"

"It's very nice to meet you April," I said. "I hope this 'crazy guy' hasn't caused you too much trouble."

"No, he's been fine," she said. "He was telling me about you and your trip."

"Really? It's not much of a trip yet. This is our first stop. We're not sure what we're doing, actually."

"You don't? Well, Chief says he's got it all planned out."

"*Chief* says he's got it all planned out? I can only hope he shares a little of his plan with me. Has he told you anything?"

"No. Just that you're here and that's about it."

The Chief sat quietly and listened to me talk to April. I was waiting for him to interject something. I didn't know what I was supposed to feel right now. I wanted to be cheery and happy in front of this woman, but I didn't know why. I'd just met her mere minutes ago.

I wanted to be angry at the Chief for putting me on the spot, but I couldn't be. Oddly enough, the more time I spent in April's presence, the more I wanted to get to know her. However, I also wanted to get our luggage out of the car and up to our rooms.

"Will you two excuse me for a moment?" I asked.

"Where are you going?" April asked.

"Yes, Louie, where *are* you going?" the Chief parroted sarcastically.

"I'm going to rescue our luggage from the unforgiving Nevada summer sun," I said. "I'll be right back."

I looked at the Chief and grumbled, "Don't get up or anything." He didn't.

As I gathered our bags, I tried to figure out what the Chief was up to and what his intentions were with April. I had an idea, but it seemed so far-fetched it couldn't be real. There was no way he was trying to set me up with her—was he? The Chief couldn't be playing matchmaker. He was too vested in me finding my own paths. Besides, I couldn't make any moves anyway, the Chief still had three more *factors* to share with me.

I dragged our luggage into the lobby, and the Chief was waiting in an alcove just inside the door.

"Hey, sorry I didn't help you," he said. "I just couldn't stop talking to that cute tomato. She was quite a looker, eh, Louie?"

"Yes, she was, Chief," I said. "Very attractive."

"Well, I'm glad you thought so."

"What's not to like? She seemed friendly enough."

"You know she's staying in this hotel. She's on the fourth floor."

"I figured she was a guest. How did you find out what floor she was on?"

"She told me. I didn't even ask. She just came right out and gave me the skinny. Well, Louie, I'm happy to hear you found her to be such a fine lass."

"Why was that so important?"

"Because you're taking her out to dinner tonight."

My jaw dropped. My half-cocked suspicions were warranted: the Chief *was* playing freakin' matchmaker. I wanted to get angry again, but I couldn't. I couldn't because I did want to talk to April a little more.

"I could've asked her out myself, you know?" I said.

"But you wouldn't have," the Chief stated. "You would've let her go and then wished you'd made the effort. I just saved you jumping one hurdle."

"Should I thank you?"

"No. Not yet. You can thank me tomorrow at breakfast. I'm hoping to join you two and hear all about your evening."

"What if there's nothing to tell?"

"Louie, you're going out for dinner and drinks with a beautiful woman. A woman named after the month of the year that represents life anew. She is your quest personified. You'll *definitely* have something to talk about in the morning."

"What if it's only me who joins you for breakfast?"

"Well, then I'll know *part* of the story—you'll fill me in on the rest."

We headed up to our rooms.

"Chief, do you want to meet for a couple of beers around 5:00 p.m.?" I asked.

"Sure. That sounds like a grand idea," he said.

"By the way, what time am I meeting April?"

"'Twenty-hundred hours, Louie. In the hotel bar."

I had to think. My knowledge of the twenty-four hour clock was sketchy.

"Eight o'clock, right?" I asked.

"Affirmative," the Chief responded.

"There's one—actually, three—more things I have to know."

"And what might those be, Louie?"

"The other 'factors' you hadn't mentioned yet."

"At seventeen-hundred over beers I will tell them to you."

"Seven ... okay, tonight at *five*. Got it. See you in a couple of hours."

"*Do svidanya*, Louie," the Chief said as he closed his door.

I shoved my suitcase into the closet. I took my shoes off and lay down on the bed. I wanted to sleep a little. It had been an early day for me. I wanted to be fresh and sharp for my date with April.

I fell asleep for about forty-five minutes. When I woke up, I felt better than I had earlier. I didn't realize I was so tired. It was close to 4:00 p.m., and I needed to get myself around to meet the Chief for beers at five.

I showered and cleaned up. I went through my suitcase to find something decent to wear on my date. All my clothes were casual, shoddy, or needed to be washed. I had nothing decent to wear. I picked out a blue polo shirt that I'd worn last week. It smelled strange. I sprayed it with some deodorant and smelled the fabric again and found it acceptable.

I went down to the lobby. The Chief was nowhere to be seen. It wasn't quite 5:00 p.m. yet, so I found a chair and sat. I read a copy of the *Elko Daily Free Press*.

I heard the bell for the elevator ring and thought it may be the Chief. I looked up and saw that it was actually April. I tucked in behind the paper. I felt like a bride before her wedding—*you can't see me now*. It was strange. April was not alone. She was with two other men and another woman. I wasn't sure what to make of this. Were these people her family? They seemed to all be of similar age. I began to wonder if the Chief had lured me into a trap—some type of socio-romantic puzzle I was supposed to solve. The solution would be a lesson in not falling for his tricks or words. That couldn't be it. Perhaps April had "agreed" to see me tonight as a way to get the Chief to leave her alone? She probably left the lobby and scoffed the old man, calling him a *masher* and a *pervert*. *Jesus, does anyone even say "masher" anymore?* I'll bet one of those guys is her husband. What stupid luck. So this is how it goes?

I watched the two couples walk into the hotel bar and disappear. That settles it. The Chief and I would get our beers elsewhere.

The Chief walked into the lobby.

"Just the man I wanted to see," I said.

"Well, it's almost seventeen hundred," the Chief remarked. "I hope I'm the man you wanted to see."

I shot the Chief a cold glance. "I saw my *date* a few minutes ago," I said.

"And what did you find out?" he asked.

"Nothing. I just watched her walk by. She wasn't alone."

"Really? Did you talk to her?"

"No. I hid from her. I wanted to wait until tonight to talk to her. I'm thinking that might not be a possibility now."

"What would make you say that, Louie?"

"I think she's married, Chief, or at the very least got something going with one of the men I saw her with."

"That can't be. There's no way."

"How do you know? Did she say anything?"

"No, but if a woman is truly spoken for, she will say so. Unless …"

I harshly finished the Chief's sentence for him. "She's a slut? She's a whore? She's a skank? Stop me when I get to the right adjective."

"None of the above, Louie. I can't believe you'd say such things about her," the Chief said. "That girl is *not* attached. I know it. Trust me."

"Nevertheless, I want to get our drinks elsewhere," I said.

"Very well. A beer is a beer is a beer—no matter where it's from."

We went to a small pub a couple of blocks from the hotel. The bartender asked us our libations, and we both ordered pints of Guinness.

"Make sure you draw it correctly," the Chief demanded. "Leave about an inch of head on the top."

The bartender glared at the Chief.

"I think he knows how to pour one, Chief," I said.

"Yeah, you'd think that, but sometimes …" he retorted.

I remembered the Chief's issue with Churchill topping a beer with a layer of foam, thereby not filling the glass completely.

"I thought getting a 'little head' was cheating you out of complete fulfillment," I commented.

"Not in this case, Louie," the Chief said. "With Guinness, the head makes the 'perfect pour.' It's the only one that gets a pass."

The bartender served our pints, and they were to the Chief's satisfaction. Both beers were equally drawn and poured. Each had an inch of the tan atop. Each one was teeming with life; the effervescence within the glasses sustained both the head and the heart of the stout.

The Chief raised his pint and saluted the bartender. He gave the Chief a smile. I'm sure at first sight, he thought the Chief was going to be trouble. This immaculate display of *tapestry* was one of both redemption and respect.

I sipped my beer and wondered if we shouldn't just stay here and drink for the rest of the night. I was certain that my date with the lovely—and now probably involved—April was not going to happen.

"Okay, Chief, we're here, we're having beers—" I started to say.

The Chief cut me off. "And you're a 'barroom balladeer'?" he asked. "Is that what you were going to say next, Louie?"

"No, not even close," I commented.

"You're a poet but don't know it," he said. "But your feet surely show it. You know why?"

"No. Why?"

"Because they're *Longfellows.*"

The bartender turned and spoke. "You walked into that, kid. That's an old one."

The Chief added to the bartender's comment. "Yes, 'walked' indeed!"

The two men had a hearty laugh at my expense.

"I get the joke," I said. "Poet. Longfellow. Henry Wadsworth. I can't say I'd ever heard it before. Very *punny.*"

I shook my head. "Okay, as I was saying … the other three 'factors.' Will you tell me what they are?" I asked the Chief.

"I will," he replied. "And I'll make it easy for you to remember them all."

"Sounds good. I'm ready to learn."

The Chief took a sip of his beer.

"Louie, we've eaten and we've drank. These two things we've discussed and you know the importance of," he said. "The aforementioned are life-sustaining acts. The other three are acts of instinct and human nature, but they are just as relevant to life as eating, drinking, and breathing—maybe even more so in certain contexts."

I was riveted. The Chief had a way of making even the mundane sound deep and philosophical. I wasn't sure what he was going to tell me, but I knew it would ring of the erudite.

"These three factors—*elements*—whatever you want to call them—are laughter, tears, and above all things: love," the Chief said. "These three, combined with the others will make you whole. Call them the Five Ls and find a mate to satisfy each one: a luncheon mate, a libation mate, a laughter mate, a lachrymal mate, and a love mate. Find the right person to share the five with and you and your life will be *complete.*

I gave the Chief a cynical look. "So eating, drinking, laughing, crying, and loving are the solutions to all of my problems?" I asked.

"No. They're not 'solutions,'" the Chief said. "They are *necessities*. You find a woman with whom you want to eat and drink with, with whom you can share laughter and tears with, and ultimately, you will find the love of your life with. It's both simple and complex, but when done properly and with the right person, they will become your *Life Mate*. Once you've found this person, your journey—your true excursion can begin."

"It sounds like a normal relationship, just broken into categories," I commented.

"In a way, but to 'categorize' it dilutes the essence," the Chief said. "These things must be experienced as a complete entity for it all to work."

"What if you can't find someone to fulfill all of the needs?"

"Then you keep looking. You can find someone who makes you happy, but if you don't want to share a meal with them, it's useless."

"Where did you come up with all of this, Chief?"

"Louie, I've spent a good part of my life looking for perfection. I can say I've only found it once, but even that was fleeting. I realized that nothing is *truly* perfect. To seek out what does not exist is a waste of time, effort, and spirit. I abandoned my search for perfection and began a quest for *completion*. I knew that I could find someone or something that embodied the true whole of being—not just an idealized perception of it."

The Chief was talking about life inasmuch as he was talking about Mariposa again. He'd spoken of her body as "perfect and divine" when he'd described it. I was now realizing that his use of the word was metaphoric. He'd found *love* with Mariposa, but perhaps that was all—and at this moment, it seemed that love was just not enough.

"That's a lot to handle," I commented. "Does anyone find this complete combination?"

"Sure they do," the Chief declared. "It just takes time. It doesn't *just* happen. If it does just happen, few people ever realize it, and by then, it's usually too late."

"Is it possible to have some without the others?"

"Yes, but it never works. You can fake your way through, but in the end, it's just plain bullshit."

"I'm sick of bullshit. That seems to be all I've got nowadays."

"See, Louie, you're already on your way."

"How so?"

"You realize what you don't want in your life anymore. Now it's time to find what you *do* want."

"It all makes sense, but I do have one question—a concern, actually. It's about the 'Love Mate.'"

"That's probably my favorite of the five."

"I'm sure. I have to know—what exactly constitutes the 'Love Mate'?"

"Well, to start, it's not about sex," the Chief said. "It's about finding one with whom you can fall asleep next to and who will still be there when you wake up in the morning. That's one of the first steps to finding love: to trust someone enough to close your eyes in their presence and see them again when your eyes are open—and without having them steal your wallet while you slept."

The look on my face did not give the Chief the impression I was amused by the prospect of being robbed in my sleep.

"I'm just kidding, Louie!" he said with a hearty laugh. "The only thing you really want them to steal is your heart. Of course, if you do end up getting a little in the process—well, that's an added bonus."

I laughed at the Chief's statement, but I knew its validity as well. I'd never thought about being with someone in that way. I'd slept with women before, but the Chief's poetic, philosophic, and semiplatonic bend on the subject gave me new insight.

"I'm nervous about April," I said suddenly. "I'm not sure about what I saw in the hotel. I'm not sure if it's even going to happen."

"You can't let your perceptions deceive you, Louie," the Chief said. "I told you she's not attached. She was too flirty and free to be another man's woman."

"Have your perceptions ever deceived you?" I asked. "You seem very confident in her availability."

"I have to be honest," the Chief proclaimed. "My perceptions in matters such as this have only failed me once. And that was a long time ago."

"Maybe you're due for the streak to be broken?"

"Not this time, son. If this woman is not your destiny, she is at least a good place to start it."

"That seems awfully presumptuous, especially when talking about a first date that hasn't even begun."

"Let me put your mind at ease, Louie. If I thought she was involved herself, I wouldn't have *involved* you. Does that make sense?"

"Yes, it does."

"Good. Now let's drink and talk about *the Islands*. Let me tell you about Samoa."

"I was in Samoa in 1976. I was fifty-four and just quit my job with the government," the Chief said. "It was the first time I'd been to a place so exotic."

"I'd imagine it was quite different," I mused.

"Oh, yes. I'd been to Cuba, saw a little time in the Dominican Republic; sipped some fine rum in Jamaica, and had a little fling in Puerto Rico," the Chief said. "Then I went to the Pacific. I was in Hawaii—before it was a state—went to Guam and all over Micronesia, but it was Samoa that really took me in."

"Wow! What was it like?" I asked.

"Ah, the Samoan people," he said. "Warrior souls but peaceful hearts, people wearing *lavalavas,* rowing *fautasi* boats and living their lives to the fullest, off of and *with* the land.

"Samoa was a separate heaven and those who dwelled upon it were angels of a God different from the one we know."

"It sounds like an amazing place," I said. "What did you do there?"

"Everything—and nothing. My life as I knew it was transformed when I was embraced by Samoa—both the island and her people. I felt like—and lived like—Paul Gauguin. You're familiar with Gauguin, right?"

"Yes. French, painter, roomed with Van Gogh for a while then went to Tahiti."

"That's him. And that was me—without the art, of course. I didn't need to paint. I could never accurately capture the beauty I saw and experienced there. Trying to visualize it and portray it in static terms would have been a gross injustice."

The Chief described the sweet scent of the tropical breezes. His words made me want to order a Mai-Tai, or any drink with coconut.

He talked about the feel of the warm sand between his toes as he walked the beaches. He spoke of how the tide had crept in and washed over his feet, making it feel as if 'a gentle spirit' pulled at his ankles.

The Chief talked of the transparent, aquamarine hues of the sea and lagoons. He said one could trace the sharp, rocky, and foreboding limestone cliffs to the surface of the water then look below and see their smooth, docile, and entrenched feet in the sand beneath.

Just as it was when he described Cuba, I felt like I was in Samoa. The Chief and I enjoying delectable, roast pig at a *fia fia*, while witnessing the awe-inspiring traditional Samoan fire knife dance: *Siva Afi*. The people were just as he'd described. I found myself assimilating into the culture. I was a stranger—a *palagi*—but was welcomed as family.

"It was easy to feel as one with the Samoan people," the Chief said. "They treated me like a king, Louie. I never needed or wanted for anything. In return for their generosity, I shared my skills and knowledge."

"Well, tell me all about it," I said.

"I used to work on computers," the Chief said. "In Samoa at the time, such advancements weren't prevalent. I called to the United States and had my old company ship the components to build one of the earliest versions of a mainframe—the first of its kind in Samoa."

"That's amazing, Chief!" I exclaimed. "What an incredible thing to do. You helped an old culture take a step into a new realm. Not many people can say they've done such a thing."

"I was revered by a great many for sure. They gave me a nickname too—*Lapo'a Fa'i*—Big Banana. It was a term of respect and endearment and had nothing to do with the size of my manhood. However, a few of the local *fafine* might have a different story!"

I got a laugh out of the Chief's dick joke but figured it was inevitable. However, I did not laugh at his story about Samoa. Again, I felt my work of words had been cheapened by the Chief's. The more he talked about places and how they made him feel, the more I realized I had to raid the thesaurus to create my imagery; the Chief just recalled his memories. Maybe that's another thing I was missing: memories? Perhaps I had no grand memories to speak of or share? I'd been and seen but never culled and collected. The Chief had lived for the places he'd spoke of. I'd only gone to mine for a paycheck.

The Chief shut down again. He'd reached the end of his yarn, and there was no more to knit. This was becoming commonplace: this cliff-hanger approach to storytelling. I didn't ask for anything additional. I knew he was done. To drive home this fact, he switched subjects.

"Not long from now, you'll be rendezvousing with the lovely April, Louie," he said. "Are you still having doubts and worries?"

"A little bit, I guess," I said. "I'm just going to go and see what happens."

"That's what life and adventures are all about."

"I know. And it doesn't instill me with a lot of confidence."

We finished our beers. The Chief wanted another round, but I needed to stop for a while. The Chief was a great libation mate, but he was not truly the one I was supposed to have tonight.

I paid the tab. The bartender asked if we'd be back again. We joked and asked him to save our spots. He laughed and set two pub mats on the bar in front of our chairs. The Chief and I nodded at the gesture. We'd definitely be back.

The Chief and I returned to the hotel and parted ways but not before he said he wanted a "full report" in the morning. He also mentioned a "debriefing." I blushed with embarrassment again. It seemed impossible for the Chief to avoid dropping innuendo into something. For the most part, it certainly gave him the last word. I was usually speechless after he'd done it.

I went to the hotel bar and found a conspicuous spot to wait for April. I looked at the clock. It was shortly before 8:00 p.m., but I felt like she was late. I wanted to order a drink but decided to delay until she'd arrived. I watched the bar patrons mill about. They smiled awkwardly as they moved past.

I noticed band equipment set up in a corner. Perhaps there would be live music tonight? From this observation, I decided that April and I would dine elsewhere—trying to get to know someone while yelling over a band is difficult and can be disastrous. Loud talkers tend to spit unexpectedly and they always seem to sound slightly drunk.

I kept rising from my chair to catch a glimpse of my date. It was now after 8:00 p.m., and I was slightly annoyed. I had been worried all day about what I'd seen earlier. I let my suspicions run roughshod over an evening that had yet to begin.

"Good evening, sir," a waiter said. "Is there something I can get for you?"

"No. I'm okay for now," I said.

The waiter nodded.

"You know what? On second thought, I think I will order something," I said.

"What can I get for you?" the waiter asked.

"I'll have a scotch and soda. And an extra glass of sparkling water."

"Coming right up."

The waiter left to get my drinks, and I was left to stew. It was 8:30 p.m., and I was still dateless.

I'd quit smoking a couple of years ago; however, now I craved a cigarette. One of the patrons had a pack of Marlboro *Reds* sitting next to his drink. The pack was calling to me. I asked the gentleman for a cigarette. He obliged my request. I thanked him and took a matchbook from the bar. I left the bar to go outside and smoke.

I walked out and stood at the edge of the valet roundabout. I found a spot with a great view of the western sky. I watched the beginnings of a picturesque Nevada dusk unfold, and I smoked my cigarette. It was a pleasant, relaxing feeling. The sun slinked down to the tops of the mountains, changing color and size as it inched to fall below the horizon. I thought of postcards and how they always seemed so contrived, their images overly enhanced by photographic filters. Witnessing this scene made me rethink my presumptuous attitude toward them. This was real. I was a part of it.

I pulled a long drag off the cigarette and could feel my attitude change. I was seeing the night seduce the day by drawing it in with vibrant colors and the promise of tomorrow. I wished I had that same type of promise. All I knew was that when I finished this smoke, I had a cold, crisp, noncommittal scotch and soda inviting me to partake of her essence.

I smoked the nail down to its filter and crushed the butt in the sand-filled receptacle by the curb. I was looking forward to my drink and cashing out on my date prospects. Perhaps the Chief and I could mosey on back to our newfound watering hole and tie one on? The Chief could tell me about Australia, Papua New Guinea, or some other place he'd been, all while I pretended I was there and cried in my beer, lamenting being stood up tonight.

Just as I made my way to the lobby, I saw April. She was in a lovely black dress and high stiletto heels. She looked different—more beautiful than I remembered. She didn't see me at first, but once she recognized me, she smiled and waved frantically.

"Oh my God, Louis! Please forgive me," she begged. "I'm so sorry I'm late. You must think I'm so flighty and a dreadful flake."

"No ... not quite," I said. "I was a little worried you wouldn't show."

"Oh, heavens no!" she said. "I've been looking forward to seeing you all day."

"So much so, you lost track of time?" I joked.

April giggled and blushed. "Not really," she said. "I just got back from getting my hair done."

I felt bad now. She had gone to trouble for me and I was scoffing her. She was dressed quite nicely. I was wearing an aerosol-coated polo shirt. She went and got her hair done. I got pissed off, ordered a drink for myself, and smoked a cigarette I'd acquired from a stranger. She looked grand. I wore the face of assumption and bitter doubt.

"Let's go to the bar for a moment," I said. "I ordered us a drink to start."

"What did you get me?" April asked.

"Sadly, just a Perrier. I didn't want to appear presumptuous."

"Well, Perrier's not bad. I really like Manhattans, though—just for future reference!"

I smiled and escorted April into the lobby. I softly put my hand to the small of her back. She smiled and quickly glanced over her shoulder. I felt her reciprocating my touch as she leaned back into my hand.

We went to the bar, and I called out to the bartender as we approached.

"Can I get a Manhattan as well?" I asked.

I grabbed the drinks from the bar and showed April to a table toward the back. I pulled her chair out for her. The waiter brought her Manhattan. I asked April if she wanted to get something to eat.

"I am hungry, but I'm not sure what I want," she said.

We asked for menus. The waiter brought them to us and suggested a few of the specials.

"It all sounds wonderful," April commented. "What would you like, Louis?"

I had to think. When April hadn't shown up at 8:15, I was thinking a burger is good enough. At eight thirty, I was wishing there was an Ed Debevic's restaurant nearby. I would've dragged her there. I was loving the thought of her squirming nervously as the waitresses rudely lambasted her for ordering too slow, or mispronouncing an entrée. Now that she was here and we were together, I no longer harbored the animosity from earlier. Strangely, though a hamburger sounded quite good to me at the moment.

"I don't know. How about something fun?" I suggested.

"Like what? What sounds 'fun'?" she asked.

"How about a diner? One of those fifties throwbacks. You know … something nostalgic?"

"Oh my, that does sound fun. Is there one here in town?"

"This is old Nevada. There has to be."

I was a little surprised that April would agree to such casual dining. She was dressed way too nice for a burger joint. Then again, I was getting the feeling that she was the kind of girl who didn't care. She wanted to look nice for the date, no matter where it was.

April noticed the band equipment. "I think they're going to have a band," she said. "It's probably going to get noisy in here. Maybe we should go somewhere else?"

"I thought that same thing earlier," I said. "We can always come back later. So yeah, let's go grab dinner elsewhere. We can eat, talk, and then come back here. Maybe even dance?"

April giggled. "I'd like that," she said. "No one's taken me to dance in forever."

"Well, what I do can hardly be considered dancing," I said. "It's pretty tragic."

"I'll be the judge of that."

"Okay. But I'm giving you an advance warning."

We finished our drinks, I paid our tab, and we left for dinner.

We drove around town and eventually found a place like we'd talked about. It was cute and not crowded. The décor was shiny metallic and red. The booths looked like the interiors of 1950s cars. The tables were rounded and fat with marbled Formica tops. The bar extended the entire length of the restaurant; twenty tall, red-glitter-upholstered barstools lined the front of the counter.

A waitress called out from behind the order wheel and told us to find a seat.

We found a booth and tucked all the way in next to the window. As soon as we were settled, the waitress came to our table and to take our drink orders. She looked at us. She was trying to write a story for this couple seated in the booth before her. April and I ordered cherry colas. They sounded good and just fit the situation.

"You kids know these ain't diet, right?" the waitress asked.

"I didn't think they were," I said. My tone sounded passive and unsure.

"Well, you never know nowadays," she said. "Everyone's trying to be Twiggy—watchin' their figure and all. Twiggy stole my look, you know. Now she's all rich and famous and I'm working here, getting nothing but fat and bad tips."

The waitress left to get our drinks. April pulled a face. It was a look of uncertainty.

"What's wrong?" I asked.

"I think our waitress is unhappy," she whispered.

"I don't know. I think it's part of the *charm,*" I said.

"Really?"

"Yeah, it's …" I paused. "Have you ever been to Ed Debevic's?"

The waitress brought our drinks. They were in tall, vintage bell glasses filled to the brim and adorned with a red straw. April's had a Maraschino cherry in it as well. I almost asked why I didn't have one in my drink. I considered the establishment and our waitress. Silence was warranted. It did make me smile.

"Here you go, sweets," the waitress said.

"Thank you," I said.

"I like the manners, honey," the waitress said with a smile. She looked at April and pointed to me. "He's a class act. Why'd ya let him drag you here?"

April tried to respond, but she was three kinds of speechless.

The waitress winked at her as she said, "It's okay, I still like him anyway." She walked away from the table and turned back toward us. "Compliments!" she yelled. "That should add another 5 percent to my tip!"

April and I shook our heads and laughed again.

We sipped our cherry colas and looked around the place. We pointed out the various posters and flyers to each other. We chatted about some of the movie posters.

Our discussion switched to music. She asked about some of the groups in the posters, and I told her what I knew. The poster of the Winter Dance Party of 1959 caught our eyes; however, it may have been more for the framed document beneath it. It was a copy of the front page of a newspaper dated February 3, 1959, known as "The Day the Music Died." Pictures of Buddy Holly, Richie Valens, and J.P. "The Big Bopper" Richardson stared out beneath the bold head-line "Top Rock and Roll Trio Killed in Airplane Crash."

"You hear about these things," April said. "But when you see them in print, it really brings them to life." She caught her faux pas. "Oh, God. I didn't mean it like that …"

"I know what you meant, April," I said. "And yes—it absolutely does."

After a couple of minutes of reflection, we went back to talking and moved onto less dark subject matter.

"What brings you to Elko?" I asked.

"My brother has a business here," April said. "He was looking for a marketing rep to handle a business deal."

"You're in marketing? What's that like?"

"It's a nice job. Sometimes it's hard to be ruthless, but you have to be to get the numbers."

"You don't strike me as the tough, hammer-dropping business woman—no offense," I said.

"None taken. I like to keep my competition guessing. It's easy to play dirty and win ugly but still have a pretty face."

I let my inhibitions down. "And you *do* have a very pretty face," realizing what I'd said before I could stop myself.

"Oh my God, April … I'm so sorry. That was a little forward of me," I said as my face reddened.

"No need to apologize," she said. "A girl likes to hear such things."

"I know, but we just met."

"That shouldn't matter, Louis. We're so damn afraid to compliment one another anymore."

"That's true. I wonder why that is?"

"Blame *feminism, chauvinism,* their bastard child *sexism,* and their little dog *political correctness,*" April said. "Women are supposed to adhere to a set of rules but can't be told they're attractive. It's okay to call me a bitch without knowing me. You just can't tell me I'm beautiful. It's stupid."

I smiled. I liked the fact that April felt comfortable around me to speak so freely. This was certainly not the same girl I'd met in the hotel lobby earlier today. That girl seemed naïve and flighty. First impressions …

I confessed. "I'm sorry about being so brazen, but I'm *not* sorry for what I said."

"Thank you," April said. She blushed and coyly looked away. The smile on her face was magical.

The waitress came back to our table and took our order. We ordered the Diner Double Deluxe. The waitress suggested we share the platter.

"Is it really that big?" April asked.

"Honey, your little petite frame will become an instant size 18 if you eat it by yourself," the waitress cautioned. "You're going to be at least a size 8 just by sharing it."

April covered her mouth and giggled.

"It's a big ol' pile of meat and everything that's bad for you," the waitress proclaimed. She looked me dead in the eye and said, "You may not be man enough to handle it, stud."

"I'm tougher than I look," I said. "My metabolism is high."

"Doll-face, after this, you'll have high cholesterol and high blood pressure too," she warned. "Hope your will is up to date."

Our dinner arrived, and the waitress was not joking about the size of this platter. April and I sat wide-eyed and burst into raucous laughter. There was no way one person could truly eat this entire plate of food. It was nothing short of a gastronomical disaster.

The meat on the burger was about three-fourths of an inch thick. It was grilled and greasy. It was capped with an oozing blend of five different molten cheeses: American, cheddar, Colby-Jack, white cheddar, and of course, Swiss—*very international.*

To counter the adverse effects of the meat and cheese were several nice, crisp leaves of Romaine Lettuce and three thickly sliced beef-steak tomatoes. Large rings of red onion and two huge pickle spears sat to the side of the burger. The bun was fat and shiny and looked to be whole wheat. Unfortunately, it had lost all of its healthy attributes long ago. There was another bun buried beneath everything.

The fries were definitely not French. They were very much American—big, bold, defiant, and against all convention. They were oval and looked more like thick potato chips than "fries." They still wore their skins, and there were a lot of them. I wondered if the cook used an entire ten-pound bag for this plate.

I cut the burger in half for April and me to share. I took my knife and fork and cut piece from my half. I brought the fork to April so she could have the first taste. She did not resist my gesture and leaned across the table to meet the suspended sample. Her eyes sparkled as she demurely took the bite.

She smiled as she chewed. Her eyes looked about first as she contemplated the quality and flavor of the food. She closed her eyes as she swallowed the morsel. She smiled again and let out a soft sigh followed by a subtle "Mmmmmm."

"How is it?" I asked.

"Oh my God," she said. "You have to try it!"

I cut off another piece to try it for myself.

"Well …?" April asked. "Wasn't it great?"

"It was amazing," I replied.

We ate as much as we could. We spent more time chatting than we did eating. Every so often the waitress came by and refreshed our drinks. She was becoming less abrasive with each stop. I got the feeling she knew something about April and me that neither of us were aware of yet.

So far in the last hour, I'd drank a little with April and shared quite a few laughs with her. We'd had an emotional connection over "The Day the Music Died" and now we were tackling this monstrous meal together. They were small steps, but they covered four of the Chief's Five Ls.

We had coffee after dinner and shared a slice of banana cream pie. It was the biggest "small" slice of pie I'd ever seen. The top was covered in thick whipped cream—definitely not from a can—and generous slices of fresh banana. Every bite tasted of lust.

"We're going to hell for eating this pie," I commented.

April didn't verbally respond to me. Her eyes rolled back in her head as she put another piece in her mouth.

When we'd finished the pie, the waitress brought the check and sat down in the booth next to April.

"Okay, you two, lay it on me," she said. "How was the grub? We've got a reputation, you know?"

"It was great," I said. "This was some of the best food I've ever had." I looked at April and asked, "Wouldn't you agree?"

"Oh yes! Absolutely!" she answered.

"Why'd you come here?" the waitress asked. "Of all the places you could go and dressed like you are. It just seems weird."

"We wanted to have some fun," April said. "We just met today and wanted to do something—not too *stuffy*, you know? This fit what we were looking for."

"Well, *beautiful,* this place isn't stuffy," the waitress stated. "But the food certainly is!"

"It's a lot for sure," April said. "But it was so amazing."

"Well, that's swell! It's just the *bee's knees,*" the waitress said. "Here's the damage and a couple of mints to help you on your date."

The waitress slid me the folded ticket. There were two huge, unwrapped, chalky butter mints sitting atop of it. I looked at the bill and thought nothing of it. April offered to chip in. I refused her money. It was our date but my treat. I left our waitress a ten-dollar tip.

I handed a mint to April. She pointed to her mouth, gesturing for me to feed it to her. I gently placed it behind her lips. She softly bit down on the mint, and I felt a strange sensation build in my body. I had an idea what I was feeling but wasn't sure if it was the right time to be feeling it.

We drove back to the hotel and talked about how great the evening had been so far. Everything seemed so free and easy between us. A thought crossed my mind, and although I was hesitant to ask it, I had to know. I had to know about the people April had been with earlier this afternoon. *Let it go. This is too good to ruin with stupid curiosities*, I said to myself. However, I was not going to let it go. I needed an answer.

"It's weird how everything has gone, don't you think?" I asked. "It's been such a great evening. I've never hit it off so well with someone so quickly."

"We seem to be doing pretty well, aren't we?" April agreed.

"Yeah, when I saw you and the Chief talking today, I didn't know what was going on."

"He's such a crazy guy. I thought he was your uncle or grandpa or something."

"No, not really. He's … he's kind of like my mentor."

"How so?"

"You ever watch *Shazam* on Saturday mornings as a kid?"

"Oh yes! *Shazam* was so great! And I absolutely loved Isis. She was so cool!"

"Well, the Chief is to me what Mentor was to Billy, I guess. It's an interesting story."

"I'd love to hear it."

"I'll tell you when we get back to the hotel."

I saw my window of opportunity open.

"By the way," I said. "I was wondering ... those people I saw you with earlier. Was that your brother and his friends?"

"Which people?" April asked. "When did you see me?"

I couldn't drop the subject now. I was too far gone.

"I was in the lobby this afternoon and saw you with another couple and a guy," I said. "You talked about your brother. I thought maybe one of the guys might've been him."

My words sounded probing and nervous.

April had a slightly sullen but stern look. She probably thought I was spying on her. Why didn't I keep my mouth shut?

"No, it wasn't my brother," she said. "I'm not even sure what—or who—you're talking about."

"Nothing. I'm sorry I brought it up," I said. "I was just wondering. It's none of my business."

"It isn't ... but I'm still not sure what you're talking about."

"I just saw you walking with a woman and two other men earlier. That's all. I'm sorry. I'm just a freakin' Nosy Nate. I'm so stupid."

Suddenly April's face changed. Her look went from "How dare you?" to "Oh, *now* I know." She laughed out loud and shook her head.

"What? Did you think I was *with* someone?" she asked.

I lied and said, "No. Not at all."

"Yes, you did! You thought I was with someone. At the very least, you thought one of the guys was my brother."

"That's true. I am sorry, April. I know I sound like I'm interrogating you. I'm not."

"Well, to ease your mind, I'm staying at the hotel alone. Do you think I would've gone out with you if I was spoken for? I mean—really? I'm single and out with you. The Chief asked me to see you and I said yes. I liked you from the start. He told me about you and I wanted to get to know you. Well … here I am."

"Here you are indeed. And I'm glad of it. I hope I didn't screw up the rest of our night."

"It's nothing a little fawning and a couple Manhattans can't fix."

"Fawning and Manhattans I can do."

"Good. All is then sort of forgiven," she said with a sly smirk.

"So now that we're okay—who were those people?" I wondered.

"Nobody," she said. "They were just three hotel guests I rode in the elevator with. We were all heading to the same place."

I parked the car and we walked toward the hotel. April extended her hand to me. She touched my fingers with hers. It took me a second to realize she was trying to hold my hand.

"I never thought you'd take it," she said of my slow reaction.

"I'm just not used to holding hands on a first date," I said.

"I could let go."

"I would prefer that you didn't."

April moved toward me and put her head on my shoulder.

We went to the hotel bar and ordered drinks. I got another scotch and soda and a pint of red ale. April got a Manhattan and a single shot of tequila. We found a table away from the dance floor and sat to enjoy our libations. The band was on break, and the bar was crowded.

I watched April sip her drink. She was beautiful. The soft candlelight from the table and the subtle ambient lights in the room made her look even more so. I had only met her today, but there was something between us—something very strong and real.

I didn't want to fall in love with the first girl I had met on this trip. That couldn't happen. No. We were just really good together. It was way too soon to even consider the mere possibility of *intense like*, let alone *love*. This was just a place to start. It was only the beginning of my journey. I couldn't, as the Chief said, "drop anchor" here.

I took a drink. Scotch and soda is not supposed to taste sweet, but this one did. *Oh no.*

April and I danced to a few songs. We drank several more drinks and both felt a little tipsy. We talked, laughed, and had a great time. It was everything a good date was supposed to be. The bar closed at 2:00 a.m. The band had quit an hour earlier and the house lights had slowly come up. We didn't even notice. We'd been lost in each other's company the whole night. The waiter broke us out of our daze and brought us back to reality. We were both a little embarrassed. We chuckled about closing the place down. I paid the tab and felt a sad twinge of finality. I started thinking that this was it—at least for the night. I wanted to stay with April. I didn't want any of this to end. I wanted to spend the night with her. I just didn't know how to tell her so.

We staggered slightly to the elevators. We laughed like a couple of high school kids, while simultaneously shushing each other. April pushed the buttons for all the floors.

"Oops!" she exclaimed.

"What floor are we going to?" I asked.

"All of them now," she said.

"Should we get off on our floors?"

"Maybe, but it would be fun to ride through them all, don't you think?"

I had a moment of clarity in my hazy drunken mind-set: April was trying to prolong our night. Riding from the first to the tenth floor and eventually back to our respective floors could take a little time. It wasn't a lot, but it was something extra.

We laughed loud as the elevator doors opened on each floor. Our drunken laughter echoed in the sleeping, empty halls. We could hear the reverberation muffle as the doors closed, and we lifted to the next floor. I kept worrying that hotel security was going to meet us at a stop. April didn't seem to care. The more I heard her laugh, the less I worried.

The car eventually stopped on the fourth floor. I held the door for April. I got out of the elevator and walked her to her room.

"Are you on this floor too?" she asked.

"No, I'm on the fifth," I said.

"Oh dear! Now you have to wait for the elevator to come back."

"I'll take the stairs. It's one floor."

I looked at April, and she returned my gaze. I wanted to kiss her, but I dared not.

"I had a great time tonight," I said. "I haven't had so much fun on a date in a long time."

"Me too, Louis," April responded. "You are such a great guy."

"Well … OK … um …" I stumbled through my words. "I really don't want this to end," I said.

"I don't either," she replied.

"What should we do?"

"This might be forward, but we could go to my room."

"We could. But we're right outside of my door."

April and I looked into each other's eyes. We didn't say a word. I moved toward her to kiss her. She smiled and turned away. I thought I'd screwed things up again. She slid her keycard into the slot and opened the door.

"We should continue this inside," she said.

I held the door for her and walked in after she entered the room.

"Would you like a beer?" she asked. "I have a couple Sam Adams in the fridge. My brother brought them up."

"Yes please," I said. "I'll get them. Do you want one too?"

"Sure."

I pulled two well-chilled Boston Lagers from the fridge and popped them open. I didn't ask if April wanted a cup; I just poured our beers into the flimsy plastic vessels and set them atop the dresser.

"Thank you, Louis," she said. "Oh, and a cup too–very classy!"

"Nothin' but the best," I said.

April dug through her suitcase.

"I'm going to put on my night clothes," she said. "I hope you don't mind. I just want to get comfy."

"I'm okay," I said. "Comfy is good."

April went into the bathroom. I sipped my beer as she changed. I heard water running and the sound of tooth brushing. My mouth began to feel disgusting as I thought of April having clean teeth and breath, when I did not. I started to get a little self-conscious.

She came out of the bathroom and was dressed in a huge pink T-shirt and pair of tight, black leggings. Her hair was mussed a bit. She looked relaxed but still amazing. I stood and stared at her.

She turned the TV on, found a channel that played music, and turned the volume down low. She turned on the light by the desk.

April walked around behind me. She didn't touch me or say a word. I could feel her presence. I didn't move. I wasn't sure what to do. She sat down on the edge of the bed, patted the mattress, and smiled. I had no idea what was going to happen next.

"Would you like your beer?" I asked. I sounded like a nervous teenager.

"Sure. Then come sit with me," she said, as she patted the mattress again.

I handed her the cup and slowly sat next to her on the bed. It was strange. The first thought I had—and the one that seemed to ease my mind—was how much firmer my mattress was than hers.

We sat quietly and sipped our beers. We hadn't run out of things to talk about—we just didn't want to say *goodnight* yet.

April broke the silence. "Louis, you never told me what you did," she said. "The Chief told me you were an artist, but he wasn't specific."

"I'm a writer, actually," I said. "I write travelogues and stuff like that."

"Have I seen anything you've written?"

"I don't know. I get published randomly. Maybe you have."

"Like in magazines and such?"

"Sometimes. It's usually trade press type stuff. Nothing like *Lonely Planet*, though."

"Where's some places you've been?"

"Well, my last stop was Crater Lake, Oregon. That trip is the reason I'm here now."

April shook her head. "Really?" she said. "I don't understand."

"It's a long story, but I'll condense it as much as I can," I said. "I went to Crater Lake and thought about it. I drove to Sacramento, put my thoughts on paper, and they sucked."

I took an angry sip of my beer and continued. "It sounded like shit. I went for a drink, and I met the Chief."

"That's pretty condensed," April commented. "And it opened the door for my next question."

"What's that?" I asked.

"How you met the Chief."

I smiled. "Our meeting was interesting," I said. "He was loud, obnoxious, and quite intimidating to start with."

"Really? He was so nice when he talked to me," April said.

"That's because he wasn't drunk."

"Oh. My."

"Yeah. So anyway, he starts talking to me and asking all kinds of questions. We have a couple of drinks and I showed him the work I was doing—the stuff that was giving me fits."

"Did he like it?"

"He did. However, he told me I could be doing better."

"How could he know you weren't doing your best? You just met."

"Oh, he knew. He saw right through me. He said my writing lacked 'soul.'"

April scowled. "Did that upset you?" she asked. "It sounds kind of harsh."

"It was, but it didn't upset me," I said. "He was absolutely right. There *was* no soul in my writing.

"Anyway, we got to talking, and the Chief tells me and the bartender about Cuba. I was fascinated. I felt like I was there. He talked about his first love: this Cuban girl named Mariposa. Did you know mariposa is Spanish for *butterfly?*"

"No, I didn't," April said.

"It is. It was such a beautiful story," I said as my eyes welled with tears. "A beautiful story like that always has a girl with a beautiful name. Mariposa … De Las Flores—*Butterfly of the Flowers*. That was her whole name. Can you imagine?"

"That is beautiful," April said. "It sounds so poetic—so romantic."

I started crying in front of April. I was so embarrassed. She took my beer and set it with hers on the nightstand. She held me as I cried. I couldn't believe I was weeping over a story about a girl I'd never met—in the arms of one I just had.

"So what else happened?" April asked gently.

"Oh my God. He told us about him and Mariposa …" I stopped. I wasn't sure if I should delve into the Chief's sexual exploits or not. April already knew.

"Did they make love?" She asked. "They *did, didn't they*? It must've been a most romantic tale."

"It was. It absolutely was, April," I said. "But I can't say any more. It's only for the Chief to tell. As strange as it all seems, that was what made me ask the Chief to travel with me."

"It does seem odd," April said. "But not that odd."

"I needed his wisdom," I said. "And he needed to get out of that bar. It was as simple as that."

April finished her beer and set the empty cup down. She turned toward me. She gave me a contemplative look that I had no idea how to read. She placed her hands on my legs. I was afraid of what she was going to ask me. When she spoke, it was not what I expected.

"Why does he go by *Chief*?" she asked. "Was he in the military or a cop or something?"

I laughed. "I thought the same thing," I said. "But I figured a fireman."

"Does he have a real name?" April wondered.

"I'm sure he does, but I don't think he'll tell anyone."

"Did you think it was weird to call him Chief?"

"No, not after I got used to it."

I was waiting for April to ask me how she fit into all this. She didn't. I was glad. I wasn't ready to explain the 5 Ls right now. I didn't want her to think she'd been reduced to some kind of litmus test, angrily wondering if she'd "made the grade." She definitely had. What was happening between us was so much more than I could have imagined. It went way beyond the basic premise of the 5 Ls. The social experiment ended a long time ago.

April yawned. It was not a bored yawn—it was a 4:00 a.m. yawn. I was tired as well, but all my gum-flapping had given me a second wind.

"I'm sorry for keeping you up so late, April," I said. "Maybe I should go so you can get some sleep."

April pushed her hands tighter on my legs. She shook her head and said, "No. I want you to stay with me, okay?"

I wanted to stay, but I didn't know the protocol—what to say? What to do? We'd had fun and laughed. We talked about so much and were still talking. We ate a big meal and drank enough to get properly drunk and feeling good. I'd even cried in front of her. We wanted to be together for the night. What did that mean at this moment? We'd held hands earlier but had yet to kiss.

The thought of making love with April was way in the back of my mind. I was crazy about her, even though it seemed too soon to be. I liked where things had gone. I was hoping to continue them when we woke up in a couple of hours—if we went to sleep at all. I wanted to be whatever April needed me to be. If she wanted me to make love to her, I would, but she hadn't said. I wasn't going to bring it up.

"Let's go to bed," she said. "Let's get some sleep, okay?"

"Sleep is good," I said. "I am pretty tired."

We said *good night* to each other. April shut the light off. The room was not dark. There was an ambient glow from the TV. A long, silver beam of light from the parking lot crept through a slit in the curtains and cut the room in half.

We curled up together, fully clothed, beneath the covers on her bed. She nestled tightly against me and shifted her body until she felt secure. I suddenly regained sobriety.

I could smell the fragrance of her shampoo as the top of her head settled just below my chin. I touched her hair. I realized I just wanted to touch *her*. She seemed comforted and I could feel her body sink into mine. I heard a soft, timid snore and then another. April had fallen asleep in my arms.

I closed my eyes but could not sleep. I turned slowly and kissed her forehead. She stirred and mumbled something. I kissed her again. She nuzzled closer and pulled her leg over my waist.

I started to fall asleep. I could faintly hear Jane Child's song "Don't Wanna Fall in Love" playing on the TV. *Too late, Jane … I think it's already happened.*

I woke up to a wonderful fragrance. However, the sounds I heard made the beautiful scent fade. My eyes were still closed. I didn't need to see. I knew I was hearing the sound of zippers and snaps—luggage being secured. It was the sound of *goodbye*. I opened my eyes. I saw April putting things into a tote bag. I stayed down in the bed so she wouldn't see me awake. I watched her finish tending to her packing and I sat up.

"Oh, good morning, sweetheart," April said softly. "I didn't mean to wake you."

"What time is it?" I asked.

"It's a little after seven. You can go back to sleep if you'd like."

"No. I'm up. I shouldn't be, but I am."

I brought myself up completely and sat on the edge of the bed. I watched April fuss with her hair in the big mirror above the dresser. She looked fantastic for someone who'd only gotten an hour and a half of sleep at best.

"What's with all the fanciness so early in the morning?" I asked half-jokingly.

"I have to leave," April said. "I've got a flight to catch at 9:30."

I was stunned. I was not expecting to hear that. I thought she was getting ready to go and work with her brother again.

"*A flight?* Where are you going?" I asked.

"Honey, I'm going home," she said. "I was just here for business."

"I thought you were here for a few more days."

"No, I'd already been here a week."

"You can't go, April … not yet … This isn't …"

April came and sat with me on the bed. She pulled me close to her and held me.

"If it's any consolation to you," she said, "I'll be back to Elko next month."

"I won't be here then," I replied coldly. "There's so much more ... I ..."

"Don't say anything, okay. I know. I know."

I wanted to tell April how I felt—*how she made me feel*—but I knew I had to keep it to myself. I could tell by her actions and the look on her face she was feeling the same about me. We weren't supposed to fall in love, but I think we had. If we hadn't, we came as close as humanly possible. This could not end. Unfortunately, it had to.

April got up. Her leaving my side made me feel as if my arm had been maliciously torn from my body. I'd never felt so strongly about a woman I'd known for less than twenty-four hours.

It was just one girl and just one night. We hit it off. There would be others. I'm a seeker—I'm on an adventure. These were the lies I told myself to hold back my tears. These were the lies I told myself to make me believe I had not fallen in love.

April gathered her luggage and stood in the middle of the room. She didn't say anything, but she looked distraught.

"Let me drive you to the airport," I offered. "I just want to be with you a little longer."

April dropped her head. "No. It's okay," she said. "I've already hired a cab."

"Save the money. I can take you. It's no big deal. I want to. Please?"

"No. You can't, Louis. You just can't."

"Why? Oh, April, please ..."

"Because, Louis. You say it's 'no big deal,' but that's just not true. It is *such* a big deal. I have to go ..."

April sniffled. It was getting harder to fight the tears.

"This wasn't supposed to happen, you know?" she said. "I was here, helping my brother. I was going to leave and go back to my boring life. You ruined all of that. You made me—"

"I made you what?" I implored. "What did I do?"

"You made me feel like *this*. I wasn't supposed to feel like *this*."

"I feel the same. I'm sorry for dragging you into whatever *this* is."

April sniffled again and laughed behind her tears. "You apologize too much," she said. "Did you realize that? You apologize for everything you do."

"I'm sorry," I said.

"Well, there you go again!"

April looked at the clock. "I have to go," she said. "My cab is downstairs for sure."

"I can't believe this is goodbye," I said. "I loved every minute we had together. Please know that."

"I do know it, because I feel the same."

"Are you sure I can't drive you to the airport?" I asked again.

"I'm sure," she replied somberly. "It's for the best."

"How so?"

"There'll be too much sadness. We don't want too much sadness."

"But there's too much sadness right now. What's a little more?"

"A little more is more than we can handle."

"It won't make a difference, April."

"Yes, it will."

"How?"

"We have our sadness now. When I leave, it will be gone."

"No, it won't. It'll still be with us."

"That's true, but this way—we won't have to *see* it any longer."

I offered to walk April to the lobby. I wanted just a few more precious minutes with her. She refused me again. This was indeed it. This was goodbye.

"Will I ever see you again?" I asked.

"I hope so," she whispered. "I'd like that very much."

April handed me a business card from her purse.

"This has all of my info on it," she said. "Oh, Louis, I have to go ..."

She kissed me softly on the lips. I tried to kiss her back, but she was in a rush to leave. She pulled away and walked out the door. She stood in the hall and gave me one last look.

"You can stay here a little longer, if you'd like," she said. "At least till I'm gone."

April turned and walked down the hall. She did not look back. Her head was hung low. Her sadness seemed to darken the hallway. The droning, rolling sound of her suitcase wheels on the carpet were the tones of sorrow and withdrawal.

I listened for the elevator car. I was so tempted to run down the hall and see her one more time just as the doors shut, but I did not.

It was very romantic, really. I'd woken up in her bed. We'd literally slept together, and her wanting to see me—to remember me—this way expressed things I understood but could not put into words. This was the way she left me: certainly not at my best. It was ironic—she refused to let me see her at her worst.

I heard the elevator bell ring, and I knew April was in the car and on her way to the lobby. I let the door shut, and I walked to the window. I peered through the curtains and kept a short vigil for her. I saw her walk into the valet roundabout and get into her cab. She never looked back toward the hotel. I watched her cab as it left the lot and drove to the street. I followed it as far as I could. It had disappeared from my sight—and so had April.

I closed the curtains and stepped to the bed. I fell onto the mattress and cried into April's pillow. I could smell her shampoo and faint hints of hairspray. I had indeed fallen in love with her. I don't think this was supposed to happen.

What was I going to tell the Chief? He wanted a "full report." I could not tell him I had fallen in love with the first girl I'd met. I lied to myself and tried filling my head with all the adventure bullshit again. Such talk made everything sound tough and robust; manly and powerful—certainly no place for weakness, delicate sentiments, and above all, tears.

I sat up and tried to collect myself. It was just past 8:00 a.m. I needed to get cleaned up and ready to meet the Chief. I went to the bathroom and looked in the mirror. I had to piss. I felt strange using April's bathroom, but then again, it was no longer hers.

I left this now anonymous furnished cubicle on the fourth floor and walked to the stairs. I didn't want to ride in the elevator yet. April's attar and essence were still inside of the car; I had to let them dissipate so I could let her go. I climbed the flight and entered the fifth-floor hall.

I opened the door to my room and it was just as I'd left it. I looked at myself in the mirror and sighed.

"Okay, Big Louie … get your shit together," I said to my reflection. "You've got lots more to see and do."

I smacked myself in the face. "It was good," I said. "It was *really* good. But it was just one and there will be more just like it—probably even better.

"This is just one stop; one step through a door, one cobblestone on a massive path."

I had one final crass comment: "It couldn't have been all that great," I said. "You didn't even want to fuck her." *There. You've sacked up.* I felt worse than before.

I went to the restaurant and spied the Chief sitting alone at a small table. He was reading the papers and had three cups of coffee in front of him.

"Good morning, Louie," he said. "What long lion tails do you have for me today?"

"Lion tails?" I asked.

"Yes. I want to know how you fared with the lovely April last night."

"Well, do you want *lion*—or *truthin'*?"

The Chief laughed. "You're getting better at this, me boy!" he said.

"Too bad it's not Sunday," the Chief lamented. "We could have *mimosas.*"

"Sorry, but it's Thursday," I said.

"Will an extra place at our table be required?"

"I'm afraid not. It's just the two of us today."

The Chief studied my face. I returned his gaze. I knew he was dying to know why I was alone.

"How did you make out last night, Louie?" the Chief asked. "You must know that by 'make out' I mean how did everything go? I'm not concerned about any *exploits* just yet."

"I appreciate that," I said. "Well, in a nutshell—things went okay."

"*Okay?* That's not a full report, son."

"If it means anything to you, she fulfilled the five Ls."

The Chief looked intrigued, but I didn't want to say any more.

"I'm sorry, Chief," I said. "I'm just not in the right mind today."

"Long night?" he asked.

"You could say that. I didn't get much sleep."

I saw a lecherous grin draw up on the Chief's face. I could smell the toast burning in his brain. I knew what he was thinking.

"Okay. Where do you want me to start?" I asked.

"From the beginning, me boy," he said. "Remember, I requested a *full report*—full disclosure."

"Is it wrong for me to leave out details?"

"I just want the facts, that's all. Any *detail* details are entirely at your discretion to share."

"Well, I'll start where we started. She was late, and I was pissed off. I almost bailed," I said. "I was at a point where I'd wanted to take you back to that pub and drain their cask of Guinness."

"You obviously waited?" the Chief asked.

"I did."

"She did show, even though she was late. Correct?"

"Yes, she did. She looked stunning. She was late because she was getting her hair done—*for me.* For our date. I was going to take a breeze and she got gussied up."

"How did you feel about that?"

"Like a damn heel at first. I'd felt like that all day. You know why."

"Yes I do. You said some mighty unsavory things about her."

"I did. And I felt horrible about it all."

The Chief stopped me and called the waiter over.

"My good man, I would like to order some grub," he said.

"Very well, sir, what can I get for you?" the waiter asked.

"I'll have the Eggs Benedict. Could you have the chef put a drop of Tabasco into the top of each egg? Only a drop now—and one per egg."

"Yes sir. I will see to it personally. What sides would you like?"

The Chief scanned the meats and fruit sides that came with the breakfast entrées.

"Quiero la fruta: piña y fresas, por favor," the Chief said in perfect Spanish.

The waiter smiled and asked, "Algo mas, Señor?"

"Si, si. Quiero carne, aa—Portugee …? I'm sorry … lo siento … aa … Linguica?"

The waiter nodded and smiled. He looked at the Chief and responded in English, "Would you rather have Linguica or chorizo?"

The Chief laughed. "I'm trying to impress you with my Spanish here," he said. "I like you, kid! Mi amigo … este niño!"

The waiter laughed too and assured him an extra serving of everything.

The waiter took my order. I didn't attempt any Spanish. I kept it simple: a large glass of tomato juice and some buttered sourdough toast.

"That was quite impressive," I said. "You speak Spanish very well."

"I did. I'm out of practice," the Chief said. "That waiter is probably gonna poison my food the way I poisoned his native tongue."

"I doubt that. You seem to know Russian too. You said *do svidanya* to me yesterday."

"Well, Louie, when you've been around like I have, you pick up a word or two."

"Nevertheless, it's pretty cool."

The Chief nodded and began scoping out the scene.

"Did you want something?" I asked. "You seem to be on the hunt."

"I am and I'm not, Louie," he said. "We could use a third at this table, but I'm not sure if it's appropriate right now."

"I think we're okay, Chief," I said. I knew he couldn't wait to put another girl in my lap.

"We are—for the moment," he said. "You still haven't finished telling me about your night."

"What more do you want to know?" I asked.

"The rest of it. Dinner, drinks—debauchery! The details!"

"You said I could leave out details."

"That's true. I did say that. okay, back to the facts."

"We went to a diner to eat. I really wanted a hamburger. She liked the idea."

"Sounds good," the Chief said. "How was the meal?"

"It was wonderful. The food was amazing, but it was enhanced by the conversation."

"As it should be when you're with a classy tomato like that."

"Indeed."

Our food arrived. The Chief's eyes beamed when he saw the two perfectly placed drops of Tabasco on the yolks of the eggs. The red appeared pink as it gently pushed through the light topping of Hollandaise Sauce. He nodded in approval. What seemed to make his eyes light up even more was the gorgeous young waitress of Polynesian descent who'd replaced our dapper—and linguistically forgiving Hispanic waiter.

The waitress placed the Chief's breakfast in front of him and smiled brightly. I knew she was in for trouble. I didn't know where this girl was from, but the Chief did.

"Mahalo nui loa," he said. "'O wai kou inoa?"

The waitress giggled and blushed and replied, "'O Ruby ko'u inoa."

"Ruby. Auê ka nani," the Chief responded.

Ruby giggled again and blushed even harder. I couldn't help but smile and roll my eyes. Two days ago, this man seated across me had complained about losing his edge, yet here we were at breakfast and he was charming the apron off our waitress—and in her native language at that. I hadn't forgotten how he'd played the lobby yesterday either. He'd talked to every woman that would listen. The Chief still had his mojo working. I couldn't figure out why he wasn't trying to find someone for himself instead of wasting his time and talent on me.

Ruby set my plate down. She placed a large bowl of fruit in the center of the table.

"From Ramon, with his compliments," Ruby said.

The Chief looked at the fruit and approved of the size and equal distribution of pineapple and strawberries.

"You still have an extra plate coming too, sir," Ruby said.

"Must be the *Portugee*," the Chief remarked.

"Ah, yes, it's is the *Portugee*," she said, pronouncing *Portugee* exactly like the Chief.

Ruby left the table. When she returned, she was carrying a huge plate loaded with dark red sausages. They looked and smelled divine. She asked if we were set with our meals.

The Chief smiled at her and said, "Hemolele!"

Once again, she giggled and blushed before replying, "E 'ai kaua."

Ruby left the table. I was still in awe of the Chief and his ability to talk to everyone in a different language.

"Louie, help yourself to some *Portugee*," the Chief said. "There's plenty of it."

"What exactly is *Portugee?*" I asked.

"It's pidgin. It's what the Hawaiians call the Portuguese sausage. You probably know it as *Linguica*."

"That one I'm familiar with," I said. I partook of a link of the *Portugee*. I hoped it tasted as good as it looked and smelled.

"What language was that you were speaking to the waitress?" I asked the Chief.

"Hawaiian," he said. "She's a *wahine*."

"A what?"

"A *wahine*—it's broad-brush Hawaiian for girl or woman."

"What exactly did you say to her?"

"I thanked her for the food, and I asked her what her name was. When she told me, I said it was *beautiful*. When she asked about our meals, I told her they were *perfect*. She bid us *'Bon appetit.'*"

"How did you know she was Hawaiian?" I asked.

"Louie, I've been to the Islands," he stated. "I know these things."

"Yeah, I know, but Hawaiian … that's pretty specific," I said.

"Okay. You got me. She had a tattoo of a hibiscus with the word *Ohana* on her wrist," the Chief confessed.

"How the hell did you see that?"

"Louie, when I look at a woman, I look at *all* of her. It's not just about faces and fannies. It's about finding every detail and learning all you can. This is why we're here now, remember?"

"I remember. I still don't know how you saw her tattoo."

Ruby came back to the table to ask if we needed anything. The Chief chatted and charmed her in Hawaiian again, and I tried to find her tattoo. I did, but I couldn't make it out right away. I had to focus on it, and even then, I still couldn't read it. The more time I spent with the Chief, the more I was beginning to wonder if he was superhuman.

The Chief took a sip of his coffee. He placed the cup on the table and continued asking me about last night.

"You and April ate well?" he asked. "Did you actually have a burger?"

"Yes. We shared a plate," I said. "It was too big for one person."

"I'll bet that was nice. How did she eat?"

"What do you mean?"

"How did she look when she ate? Was she a grazer or a proper *gourmand*?"

"She ate like a normal person—maybe slightly more dignified? I don't know. I fed her the first bite. That was pretty cool and romantic."

"Louie, one might say you had her eating out of your hand."

"But from a fork."

"Oh, but of course!"

"So you found her to be a suitable luncheon mate?"

"Yes, definitely. We shared a slice of banana cream pie for dessert as well."

"There was a lot of sharing going on."

"That's because there was a lot of damn food! I'd never seen portions so big."

"What else did you share? Did you have a 'moment' at dinner?"

"We may have, I suppose. We laughed a lot."

"She's a laugh mate too? Splendid, Louie!"

I started to find it difficult to keep talking about April, but I knew he was going to keep pestering me about everything. I thought I could give him a *Readers' Digest* version of the date, but he'd see through it. I had to keep him informed while keeping my emotions in check.

"After dinner, we came back here and had drinks," I said. "She likes Manhattans. We had several drinks. More than we should have. We danced too. I'm a terrible dancer, but she danced with me. It was … yeah …"

"Louie, you're rambling a little," the Chief said. "Are you okay, son?"

"Yeah. I am."

The Chief saw straight into my heart.

"You spent the night with her, didn't you?" the Chief asked.

"In a manner of speaking, yes," I said.

The Chief looked at my eyes. I had no way to defend his gaze. I was hoping he'd sit back and think that good ol' Louie 'got a little' last night. I wouldn't say yes or no—just let him think what he wanted. The Chief was too adept at this. I felt like I was being profiled for a crime.

"That's not the face of a man who spent the night with a woman and made love to her," he said. "That's the face of a man who spent the night with a woman and had his heart broken."

I sat silent. I was busted. I knew I couldn't hide anything from him. I dropped my head slightly.

"What happened, son?" he asked. "You just tell me when you're ready."

"I'm not sure," I said. "I don't think it was supposed to go like it did."

"What do you mean? It sounds like it went just as it should've— up to the end at least."

"The end was bad but not like it could've been. Not like what you think."

"You had dinner and drinks. You had some laughs. You went to bed with her. What happened after that?"

"Well, to clarify: I went to bed with her, but we didn't have sex. There was a great intimacy between us, but we didn't make love."

"You don't have to make love, Louie. Intimacy does not always mean intercourse."

I looked around the restaurant. No one was paying attention to our conversation, but I was still uncomfortable.

"I forgot to mention ... I cried too," I said. "Add lachrymal mate as well."

The Chief shook his head. "This wasn't where it went bad, was it?" he asked.

"Oh, God, no!" I said. "I teared up before we went to sleep."

"What upset you?"

"Nothing, really. I was telling April how your story about Mariposa made me feel."

"How *did* it make you feel?"

"Chief, it changed my way of thinking. Obviously, it really struck me."

"Obviously! Well, I'll be a mare's ass. I didn't know that."

"How could you? I never really told you much beyond how amazing it was to hear."

The Chief shut down again. It was strange this time because he'd done it while I was retelling *my* story. He resumed eating his breakfast and didn't say a word. Between bites, he would point his fork at the fruit and *Portugee,* gesturing for me to help myself to more. I did just to appease him.

Ruby came back and brought me another glass of tomato juice. She topped off the Chief's coffee as well. I had figured I'd lost him for the rest of the day, but seeing his little *wahine* again snapped him out of his funk and back into our conversation.

"Where did you two go wrong?" the Chief asked. "Something must've happened."

"No, it was nothing like that," I said. "Things couldn't have been better."

"Well, why isn't she here? And why are you so goddamned upset?"

"Because she's gone, Chief. She left."

"Gone? Where'd she go?"

"She went home. She had a flight this morning. She's thirty-five thousand feet in the air right now going God-knows-where."

"Did she tell you where she was heading? Where home was?"

"No. She didn't. She just gave me a business card."

"Did you read it?"

"No. I couldn't. I was devastated watching her go. I offered to drive her to the airport, but she wouldn't have it. She left me and I looked a wreck—she was so beautiful."

"Well, read the damn card, Louie. Find out where she's headed."

"I can't. I just can't, Chief."

"*Why the hell not?*" the Chief yelled and slammed his fist on the table.

Our dishes bounced, and the silverware clanked and rattled dully against the fabric of the tablecloth. This attracted the attention of the restaurant patrons. Everyone turned our way. There was a quick and very noticeable silence within the room. The Chief looked around and nervously pulled at his collar. He leaned across the table and, using a more subdued tone, repeated himself. "Why the hell not, Louie?"

I didn't answer him. I reached into my pocket and pulled April's business card out. It was facedown, and I refused to turn it over. I slid it across the table to the Chief.

"Here," I said. "You read it."

The Chief looked at me and then at the overturned card.

"Well, go on," I said. "Take a look at it. See what it says."

"No see on all dry land, Louie—you know that," the Chief replied. "This is not for me to do."

"I want you to look at it. I just don't want to know what it says."

"Are you sure? It may hold great promise."

"I'm sure. If it's the key to my happiness, I'll know when the time is right."

The Chief turned the card over. He read the print. When he was finished, he slid the card back to me. I shook my head refusing it. I couldn't stand to have it in my possession. The Chief took the card and slowly placed it in his pocket. He looked at me and shook his head. The head shake didn't mesh with the look on his face. I was caught between the devil and deep, blue sea.

"Everything you could want to know is on that card, Louie," the Chief said.

"April kind of said that as well," I replied.

"Well, son, if she's your girl, your destiny is a hell of a lot closer than you think."

"What does that mean?"

"It means nothing now—unless you fell in love with her. Did you fall in love with her?"

I shook my head and scowled—and lied my ass off. "No … I didn't … You can't possibly think … *Come on!*" I stuttered. "We've got too much to see and do and too many other women to meet. I'm certainly not going to fall in love with the first one I'm with."

There was no way the Chief was convinced with what I'd said. He just nodded and finished eating his breakfast.

Just as April and I had done in the darker hours of this morning, the Chief and I closed the restaurant down. We were the last to leave after the breakfast service. The manager had to tell us it was time to go.

When I paid the check, the manager had a mischievous look on his face.

"What's that all about?" I asked.

"You, sir. You're becoming a fixture here," he said.

"How do you mean?"

"You closed my bar last night, and you closed my breakfast down as well."

I laughed and said, "I can't get enough of this place."

The manager tore up my bill and gave me my money back. I was surprised.

"What's the deal?" I asked.

"Breakfast is on the house. You and your friend were so good to my servers this morning," he said. "And you and your lady friend were so kind last night to everyone. Just put a tip on the table and you're set."

"Oh my God, thank you so much! Are you sure?"

"Yes, sir—I am quite sure."

I walked to the table and took out my wallet. I filed through the bills. I left a fifty-dollar tip: twenty-five for Ramon and twenty-five for Ruby.

I met the Chief in the lobby and told him about the complimentary breakfast.

"Louie, there's good out there," the Chief said. "We'll come across more as we venture, I guarantee it."

"I'm looking forward to it, Chief," I said. "I just can't let the comps go to my head."

The Chief laughed. "No, you can't," he said. "But they sure are damn nice when they come around."

The Chief and I sat down in the lobby. We tried to figure out the rest of our day. We'd been in Elko for about twenty-four hours and hadn't done one thing to enhance and enrich my artistic soul. I'd gotten lost in love and successfully fulfilled the Five Ls for one day, but that was only part of why we were here. We needed to get out and see something. I needed something to write about and absorb its essence. The Chief needed to discover something new. More than anything, I needed to get my mind off April.

I found a brochure of events and sights in the Elko area. The Chief and I went through it and looked for something that satisfied all our needs. Nothing seemed to strike our fancy at first, but then something in the brochure hit the Chief.

"Louie. Look at this," he said.

I looked at the page, and a huge smile drew across my face.

"The Ruby Mountains," the Chief said. "That's where we're going. See, there was a reason I chatted up that *wahine* at breakfast."

"I think you're right," I said. "This is too perfect."

"Inasmuch as there's no such thing as perfection."

"Right, but you have to admit it is a pretty cool coincidence, eh?"

"It is, me boy—it is!"

Even though I knew I'd find captivating sights and natural beauty within the confines of the Ruby Mountains, I was no outdoorsman in any sense. My trip to Crater Lake was the most I'd been *in nature* in my entire life.

"Maybe this is not such a good idea," I said. "What are we going to do in the mountains?"

"We're going to see things, Louie," the Chief said. "And you're going to let them envelope you. And you're going to write a *razz-babler* of a story about them."

It sounded easy enough. I needed to start somewhere—even if that somewhere involved tripping over rocks and branches and kicking rattlesnakes.

"I'm no hiker, Chief. Just so you know," I said.

"Neither am I," he replied. "We're not going to kill ourselves. We're just going to look at some natural beauty that's sharp and craggy, instead of soft and curvy. We'll take care of *that* later."

The Chief and I left the hotel and made our way toward the Ruby Mountains.

"We're heading to a town called Wells," the Chief said.

"What's there?" I asked.

"US 93 to start and a place called Secret Pass."

We drove for about forty-five minutes. We got to Wells and picked up US 93—the Great Basin Highway. We headed south and ran along the eastern edge of the Ruby Mountains. We were looking for Nevada State Route 229. This would take us to Secret Pass.

I was in awe of what I was seeing. The mountains were so beautiful even in their current state of dry, desert summer colors. Their peaks were still snow-capped.

"I'm going to want to stop at some point," I said. "My spirit needs to have a conversation with God and Mother Nature."

The Chief seemed confused by my words. "You gotta take a shit, Louie?" he asked unabashedly.

"No. I just think I can cull something from this," I said.

"Okay. It just sounded like …"

I cut the Chief off. "I know what it sounded like," I said.

We continued driving until we got to Secret Pass. We made stops along the way, and I wrote quick notes about what I saw. At some points, I sat and stared and wrote nothing. I didn't know what to say. There were no words I could conjure up to describe what I saw and how it made me feel.

"So what have God and Mother Nature said to you?" the Chief asked.

"I don't know," I said. "But they've been speaking to me."

"When you figure it all out, hopefully it's what you wanted to hear."

I nodded. "That would be nice," I said.

I gathered what I could from the places we'd stopped. I'd seen a lot and felt even more. I was hoping that this would be the first of many inspirational detours as the Chief and I made our way across the US of E.

"Louie, I think it's time for a belt," the Chief said. "Although out here, there probably isn't much."

"Not much of what?" I wondered. "Civilization? Or places to get a beer?"

"Both."

We leaned into a few curves and began heading north again. The Chief was still talking about libations, and it was starting to sound good to me as well. It didn't take long, and we happened upon a town—a place called Jiggs. The Chief smiled brightly, and looked like a little kid who'd hit the motherlode on Christmas morning.

"Hell yes, Louie!" he exclaimed. "This is my kind of town. It's just a fucking bar!"

Indeed it was. Jiggs, Nevada, was nothing more than a bar—an Old West style saloon, actually.

The Chief was chomping at the bit to go in. I dropped him off and pulled the car around to park. I got out and looked at the place. I felt like I was underdressed, and by that, I mean I needed a ten-gallon hat, some spurs, a belt of bullets, and a holster for my shootin' eye-urn.

I had to wonder if at any second some green horn, lily liver, or tenderfoot was going to come flying through the door—landing hard on his ass in a cloud of dust. Would it have been because he stiffed the barkeep out of two bits? Or was it because he eyeballed one of the barmaids the wrong way? It was probably because he complained too much about the rotgut—*yeah, that'll get ya tossed every time.* I stood waiting. No one came flying out, so I walked on in.

The interior of Jiggs's Bar was open and bright. The bar itself was old and long and the stools had seen better days. A couple of them had tears in their worn, faded black vinyl, while others had red vinyl. I took a seat next to the Chief. I found this ratty, well-worn, and half-shredded barstool to be one of the most comfortable pieces of furniture I've had the pleasure of parking my ass on—ever!

I looked at the Chief. There were three empty shot glasses in front of him. In the time it took for me to park and peruse the establishment, he'd already had three gulps of God knows what.

"Can I get two Budweiser's, please?" I asked. "And put this old man's stuff on my tab." I said pointing to the Chief.

"He's already got your tab going," the bartender said. "He said it was okay."

"I guess it is. He's always one step ahead of me."

The bartender laughed. "You gentlemen from out of town?" he asked.

"Yep, we're here for a couple of days exploring," I said. "I'm trying to make myself a better person. Weird, I know."

"Not really. You won't believe the kinds that come through those doors."

"I'd like to find out. They could probably help me."

"How so? You writin' a book?"

"In a way, yes. I'm trying to discover interesting things. The old man here—the Chief—he's keeping me on point."

"Damn, son, you sure came to the right place. You want interesting? We got it by the barrelful. Every five minutes it's another adventure."

I took a swig of my beer and looked at the Chief. He hadn't said a word since I came in.

"Chief. Are you okay?" I asked.

He looked at me and asked, "Louie—how's your *chung-mung-fung-gooer?*"

"Um, I suppose it's just fine," I said. I had no idea what the hell he was talking about.

"Ya, damn straight it is," he said. "You know that cute little tomato you went out with last night?"

"April? Yes, Chief, I know her quite well."

"She's a good woman, Louie. A damn good woman. She's a keeper."

I put my defenses up. "That she is, Chief," I said. "She's something amazing."

"Can I tell you something about her?" he asked. "It's pretty good, I promise."

I was a bit apprehensive to hear what the Chief had to say, but I acquiesced and let him tell me his "good" secret.

"What is it?" I asked.

"She's closer than you think, Louie," he said. "She's not far from you."

"I know, Chief, it's all semantics and perception," I said. "I wish she was here, but she's not."

"No, Louie, you're right, she's not *here*," the Chief said. "But she is close. Don't forget that. She's so damn close."

I still didn't understand what he was saying. I waved it off. Now I could feel April somewhere in the bar.

I finished my two beers and ordered a couple more. The Chief had two more as well. Dusk was slowly setting in, and so were other patrons. For a town of none, there were sure a lot of people filing into Jiggs for the evening shift.

I did quite a bit of people watching. I listened to tales of everything from fishing to farming. One gentleman was decked out in cowboy gear and talked about how he couldn't find a place to "park" his horse. I chuckled at this. It sounded ridiculous. Another patron asked where he'd eventually found a spot. The cowboy replied that he had and that his horse was "right cozy" with Tubby's old Shivee.

We'd been at the bar for almost three hours. The Chief was tanked, even though he swore he was not. I helped him up, and he wobbled a bit before he got his footing. I paid our tab and thanked the bartender.

The Chief and I walked out just as a new crowd of folks were streaming in. As we made our way to the car, I saw the damnedest thing—a true case of the word and the deed going hand in hand. I saw a huge Belgian horse, his reins loosely tied around a welded armature of thick pipes. These pipes were in the bed of an old Chevrolet pickup truck. I had to imagine that this was Tubby's truck, and sure enough, this horse was "right cozy" with it. I came to a realization: if you hear it at Jiggs' Bar—you just might want to believe it.

The drive back to town was quiet. We came up over a ridge. The sun had not fully set. The western sky was still painted with all the colors of festivity and warmth and joy. As I viewed them and drove closer, these swaths of yellow, orange, red, and varying shades of violet stacked atop one another made me feel tiny and insignificant. The Chief talked about "going beyond." Could this be what he meant?

"Chief, are you up for another round?" I asked. "Let's hit that tavern we popped into last night. Think you can walk there and back?"

"Louie, I'm as sober as a goddamned judge, kid," the Chief said.

We walked to the bar, and the same crowd that had graced the place last night was there this evening as well. They greeted us as we walked in. I felt like a barfly on the TV show *Cheers*. The bartender pointed us to our spots and dropped our pub mats down.

"After you, Mr. Hemingway," the Chief said as he gestured to my barstool.

I blushed at the highly endearing and most undeserving accolade. I had to counter.

"No, no, after you, Mr. Sinatra—I must insist," I said as I waved the Chief to his chair.

The Chief and I had a hearty laugh at our bestowment of titles. *Where is Ava Gardner when you need her?*

The bartender drew another two perfect pints of Guinness for the Chief and me.

"An army travels on its stomach," the Chief said, out of the blue. "It's time for a little grub."

He called the bartender over and inquired about food.

"*Bradford,* my good man," he said. "How's the mess looking tonight?"

The bartender—whose name may or may not be Bradford—handed us a couple of menus.

"We don't have a lot," he said. "But what we have is pretty good."

"Pretty good is good enough," the Chief said.

The Chief and I scanned the selections. He wasn't kidding—there really wasn't much, but it did sound good. There was a burger and fries. The description of the burger reminded me of the one I'd had at the diner. There was a steak and eggs combination. The eggs were cooked to order—as long as they were sunny-side up or scrambled. The fish and chips sounded nice. It was the only the only dish to come with "greens"—those being a scoop of coleslaw. *Nice try.* The "suds soaker" appetizers were a platter of French Fries, onion rings, and fried cheese curds. I was up for anything.

"I'd like to get the fish and chips, please," I said.

"Do you want *authentic* or *Yankee style?*" 'Bradford' asked.

"What's the difference?"

"*Authentic* comes with fries, like they do it in England. *Yankee style* comes with potato chips."

"I'll take the authentic."

'Bradford' asked the Chief, "and for you, sir?"

"I'll have the steak and eggs," the Chief said.

"How do you want them cooked?" Bradford asked.

"I'll take them both rare. I want to cut into each and hear them loudly sing out their barnyard songs."

Bradford nodded and laughed. "Very well, sir," he said. "Bloody and bursting!"

He called to one of the men sitting in a back corner of the tavern. This must've been the cook. Apparently, they didn't get much in the way of food orders, as the cook seemed surprised his presence was requested in the kitchen. Bradford seemed surprised the cook actually got up to do his job.

The Chief and I drained our pints. He ordered another Guinness while I ordered a scotch and soda. As we sat and chatted and waited for our food, we watched two very beautiful women walk into the bar. They seemed out of place. The Chief zeroed in on the older woman. She had thick black hair, about shoulder-length and shimmering. Her skin had an olive tone, and her eyes were deep brown and alluring. She was wearing very little makeup. She didn't even need what she had on.

The Chief leaned against me. "Louie, do you see that?" he asked. "I think I'm in love."

"Yes, I see her," I said. "And her sidekick too."

The woman accompanying the Chief's new found love interest was much younger but certainly of age to be in a bar. She had dark-brown hair, streaked with chestnut highlights. It was much longer and fuller than the other woman's. Her skin, albeit lighter than the older woman's, had an olive tone as well. Her eyes were jade green.

The women flashed knowing smiles in our direction as they glided past us. The younger of the two winked at us.

"This is indeed a dilemma, Louie," the Chief said. "I've got things moving that I thought quit, died, or broke off years ago."

The women sat at a table near the center of the bar. The older woman read the "Specials" aloud from the laminated place card, while the younger one looked around the room and scanned faces. No one seemed fussed or fazed by them like the Chief and I were. This was strange to me. In a place like this, women of such stunning beauty are usually attacked the moment the aroma of their perfume permeates beyond the threshold of the door. They don't have to be physically present to attract attention. This was not the case with these two. I had to wonder if they were regulars.

"Bradford, come here," the Chief whispered. He waved the bartender over.

"Yes, sir?" Bradford inquired.

"What's the skinny on those two tomatoes?"

"Their names are Estelle and Cindy."

"Which one's which?"

"Estelle is the older one. Cindy is her daughter."

The Chief's eyes got big. He was no doubt imagining some twisted, forbidden mother-daughter tryst that only occurs in adult films and fake letters in *Penthouse Magazine.* I know the thought because for a brief second, I had it too.

"They come here often?" the Chief asked.

"Often? Not really," Bradford said. "Maybe every couple weeks or so."

"Not to be rude, but—why? Why here? Those are two classy broads."

Bradford took no offense to the Chief's comment. "Because they like the drinks," he said. He jabbed back at the Chief. "And I make some pretty 'classy' drinks."

"What types of *classy* drinks would you whip up for ladies of such caliber?" the Chief asked.

"Whatever they want," Bradford said. "They always get something different."

The Chief and I were stupefied. None of this made sense. These ladies didn't belong here, yet they came in with a minor semblance of frequency. They ordered a variety of drinks, but there was no list of cocktails or other mixed fare to be found. The "Specials" on the place card read, "Well drinks, big beers (excludes imports)"—Guinness was the only "import" we'd noticed, you call it shots, and my favorite—"the managers' special (ask about it. Only available 6:00 to 9:00 p.m.)." We were missing something.

The women hadn't ordered drinks yet. Our food had just arrived, and we were set to get another round. The Chief added two extras to the tab.

"We'd like send a couple of libations to those gals," the Chief said to Bradford. "Something good, sweet and classic. Something they've never had before. You got a recommendation?"

Bradford thought. "They never get the same thing," he said. "So guess whatever you send them would be fine."

"Bradford, I think we'd like to order up an old-fashioned for Mama-san and a margarita for her lovely daughter," the Chief said.

"Sounds good, sir," Bradford said. "I don't think they've ordered either one of those before."

"Well, damn it all!" the Chief exclaimed. "I'm one innovative son of a bitch."

Bradford went behind the bar to prepare Estelle and Cindy's drinks. He dropped down and disappeared for a moment. When he popped back up, he had several bottles of liquor that had been nowhere in sight earlier.

"What the hell?" I asked. "You've been holding out on us."

"What do you mean?" Bradford asked.

"That's false advertising, man. You park the Yugos out front while hiding Ferraris in the garage?"

"I have to. If I let everyone know I had the good stuff, I couldn't sell the other."

I looked at Bradford and shook my head.

"Have you really seen your crew?" I asked. "There's not one person in here who's gonna order top-shelf stuff—except for those two ladies. Am I right?"

Bradford laughed. "Probably," he said. "But I still gotta keep up appearances."

The Chief kept casting his gaze toward Estelle and Cindy's table. He tried to be clandestine but was failing. His expression was impossible to deny—he was smitten with Estelle.

"Chief, why don't you go talk to her?" I asked. "Their drinks will be ready in a minute. Just take them to the table."

"Nope, Louie. I've got to eat my steak," the Chief insisted. "This choice cut of beef is too good to let grow cold."

"You're stalling. You know that, right?"

"Stalling? Surely you jest. I don't stall, son. I take my time. I assess and ascertain. Such matters must be dealt with accordingly and in due time."

"You're fucking stalling. That was all just double-talk for stalling, Chief."

I called to Bradford. "Will you tell him he's stalling?" I asked.

"He's right," Bradford said. "You are stalling."

The Chief blushed. I'd only known this man for a couple of days, but we'd had some pretty heady conversations in that short time. I'd gone red-faced on numerous occasions, but this was the first time I'd seen the Chief do it.

Bradford finished mixing the drinks and started to the ladies' table.

"Hold up a second," I said. "Should we take them over there?"

"That's not how it works," Bradford said. "I take 'em and tip 'em off—then you talk 'em up. That way, it alleviates any uncomfortable scenes."

"How so?"

"You never look good standing before a couple of ladies holding drinks they didn't order."

"They didn't order these."

"True, but this way, if they don't accept them, you're just out the drinks. It saves a little face—and a lot of embarrassment."

"I never thought of it like that."

"Nobody ever does."

"If they don't accept it, you are out the booze, though."

"Sure. But pitching out a little rejected hooch hurts much less than getting your heart broken."

I had no response. Bradford's words sounded sage to me. I filed them with the other affirmations, musings, and things I'd learned today.

The Chief and I stealthily watched as Bradford presented Estelle and Cindy with their drinks. I took sips of my scotch and soda between bites of my food.

Bradford pointed toward us. The women seemed pleased with our unsolicited offerings. Estelle smiled and raised her glass. Cindy tucked her head down slightly and coyly grinned.

"Well, what do you think?" I asked. "Should we go talk to them?"

The Chief was still nervous. I couldn't figure him out right now. He talked about love and sex and made it pure poetry. He chatted up several women in the hotel lobby yesterday, not to mention securing a date for me. He spoke free and easy and *in Hawaiian* to our waitress this morning at breakfast. However, at this moment, he was lost. He was overcome by feelings he probably had not actually felt in a very long time. He saw something in Estelle that stirred him deeply, and it was something much more than just her aesthetics. The Chief was moved by her soul. He had never met this woman before—*or had he?*

"Louie, I'm going to stay right here," he said. "I'm not going to cause any problems."

"What's the matter?" I asked.

"I've got to finish my dinner."

"We've gone over this, Chief."

"Well, it's the decision I've made, and I can't break from it. That would make me a hypocrite."

"No, Chief—not following your feelings makes you a hypocrite."

"You go talk to the tomatoes. Put in a good word for the ol' boy, will ya?"

"Put in your own good word. You brought this on yourself, you know?"

"The hell you say!"

"No, you did. You bought them the drinks. I was fine to just sit and be a lump. You had to stir the glass, as it were."

I looked over to the ladies' table and saw Estelle gesture to us.

"We're being paged, Chief," I said. "Mom just gave us the all-clear."

I got up and headed to the table. The Chief watched. I believe he was surprised at my sudden adventurous streak. It wasn't as grand as he may have thought. I was no doubt, attracted to Cindy, but my heart was still with April. I was just looking for someone to casually talk and drink with—nothing more.

"Good evening, ladies," I said. "How are you tonight?"

Estelle smiled and gestured to an empty chair. "Have a seat," she said.

"Thank you," I said as I sat down. "My name is Louis. I hope you don't mind the drinks."

"Oh, not at all," Estelle said. "They are lovely, as was the gesture."

"I'm glad you like them. They were my friend's idea. He gets the credit."

"Well, I certainly hope he'll join us so I can thank him personally."

"He'll be over. He's just a little shy."

Cindy kept blushing and looking away.

"Where are my manners?" Estelle asked. "My name is Stella, and this shrinking violet here is my daughter Cynthia."

I didn't make corrections. I held my hand out to each of them and greeted them just as they'd been introduced.

"It is very nice to meet you Stella, Cynthia," I said after shaking their hands. Cynthia informed me that I could call her Cindy.

The Chief looked over at us. He remained at bay and continued tending to his dinner. I kept sending him subtle gestures that it was okay for him to join us. After a while, I couldn't stand his shy routine anymore.

"Stella, my friend is interminably reluctant to grace us with his company," I said. "Would you mind telling him that everything is fine and we'd like him to come and sit with us?"

Stella smiled and got up. She sashayed to the bar and began talking to the Chief. It was a sight to see. He fidgeted nervously in her presence. This woman had turned the Casanova of Old Cuba in to a gushing, crushing high-schooler.

I'd never have believed this was the same man who'd built lush landscapes and scenery of passion, potency, and prowess. The Chief's testosterone levels seemed to have dropped to zero. The longer Stella kept his company, the more he melted. Stella referred to her daughter as a "shrinking violet." She was turning the Chief into a wilting lily.

"What's wrong with your friend?" Cindy asked. "He couldn't take his eyes off my mother before, and now he can't look at her."

"He's fine," I said. "He's just a little out of practice is all."

"How so?"

"He's been holed up in a bar in California for too long. I brought him out to see the world. It's changed a bit for him."

"That sounds interesting. Are you from California?"

"I lived there when I was a kid. Are you and your mom from here in Nevada?"

"We are. We used to live in Reno but moved to Elko for my dad's job."

"What does your dad do?"

"He used to be a miner. He died about nine years ago."

Cindy's statement about her father seemed cold and distant. I wasn't sure what to make of it.

"I'm very sorry to hear that," I said.

"It's okay. He wasn't around much for us," she said. "If he wasn't down in a shaft for work, he was down in one of the local girls."

I took a sip of my drink. What the hell else was I going to do?

Stella finally got the Chief to come and join us. I was quite happy to have him at the table. My conversation with Cindy had just taken an odd turn. I didn't know what to say or how to feel about her comments on her dad. I began to wonder if Cindy and her mom coming here wasn't some way of exacting revenge on this deceased man. The longer I sat with these two femme fatales, the more uncomfortable I was getting. Perhaps the Chief was right to keep his distance? Maybe he knew something?

"So where are you boys from?" Stella asked. "We know most of the folks around here, and we've never seen you two before."

"We're from parts unknown, ma'am," the Chief said. He opened his arms, depicting some vast expanse.

I rolled my eyes. The ladies seemed to love it. I think I knew why. They were going to kill the Chief with their wiles.

"Well, what brings you to our little corner of the world?" Stella asked.

"The lad here," the Chief said, pointing to me. "He's a literary genius in search of the next great tome. He and I have taken to the road to find his muse."

I shook my head and dropped it slightly. Under my breath, I said, "Fucking bullshit …"

"Louie, tell these ladies your tales of travel," the Chief said.

"There's not much to tell, really," I quipped. "I am, as the man said, trying to find my muse. We're going here and there, and I'm jotting it down."

The Chief took drink requests, and Bradford brought us another round. The ladies seemed just as happy as the Chief to not have to pay for drinks tonight. I felt like a Gin John—just paying for the privilege.

It wasn't long after the second round came that the Chief ordered the snack platter as well. We were on the verge of hitting three of the Five Ls tonight. I was sure I'd be my own lachrymal mate when I saw the tab.

"I have to ask, what brings two beautiful dames like yourselves into an establishment such as this?" the Chief inquired. He half-assed waxed Bogart. "'Of all the gin joints ...' You know the rest, right?"

The ladies didn't know the line, but I did. I found myself contemplating the statement personally. The longer the night went on, the more I could feel my defenses strengthening. I'd been intrigued by these women earlier. Now I was afraid of them.

When Bradford took orders for the next round, I got myself two glasses of scotch—neat: one for me and one to quiet the voices in my head.

I fell out of the conversation. I was tired from the day. I was scared of the women at the table, and above all, I was drunk. I poured the first neat scotch down my gullet, and it hit me like a hot hammer to the face and chest. I flushed out as blood rushed to my cheeks. It felt like my face was in front of a furnace. My chest warmed, and I could swear it was glowing. I thought I looked like E.T., my heart light illuminating red through my shirt.

"Louie, are you feeling all right?" the Chief asked. "You're on the *China Clipper.*"

I didn't know what he meant, but I knew it had to do with traveling—which I was.

"I'm as *jober* as a *sudge, Chief-a-ree-no*," I said. "It's been a long day, you know? I'm ready to hit the sack."

"No, you can't cash out yet," he said. "These fine ladies are going to show us a good time."

I found myself at that point of inebriation where you say what you feel with no pretense or fear of repercussion.

"So what do we have going on here?" I asked. "You two are gorgeous. You so totally are. I'm just not sure what's going on. Chief! What's up? Do you know?"

The Chief shot me a look. "Louie, we're enjoying the company of lovely ladies," he said. "What more could you want?"

"I want to go back to the hotel and go to sleep. I'm drunk. I'm freaking out and I'm—"

"You're what?"

"I'm just ..."

The Chief intervened on my behalf. "You'll have to excuse the lad," he said. "When he drinks like this, he's akin to a dog with his tail in a blender."

Stella looked dumbfounded. "What does that mean?" she asked.

"When the gears start to turn," the Chief said, "the old dog utters: 'It won't be long now.'"

Cindy interjected, "That's disgusting!"

"Disgusting but true," the Chief said. "I think we are indeed finished for the night. I apologize."

I chimed in. "*You* apologize?" I asked. "No. *I* do. That's *all* I do. April said that's all I do. I'm fucking doing it again."

I started to break down. "Goddammit, Chief," I said. "She was right. She was so right about me."

"Who the hell is April?" Cindy asked rudely.

"She's an old friend," the Chief replied. "Just a stranger in the night."

"Fuck you, *Ol' Booze Eyes*!" I yelled. "She was more than that. She was …"

Bradford grabbed me and pulled me from the table. I was so drunk, distraught, tired, and lovesick I didn't care I was being man-handled. As he dragged me to God knows where, I asked about the tab and how expensive it was going to be. I also asked about the ladies and how dangerous they were. He answered neither question.

He brewed up a pot of coffee. My head was flying in every direction. I just wanted to find a single place to land—just not at the ladies' table.

"Talk to me, kid," Bradford said. "I gotta get you somewhat vertical."

I looked through red, tear-swollen eyes at the man who'd been serving my drinks the last two nights and asked him his real name, his Christian name.

"My name is Davis," he said.

I smiled through my tears. "Davis? Not Bradford?" I asked.

"Nope. Never Bradford," he said.

"I'm so sorry," I said. "The Chief. He just—*fuckin' outta' nowhere*—called you *Bradford*."

Davis said, "I gotta admit, though, Bradford is way cooler than Davis."

I smiled. "Yeah, being called Louie sucks," I slurred. "But the Chief makes it sound legit, respectable. I feel like a made man, a total gangster."

Davis dumped coffee down my throat. I was chatty and lucid and becoming more coherent and sober. *Jesus. I don't remember drinking so much. What the hell happened?* I tried to collect my thoughts. As I did, I wondered how the Chief was fairing with Stella. I was just hoping the old man was still alive.

Davis, whom I still wanted to call Bradford, left me alone with my coffee and my thoughts. I don't know where he went. The coffee was quite good—strong and bitter—just the way I like it. I sat and sipped with my hands tightly wrapped around the mug. I was so upset and in so many ways. I just wanted to go to sleep. Today, which may very well be yesterday now, was long and harrowing for me. I'd gone through the gamut of human emotions, and now I was *physically* hurting as a result.

I drank the rest of my coffee. It had cooled, but was still strong. *When Davis comes back, I'll ask him what brand it is. I want to have this at home.*

The Chief came into the room where Davis had brought me.

"Here's your charge," Davis said. "I've given him some coffee, so he should be okay."

"Thank you, Bradford," the Chief said. "I've got him from here."

"Would you like me to call you two a cab?"

"No. I think we can walk it. We're staying just up the road at the Best Western."

I looked at the Chief and then at Davis. Their faces were expressionless. I had no idea if I was in trouble or not.

"I'm sorry, guys," I said. "I've caused an awful stir and I apologize."

"It's nothing I haven't seen before," Davis said. "You oughta come in here on Saturday!"

"Louie, you should've seen me in the fifties ... that was something!" the Chief proclaimed.

"Where are the women?" I asked.

"They're gone, son. And good riddance to them," the Chief said. He quickly looked at Davis. "No offense, Bradford. I know you're acquainted with them," he apologized.

"None taken," Davis said. "I just serve them, I don't judge them."

I pulled myself up to leave. There was still the matter of the tab to settle.

"Davis, I believe I owe you some money?" I said.

Davis nodded and smiled. "Let me ring you up," he said. He went to the front of the bar to get my ticket.

"Who's Davis?" the Chief asked.

"Bradford is Davis," I said.

"Why the hell did I call him *Bradford*?"

"I don't know, Chief. Why do you call anybody anything?"

"Well, he looks like a Bradford, don't you think?"

"He likes the name too. That's a plus."

The Chief laughed. "Then I'll keep calling him Bradford," he said.

The Chief and I walked to the front of the bar and met Davis. He gave me the bill.

"Not as bad as I thought," I said. "I figured I'd have to take out a loan."

"I cut you a break on the ladies' drinks," Davis said. "I watered them down a bit."

"I appreciate that."

I had to know the ladies' story.

Davis told us everything he knew, and as I expected, none of it was good.

The Chief had a disappointed look. I found his expression confusing. He himself had bid them good riddance.

"Something wrong, Chief?" I wondered.

"No. Not really," he said. "I just liked being with Mama-san."

"She would've killed you."

"Perhaps, but what a way to die: in the arms and at the hands of a beautiful woman."

If there was ever stupidity spoken in the guise of profundity, I'd just heard it.

I paid the tab and tipped Davis twenty dollars. I'd sobered enough to not look foolish walking back to the hotel.

As we walked, the Chief mumbled every so often. When I'd ask what he was saying he'd say "nothing" or that I was "hearing things." No doubt he was lamenting my behavior and how it had inadvertently ruined his evening. He should have thanked me. I'd rescued him once again.

When we got back to the hotel, the Chief wanted to get another drink. I did not. I was exhausted from the day and was ready to go to sleep. We had one more day left in Elko. I wanted to be rested and refreshed so I could fully enjoy whatever we were going to do.

"Good night, Chief," I said. "I'm taxed. I apologize."

"It's okay, Louie," he responded. "I should turn in myself, but I want one more for the road."

"Go ahead on. I'll see you tomorrow at breakfast."

I went up to my room. I got inside and looked at the clock. It was just past midnight. I kicked my shoes off and got undressed. I turned on the TV and found the music channel that April and I had listened to. I lowered the volume to where she'd set it. I crawled into bed and pulled the covers and a pillow tight to my body. I started to cry. I was alone in this bed. I wanted to be with April. I wanted to go home.

I woke up and glanced at the clock and noticed it was 11:00 a.m. I hadn't planned to sleep so late. I'd missed "build your own" omelets and *Portugee* breakfast down at the restaurant.

I was surprised the Chief hadn't knocked on my door to see if I was alive and yell some kind of boot camp wake-up phrase like "Rise and shine and start the grind" or "Hands off your cock and grab your socks." Maybe he had and I'd slept through it? I have no idea.

I sat up in bed and felt sloshy. I'd gone to sleep with a head full of jagged little fragments that did not play well with my stomach full of booze. I should be hungover, but wasn't—and that was *very* good.

I stared at the TV. The workday sounds outside of the hotel were louder than the volume, and I could not hear the song that was playing. I turned the TV up a couple of notches to hear it. I caught the last verse of Material Issue's "Valerie Loves Me." I found myself bobbing my head to the choppy guitar riff and miming the words. For all of its punk attitude, I've always thought it was such a sad song.

I got out of bed and went to take a shower. I was still singing "Valerie Loves Me" as I stood beneath the hot spray and soaped myself up. That song was going to be stuck in my head all day.

I wondered what the Chief and I might do today. So far, what we'd managed to do was inspiring, to say the least. I'd taken some great mental pictures. The collection of photos floating in my brain was quite motivating. I couldn't wait to see if my words would do them proper justice. The more I thought about it, the more I realized I needed to get to work.

I heard a knock on the door. I looked through the peephole and caught a fish-eyed view of the Chief standing outside the door. He looked lost.

"Chief. Give me a second, okay?" I said. "I'm not dressed. Just hold on."

"You in there, Louie?" he asked. "Just wanted to make sure you were alive."

I shook my head. "Okay, Chief," I said. "Give me two minutes."

I put on my clothes and pulled the covers up on my bed. I opened the door, and the Chief poured into my room and dropped down in the chair by the window.

"You okay?" I asked.

"Sure. I'm fine," he said.

"You're acting like you're being chased."

"No. Just antsy. The day's half over. Time's a-wasting."

"I know. I'm sorry. I slept late. I was very tired."

"You had a big day yesterday. What's on the agenda for today?"

"Nothing. I'd actually like to write a little. I've got some great stuff from yesterday to put down. I don't want to lose it."

The Chief seemed upset by my not wanting to venture out. I know we're supposed to be exploring and seeking and adventuring, but I am also supposed to be writing as well. I needed some time to get my thoughts out.

"Maybe we can do something later?" I proposed.

The Chief still looked sad. I wasn't sure how to appease him.

"Let's get lunch," I suggested. "We'll figure out something to do then, okay?"

The Chief nodded. This pleased him, and it worked for me too. I could write later. My creative stimuli were working overtime. The muses were plentiful, and they were not going anywhere.

"Chief, what sounds good for lunch?" I asked.

"I think I want a panini," he said. "That sounds good."

"Let's find out a good place to go," I said.

We stopped at the hotel desk and asked the clerk if he had any suggestions about where to track down Paninis.

"You guys want a good panini," he said. "You gotta check out this place called Two Dames and a Deli."

The Chief's face lit up when he heard the name of the restaurant.

"Say no more, Hop," the Chief said. "I don't care if all they serve is dirt and prune juice. With a name like that, you can't go wrong!"

"Sounds like we're dining with the dames," I said.

The Chief and I drove to the restaurant. The parking lot had five cars in it. The owners of the cars probably filled the establishment to capacity. It was a charming, diner-like small building, and we could smell the food from outside.

"This is going to be good," the Chief said. "The dames are in there, just rarin' to stuff our gullets."

We walked into the restaurant and looked around. The place was bigger than it seemed. There were plenty of places to sit. The patrons turned as we moved toward an empty table. Music played quietly overhead. The Chief admired the huge metal utensils on the wall.

"You've got to be one big son of a bitch to use those," he murmured.

We sat down and looked over the menu. The sandwiches and paninis all sounded absolutely delicious. It was hard to choose.

Our waitress came by and brought us glasses of water. I drank half of mine while I tried to decide on what to eat.

"Damn, Chief, what sounds good?" I asked. "Besides everything?"

"I don't know," he said. "Maybe this was a bad idea."

"How so?"

"Well, it all looks and sounds—and smells great. How the hell is a man to decide? What are these dames trying to do to us?"

"Perhaps we should ask for recommendations?"

"Good thinking, Louie."

The waitress came back to the table and could tell we were still undecided.

"I know that look," she said. "You boys are having some trouble."

I nodded. "That we are," I said. "Do you have any suggestions?"

The Chief looked the waitress up and down. "Chile, right?" he asked. "You're from Chile?"

My facial expression changed from indecision to embarrassment. How the hell the Chief discerned her as Chilean I don't know—but he was right.

"Why, yes I am!" she said excitedly. "How did you know?"

"The color of your skin and those eyes," he said. "That soft, warm penny brown. Only Chileans have eyes that color."

The waitress blushed. Her lovely penny brown eyes crinkled as she smiled. I kept waiting for the Chief to start speaking Spanish to her. He did not, and that surprised me.

"Where were we?" she asked.

"Recommendations," I said.

"Oh, yes. Well, it's all quite good, really."

"What's the best panini you have?"

"My favorite is probably the pastrami panini. It's very tasty."

"Which one is it? I don't see just a pastrami."

104

"It's here," she said, pointing to the menu. "It's called the Californian."

"Does it have avocado?" I asked.

"It does," she replied. "How'd you know?"

"Because every California-named food item has avocado on it."

"Really? Is that true?"

"It's true everywhere but in California," I said with a laugh. "Well, that's what I'm getting."

The waitress smiled. "Very nice," she said. She looked at the Chief and said, "And for you, sir?"

"I'm feeling piquant," he said. He seemed to puff with slight machismo. "I'll have this one with horseradish and beef. How's it fair with the others?"

"Oh, it's spicy," the waitress said. "The zing of the horseradish tickles me right here." She crinkled her eyes again and tapped the tip of her nose. It was an adorable gesture. The Chief liked this girl before. He was quite smitten with her now. Sadly, he was old enough to be her grandfather.

The waitress left to put our orders in. The Chief followed every single step she took. He craned his neck to get a last glimpse of her as she disappeared into the kitchen.

"Don't hurt yourself, Chief," I said. "She's coming back, you know?"

"Oh, I know," he said. "I just don't want to miss a single moment."

"She's a little young, don't you think?"

"Maybe, but she's over twenty-one. The law says it's okay to ogle if they're over twenty-one. Even for an old, horny bastard like me."

I laughed at the Chief's logic. He was an old, horny bastard of the highest order.

"Louie, shall we see if our *poco de tomate Chilena* would like to join us for lunch?" the Chief asked.

"No!" I said, in a whispered yell. "She's working. She doesn't want to eat with us."

"How do you know?" he asked. "She's probably hungry too."

"Maybe, but still. It's okay if we have one meal that's not a set-up, you know?"

"It's no setup at all."

"What do *you* call it? It's all about the Five Ls, right? That's the setup."

"It is, but it's just the one *L* this time. Just lunch."

I leaned in close. "You can flirt all you want, Chief," I said. "Just please don't ask her to eat with us, okay?"

"She's a beauty, Louie," he said. "Don't you want to feast on delicious food with a beautiful woman?"

"It's a nice idea, Chief, but there's probably a rule about dining with customers while on duty."

"You're too ethical," the Chief said with a scowl.

"No, I'm far from 'ethical,'" I stated. "I'm *practical*."

"Practical, ethical—I call it boring."

"Well, then I'm boring too. I can handle that."

"What happened to your sense of adventure, Louie?"

"It's still here. I'm just choosing to quell it for lunch."

The Chief folded his arms and huffed at me. His actions were so childish. I shook my head, but I had to laugh. He kept turning away, trying to avoid me. It was going to be a long day if he kept this up.

Our waitress returned and served us our food. The sandwiches were big, warm, and smelled divine. She apologized for the orders taking so long and not finding out if we wanted something besides water to drink.

"It didn't take that long," I said. "If it all tastes as great as it looks and smells, it was certainly worth the wait."

The waitress smiled. "Can I get you guys sodas or something?" she asked.

"I'll have a diet cola, please," I said. "Grumpy Gramps here probably wants a ginger ale."

"Would you like a ginger ale, sir?" the waitress asked.

The Chief scowled at me again. He timidly nodded at the waitress. She smiled at him and her eyes sparkled. He warmed up a bit, though he was still ignoring me.

The Chief stared at his plate.

"You should eat," I said. "It's going to get cold."

He mumbled something.

"I'll bet your sandwich is amazing," I said. "With the horserad-ish and all."

He continued his moratorium against me.

The waitress came back and brought us our drinks. She set them on the table, and the Chief stared at her lovingly and whispered "Thank you" to her. I wanted to kick him under the table.

"Is there anything else I can do for you right now?" the waitress asked.

The Chief spoke up. "Yes, there is *mi ángel querido—por favor, comer con nosotros.*"

My face went red again with embarrassment. I figured it was only a matter of time before the Chief came out of his shell and spoke Spanish to our waitress. I looked at her face as well. She too was blushing. Her blush was one of embarrassment as well, but of a different nature than mine.

"I'm so sorry," she said. "I don't speak Spanish."

The look on the Chief's face was one of pure disappointment. He'd always been correct in his reads of people. This time was a miss. He'd fallen into a definite linguistic generation gap.

I had to imagine that years ago, this girl's family spoke Spanish. However, her parents, though Chilean in descent, had never lived in Chile, nor did they speak the language of their homeland. They had brought their daughter up in an assimilated, English-speaking world. She knew a couple of greetings and holiday salutations, maybe.

"No, my dear," he said. "I am the one who should apologize. It was callous and ignorant of me to just suppose things."

"What did you say to me?" she asked. "I don't understand, but it sounded wonderful."

The Chief picked his pride up from the floor, dusted it off, and shared his words with the waitress.

"I called you, my dearest angel," he said subtly. "And I asked if you'd please join us to eat."

The waitress blushed even harder. She sat down next to the Chief and patted his hand.

"Oh, what a grand gesture. You're so very kind," she said. "I'd love to have lunch with you, but we're not allowed to dine with the customers."

"I told you, Chief," I said.

"Yes … You did, Louie," he replied. "Ethics and all."

"No, you made the crack about 'ethics,'" I reminded him. "After which you called me *boring*."

The waitress smiled. "You guys are too much!" she said.

The Chief wanted one more try at asking her join us. "Well, since you can't frolic with the paying customers," he said, "perhaps you could join us for a drink this evening? Just a friendly libation to unwind after your shift."

The waitress smiled uneasily at the Chief's request. She put her head down slightly and sighed.

"I'm so flattered by your invitation," she said. "But I'll have to pass."

"May I ask why?" the Chief implored.

"Because my husband would not be too happy."

"Husband? You're married?"

I chimed in, "That's how women get a husband, Chief—by being married."

"Louie, if I want any shit from you, I'll squeeze your head," the Chief replied crossly.

He looked back at the waitress and donned his dejected look again.

"That's such a shame—for us," he said. "Your husband is quite a lucky man."

The waitress apologized again. "I'm so terribly sorry. I didn't mean to cause trouble."

"Oh no, my dear. Please don't apologize," the Chief said. "You're married. You should never, *ever* apologize for loving someone." He touched her wrist as she walked away and told her: "And you were no trouble at all."

We continued eating our lunch. The Chief quietly cursed his actions. How was he to know? We make mistakes. It's part of being human. The waitress was not offended. I had to believe she felt a sense of ethnic pride she'd never realized when the Chief spoke Spanish to her.

"Chief, if it's any consolation," I said. "I think it's better to have assumed someone spoke a foreign language and be wrong than just assume everyone speaks English."

"Thanks, Louie," he muttered. "That does make sense."

After finishing our lunch, we sat for a few minutes and tried to figure out the rest of our day.

"What should we do?" I asked. "We could go see something in town. There has to be some old stuff around that's worth a look."

The Chief sat and sulked. "Nah, let's go back to the hotel," he said. "You want to write, and I just need to think about things."

"Actually, that's the last thing you need," I said. "What you're thinking about isn't worth the effort. Everything's okay."

"I know. I just … I …"

"What is it?"

"I don't know. All I know is we're leaving tomorrow and we don't know where we're going."

"Don't worry, I'll figure that out tonight."

I got up to pay the bill, and the Chief wandered out to the parking lot. It was the convenience store outside of Reno all over again. Unlike Reno, he didn't steal anything. At the very least, *he'd had* something stolen: his heart, at the hands of our waitress. Also unlike Reno, I didn't think he was going to flip her off as we drove away. I could be wrong, though. He *was* upset.

I went back to the table to place a tip. There was a folded ten-dollar bill under the pepper shaker. *Did I leave a tip already?* I asked myself. I was throwing so much money around the last few days, I couldn't keep track.

We pulled into the hotel parking lot, and the Chief opened his door before I'd stopped the car.

"What are you doing?" I asked. "At least let me park."

"I need to get out, Louie," he said. His voice sounded slightly frantic.

"Are you okay?"

"I'm not sure, son. I've been feeling strange all day."

"It's not what happened at the restaurant, was it?"

"No. No. This started while I was at breakfast. You remember breakfast, right?"

"No, Chief. I slept through breakfast."

"Oh, that's right you did. You slept through breakfast and left an old man to die."

"You're not dying. Your ego got a little bruised."

"No, kid. I am dying. Hell, we're all dying. Some are just a little closer than others."

"Stop that. I'm not going to hear it."

The Chief looked at me. There was a frightening flare in his eyes.

"It has to be said. You can choose to ignore it, but the god-damned Reaper is taking swings at me," he said. "He's got a big scythe. You best be careful. He's liable to miss me and hit you. He's a blind son of a bitch, you know? That's why innocent people die."

The Chief was talking crazy, and I wasn't sure how to deal with it. Perhaps we needed to take today and truly *rest*. We still had a long way to go on this trip, many more stops and lots of adventures and seeking. Last night I'd wanted to go home. Right now, the Chief was ready to punch his ticket.

"Louie, I'm going to hit the rack," he said. "Get some shut-eye. Maybe I'll feel better. It's a bitch being old."

The Chief's sudden face-to-face with his mortality and his urge to go to sleep so early in the day scared me. I had this impression that when you reached a certain age, sleep was an enemy. One may go to sleep and not wake up. A twinge of fear shot through me. This could not be what the Chief wanted—could it? There was no way. He had too much life left in him. I reverted back to him just having a bruised ego and damaged pride from the events at lunch.

"You gonna be okay?" I asked.

The Chief nodded. "As well as can be expected," he said. "Don't worry, kid—you're not getting rid of me that easy."

The Chief and I were leaving tomorrow morning. No doubt we'd have an early, predawn departure; ironically, even that absolute was uncertain at the moment. We'd decided on nothing else. It was impossible to make any plans. I went down to the car and got the atlas from the backseat.

I opened the atlas to Nevada and thumbed to adjoining states, looking for cities that began with *E*. I was also looking for E-cities with populations of at least two thousand people. This was my personal addition to the adventure. I figured if we were supposed to be exploring, enjoying, and enriching our lives as well meeting people, we'd need to go to places with a modest population.

I wanted to continue heading east. I ran across a couple of places in Utah and Idaho, but nothing struck me. I was also looking to get out of the desert. I wanted a change of scene.

The next logical state was Wyoming. It fit the criteria of *change of scene*. The town I'd picked to hit next was Evansville. I looked up the population, and it was perfect.

I calculated the drive. It was going to take over nine hours to get from Elko to Evansville. That was okay. The long stretch would give the Chief and me some time to talk and devise plans for the days we'd spend in town. Such quality conversation would make the drive seem shorter as well.

I went across the hall and knocked on the Chief's door. There was no answer. I tried again. After three times, I quit. I returned to my room and wrote the Chief a note. I put it under his door. I stepped back into my room and decided I was going to finally get some writing done. I sat down at the desk, opened my notebook, put pen to paper, and nothing happened. The ideas, the memories, the mental photos were all there, but the drive was not.

What the hell was going on? I thought. I'd been anticipating doing this all day. When I woke up this morning, this was what I'd planned to do and now I was stifled. Stuck, paralyzed, and *polarized* by what I wanted to do and where I was now. My will to work was greater than my willingness to apply it. This was a most perplexing situation. It was beginning to frustrate me.

I was supposed to be finding my soul, but instead, I was finding reasons to revert to failures and the banality I'd sought to expunge. *So much for great expectations.* Self-improvement sounds like a good thing, but for me, it has the opposite result: I build myself up just to tear myself down.

Elko, Nevada, provided me with what I was supposed to find on this journey; unfortunately, all those elements that seemed so grand were now destructive. It was definitely time to leave this place.

I continued to sit and stare at the blank page in my notebook. By now, there should have been lines and curves of ink from the letters I'd written. These letters should have formed numerous words. These words should have filled several pages. There should have been an inordinate amount of thick, hasty, inky scratch marks from where I'd decided I hated what I'd written and heatedly obliterated it. There was none of that. There was only white, faintly pulpy, lined, and margined paper in front of me. My pen wasn't even in my hand.

Nothing was making the words flow. I was just going to have to deal with this *writer's block* again. Dammit. I have a head full of memories, but no way to share them.

I heard a knock on the door. I got up to answer it. I didn't even look in the peephole.

A man was standing outside the door. He was one of the desk clerks.

"Sorry to bother you, sir," he said.

"It's no problem," I said. "What can I do for you?"

"There's a gentleman in the lobby who ..." he paused. He opened a piece of paper and rolled his eyes. He continued, "'requests the honor of your presence in the establishment's lounge.'"

"Would this perhaps be an older gentleman?" I asked. "Curly white hair, probably speaking Swahili or French to someone?"

"That would be him."

"He's not drunk, is he?"

"Oh, no. He's fine. He just asked me to give you this message."

"So he's sober—and speaking English?"

"Yes, sir."

"All right then. Let's go fulfill his request."

"He's in the restaurant," the clerk said.

"I figured as much," I noted. "It's after six as well. I'm surprised he's not drinking yet."

"That's none of my business, sir."

"True, but now it might be mine!" I said with a laugh.

I walked into the restaurant, and the Chief was seated at the bar. He had a full glass of beer in front of him. There was a short glistening vessel cradling the ingredients of what looked to be a scotch and soda parked in front of the barstool next to him. *Is that seat taken?* I joked to myself. *Well, it is now,* I answered back—seriously this time.

"Good evening, Chief," I said as I took the seat next to him.

"Louie, me boy," he said. "It's time to leave."

I nodded in agreement. "I've been working on that," I said. "I think I've found our next stop."

The Chief put his hand up. "Tut-tut. All events and related information to be revealed at their due and most appropriate time," he said.

I nodded. I couldn't understand why half the time the Chief talked like a normal person, and the other half, he sounded like he was reading a script from a 1950s war movie.

"I'll keep it to myself, Chief," I assured him.

"On the QT, Louie—on the QT," he replied.

"That too."

"I feel like doing a couple of shots, kid," the Chief said. "I need a little something extra tonight. It's been a hell of a day."

"Yes, it has," I responded. "I can't coordinate my head and my hands."

"Son, that sounds like a personal problem."

"It is. It's …" I paused. "Let me rephrase that. I'm having writer's block again."

"That too is a personal problem," the Chief noted. "However, it is one without *blue* connotations."

"Glad I could add a little civility to the conversation."

"Civility is a wonderful thing."

The bartender stopped to check on us. "You gentlemen doing all right?" he asked.

"We'd like a couple of shots," the Chief said. "Give us your top shelf rye."

"Very well, sir. Two ryes."

I looked at the Chief with uncertainty. "Rye?" I asked. "Couldn't that be dangerous?"

"No. Not a chance," he said. "It's just got a bite, that's all. We all can stand to get bit every so often, right?"

"I suppose."

"You like that liquid peat moss, right? You'll like the rye just as much."

The bartender brought our shots.

"Enjoy, gentlemen," he said.

I sipped my scotch and soda. The act seemed like some odd defense mechanism—as if the familiarity of the watered-down scotch would cushion the possible blow of the unknown, intimidating swig of straight rye bourbon. I looked at the shot and began to wonder if I shouldn't order a beer to chase it.

The Chief watched me negotiate the shot. "That's the nice thing about a shot," the Chief said vaguely.

"What's that?" I asked.

"You don't have to worry about it getting warm or cold while you meditate on it. It'll just age a little more."

"What do you mean?"

"Well, son, you've been looking at that glass for a long time. It's already about twelve years old. Are you waiting for it to get legal so you can marry it?"

"No. I just need a beer to chase it."

The Chief slid his glass over. "Here, take a snort from mine," he said.

"You can do this, Louie. Let's lift 'em up and put 'em down."

We raised our shot glasses. The Chief got a contemplative look on his face and slapped his hand to the bar.

"*Na zdorob'ye, Salud, Kampai, Le Chaim, Biba, Huli Pau,* and down the hatch!" the Chief shouted as he clinked his glass to mine and threw the rye down his throat.

He shuddered and slammed the glass on the bar. He hit my arm and waved his hand for me to take my shot.

I swilled the booze down with no further hesitation. It burned a path from my mouth, down my throat, and finally, it firebombed in my stomach. It was spicier than any bourbon I'd even had before, which added to the heat. I slammed my glass down as well.

"Motherfucker!" I exclaimed in a whisper. I closed my eyes tight as I shook my head—and the ghosts right out of me.

"Good stuff, eh, Louie?" the Chief asked.

"It was different. Not too bad," I said. "I was right to be a little concerned, though."

"Sure you were. But now you're an old whore. Your *ryeman* has been busted. How about another?"

I took a drink of the Chief's beer. We called the bartender over and got two more shots of rye, and I ordered two more beers. It was an off night. I was neglecting my scotch.

Our drinks came, and we fired them down with no great fanfare. The Chief didn't belt out "Cheers" like he was at a United Nations meeting, and I didn't feel my drink was going to kill me. Glasses drained, we dropped their bottoms on the bar. I was feeling pretty good after just two shots. I started to think about tomorrow and getting an early start. At this rate, that may not be a possibility. I looked at the clock. It wasn't even 7:00 p.m. yet. The night was young.

The Chief drank some of his beer. I chased the burn of the rye with mine and had a little of my scotch. My stomach was turning into a liquor cabinet; my digestive acids being replaced by top-shelf alcohol and hoppy ale.

The Chief looked at me. He squinted his eyes. It was as if he was trying to read my mind. *Good luck.* Right now, my mind was blank.

"Louie, have you ever *made love?*" the Chief asked.

I was caught off guard by his rather odd question. I'd gone from *zero to sex* with no warning. I wasn't sure how to respond. The alcohol and a slightly inflated testosterone level helped influence my reply.

"Yeah, quite a few times," I said, somewhat proudly. "I've had my share—some crazy moments along the way too."

The Chief elaborated. "You've obviously *fucked,* but have you ever truly *made love?*" The Chief ordered another round, awaiting my answer.

Now I wasn't so sure of what I wanted to say.

The Chief passed me my shot and spoke. "Do you know what separates us from the animals?" he asked. "What makes us human?"

I mused silently and shook my head. I felt anything I'd say would be wrong.

"Opposable thumbs and sexual passion: those are the dividers between human and pure beast," he explained. "We have the incredible ability to feel a connection during sex that no other animal experiences, and make no mistake—we *are* animals.

"Oh sure, we can be savage, but we're also subjected to a realized pleasure through sexual congress as well. We express a love and a deeper sense that goes beyond anything the other species in the animal kingdom can ever comprehend. That's why we can make love and all of God's other creatures can't. They just smell the stink of heat and mate—theirs is to strictly fuck and propagate the species.

"We also have the inherent need to procreate, but that's the *primal* primal—we also know how to have fun and love. There's another element of that 'civility' you mentioned earlier."

I smiled at his assessment. I found it interesting that the word *civility* had found its way into a full-blown sex talk; it had cropped up earlier as part of an odd, inadvertent double entendre.

"Well, thank God for the gift of civility," I said.

We clinked our glasses together in another toast.

"Goddammit! Here's to 'civility'!" the Chief announced.

We swilled our shots down and simultaneously slammed our glasses onto the bar.

Although I was enjoying this philosophical rant about pleasures of the flesh, it was time I changed the subject.

"Okay, Chief. What time do you want to leave tomorrow?" I asked.

He switched gears with no problem at all.

"Bright and early—like last time," he said emphatically. "Why do you ask?"

"Because I need to know when I should stop drinking."

"Why the hell would you want to do that?"

"I don't know? Maybe it's because I want to be able to function in the morning."

"You did okay coming here."

"I did. But I wasn't doing shots all night either."

"That is true, Louie. Are you suggesting we retire at such an early hour?"

"No, not really. I just want to be able to get up and not hate myself."

"Fair enough. Shall we take ourselves to 'Bradford's' to cap the evening and tell our friend 'fare thee well'? Or is it time to tuck ourselves in and go *nighty-night*?"

"I'm going 'nighty-night,' Chief," I said. "I need to be clear to drive. We've got a long haul."

"Dammit, Louie—don't tell me anything," the Chief said. "The QT—keep it on the QT!"

"I am. The only thing I'm revealing now is that I want to go to sleep."

"All right, kid. I've got to respect that. But won't you have one more rye with the Old Boy?"

I smiled and shook my head. "Sure. Why the hell not," I said merrily. "One more isn't going to kill me."

I woke up to an incessant pounding—both in my head and at my door. I rolled over and let out some strange sound. It was one I can't recall ever making in my life. It was a death moan of sorts. I looked at the clock. The illuminated digits were blurred, glowing red blobs, indiscernible and spinning slowly. I squinted to make out the time. It only made the situation—and my head feel worse.

"Stop it!" I shouted somewhat incoherently.

The knock seemed to get louder. It had to be my imagination. There was no way anything could get louder than the whirring sound going on in my head.

"*Didnyahearme? I sattastopit, dammit*," I slurred.

I tried to sit up in bed, and that turned out to be a mistake. My head expanded, and it felt like it would explode. The whirring sound was now accompanied by a throbbing that was not only noisy but painful as well. Nothing was still. The room and everything in it shifted and floated slowly back and forth.

The person knocking at my door began to speak. The voice and the knock were making my nausea increase.

"Louie!" The voice rasped outside my door. "Louie. It's the Big Banana!"

I shook my head and crunched my eyes together hard. I put my face into my hands and let out a hoarse shout of disapproval. I was hoping that my caller heard me.

"Louie. Louie. Open the door," the voice rasped again.

"Who the hell is it?" I asked.

"It's your old pappy from across the hall," the voice answered.

"Fucking hell. Is that you, Chief?"

"Who the hell do you think it is?"

I sat up again and dropped my feet to the floor. I hadn't realized I was still fully dressed from the previous night. Oh and what a night it must've been. I forced myself to my feet. I stumbled to the door to open it and let the Chief in.

He took one look at me and stepped back. "Jesus H. Christ the Fourth," he blurted. "What kinds of trouble did you get yourself into last night?"

"You tell me, and we'll both know," I said, blearily.

"Lots of rye, kid. That's all I can tell you. Lots and lots of rye."

The Chief walked into my room and sat down. He had his bag with him, and it appeared as if he was ready to travel. I was definitely not, nor would I be for quite some time.

"Can we get a light on the subject?" the Chief asked.

"No. That's not a good idea," I said flatly.

"Dammit, Louie, I can't see a freakin' thing in here."

"I'd like to keep it that way if you don't mind."

The Chief wasn't totally blind. There was enough scant light to see him to the chair by the desk. He sat down and then quickly stood up again.

"There's some stuff on this chair," he said. "I think I sat on your work."

"What? What work?" I asked.

"There's a bunch of papers in this chair," the Chief said. He leaned toward the desk and noticed more sitting atop of it.

I couldn't fathom why there were papers all over the place. I didn't want to deal with anything except going back to sleep for another six or seven hours.

"What time is it?" I foolishly asked.

"Do you want the actual time?" the Chief asked.

"It doesn't matter," I said. "It's fuckin' oh-dark-thirty regardless. It better not be four a.m. Is it four a.m.? It is, isn't it?"

"It is what it is."

"What the hell does that mean? *It is what it is?* That's the stupidest thing I've ever heard anyone say. What else would it be? It's too damn early, and I'm still too fucked up to play this game."

I dropped back on to the bed. I closed my eyes and rolled over. The Chief turned on the light. Even though my eyes were shut tight, the radiance in the room sliced through the miniscule slits of my eyelids.

"What the fuck!" I shouted. "Goddammit, Chief! The light! Turn off the light!"

The Chief made a strange noise. It sounded pensive and worrisome.

"Louie, you might want to see this," he said.

I slowly opened my blood-filled, burned-out, tired, and blurred eyes to see what the Chief was on about. It had to be something big. I was more afraid than anything to see it.

I looked through the rye-induced film of my hangover. What I witnessed was some type of crime scene. It was as if an innocent notebook had been violated, disemboweled, and left to die, its contents strewn wildly about the area. The cryptic scrawling on the pages were meaningless at first glance but may hold a key to the mystery and thus be imperative in solving the crime.

"What the hell did I do?" I wondered aloud. "I don't remember any of this."

"You were pretty trashed, Louie," the Chief offered up. "I had to help you to your room."

"No shit? I'm sorry about that."

"It's no problem, kid. You've helped this old boy out—just returning the favor."

"I've got to clean this mess up. I'd like to see if I can salvage any of the writings. My head is so … yeah. I can't see straight. I need a few minutes. Is that okay?"

"Do what you have to. You've got plenty of time. It's only three a.m."

I didn't say a word. The Chief had seen to me and made sure I'd gotten home safely. For that reason alone, I decided to keep my anger and harsh comments about the time to myself.

I started picking up the papers. There was nothing on them that I could read. My drunken handwriting was illegible and juvenile. The words that I could read made no sense in their placement, and I wanted to pull every torn page together into a pile and burn them all.

I—in a stupor, a rage, or a *whatever*—wasted time, paper, and ink on something I'll never be able to read or ever remember doing. I was so pissed off right now. I'd finally sat down to write, and it was a worthless endeavor.

The Chief grabbed a couple of sheets and tried to read them. I couldn't get mad at him—there was nothing comprehensible on those pages. However, he started to make out words. He mumbled and grunted as he read what was on the paper. This had to be a joke. There was no way the old man could decipher my inebriated chicken scratch. All of a sudden, he stumbled upon something that rang out undeniably loud and clear—*April.*

I maliciously yanked the papers from the Chief's hands. I didn't want him to read any further. I did not look at what I'd scribbled. I couldn't bear the sight of the words I'd written about April. I was afraid I'd blasphemed her. I was afraid I'd revealed how hard I'd fallen for her. Whatever, it didn't matter. No more reading. *No see on all dry land* for either of us—at least not until I sobered up and could try to make some sense of all this.

"I'm going back to bed," I said. "It's too early. I can't function."

"I can come back in an hour," the Chief offered.

"An hour? No. How about three or four hours? How about when it's daylight? How about when I'm freakin' sober?"

"You're the boss, Louie. But the longer we wait, the longer it takes."

"Fair enough, Chief. Check out is at ten a.m. Can we leave at nine?"

"Oh-eight-hundred. No later. That's five hours."

I squinted again at the clock. "No, that's about *four* hours," I noted.

"Well then, son, you better get to sleep," the Chief said, as he kicked his feet up onto the desk.

I shut the light off and crawled back in bed. All I cared about was sleeping off this drunk. I hadn't had time to do that yet. I didn't even know what time I'd gotten back to the room—or how much I'd actually drank.

I woke up later to the most bizarre sounds: the sounds of violent scrubbing and weird humming. I listened to the humming to figure out what it was and where it was coming from. It was a song but nothing I knew. It was coming from the bathroom.

I rolled over. I could see the clock a little better now. It was 7:30 a.m., and even though I still felt like shit, the extra sleep was amazing.

I spied the chair by the desk. The Chief was sitting there when I went to sleep. His luggage was still in the room. He'd turned the TV on and was watching CNN with the volume down. The humming and scrubbing noises provided an eerie and ironically fitting soundtrack to the story being broadcast.

"Chief? You still here?" I said in a half-groan.

From the bathroom, I heard a full-mouthed, flappy-gummed response. "Yab, Boowie. Umjuss wabbin muh teet."

What the hell did he say? I thought.

"What are you doing?" I asked.

The Chief responded, "I ted umma wabbin MUT TEET!"

"You're 'washing your teeth'?" I asked.

"Yowp."

The Chief came out of the bathroom and looked quite spiffy. He was dressed, clean, and had nice, washed teeth.

"You appear travel-ready," I said, peering from behind my bloodshot eyes.

"The road is calling, kid," he replied. "I've done all I can for the good folks of Elko, Nevada."

"I agree. It is time to go."

I got out of bed and pulled some clothes from my bag. I locked myself in the bathroom and took care of everything. In the shower, I was in pain. My extra respite was great, but now I was realizing it was not enough. I'd need several more hours to sleep the rye out of my system.

I wanted to throw up, but I couldn't. My body was so full of toxins. Every nausea-inducing receptacle was causing my stomach to slosh. My gut felt like it was jammed full of ramen noodles ready to be forced out with a jagged stone. It sounds disgusting. It feels much worse—especially when you can't purge the poison.

I knew we had to leave, but driving like this was dangerous. I was still slightly drunk, but that was not my concern. My concern was losing control of my bilge pump and blowing out at both stem and stern while I was in the car. *Did I just say that? Bilge pump? My God, I'm turning into the Chief.*

I packed my clothes and tended to the mess that was still atop the desk. I glanced at a couple sheets of paper but wasn't trying to read them just yet. I wanted to sort them all out, but that would take some time and a clear head. I was hoping to have both in Evansville, Wyoming.

The Chief watched as I finished gathering my belongings. It was nearly 8:00 a.m., and he was chomping at the bit to leave. I didn't understand his rush to do things so early. At his age, you'd think he would just say "Forget it," and catch a few extra hours of sleep. No. He was still getting up at stupid early times and involving me in the schedule. In all fairness, though—I asked for this and I could handle it. I just needed to learn to handle my drink a little better—especially on nights prior to traveling.

I went to check us out, and the Chief was talking to three women in the lobby.

"Christ, does that man ever quit?" I wondered aloud.

"Louie!" he shouted. "I want you to meet someone."

"Chief, we have to go," I said emphatically. "We're late as it is."

"I know Louie, but this'll only take a second," he said, waving me over again.

"Yeah? So will this …"

I grabbed my suitcase up, and headed out the door. I didn't want to deal with any matchmaking bullshit today. I wanted to leave Elko. Hell, the Chief did too until about ten minutes ago.

I stormed out to the car. I figured he'd follow right behind. If not? Oh well. He could stay in Elko with this "tomato," start a new life and do whatever it is he did, and I could get back to normal—writing fluff and bullshit—get paid for it and live my nice, banal existence in Valdosta. *Practical is boring.*

The Chief walked outside and stood in the valet roundabout. He had his arms out and palms up. I could put the look into two words: *as if*. As *if* I'm bailing on you. As *if* our adventures are over. As *if* I don't know you fell in love with April and won't be happy with another girl on this trip. *As if…*

"Get in the car, old man," I said with a smile. "I ain't leaving you."

"I was worried there," he said. "I'm getting left behind, and I don't even know where the hell I'm going."

"Evansville."

"Dammit, Louie. You weren't supposed to say anything."

"I know. The QT."

"Yes. The QT."

"Well, Chief, if it makes you feel better, I don't have a clue what's in Evansville."

"Neither do I, but I know it's *in* Indiana."

"Yes, but we're going to Wyoming."

"Good," the Chief scowled. "Because I fucking hate Indiana."

Our drive was quiet and uneventful for a couple of hours. The Chief found radio stations that played 1940s swing and jazz music, but no sooner did he tune them in and we'd lose them. Radio silence was rampant as we moved from Nevada into Utah.

All of a sudden I went cold—my entire body temperature dropped. My blood rushed from my head to tend to other parts of my body. My forehead beaded with a cool film of perspiration. My stomach churned, and I knew I was done for.

I stomped on the throttle. It's human nature to drive faster when seeking out a place to expel bodily fluids or solids. We may have no idea where we're going, but dammit, we wanted to get there as quickly as possible.

"Louie, are you okay?" the Chief asked. "You look like a sheet."

"I'm gonna be sick," I said. "I knew this was gonna happen."

"Well, just pull over and heave or shit or whatever you have to do."

"I can't. I've got to get to a rest area or something."

"Why? You're really gonna stick your mug in some roadside shitter to vomit? Just do it here on the road. No one's gonna care."

"I said I can't! What if someone sees me?"

"How many cars have you seen yet? We're in the goddamned desert. Just puke. The sun will dry it and you'll feel better."

I couldn't hold myself any longer. I pulled the car off in a turnabout, opened the door, and fell forward. I was still strapped in, so I was suspended and swaying. The Chief popped my seatbelt button, and I fell out of the car fully. My palms hit the scorching, rocky ground first. My legs followed close behind, and within seconds, I was lying sideways on the hot desert floor projectile-vomiting a chartreuse and pink fountain of acid and alcohol.

The stench was deplorable but lasted only a split second as the heat of the ground instantaneously baked every bit of foulness that came out of my mouth.

"Oh. My. God … *Oh my fucking God …* " I said as I rolled onto my back.

My eyes were closed tight as my face pointed toward the sky. The burning surface beneath me felt good and helped bring my body temperature back to normal. I still felt sick inside, but on the surface, I felt dry. My face hurt, and my throat burned from the bile.

"I'm sorry. I wasn't planning for this," I said, as I put my head in my hands.

"You overindulged," the Chief said. "No one plans for that. It's life. You had fun. Don't be ashamed of letting yourself go."

"I threw up on the state of Utah."

"The Mormons will forgive you. They like doing that shit."

I laughed, and it hurt. The Chief helped me up.

"I'm sorry. I'm so, so sorry," I said again.

"Dammit, Louie. Stop apologizing," the Chief said. "You don't have to say you're sorry for everything you do."

"That's what April said …" I confessed. I started crying. "She said I apologized for everything—including apologizing for apologizing."

"She's a smart gal," the Chief said. "She knows you too well."

"Goddammit. Stop. She's gone. She's out of my life."

"I don't think she is, Louie."

"No, Chief. She's gone. All she left me with was empty arms and a business card."

"Son," the Chief said, solemnly. "Sometimes a business card is all you need."

"What? Fancy printed words and an e-mail address?" I asked. "It's cold. It's corporate. It's a fucking *business card*. It's not her. It won't … It just won't …"

I turned to throw up again. It was more dry-heaving than any-thing—barely any content but a lot more pain. When my stomach finished contracting and trying to evict the tenants it had already thrown out, I pulled myself up and staggered back into the car. My eyes were sore and tearing. My throat was burning, and my mouth was filled with the worst flavors I'd tasted in a while.

"I need some water," I said. "I have to get this taste out of my mouth and this desert out of my system."

My mouth was dry and smacked of pennies, warm, soggy Wheaties, and turpentine.

We stopped in a town called Delle. It was very much like Jiggs, Nevada, but with a gas station instead of a bar and an abandoned, heavily graffitied school bus.

We were so close to Salt Lake City, but this place called out to us. It seemed the type of spot where a couple of seekers or lost souls might stop in for a spell—or at least a fill-up and some provisions. I bought lots of beverages and very little food. The Chief grabbed a bag of beef jerky, opened it, and began to eat it as he wandered the store.

"You gotta pay for that," the cashier said.

"Hear that, Louie?" the Chief said. "You gotta pay for this."

I didn't respond to the Chief's remark. I knew I had to pay for it. I had to pay for everything. The Chief still hadn't offered to pick up a tab or even split a bill. Churchill said he was "broke," but I thought he was speaking figuratively. I had no idea the old man truly did not have a dime to his name.

For the first time since the Chief and I began our trip, I felt genuine anger toward him. He had gotten me drunk a lot, and now I was sick. He had set me up with a woman whom I *may* have fallen deeply in love with and will never see again. He had rousted me out of bed at ridiculously early hours and pulled me to and fro and on "adventures" that seem to never take place. These same "adventures" have kept me from the very work they were supposed to inspire.

"Something wrong, Louie?" the Chief asked. "You look a tad peeved."

"You could say that," I responded coldly.

"What's stuck in your craw, kid? Tell the old boy your tale of woe."

"It's nothing really."

"It's got to be something or you wouldn't be irked."

"I'm probably just tired. It was a long night with a short rest."

"Sorry about that, kid."

"It'll happen again I'm sure. I'll be kicking myself then too."

"I can tell you from experience that there's nothing but truth in such a statement."

I chuckled. "I just need some coffee," I said. "That's why I'm so ... you know?"

"Coffee? Good luck with that," the Chief said. "This is Utah. Brigham's Boys don't drink the java."

We drove into Salt Lake City about forty-five minutes later. The skyline and the Wasatch Mountains made for great viewing after such a long, desolate stretch. I'd always found Salt Lake City a fasci-

126

nating place—it didn't make sense that a city so "holy" and revered would be so modern and progressive.

It was early afternoon on Saturday, and traffic was fair on the interstate. This made it easier to enjoy the scenery as we made our way around the town.

"'This is the place,'" the Chief said. "Why here? Only God and Mr. Young know the truth."

"Didn't he have a dream or something?" I asked. "Young saw this place in a dream."

"No, Louie. That was Martin Luther King. *He* had a dream."

"That's true, but I think King's was more emblematic, figurative. I don't he woke up in a sweat in the middle of the night from it."

"How do you know that? Maybe he did."

"Okay, maybe he did. Brigham Young allegedly woke up from a dream about the desert."

The Chief huffed. "Well, that's a matter of semantics," he said. "By the way, where do you find out all this stuff? You're not a Mormon, are you?"

"No. I'm not," I said. "I just read things. That's usually how we learn."

"Yeah. Reading the damn *Book of Mormon*."

"I've never read it. I'm not a freakin' Mormon."

"I think you were, but you strayed. Now you're drinking coffee, hanging out in taverns swilling booze, gallivanting with broads, and writing claptrap about places you've been to but don't care about."

"That's an unfair assessment, don't you think?"

"Not if it's true."

"It is not true. I'm not, nor have I ever been a Mormon. I have not strayed from anything—except my work. That part is true."

"Stick with me, kid, and you'll stray from a hell of a lot more than just your work. I can guarantee you that."

We were in Wyoming now and about halfway to our destination. The Chief nodded off to sleep. Our talks had been sparse and my side a bit hostile, but the son of a bitch kept me company regardless, and now he was asleep and snoring.

My choice of Evansville as our next destination took us off the familiar route of Interstate 80 and onto new roads. We came to a town called Walcott and got onto US 287 and US 30. We drove through towns called Hanna, Elmo, and Medicine Bow. I stopped in Medicine bow to stretch and fill the car up.

"Where are we, Louie?" the Chief groggily asked. I didn't know he was awake.

"A town called Medicine Bow, Wyoming," I said.

"Holy shit! Medicine Bow? You don't say."

"You know it?"

"I sure as hell do, son. So should you. It's famous."

"Famous? It's got a cool name, for sure. Why should I know it?"

"Because of *The Virginian*—the first novel ever written about the Old West."

"I thought that was a TV show."

The Chief glowed. He had a story to tell.

"Yes, it was—and it was all inspired by this place," he explained. "Owen Wister, the author, came here, and like you, he wrote stuff down. He got a book out of it and created a whole genre."

I smiled. "Pretty impressive," I said. "I don't think I can beat that."

"Not with that defeatist attitude. You gotta think like *The Virginian* if you want to get things done, kid," he said. "He was a man who took care of business the old-fashioned way and adhered to the law of the land. He had ethics—something lacking in the Old West. He never used his title or place in society as leverage or an advantage. He was loyal to himself and especially to his woman. He had heart. *The Virginian* was a true hero in a place and time that had so few."

"Maybe I should read this book?" I wondered aloud. "It sounds pretty good."

"It is. And you definitely should," the Chief said. "Even more incentive to read it is the fact that this book was the first time one of my favorite phrases ever saw print."

"What phrase was that?" I asked.

"Son of a bitch!"

I laughed at this. "Well, ain't that a son of a bitch?!" I said.

"'When you call me that—smile!'" the Chief replied. "That's from the book too."

I filled the car and went in to pay for the gas. While in the store, I asked the cashier about all things *The Virginian*. He looked at me strangely. He obviously had no idea about his town's history any more than I did.

"There's the Virginian Hotel," he said. "It's down on Lincoln Highway. That's US 30."

"So it's not far?" I asked.

"No. Not far at all. I don't know if it's open."

"That doesn't matter. I'd just like to see it."

"It's haunted."

"That's even better. Spirits of the Old West and all that stuff."

"We're not far from Evansville," I told the Chief. "I figured we could have a look around if you want."

"It'll be late when we get to Evansville, though," he lamented.

"So what? We'll just have to make up some time."

"No, Louie we can't make up time—only waste it. We've got to move on."

I looked at the old man and smiled. "Are you saying you can't make time for *The Virginian?*" I asked.

"What do you mean?" he wondered aloud.

"Get in the car. I'll show you."

We drove around until we happened upon a behemoth of a building. This structure seemed out of place in this town. It was bigger than anything else we'd seen in a while. The Chief nodded when he read the marquee above the door. It was a contemplative nod.

"The Virginian—well, I'll be damned," the Chief said. "Louie, you sure know how to make an old man feel young, you son of a bitch."

"Hey, Chief ..." I snapped. "When you call me that—smile!"

And he did. The Chief's smile returned. It was bigger and brighter than any I'd seen on his face the whole trip. Whatever ire I'd felt toward him earlier ceased to exist at this moment.

We left Medicine Bow and made our way into the Shirley Basin on SR 487. The road was long and without curves. The land around us was dry and dotted sparsely with trees. It was as if we were driving on the moon. The ground was bright gray and craggy, while some areas were white and without texture. Perhaps people lived here somewhere? The only existence of previous human interaction with these environs was the road we were traveling on.

We went from the flat expanse of the basin and rose up into the Shirley Mountains. The scenery changed as we headed further north and into higher elevations. Wyoming is a state of mind, a state of being, and a state of confusion—its scenery going from breathtakingly beautiful to depressingly desolate and back again in mere minutes.

It was dusk, and dark shadows fell upon the land, inciting a different view of our surroundings. We were treated to the fantastic sunset that was being painted to our west. The Heavenly Palette of evening colors was like nothing I'd ever seen. Streaking sunbeams fired from behind the thick purple clouds. Their coronas flared bright, blinding orange as stray capsules of red rolling billows drifted beneath them. I wished I had a camera—my words could do this picture no justice. You can't describe something like this and have anyone believe it.

We drove northwest until we came to the terminus of our road. We paralleled and crossed over the North Platte River on our way to Casper and our final destination: Evansville. We were close. It was a good thing too. I was getting tired. Considering my condition earlier today, a drink should have been the last thing on my mind. However, I was quite ready for one now. I would be cautious.

It was dark, and the sky was filled with more stars than I had ever seen in my life. The Chief pointed and mumbled to the stars. He traced lines from one constellation to another. It was fascinating to watch him do this. He was so meticulous in his stargazing. If he couldn't remember a star's name, he'd retrace his path and say this little poem. It put him back on track.

"What is that poem, Chief?" I asked.

"It's the Skywatchers' Song," he said.

"Can you tell me the words?"

"No. I can't do that."

"Why not? It's pretty cool and catchy."

"There's really no 'words' to it."

"But you keep singing them."

"I do. But they're just gibberish. I just replace the nonsense words with the names of the stars, planets, and constellations."

"So it's just a melody, then?"

"Yep, Louie. It's just a melody."

"What is it? Do I know it?"

"No. You probably don't."

"Where is it from? Where'd you learn it?"

"From my father. It was one of the few things I remember about him."

The Chief got quiet. I felt like a fool now, but how was I to know? I was just curious about this strange little ditty he kept singing as he looked to the heavens. There was much more to this than just a silly rhyme to remember the stars.

"I'm sorry," I said. "I didn't mean to upset you."

"You didn't upset me, kid," the Chief said. "I just lost my train of thought. I had to start over again."

I heaved a sigh of relief. "You never cease to amaze me, you know that?" I said.

"It's a gift, Louie. Most people call it bullshitting or shenanigans," the Chief stated. "Then you gotta go and compliment it and make it sound legitimate."

"Is that bad—to be legitimate?"

"Not if you want to be an old bastard—which I am. You have to be *illegitimate*. You've got to keep up your reputation."

"I'll remember that."

We came into Casper and picked up Interstate 25. Evansville was only a few minutes away, and the old bastard and his son of a bitch driver were ready to be out of this car.

Evansville, Wyoming

I found a hotel and checked us in. This time as I was finishing up the details, I looked back and saw the Chief sitting alone. It was odd to see him in a hotel lobby and not striking up conversations with every woman who'd listen to him. Then again, there were no women in the lobby to speak of, only a couple of men who were engaged in reading magazines and pretending no one else existed but them.

"Two rooms for two nights, Mister DeCarlo?" the desk clerk asked.

"Yep. That's it," I said.

"Third floor, sir. Rooms 312 and 313."

"Sounds great. Is the restaurant open?"

"No, sir. It is only open for breakfast from six to ten a.m."

"Thank you. Is there any place to go and get some food and drinks close by?"

"Sure. There is a barbecue place about a block away. They have a bar. There's more places in Casper than here, to be honest."

"Okay. Thank you for the info."

I walked over to the Chief and gave him his room key. He looked dejected.

"What's wrong?" I asked.

"I'm not thinking this going to be good for our adventures," the Chief said.

"Well, we won't know until tomorrow. I found us a place to eat and drink, though."

The Chief nodded. "Well, right now, that's all that matters," he said.

We took our luggage up to our rooms and just shoved it into the door. We left to go get some food and have a couple of drinks. I told myself I would *be good* tonight. I had a feeling around here that would be easy to do.

I called us a cab, and the Chief and I went to a place called Butch's. It was a small bar, but it was jumping. It was loud and one of the most crowded places we'd been to. The bar staff was great, and the clientele were quite friendly, and a lot of them were decked out in Western wear. If it wasn't for the jovial demeanor of the place, I'd swear a good ol'-fashioned cowboy brawl was going to break out any minute.

"What can I get you boys?" the server asked. "We've got some great specials tonight on mixers. If that ain't your taste, we've got a hell of a lot of beers."

I smiled at our server. She was beyond cute, and her bubbly attitude made her even more so. Her looks weren't lost on the Chief either.

"I'd like a scotch and soda and your best local beer," I said.

The Chief looked at the taps and the bottles along the back of the bar.

"Doll, I'll have whatever beer the kid's having and a *Wyoming-sized* snort of some of that Evan Williams white label."

"You got it guys," the server said. She smiled, and I responded in kind. The Chief, however, completely melted.

"Don't get too attached," I said. "We're only here for two days."

"Louie, there may not be a damn thing to do in this town, but that gal—she's worth an extra day."

"No. Not this time. We'll come and see her again tomorrow."

"Do you think she'd have a drink with us?"

I looked dead at the Chief. "Do the words *Chilean* and *waitress* mean anything to you?" I asked.

The Chief sighed. "Do you have to break an old man's heart, Louie?" he pondered.

"That's not my intention."

"I know, kid. I'd just like a moment of her company."

"She'll be back with our drinks. We'll order a lot so we can see her more. Sound fair?"

"It ain't the same thing."

I couldn't understand why the Chief was so hell-bent on conversing with this woman beyond the normal patron/professional capacity. What did he see in her that intrigued him so greatly?

Granted, she was—as the Chief might say—quite a looker, but there was something more to it. I was also curious about his drink order.

"Chief, why the Evan Williams?" I asked. "And one hundred proof, at that."

"I'm celebrating, Louie," he said. "We're in this bar. Our waitress is one fine tomato. And well, we're in *Evansville*. Mr. Williams is responsible for making all these scenarios possible."

"I never thought of it like that. You're absolutely right, though."

"Well, that's one for me, kid. Lately, I haven't been right about much."

"What do you mean by that?"

"Nothing. It's not important. Life, Louie—that's what's important. We drink to it and revel in it. It's all we have. Mine is getting short. Yours will be too if you don't get that stick out of your ass and loosen up. You're running out of time, son. You've got things you want to do, so why aren't you doing them? It's okay to chase dreams, but goddamn it, eventually—you need to fucking catch one."

I was beginning to sense a trend with the Chief and how he reacted to the possibility of rejection. When it happened, it hit him hard, and oddly, he took it out on me. This time, however, I was trying to prepare him for it. I didn't want to see him hurt or embarrassed. I also didn't want another dark-tinged lecture about life, death, and which one of us was going to cash out first.

Our waitress returned with our drinks, and the Chief returned to his jovial, flirtatious self.

"Okay, guys, we have two pints of Grand Teton, one scotch and soda, and one 'Wyoming-sized snort' of Evan white," the waitress said as she spun around our table.

She set the drinks down, and I have to say, they were quite generous. I'm not sure, but I'd venture a guess that no set measuring is considered when pouring a "Wyoming-sized snort" of booze. The bourbon was in a lowball glass, and it took a steady hand to keep it from spilling. My scotch and soda was a decent size too but nothing compared to the Chief's "snort."

"I want to marry you, sweetheart," the Chief said. "Any woman that can serve 'em up that big and not spill a drop needs to be my wife."

The waitress blushed and giggled. I blushed too—from embarrassment.

"Oh, aren't you just the charmer?" she said to the Chief. "I don't know what I'm gonna do with you."

"Darling, I can think of a hundred things. Ninety-nine of them are moral, righteous, and honest."

"What about the one?" she asked. An intrigued expression flashed across her face.

The Chief winked at her. "Well, there has to be *something fun,* right?" he said slyly.

I shook my head. I'd gone from embarrassed to mortified. The Chief was too damn old to be hitting on these young girls. What sucked about it all was when he went from Happy Gramps to Grumpy Geezer, I had to listen to his lamenting and philosophizing.

I looked at the waitress and watched as she flirted back with the Chief. I didn't want to deal with the Chief moody and brooding tonight. We just got here and just got our drinks. *Please let this night go smoothly,* I said to God as I heard our waitress let out a loud laugh.

"Oh, cowboy, you are just too much!" she said as patted the Chief on his shoulder.

"It's a good thing you can never get too much," the Chief responded.

"Is that backward? Doesn't the saying go 'You can never get too much of a good thing'?"

"Maybe, but whoever said that never had too much of *any-thing*—let alone anything good!"

"I'm gonna have to keep my eye on you."

"You can keep anything you want on me, darling—just keep it respectable."

The waitress laughed again and went to help other customers.

The Chief leaned across the table. "Louie, if I were half my age …" I cut him off.

"You'd *still* be too old for her," I said.

"If it's any consolation to you, kid," the Chief said. "I didn't ask her to join us for drinks."

"That's true," I noted. "You were jumping straight from 'libation' to 'love.'"

"Louie, let an old man have his fun. I ain't got much more."

I put my head down. I didn't know what to say. The Chief was an old soul and a hopeless romantic. He was the type of man Sinatra sang of and characterized in his songs. It's no wonder the Chief loved Ol' Blue Eyes so much. I wanted to give the old man some space to have his fun, but I couldn't deal with the repercussions when things went south. Maybe they wouldn't? I don't know if I was willing to take that chance.

"I'm sorry, Chief," I said. "I do need to lighten up."

"Just a little, kid," he said. "I've nothing but good intentions."

"Really? Not from where I'm sitting," I said with a smile.

"Louie, let me tell you something about this old bastard. I'm as pure as the snow ..."

I looked at him. I knew he had something else to say. He always did. "But?" I asked.

"But I tend to drift," he said. "Only a little, though!"

The Chief took a long drink of his Evan white. I'd never seen a man draw so much of such strong liquor in one shot before. He set the glass down and winced.

"Good stuff?" I asked.

"It's like a little shot of hell," the Chief said, "but a big shot of heaven."

"That was a *gulp*. I'm drunk from just watching you."

"I'll bet. There's a lot going on in this drink."

The Chief chased his Evan white with a sip of his beer. He seemed disappointed at the result. The warm, strong, flavorful fire the Old Kentuckian had lit in his belly was being coldly doused by this western cowpoke. He'd been invited to the party, but now seemed to be an unwanted guest.

I started to draw parallels between how the drinks were treating the Chief and how I was as well. I decided to stop being the cold beer and let the Chief enjoy that fire in his gut—and wherever else it was burning.

"Excuse me, Chief," I said. "I'll be right back."

He nodded and took another, much smaller sip of his drink. I was beginning to feel him slipping back into a funk. I wanted to try and put a stop to it. I owed him that much.

I went to the end of the bar. I tried to make sure I was out of the Chief's field of view. It wasn't difficult. This place was packed, and it was easy to disappear into the crowd. I don't know who Butch is, but he's got a hell of a lot of friends—including the Chief and me among them tonight.

I wanted get a word with the bartender. It took a minute, but I finally got his attention.

"Hey, I'm sorry to bug you," I said.

"Not a problem, whatcha need?" the bartender asked.

"Nothing really, our waitress has been taking great care of us."

"Well ya gotta want something!"

"I do. Can you tell me our waitress's name? She's about five-five, blond-black streaked hair, ponytail. She's …"

The bartender nodded and smiled. "That's Gretchen," he said. "She's a favorite around here."

"That makes perfect sense," I said. "She's pretty amazing. My friend has taken quite a shine to her."

"She's one of my best servers."

"I know I'm asking a lot, but is she spoken for?"

"No, not really. Unless you count three-quarters of the swingin' dicks in this place. They all love her and would love to spend a little time with her."

"My friend does too. He's an original. A little older than she may be used to."

"That sounds a bit odd."

"Well, he is that, but a great man. He just wants to talk to her. What time is she off? Can you tell me that? I don't want to get her in trouble while she's working."

"Her shift's over at one a.m. Your friend's gonna have some competition, though."

I laughed. "That's his concern," I said. "I just want to do something nice for the old man. He's been down a bit. Gretchen would really lift his spirits."

"Well, as long as his spirits are all that's being lifted," the bartender commented.

"I don't think that's an issue," I said, a bit coldly. I felt that the bartender's remark was a little off-color. So what if the Chief wanted to have a romp in the rack with Gretchen?

I returned to my seat and saw the Chief had been topped off and was a little sloshy.

"You okay?" I asked. "You got new drinks."

"That's what happens when the glasses get empty," the Chief said, matter-of-factly. "They get filled right back up again."

My scotch and my beer remained as they were. I was surprised the Chief hadn't gotten me new drinks as well. He was never one to shy away from getting the next round and increasing my tab.

"I'm good, Chief," I said sarcastically. "I'm not ready for another just yet."

The Chief said nothing.

"I've got a surprise for you, Chief," I said. "But you can't have it till about one."

"That's not too far-off, but it is pretty damn late," he said. "It better be something good, Louie."

"It'll be worth the wait, I promise."

As soon as the words *I promise* came out of my mouth, I realized I hadn't asked the one person who was most involved if this was even remotely okay; I needed to chat with Gretchen.

I excused myself again and went to look for our lovely server. She was ringing up tabs at the bar. Perfect. At least for a moment, she was not completely busy and was not with a patron.

"Hi, I'm sorry to bother you," I said.

She smiled. "Oh, it's not a problem," she said. "What can I do for you?"

"I know you're busy …" I paused. I pretended I didn't know her name.

"It's Gretchen," she said. "Some people call me Gretta, or Gree-Gree. Weird, I know!"

"Well, it's nice to meet you Gretchen. You have a great name. I'm Louis."

Gretchen smiled again. "Your dad called you Louie," she said.

I nodded. "Yep, he does call me that," I said. "He's not really my dad. He's more of my traveling companion. Did he tell you anything else about me—or us?"

"No, he's just the sweetest man, though," she said. "He seems like a lot of fun."

"He is. He's a little odd, but he's great. Lots of stories and adventures to share."

"I can imagine. He looks like an old-time movie star."

"He'd like to hear that, I'm sure. Listen, I don't want to take up a lot of your time, and I don't know how to ask what I'm about to, so I'll just come out with it."

Gretchen's face took on an uncertain look. I know she'd been hit on countless times, but my words sounded like the beginnings of a marriage proposal.

"I'm sorry, I'm not good at this stuff," I said.

"Just say it," she said. "I've heard a lot of stuff, honey. It's okay."

I laughed. "I'm sure! okay. My friend would like to have a drink with you," I said. "He's taken quite a shine to you, if you don't mind me saying."

Gretchen blushed. "I'd love to," she said. "I'm off at one a.m. Can he wait till then?"

My face beamed, and I chuckled. "He can," I said. "So long as Mr. Williams stops coming by for a while."

Gretchen winked and nodded. "I can make sure his visits are over for now," she said.

"Thank you, Gretchen," I said. "You have no idea what this means to me—*and to him.*"

"It's not a problem, Louis. He seems like such a great old guy. What's his name?"

"He likes to be called *Chief.*"

"Really? Why?"

"Beats me. That's what everyone has called him since we met."

"Okay. *Chief* it is!"

"Thank you again. You're truly an angel on Earth."

Gretchen blushed again and turned away. She didn't have to say any more.

I sat down again, and the Chief gave me a scowl.

"Where you been, Louie?" he asked. "Mister Williams and I have been lonely without your grand company."

"I had to find out something," I said.

"What the hell was it? You've been gone for hours."

"Not really. It's only been a few minutes. I have to keep it on the QT, though."

"Fuck the QT, Louie. You just left an old man to fucking die again."

"Chief, calm down," I said. "I didn't leave you to die. It was just the opposite."

"That's bullshit, kid!" the Chief shouted. "You get me all drunk, then you try to kill me. I know what that's about."

"So do I, you old son of a bitch! You got me loaded as fuck on rye last night, woke me up at three a.m. and expected me to drive you across state lines. I'm trying to do something nice here and ..."

I was interrupted by Gretchen. "Boys! Boys! Stop this!" she said, sounding like a referee in a fight. "Now you listen. Settle down, or my boss is gonna throw you out. None of us wants that, right?"

The Chief and I hung our heads like a couple of scolded children.

"No, ma'am," we said in unison.

Gretchen looked right at the Chief and said, "As for you, if you can't be a gentleman, I can't see you after work, okay?"

The Chief looked like he'd been knocked out of his chair. He wasn't certain he'd actually heard what Gretchen had said. He didn't ask her to repeat herself for fear it he'd imagined it. She winked at him and turned away to go back to work. The Chief watched her sashay from the table. His eyes were fixed on the rolling, sensual swing of the pockets and fabric of her tight blue jeans, as they tried to keep up with the curvy flesh inside them.

"Am I dead, kid?" the Chief asked. "I've got to be. I'm in heaven."

"No, Chief, you're quite alive," I said. "And you're not in heaven—you're in Evansville."

I sat down and sipped my scotch and soda. It was warm and seemed more soda—more water, really—than scotch. My beer was still a little cold but was bordering on acceptable English drinking temperature. I drank it down in two large, long swallows. I didn't wait for Gretchen to return. I went to the bar and ordered a pint of Red Hook ESB for myself and another Grand Teton for the Chief. I got myself a small glass of Evan white as well. I decided to celebrate the man as well.

When I returned to our table, the Chief was chatting with two men at an adjacent table. They were talking about baseball. Moreover, they were talking Chicago Baseball: Cubs and White Sox.

"Well, the South Siders won it all last year," one of the men said. "As for your Cubbies? Not such a good record."

"That's true," the Chief said. "But I'm not talking about last year. I'm talking about the years when baseball meant something."

"It still means something. It's just a different game," the other man said.

"Yeah. It is different. It's all about the damn money and celebrity," the Chief stated. "These punks today couldn't hit 'the Great Man' Dizzy Dean. Hell, they probably couldn't get one off of Bill Fleming and he was terrible."

"Things change. You've got to accept that. It's still the Grand Old Game."

"Yeah, and think about it like this, Chief," the first man said. "Your guys still have a park to play in that represents just how old and grand it is."

The Chief smiled. "Yeah, Lefty, you got me there," he said.

The man the Chief called Lefty gave me a nod. "You want in on this, kid?" he asked. "This old boy's got us in a pickle for sure."

I shook my head and waved him off. "No thanks. I'm not sure I can keep up," I said.

"What? You don't like baseball?" the other man asked.

"I do. I'm just not a historian of the game," I said.

"Well, at least tell us who you like. You gotta have a team."

The Chief looked at me quick and then back to the other men. "Louie here is a Braves fan," he said without knowing if I was or wasn't. "He's a *Joe-jah* boy. He ain't got much choice."

The other men laughed. "Well, that's true, but you got yourself a damn good team," Lefty said. "Who's your favorite Brave? Hammerin' Hank? Warren Spahn?"

"Tom Glavine," I said.

"All time? He's too new," the other man said. "Who's your *all-time* favorite player?"

"Steve Garvey," I answered.

"Garvey? He wasn't a Brave. He was a Dodger."

"He was. And a Padre too—unfortunately."

Lefty laughed. "Being a Braves fan, how'd you get Garvey on your roster?"

"I grew up a Dodgers fan," I said.

"What happened?"

"I remembered where I came from."

Lefty, his buddy, and the Chief all burst out laughing. It was raucous but civil. I'd never seen the Chief interact with other men like this who weren't bartenders or waiters. It was interesting. Even more so, I didn't realize he was any kind of sports fan. We never talked about such things. Our conversations were dominated by travel, booze, and sex. I'd just learned something new about the man—and I wasn't even trying.

It was getting close to 1:00 a.m. Saturday night had segued into early Sunday morning. The crowd began to thin a little, but Butch's still seemed the place to be.

"Where's everybody going?" the Chief asked. "The night is still young."

"Well, the night's old. The day is young," I said. "It's almost one. These people probably have church in a few hours."

"Church? Why the hell would they want to go and do a damn fool thing like that?"

I looked at the Chief and shook my head. "I think you just answered your own question," I said.

I peered around the bar and saw no sign of Gretchen. She probably decided to go home and leave an old drunk man to his dreams. I had to believe it was better that way. What were those two going to talk about anyway? Hell, the Chief was old enough to be her grandfather.

"So what's this special thing that supposed to happen at oh-one-hundred?" the Chief asked.

"It was nothing, really," I said. "I was just trying to get you to relax."

"I was relaxed. Now I'm riled up. I should've been in bed, Louie."

"I know, Chief. I'm sorry."

"Damn, kid, that filly you saw in Elko was right—you do apologize a lot."

"Yeah, well … sometimes, it's quite warranted."

The Chief was angry with me—and with good reason. I'd gotten his hopes up for something that he wasn't sure about but was still anticipating. I never should've talked to Gretchen. I put her and the Chief into awkward positions.

I was about to get up when I felt a hand on my shoulder and heard a familiar voice.

"Where you going, cowboy?" Gretchen asked. "I thought we had a *ron-day-voo* to *ron-day*?"

Gretchen pulled a chair around and sat front to back. I glanced down and noticed the wide spread of her legs across the chair. The Chief noticed it too and made a comment.

"Dearest, you ride a bit, don't you?" the Chief asked.

My eyes got big with embarrassment. I couldn't believe he said that. There are things you don't say to a lady, and I'm sure mentioning the spread of her thighs may be one of them. I figured the Chief was a goner and would be leaving with a face soaked with Evan white.

"Why yes, I do. You must've noticed my *bow?*" Gretchen fired back. She laughed out loud and grabbed the Chief's knee.

She leaned toward me and put her hand on my shoulder. She looked at the Chief and spoke to him while she shook me.

"Your friend told me you'd taken quite a shine to me," she said. "If it's true, why haven't you bought me a drink yet?"

The Chief sat dumbfounded. I looked at the clock.

"Isn't it too late?" I asked.

"Nope. Freddy hasn't blown last call yet," Gretchen said.

"Chief?" I said, waving my hand in front of his face. "You want to find out what the lady would like to drink?"

He didn't answer. I did the leg work for him.

"He's a little shy, Gretchen. What would you like to drink?" I asked.

Gretchen thought. "I'll have a whiskey sour," she said. "Heavy on the whiskey."

I got up and went to the bar. I looked over my shoulder and watched as Gretchen chatted with the Chief. He sat there like a damn zombie. He was so taken by her he couldn't muster an intelligible word or thought. She was vibrant and animated. He was just plain dead. It was like a case of platonic semi-necrophilia.

Freddy was wiping the bar down when I got there. He looked as if he was not interested in taking my order. That was not the case. He was just keeping an eye on his star server.

"The old boy, is he legit and on the level?" Freddy asked.

"Straight as they come," I said. "He's just an old man with a young heart."

Freddy nodded in what seemed to be approval. "Just make sure he treats her right," he said.

"That won't be a problem. They'll chat. We'll leave. It's all good."

"I'mma hold you to that, kid."

"Go ahead. My word is gold, and it's all I've got."

Freddy gave me a look of disbelief. "What are you having?" he asked, ready to take our orders.

"I want a dry-ass Gibson Martini," I said. "Give the Chief another small glass of Evan white and you probably know what Gretchen likes."

Freddy gave me a perplexed look. "Can't say I do," he said. "In all the time she's been here, I've never served her a drink before."

"No shit?" I said.

"Hell, I've never even *seen* her drink," Freddy said. "Let alone order one."

I smiled big and chuckled. "Imagine that," I said. "A couple of *greenhorns* blow into your saloon for a few drinks and they know more about your 'star server' than you do?"

Freddy laughed. "It was bound to happen sometime, I suppose," he said as he violently made my martini.

"Gibson. Onions, right?" Freddy asked.

"Yes. Frozen," I said.

"Who are you? Freakin' Ernest Hemingway? First time I'd ever heard of frozen onions in a drink was from something I'd read about him."

"You know his work?" I asked excitedly.

"No. Not his writing. They teach you about famous drunks in bartenders' school," he said. "I got a half a week on him and all those other 'Lost Generation' guys and their archaic drinks."

Freddy poured my martini, and it looked good. It looked crisp and clean the way a martini should. He garnished it with three frozen pearl onions and went to pour the Chief's drink. I stopped him.

"Hang on a second," I said. "Make that a small glass of Jack Daniels instead of Evan white."

"Why the change?" Freddy asked.

"Because, the Evan white is too much for him, and I want the old bastard to feel like Frank Sinatra."

Freddy smiled. He knew the story. I watched him pour a healthy dose of Old No. 7 for the Chief.

"Hope he likes it," Freddy said. "It's definitely not Evan white."

"He'll be fine," I assured. "If it was good enough for Ol' Blue Eyes, it's good enough for him."

"Okay. Now, Gretchen," Freddy said. "What's her poison?"

"Whiskey sour," I said. "And per her words, 'heavy on the whiskey.'"

Freddy set our drinks up. They were perfect. I took a sip of my martini, and it tasted good and right. He knew how to mix a drink for sure. I brought them to the table. The Chief and Gretchen laughed at me. They sang some old chantey. The Chief sang it in German while Gretchen sang it in English.

I sat down and doled out the libations. The Chief seemed miffed that his glass wasn't filled to the brim. I pointed back to the bar. Blame Freddy.

"What is that you're drinking, Louie?" the Chief asked. "You put ice water in a martini glass just to throw me off?"

"It's a Gibson martini, Chief," I said. "Those are onions. Not ice cubes. I haven't cashed out for the night just yet."

Gretchen sipped her whiskey sour. She was pleased with the booze to mixer ratio. The Chief took a quick sip of his drink.

"This isn't what I had before," he said.

"No, it's not," I said.

Gretchen smelled the liquid in the Chief's glass. "Honey, that's Jack Daniels," she said. "It's not as rough and tumble as the Evan white, and it's from Tennessee."

"I know that, missy," the Chief said to Gretchen. "I'm just trying to figure out the switcheroo."

"No switcheroo, Chief," I assured him. "I wanted to get you something different. Something nostalgic and special."

The Chief winked and nodded. "And I appreciate the sentiment, son."

The three of us chatted for a few minutes. The Chief and Gretchen seemed to be getting on quite well. She laughed at his jokes and touched him a lot. I watched his face change. The last time I'd seen him look this way was when he told Churchill and me about Mariposa and Cuba. Gretchen made him feel young again.

I was happy for the Chief but a bit scared as well. The age difference between these two people was vast. For what it's worth; however, at this moment, the Chief was in his twenties again.

Freddy finally "blew" last call. The crowd had thinned even more—especially since Gretchen's shift had ended. We continued to sit and talk. No one had made much of a dent in their drinks, so there was no need to replenish them.

I got up and walked to the bar. I left the Chief alone to woo Gretchen with his tales of adventure and travel. She'd probably never been out of Wyoming. I sat down and looked back at them. I thought about her face lighting up when he told her of tropical locales, throwing in a couple of native phrases just for good measure.

Freddy asked how my martini was. I told him it was perfect—as a martini should be. He laughed and nodded and thanked me. How hard can it be: drop of dry vermouth and a whole lot of gin? Hell, I could whip that up.

"So what's the story with the old man?" Freddy asked. "You said he's on the level. What's his crush with my waitress?"

"She makes him feel something," I said. "I don't get it, but that's between them. She's like a fountain of youth for him."

"Whatever you say."

"Don't worry, man. He's harmless. He just wants to talk to a beautiful girl. Gretchen fits the criteria for him."

"Well, I close at two a.m. You'll have to clear out by then."

"Understood. We'll be gone."

Freddy walked over and popped some money into the jukebox. The first song he played was "Treat Me Right" by Pat Benatar. I got the message. It seemed that no matter what I told him about the Chief, this man just didn't want to believe it.

Freddy and I both looked over at the Chief and Gretchen. They seemed to be having a great time. It appeared as if Gretchen was doing most of the talking. I found that odd, but maybe the Chief wanted to hear *her* story. I'm pretty sure he's told his enough.

The clock was fast approaching 2:00 a.m. I went back to the table and sat down to finish my drink. The Chief and Gretchen moved to the table where Lefty and his pal had been. They'd created their own little world inside this bar. It was nice.

I threw forty dollars on the table and took my empty glass back to the bar.

I pointed to the money. "Forty bones cover the damage?" I asked Freddy.

"It'll cover it and then some," he said. "You're tipping generous, I guess?"

"Call it that. She's worth it, if just for the service alone."

"A lot of people come in this place and ogle and touch that girl. This is the first time I've seen her converse this much."

"Maybe there's something there? Maybe she sees something in the old man. He's definitely like no one else I've ever met."

Freddy grabbed a glass and asked me if I wanted another—"for the road."

"What about 'last call'?" I asked.

"I run this place," he said. "I'm taking back the previous last call."

"Isn't that illegal? You know—state laws and shit?"

"You a cop, or you see one in here?"

"Nope to both questions."

"Good, then tell me what you're having and shut up and drink!" Freddy said with a laugh.

"You about done with my travel buddy?" I asked Gretchen. "It's past his bedtime."

Gretchen looked at me. "Would you mind if I borrow him for just a little longer?" she asked.

"What do you mean?" I wondered.

"Well, I can bring him back to the hotel," Gretchen said. "It's not that far from here. I just want to talk with him a little longer."

"He's a grown-ass man. If he wants to stay, he can."

Gretchen smiled. "Thank you," she said. "I've really liked spending time with him. I just need a little more."

I saw the Chief sitting and still looking young. I couldn't tax this man's gig. I went to the table and told him I was leaving.

"Okay, Louie. I'll see you back at the ranch," he said. "I won't be long. I've just got to tell *Gretel* about the islands—then I'll be home."

"That's fine, Chief," I said. "Oh, and it's *Gretchen*—not *Gretel.*"

The Chief waved me off as if I'd lied to him about the pronunciation of Gretchen's name. As a member of the Chief's Redub Club, it shouldn't have surprised me that he called her something different.

I stopped Gretchen as I was leaving. I took her wrists into my hands and looked her straight in the eyes.

"Don't hurt him, okay?" I said. "He's a great man, and when he's drunk, he's a little fragile."

"I just want to hear about 'the islands,'" she said. "They sound fascinating."

"Oh, they are. You're gonna be up for a while."

"That's okay. I've got nowhere special to be. Except here—and I've got Sundays off."

I called my cab and waited by the door. The only other people in the bar besides me were Freddy, Gretchen, and the Chief—and one passed out, left over. He was comatose under a speaker. The song playing was "Don't Rock the Jukebox" by Alan Jackson. It seemed fitting for some reason. Freddy went to roust him up and get him out, but he wasn't moving. I noticed a small cattle prod on the wall above the cash register. I had to wonder if it was used not just to stop fights but to wake dead customers as well. I'd never get my answer. My cab arrived, and I left the bar.

On the short ride to the hotel, I thought about the Chief. I knew he'd be okay with Gretchen, but the whole scenario still felt weird to me. I had to leave it alone. If this wasn't some random plot to kill an old man from out of town, I'd see the Chief tomorrow at breakfast and get a "full report" from him. The cab arrived at the hotel. I dug through my wallet for some cash, paid my fare, and stumbled out the door and into the hotel.

I walked in the lobby and saw it was almost three—there was no way I was getting up at six to eat. I staggered slightly to the elevator and got in. I was alone in the cab and quite tempted to push all the buttons and ride to every floor, stick my head out, and yell while my voice echoed in the quiet halls. I did nothing of the sort.

I pushed the button for the fifth floor and rode the elevator to all the way up. The bell rang, and the doors opened. I timidly peered about the empty hall. I pushed the button to close the doors. I leaned my head into the wall and began to cry. I missed April.

I envisioned her through my tears. I could see her plain as day—beautiful and vibrant and looking right at me. I didn't turn from my position. I vigorously ran my hand up and down the elevator's floor panel. I felt the car jolt and descend and then ascend. I started laughing as the bell rang, and the doors opened, stopping on every floor. I remained with my head to the wall, crying and laughing simultaneously.

"This is for you, my darling," I whispered as I traveled with my memories of April from floor to floor to floor.

I finally arrived on the third floor and shuffled to my room. I opened the door and drifted inside. I walked to my bed and fell flat on it. No lights or TV required this time. I didn't even take my shoes off. I just fell asleep.

I remained in slumber until I heard a vacuum cleaner whining in the hall a few hours later. It was time to get up.

I smiled as I remembered my dream. I dreamt about April and I making love on a picnic blanket amid a forest of Georgia Pines. It was warm and windy and fragrant and beautiful. I was painfully missing her a few hours ago when I was drunk—missing her sober hurt ten times worse.

I checked the clock and saw that it was 8:30 a.m. Not a lot of sleep, but I felt fine. My eyes were the only part of my body in pain. I got up and went to take a shower. I was looking forward to having breakfast with the Chief and in a turn of events—hearing about *his* night. I finished up, got dressed, and made my way to the restaurant.

I peered around to scope out the Chief. I didn't see him at first. There were quite a few people milling around the area. I'm not sure if this place qualified as a legitimate restaurant or not. It was just a bigger-than-average space with a few dinette sets and a row of do-it-yourself appliances, warmers and assorted vessels, and accouterments along the wall.

Light yellow, shiny, slightly textured, and perfectly round eggs sat orderly in one warmer, while plain bagels occupied another.

The selection of breads was slightly better than that of the bagels: white, wheat, or raisin. A six-slotted toaster awaited those who fancied their grained fare warmed and crisped—or even burned.

There were devices for making pancakes and American-Style Belgian Waffles. The only requirement for these mechanisms was to be filled and flipped. The desired results were light brown, soft, thin—but fluffy—aromatic pancakes from one machine; and golden-brown, crispy, thick—but airy—segmented waffles from the other.

More often than not, these results were seldom met. Kids and adults alike struggled as they negotiated the contraptions, both with the measuring and pouring of the batter, and the timing of their flips. Too raw or half-done, too crispy or completely burned were the predominant outcome.

One gentleman seemed to have a perfect system, and soon he was tasked with making pancakes and waffles for all who wanted them.

There was a large plexiglass cube with slots inside and knobs on the front. Each slot was filled with a different cereal: flakes, puffs, loops, and granola—turn a knob, get a bowl.

Coffee was pumped from large, brushed metal barrels. Each one had a sticker of an outdoor scene on it representing what coffee was inside: an aerial shot of a couple in a convertible for regular, a silhouetted couple on a beach at sunset for decaf, an overly enthusiastic couple laughing outside a café for French Roast.

The only instantly familiar objects were the decanters for juice and milk. Each vessel had a place card informing customers of what they were drinking. Someone had swapped the orange and tomato juice decanters' cards. The milk was less obvious. One percenters were going to be getting a little extra fat in their glass courtesy of that mischievous prankster!

The drinking receptacles were white Styrofoam cups for the milk and juice. Coffee could be enjoyed in thick paper cups. Both cup types had lids to cover their contents. None of them fit properly. The lips of the paper coffee cups were too thick, whereas the Styrofoam's were too thin. The sides collapsed frequently and more than one guest could be heard shouting: "Shit!" as they were suddenly splashed with cold milk, juice, or passably, hot coffee.

The utensils were white plastic, flimsy, and sterile. While a few held tightly to their respective positions, most of them were scattered and not in their proper trays. Some of the forks had damaged tines—more *threeks* and *twoks* than forks. They still worked, just not as well.

The tableware was white paper: smooth, shallow bowls and textured, corrugated plates.

A large bowl was half filled with fruit. It was labeled 'fresh' but teetering toward expiry. The apples were different types: pink ladies, red delicious, and a lone Granny Smith. There were three oranges in the mix and one peach. The peach was bruised severely.

I'd gotten so caught up in my observance of the Sunday brunch fare. I'd forgotten I was tracking down the Chief. When I saw him, he looked off, sullen, and older than usual. It was either a good night or a bad night. The fact that he was alone gave off the same vibe. I was afraid to approach him.

I sat down across him in an empty chair at his table. He was eating eggs that were doused in Tabasco sauce and ground pepper. He had three cups in front of him: one had coffee, one had milk, and the other was empty. He seemed disappointed with the eggs. He pressed the edge of his burned toast to the egg's surface and sopped up Tabasco. He wanted yolk. This was the best he would get from these eggs.

"Good morning, Chief," I said as I peeked into his empty cup.

"Morning, Louie," he responded. I felt a chill in his greeting.

"Did you sleep okay? I was so dead when I got back here."

"I did all right, son."

I was definitely sensing tension, but I didn't know how to broach the subject.

"How did things go after I left?" I asked. "You and Gretchen seemed to hit it off quite well."

"We did, Louie," he said. "We did. She's a high-class dame—a fine tomato."

"I knew that. What did you do after I left? Where did you go?"

"Kid, a man can have secrets. He doesn't need to divulge everything. Ever heard of boundaries? If not, let me tell ya about them: people put 'em up when they don't want to be fucked with."

The Chief dropped his head and went back to eating. Now I knew things had gone awry. I just didn't know how badly. I decided to honor his boundaries. I figured he'd spill something eventually.

I got up to get some food, and the Chief stared at me.

"Where you going?" he asked. "If it's my tone, I apologize. Sit down. Tell me a story."

"Okay. Once upon a time, there was a guy named Louis who was really hungry," I said. "Don't fret, Chief. I'm just going to get some food. I'll be right back."

The Chief nodded and waved me toward the buffet. The food was pretty well picked over, but I managed to snag an egg, a bagel, a bowl of Frosted Flakes with 2 percent milk and a cup of French Roast coffee.

I returned to the table, and the Chief hadn't touched anything on his plate since I'd left.

"Your food's going to get cold," I said.

"It's past cold, Louie. It's damn near frigid now," he said.

Okay. First, he lets into me; now he uses the word *frigid*. That word is only used to describe two things: cold weather—and even colder sex.

"All right, Chief. Spill it," I demanded. "You've got something bothering you, and I want to know what it is. Full report, sir, and right now."

"It's nothing," he said. "I'm just making statements that don't state or mean a goddamn thing."

"Something happened last night, Chief. You've got to tell me what it was."

"Louie, you're treading into dangerous territory."

"I don't care if it's a freakin' minefield. Something's wrong, and you need to tell me what it is."

"Piss on it, Louie. Here's a lesson for you: if you can't eat or fuck it—piss on it. That's what I'm doing with this conversation. I'm pissing on it."

"Not this time, old man. Come on. Talk to me."

"No. Drop it, or I'm liable to drop you."

"What? You gonna deck me or something? Give me a break."

I shouldn't have said that. The Chief stood up, and he looked taller and bigger than I'd ever seen him before.

"You wanna fight this old bastard? Then come on," the Chief said. "I was a member of the Chicago Golden Gloves, and let me tell you—I may have lost a step, but I ain't lost my strike."

I put my hands up. "I surrender, Chief," I said.

He shook his head in anger. "You don't even know battlefield terminology," he said. "You surrender to your enemy—unless that's what I am to you now?"

"No. No, Chief. You are definitely *not* my enemy," I swore to him. "Please sit down. Now I say this phrase a lot in jest, but at this time, it's true: *you're scaring the kids.*"

The Chief scanned the room as he settled back into his chair. All eyes were on him. The quiet cacophony of voices had been completely silenced for the moment. The only sounds that could be heard were the uncomfortable shifting of asses on chairs. And the kids present were truly scared.

"Ladies and gentlemen—my apologies," the Chief said. "Thank you for coming and drive home safely." He dropped his head and resumed eating.

The mumbling rumble of low chatter continued as if nothing had ever happened, and everyone went back to the business of breakfast.

"What was that all about?" I asked.

"Kid, I'm not in a good way," the Chief said. "That's all you need to know."

"I'm worried about you. I've never seen you like this. You're upset."

"No, I'm not 'upset.' Favorites, buckets and stomachs get 'upset.'"

"Whatever. okay, so you're *depressed*—and don't give me some weird analogy or metaphor about the word, all right?"

The Chief huffed and relented. "All right."

"Just tell me *something*," I said. "I don't need details—just *something*."

"Nothing, Louie. Nothing happened," he said. "What was supposed to happen?"

"I don't know. You and Gretchen were getting on so well. Did you have a good talk? Did you tell her about the islands?"

"Kid, we did get on well, and that was the problem. We got on *too* well, and there was nowhere to go. She was too damn young and too damn beautiful, and I was too damn old. And I did not tell her about the goddamn islands."

"I don't understand. You didn't share your stories with her? She wanted to hear them."

"I wasn't about to ruin her night with all that bullshit."

"It's not bullshit, Chief. It's history. It's incredible."

The Chief was stalling again. Before, he'd stalled out of nervousness. This time, however, I believed he was stalling out of humiliation. I just didn't know from where his humiliation stemmed. I pressed a little more.

"None of it is bullshit," I said. "When you tell me your stories, I get inspired. Hell, you had me and Churchill sipping rum and cokes on the beach in Havana when you told us about Cuba."

"You and Churchill bought that garbage because you're men. You're *pirates*," the Chief said. "And pirates, for as bold and brazen as they are, tend to be naïve and don't mind a lie or two. It's in our nature. We hunt and kill, we seek and we destroy, we build and we lie."

"That doesn't make sense. None of it."

"What do you want me to say? You want to hear another lie?"

"No, Chief, I want to know *the truth*. What happened between you and Gretchen?"

"You want to know what 'happened'?" the Chief asked. "You want the damn 'truth'?"

"Yes," I said.

"Nothing happened. Not a goddamn thing," the Chief said. "She was willing to give this old man a roll in the feathers, and I couldn't do it. *I couldn't do it in any way.* She reminded me, without saying a word, that this shit is not supposed to happen. I touched her skin, and I knew it was wrong. Even though I play the role—and I do it pretty goddamn well—I'm just an old bastard who can't ..."

The Chief paused at an awkward spot.

"'Can't what?" I asked.

"Just *can't* ... anymore," he said.

He didn't have to say another word. I knew what he meant, and I felt devastated by it. Gretchen made the Chief feel alive and young at the bar, but once they'd left and were alone, his safety net was gone. Gretchen and her youth conflicted with his age and inability. It was something the Chief had spoken of but hadn't dealt with on a level such as this.

I looked at the Chief. His head hung low. He seemed so defeated. As a man, I guess he was.

I put my hand on the Chief's. He glanced at my face then at my hand.

"What's this for?" he asked. "You wanna tell me you love me?"

"No. I just want to tell you it's all right," I said.

"It ain't all right, kid, but thanks for the sentiment."

I wasn't sure where to go next with this conversation. It was harrowing, borderline violent, and intimate all at once. I'd witnessed the Chief go through a gamut of feelings. That's difficult for any-one—even a tough old bastard like him.

As I finished my breakfast, I noticed the Chief shooting quick looks in my direction. I couldn't tell if he was angry with me, or if he was peering past me at something else. I sat up and stretched.

"I'm going to go to my room and write a bit after we're done," I said. "I haven't done a damn thing, and I need to get some kind of proof of work to my publisher."

The Chief stared at me. He seemed disappointed, but the look faded as quickly as it came.

"Really? You're going to waste this beautiful day holed up with your face in a notebook?" he asked. "Well, if that's what you want, who am I to stop you?"

I was surprised by his reaction. "Okay, what do you want to do?" I asked.

"Anything but sit around this hotel. We're seekers, Louie. Let's do what we do best. You can lie about it later."

I nodded and smiled. This was good news to me. The Chief was definitely not over what happened with Gretchen, but if he wanted to deal with it by not moping and going out to explore the environs instead, I was fine with that. He was definitely a bigger man than I.

The Chief and I decided to head out around noon to go and see the sights of Old Evansville. In the interim, I wanted to sit down and try to get some work done. I was a few days off schedule and falling farther behind. I had nothing to show for me delinquency. My publisher was lenient to a fault, but I hadn't even given him a single verbal word as to my whereabouts, let alone a written one. I'm sure his lenience with me was running out—if it hadn't already reached empty.

I opened my notebook. I filed through my scrawling. There was nothing too out of the ordinary or incriminating. I'd started several small essays that had to do with places I'd been in Elko, but there wasn't anything I could use as *work*.

I found a story about the diner where April and I had eaten. I described the food and the décor, but my words were vague and seemed interrupted. It was like I couldn't get a cohesive thought out and I just abandoned the text. There were pages and pages like this. It didn't make sense until I got to the end.

When I got to the end of the writing, I noticed I'd written a love letter to April. It was more like a formal request to take her on a vacation, but it was romantic all the same. This was where I'd seen her name so many times as the Chief was thumbing through the strewn pages. It wasn't anything to fret about, but it *was* personal.

I put the pieces together, and I had *something*. I began to cobble sentences and lines from various pages until I had a decent paragraph. I felt like I was back on my high school newspaper staff, cutting sections of paper and text and pasting them to form a unified and legitimate-looking story.

I studied the words and studied them again. I checked their placement in the puzzle, and they seemed fine. I copied them onto a page in my notebook and added what I needed as I went.

I used a pencil so I could erase new things I'd jotted. I was tired of thick black or blue blobs of mistake reminders besmirching my page and making me look like a total hack.

I chose not to read back what I'd written and stitched. The last time I did that, I ended up in a bar in Sacramento, California, and now I'm in a hotel in Evansville, Wyoming, trying to figure out what I did in Elko, Nevada, when all the while I should be home in Valdosta, Georgia.

I kept working and checking, but not repeating or reading: *That's what an editor is for,* I told myself. As I began to find my place, I was becoming less reliant on the scribbled notes. I was remembering vividly points of interest and quirky sights that made me smile—things that made this trip worthwhile. These are what I'd sought, and the reasons I'd decided to ask the Chief to come along for the ride.

Just as I stopped working, I heard a knock on my door. I peered back at the clock. It was 11:59 a.m. A second knock came just as the digits switched to 12:00 p.m. *How in the hell can a man have* that *perfect timing?* I wondered to myself. I got up to answer the door.

"Hello, Chief," I said.

"How'd you know it was me, Louie?" he asked.

"Timing. I didn't even have to look in the peephole."

"Are you ready to see what Evansville holds for us?"

"I am. Let me get my stuff, and we'll be on our way."

The Chief spied the scraps of paper laid out like a ransom note on the desk.

"What do you think?" I asked.

"About what?" the Chief replied.

"What I've got going on the desk."

"I'm not concerned about that. That's your business."

"It's okay if you want to read it."

The Chief cast his gaze elsewhere. I shook my head. I really wanted him to read what I'd put together. I was hoping he would be interested enough to inquire. He seemed to be. He just wasn't going to say anything.

We left my room and headed to the lobby. In the elevator, the Chief began to ask me questions about what I'd been doing.

"I told you, you could read the stuff," I said.

"I don't want to read it," he said. "I'm just wondering how you're getting on with your work."

"Better than I thought. I actually have something to work with."

"Did you get everything organized like you wanted?"

"A little. I just tore strips of paper and arranged them on a page. It's like a puzzle. It's fitting actually, the whole puzzle thing."

"How so?"

"This trip has been like that. Lots of pieces that need to be placed a certain way—it's just getting there."

"Well, kid, it sounds like you're finding the right pieces at least."

The Chief knew my puzzle analogy all too well. His whole life had been a series of varied pieces locked together to make a grand and glorious picture. He was continuing to add pieces. I just wanted to finish this one before I started another.

The Chief and I decided it was time to do some seeking. We headed west out of town. Our destinations were Fort Caspar and a little plot of land called Hell's Half Acre.

"Come on, let's go explore," I said.

"No. It's okay. I'll check it out from here," the Chief said.

"This is your thing: old war stuff; the Oregon Trail, cowboys and Indians. You live for this shit."

"Too many people, Louie. I'm not dealing with crowds today."

"We'll get out and find a place less crowded."

"It's all crowded. Let's go see your half acre of hell."

"Chief, we're here now. Just give it a few minutes. It'll be fine."

"No. You go on ahead. I'll wait here."

The Chief shut down again. I closed my eyes and shook my head. I didn't know what to do with the old man. He'd hit bottom this morning, perked up, and now was in the doldrums again.

"What is the matter?" I asked. "You wanted to do this. It was your idea."

"I changed my mind, goddammit," he said. "A man can change his mind, you know."

"I thought that was a woman. In this case and at a place like this, isn't a man supposed to 'stick to his guns'?"

"You're gonna persist, aren't you?"

"I am, Chief. It'll be fine, I promise. If it helps, I'll come around and open your door for you."

The Chief looked at me. His expression was hostile but not unwavering.

"I can get the door myself," he said.

I got out of the car and walked around to the passenger's side. The Chief glared at me through the glass, and I just smiled back at him.

"Are you getting out?" I asked.

The Chief turned his head and looked away from me.

"Okay, suit yourself, old man," I said.

I tapped on the glass. "You might want to roll the window down," I said. "It's pretty warm out here."

I started to walk away when I heard the car door open. I slowed my pace but did not stop. I had my back to the Chief so he couldn't see the big smile that was drawing on my face.

"Hey! Speedy—wait!" the Chief shouted. "Why you want to leave an old man to die in a hot car? What kind of a heartless bastard, are you?"

A few of the visitors looked at me. Their expressions were varied from shock to disgust to sympathy—for both me and the old man.

I stopped and turned around. "You're just fine, Chief," I said.

"Louie, it's cruel," he said. "You're trying to kill an old man. Your generation—no respect for their elders. No respect at all."

I walked over to the Chief and put my arm around his shoulder. "Do you need me to help you along, *Mr. Dangerfield*?" I asked. "Can I get you a wheelchair or would you prefer a cart?"

The Chief shook my arm off his shoulder. "I don't need your goddamn charity, kid," he said. "I can do this myself."

"I know you can."

"Why do you always make things so difficult for me?"

I looked at the Chief and smiled. "Because you make it easy for me to make it difficult for you," I said.

He chuckled at my comment. "Yeah, Louie, I guess I can be a handful sometimes," he said. "A handful of what I don't know ..." He paused. "Don't answer that."

The Chief ran across something that caught his attention.

"Hey, Louie, your people were here," he yelled. His loud voice again caught the attention of the other visitors.

"'My people'?" I asked. "Which people are those?"

"The Mormons. Mr. Young and his cronies were here, too. They're like *Kilroy*—always somewhere. Always *here.*"

I rolled my eyes as I read the rest of the sign. "This was on the way, Chief," I said. "A lot of folks passed through this area back then."

We walked the grounds, and the Chief had finally lightened up. The tourists didn't bother him as much, and he'd even imparted some of his wisdom on a couple of kids. I wasn't sure if what he was telling them was fact or fiction, but it sounded credible, and they were eating it up.

I went into a couple of the barracks rooms, and the Chief followed. He was quiet as he marveled at the displays: uniforms looking pristine and unscathed—their wearers without a clue that soon they'd be donned and covered in blood.

The Cavalry Bugle at rest on a table—it had sounded *Reveille* this morning and would sound *Retreat* tonight; unfortunately, it and its bugler would be silenced when bands of Lakota, Cheyenne, and Arapaho Indians overran the fort in the Battle of the North Platte Station.

Old state flags hung on the walls of the rooms—some from Ohio and some from Kansas. Not a one from Wyoming, however. An 1865 36-starred version of *Old Glory* was displayed on the walls of each room as well. Some fared better than others—stiff, shiny, and complete in one room; loose, stained, and threadbare in another.

Provisions were mocked up on shelves in the supply room. Old wooden barrels lined the floor, while copper pots and tin buckets hung from ceiling rafters. The Chief was quick to point out discrepancies with the labels on some of the cans. I wasn't fussed about a label on a can of tomatoes. I was just happy that *he* was happy.

As we ventured back outside, the Chief spied something that really took him in. I hadn't seen him move so rapidly toward anything. From my view, it was nothing more than a plaque about the Battle of the North Platte Station, but the Chief's eye caught something significant.

"Well, I'll be a mare's ass, Louie, check this out," he said.

I peered over his shoulder and read the gold stamped lettering on the black, granite slate. There was nothing that drew me in. It was a repeat of the information we'd already learned.

"What is it, Chief?" I asked. "I'm not seeing anything."

"Right there, kid," he said pointing his finger—almost violently—toward the plaque. "*Right there.*"

I read the words again and tried to follow the Chief's finger as he guided me along the lines. Still nothing.

"Sorry," I said. "You're gonna have to tell me what it is."

The Chief shook his head in disappointment. "*Roman Nose,* Louie," he said with an impish delight. "Roman freakin' Nose! Can you believe that?"

I wasn't getting it. The Chief found the name of this Cheyenne Warrior to be fascinating.

"What's the big deal?" I asked. "It's just a crazy-ass name. There's another guy named *Red Cloud* too."

"Yeah, kid, but Red Cloud is *not* Roman Nose," the Chief said. "When I was a boy, that was a name I heard a lot."

There was a story attached to his delight, and now I was intrigued.

"Really?" I asked. "How so?"

"My father used to talk about people having a Roman Nose," he explained. "I never knew what the hell he was talking about. It just made me laugh at first. Then I thought it had to do with a physical trait. So it wasn't as funny anymore. It sounded more like an insult."

"Sounds logical," I said.

I kept waiting for the Chief to make a crack about my ancestry and ask why I did not have such an olfactory organ gracing my visage. He did no such thing.

The Chief continued his story.

"One day, my brother and his friend were playing in the house," he said. "Father was a little tight and started in on my brother's buddy. He wasn't trying to be mean, he was just bombed and having fun. He told the poor kid he had a Roman Nose.

"When the kid asked him what he meant, he said, 'Because it's *roamin'* all over your damn face.' We all fell apart—even the friend. The kid kept touching his face to make sure his nose hadn't *roamed* away.

"My father played along with a game of 'got your nose.' That's how I've always known the expression, so to see it here, on this plaque, and the name of a great Indian warrior? Well, Louie, that just makes my goddamn day!"

The Chief put his arm around my shoulder. "Thanks for bringing me here, son," he said. "You always manage to bring the best out of me, even after you piss me off."

I smiled. "You're welcome, Chief," I said. "It's not my intention to piss you off, but I'm always fascinated when you find that *something* that makes you happy. Glad I can help."

"Are you ready to go see Satan's little plot of land?" he asked.

The drive to Hell's Half Acre was about forty-five minutes. I took in the sights along the way. The otherworldly landscapes I'd caught glimpses of as dusk fell last night were even eerier-looking in the daylight: scrubby and dry wasteland in one spot, sculpted and eroded abstractions in another. We drove up and down and curved as we made our way to our endpoint of sightseeing.

"So why are we here?" the Chief asked. "Why in the world would you want to come to a place called Hell's Half Acre?"

"I had an ex who used the term a lot," I said. "Every time she'd lose something, she said she had to search all over Hell's Half Acre to find it."

"Are you trying to find her stuff?"

"No, I just found it intriguing that the place actually exists."

The Chief nodded and looked out the window.

I pulled the car off the road to read the sign welcoming us to this little slice of hell. There was an abandoned restaurant inside of a fenced area.

"Hell's Half Acre: restaurant and souvenirs," the Chief mumbled as he read the sign on the building.

"Maybe once upon a time," I said. "I'm not here for the food or gifts, though."

I drove to the edge of the perimeter fence. We could go no further. I shut the car off.

"Are you coming along?" I asked the Chief.

"I can see it just fine from here," he said.

"Oh, Jesus Christ on the cross, you're not gonna do this again, are you?"

"Louie, I've seen the goddamn Grand Canyon already—why do I want to see its little cousin from Wyoming?"

"Okay. I'll be back."

I got out of the car and walked to the fence line. This place was amazing. The crags and ravines spread as far as the eye could see—a lot further than a mere half acre, for sure.

The first feature I noticed was the color of the clay: gray to white. It looked as if snow had covered the ground on this hot August day and the Earth had formed glaciers of tightly packed soil, sediment, and sand.

The longer I looked, the more colors and shapes I could see in the landscape. The red bands so common in terrain like this emerged as patchy afterthoughts, fading to yellow, and they disappeared into the valley below.

The air was filled with hauntingly beautiful sounds. The wind wisped and cascaded into the gorge. It moaned as it made its way through caves, juts, craters, and holes in the scenery and embraced the gnarled towers of earth as they rose from the valley's floor like fossilized dragons perpetually surveying their territory.

I took a deep breath. The air smelled clean and fresh and crisp. It was the smell of purity, finished with a hint of spirituality. I wanted to believe that I'd drawn some long, forgotten souls into my lungs. I felt a slight buzz—as if I'd been mildly possessed. It was an exhilarating feeling.

I drifted back to the car. I was still quite overcome by what I'd felt. I was hoping to carry that feeling for as long as I could.

"Welcome back, Louie," the Chief said. "Did you find what you were looking for?"

"I found something," I said. "That was amazing."

"I take it you *didn't* find your old tomato's lost clam diggers or virginity, though?"

"That's messed up."

"I'm just fucking with you, Louie."

"How the hell did you get pants and virginity out of all the stuff I told you?"

"I don't know. You talked about your ex searching Hell's Half Acre when she'd lost something. It just made sense. I'm sure she loved those pants. As for the other thing? She ain't getting that one back."

"Nope. And I know exactly where *that* is."

The Chief laughed out loud and said, "I'll bet you goddamn well do!"

As we headed back toward Evansville, I began getting curious again about the Chief's less than cordial attitude at breakfast. I was worried and I'd expressed that. It was hard to be straight sentimental or openly caring toward the Chief's feelings, if you were, he put up a shield and acted like Burt Lancaster playing a tough in some forties flick. The Chief was a gentle giant, but he could be a surly son of a bitch as well.

"Okay. Chief, give it to me straight," I said. "What the hell happened between you and Gretchen?"

The Chief looked at me and furrowed his brow. He sighed deeply and nodded. He turned again and faced forward. His fingers fell one by one onto the dash. He stared dead ahead into the straight, perpetual void that was eastbound US 26. He closed his eyes in contemplation and took a quick breath.

"Everything was okay with that gal," the Chief said. He was still staring ahead. "We laughed and talked. She made me feel young. I like feeling young, Louie."

"I know you do, Chief," I said.

He continued as though he hadn't heard my response. "I was back in a place I hadn't been in a while," he said. "A place I hadn't thought of—wasn't supposed to think of."

I looked at him. I was confused by what he'd meant.

"Why weren't you supposed to think of it?" I asked.

"Secrets, kid," he said. "Too many damn secrets. I've got a lot of 'em. These, though—they weren't mine to begin with."

"Secrets, Chief?" I asked. "Like what?"

The Chief opened up like a floodgate.

"I was sent to Colorado. This was in the very early sixties," he said. "A couple of my friends were tasked to do an assignment that would take us out west and into a world we never thought we'd see. We knew it existed, but only as an idea.

"We flew out to Peterson Field in Colorado Springs. When we arrived—even before we could have a piss or a smoke—some brass from the US Air Force whisked us into a bus and drove us off the base. There were several other men in that bus. We'd never seen them before, but they looked like us. There were a couple of other Air Force hotshots on the ride as well. They stared at us and sized us up. It felt like we were being shuttled to boot camp.

"We were driven to a site that was hard to make out. There was nothing but a road and whole lot of rocks and foothills. We were going to the mountains. None of us really knew why."

"That's wild," I said.

"*Wild* is a good word for it," the Chief commented. "Well, we get to a point and we stop. A couple of kids—young airmen—get on the bus. They're armed and look even more serious than the officers. They handed us packets and got off the bus. They didn't say a damn thing. We sit and wait. Nobody really looks at the packets. No one told us to. We were all pretty much strangers, but we all knew that with the military, you don't do anything without some kind of an order. We awaited ours.

"One of the officers started speaking. He told us to open the packets and ensure that the items within were 'accounted for' and that all of the information on them was 'accurate.' I reached in and pulled out some folded paper and a plastic badge with a clip on it. Everyone else had the same thing in their packets.

"I read the papers before I looked at the badge. It was all there— names, numbers—*everything*. Someone had done their homework on me. I flipped the badge over and was dumbfounded. I'm staring at a photograph of myself—one identical to my company work badge—except this one had the words Top Secret stamped in red on it. Every swinging dick on that bus must've finished reading the contents of those packets at the same time. It was one simultaneous mass of confused looks and peering heads. The officers just sat and watched. One cocked a half-grin. They'd obviously seen this display before."

I stared at the Chief and shook my head. I was awestruck.

"'Top secret'?" I asked. "You mean, like on the QT?"

"Oh yes," he said. "The Q-est of all Ts. This was cloak-and-dagger, 'If I tell ya I have to kill ya stuff of the highest order."

"Then why are you telling me?"

"I haven't really told you anything yet, Louie. When I do—you'll know." The Chief winked and did that Fred Flintstone laugh again. This time, it sounded sinister.

The Chief continued his story.

"The officers tell us to put our badges on, and we all do, without hesitation," he said. "Then the bus stopped at a fence, and we were met with more guards. They get on and check us out, but they stay on the bus. One radios somewhere, and this gate opens. We can hear the chain link gate rattling along its runners. We were looking at each other again, but still no one was speaking. The only voices were the ones crackling over the radios the guards were carrying.

"The bus moved through the gate, and we were heading toward a tunnel. It was a concrete tube sticking out of the mountain. None of us had ever seen anything like this, but we'd heard rumors about places like it. It was the kind of thing you tell people about and they scream 'Bullshit!' because it's just too hard to believe.

"Anyway, we drive into the mountain, and the guards usher us off the bus. We walk out into a huge space. There are computers in this place that went from floor to ceiling, desks and control boards that wrapped around the room, screens on the walls that looked like a drive-in theater. There were so many blinking lights surrounding us, I swore it was goddamn Christmas. The officers briefed us as they gave us a limited tour of the facility—specifically, the places within it where we would be working. Everything else was beyond our clearance."

"How can you get beyond 'top secret'?" I asked. "Isn't that the pinnacle of secrecy?"

"Apparently not," the Chief said. "There were upper rungs of this clandestine ladder, and we weren't allowed to climb them at this time."

"Wow. I can only imagine how freaked out you must've been," I said.

"It was pretty damn intimidating," the Chief said. "We'd heard about this stuff but never seen it. It just didn't exist outside of science fiction—at least not back then."

"So let me get this straight: you worked at NORAD?"

"Not just worked there—I was on the ground floor at NORAD. However, at that time, it wasn't called NORAD yet."

"How did you land that gig? That's not something you just happen upon."

"Louie, back in those days, it didn't take much. For me, I was the perfect candidate. I was good with numbers, had a passion for science and computers, and I loved my country. That was all it took."

"That's an amazing story, Chief," I said. "I'll bet you tell it a lot. It's something to be proud of, for sure."

"I've only told a couple of people, Louie," he said. "For a long time I couldn't tell a soul. Once our mission was declassified, I was still hesitant to tell anyone. Most people wouldn't have believed it anyway. Where the whole idea was the stuff of fiction before, to say you worked there? *That* was the stuff of *fantasy*."

I was fascinated with this story but was curious as to how Gretchen fit into it all. There was a huge bridgeless gap between the friendly barmaid in Wyoming and the mountain-constructed fortress of defense in Colorado.

The Chief shook his head. "Where was I?" he asked. It was like he'd lost his place in a book.

"NORAD," I said. "You were telling me about going there to work."

"Yeah. That was a time," the Chief said. He took a breath. "It's a good thing I was a great liar back then."

I was even more confused now.

"Great liar? How so?" I asked.

"I was a Socialist, Louie," he said.

The statement came from out of the blue.

"I was a goddamn Socialist. Do you think the government wanted someone like that working on their most prized possession against the Soviets?"

"I don't understand, Chief," I said.

"I covered my tracks," he said emphatically, as if he was confessing a sin. "I went in with a military mind-set, and I betrayed my beliefs so I wouldn't betray my country."

"That was a long time ago," I said. "You did your job, and you did it patriotically. You didn't betray anyone—especially your country."

"Yeah, kid, but you don't shake off the probability of a fucking witch hunt—even now."

"There's no one here but us. And any secret you divulge is safe with me."

"I appreciate the thought. I don't know why I brought it all up."

"You were going somewhere with this story. I don't think this was it, though."

"No. It was not. I don't know what the hell I'm rattling about. Just forget it."

I smiled and looked at the Chief. He knew he was with a confidant but when a such a deep secret from your past crops up, it's difficult not to be paranoid.

"It's all okay, Chief," I assured him. "I only have one question about it. And it's more semantic than anything."

"What's that?" he asked.

"You called Castro a *pinko*," I said. "Weren't you, kind of ..."

The Chief cut me off. "What? You calling me a *commie*?" he asked in an angry whisper. "No. Theirs was a whole set of wrongs we didn't adhere to. They wanted to take over the world—we just wanted to make it a decent place to live."

That was it. No further sociopolitical queries.

"Where was I?" the Chief asked again.

"Colorado," I said.

"Colorado, Louie. We were in Colorado."

There was a new vibrancy in his tone.

"We were taken to a remote ranch about an hour and a half from the base," the Chief said. "Some town called Karval. A lot like Delle and Jiggs. Hell, there weren't even any trees. Colorado has no damn trees past the mountains!"

"Why so far away?" I asked.

"The feds didn't want us staying close to town. There was paranoia abound and they didn't want anyone to flap their lips."

"But you could still flap your lips in Karval, right?"

"Yeah, but you'd be talking to the wind for the most part. That was semi-okay. Plus out there, if you leaked, they could kill you and no one would ever find your carcass."

"Geez. What a way to go—shot dead in the wastelands of Colorado."

"Right. And no one wants that fate. You kept it zipped."

"It still doesn't make sense, Chief," I said. "Didn't the ranchers know why you were there? They had to have an idea."

"Nope, Louie, and if they did, they never let on," he said. "I'd imagine there was some kind of deal that involved a bullet or two. Then again, it was a riding ranch. I'm sure folks came by to ride the range from time to time."

I'd heard and read about this kind of stuff but, until now, had never *met* anyone who'd been a part of anything like it. I found it all intriguing, cool, and downright terrifying.

"We get to this ranch, and there are horses and a couple of buildings," he said. "We were in the plains part of Colorado now. It was scrubby and dry, but a look to the west and you could see the Rockies. It was like a different place."

"What were you thinking?" I asked.

"Not a damn thing," he said. "We didn't know the whys and wherefores, and nobody asked. We just waited for someone to show us the way. I remember asking a co-worker for a cigarette. That was a sight. I hadn't smoked in years, and here I was, coughing up a lung out in the middle of nowhere, in front of a bunch of people I didn't know, on someone else's land and on a secret fed job. There you go

Louie, there's something for your story. Can't you just picture that? Write that shit down."

I laughed. "I'll put that to paper—most definitely!" I said.

"Yeah, kid, there I was. Green and sick all over the place," the Chief said. "I was worse for wear for sure. It didn't help matters, especially for what happened next."

"What was that?"

"*That*—was when I met her."

Finally! I knew there was some type of romantic angle to this story. With the Chief, there always was. I nodded and listened as he began to open up about another woman from his past. This particular woman, however, seemed to resonate in his present as well.

"This truck pulls up to meet us, and we're all standing around waiting," the Chief said. "That seemed to be the order of the day: just stand there and wait for something to happen. And happen it did. This world-class dame climbs out of the cab of that truck, and well …"

"Just like that?" I asked.

"Even quicker than that," the Chief replied. "One look, Louie—I was hit. That little bastard Cupid fired one into my chest lickety-split. I damn near fell over. It's happened before: Mariposa, at first, a couple of gals here and there in different places, but it had been a while since I'd felt it like this. This was love, pure and simple. I like love. Hell, I *love* love. After not having it in my life for a while, this was a damn nice way to be.

"At first, I was just captivated by the fact she was driving a truck. You see, back in those days, women hardly drove, and even fewer of them drove a truck. But there was more to it, and I knew it. I was a goner. I watched this tomato walk over to us, and I got stupid. I didn't know if it was drilled or punched at this point. All I knew was that I wanted to get to know this woman."

"Did she have the same effect on the other guys?" I asked.

"Hell if I know," the Chief said. "From here, all I gave a damn about was her, me, and a couple of drinks by the fire."

"What happened next?"

"She showed us to our bungalows. We were billeted two to a room. There was riding gear and all kinds of stuff for us to use. At this point, I had to believe those ranchers really did think we were there to ride the range for the next few days. I felt like I was part of some big, government lie. Oh, sure, it was real, but it all seemed so goddamn wrong."

"How did you manage to keep things quiet, Chief?" I asked. "There had to be some times when you wanted to reveal why you were there."

"Oh, you bet, but that was not going to happen," he said. "We were sworn to secrecy, and the fear of possibly getting executed helped us keep that promise."

"I want to know about this woman," I said. "I know the other stuff. I want to know about *her*. What was her name? What did you do? Give it to me straight—*full report!*"

"Okay, kid. You want the sappy stuff? I'll give you the sappy stuff. We spent a lot of time in our rooms when we were at the ranch. One day, I was bored and getting cabin fever. I took a walk out by the horse stables. I wasn't doing anything, just admiring these beautiful creatures that roamed the acreage.

"I was petting the muzzle of an Arabian when *she* called me over to talk. I introduced myself, and she responded in kind. Her name was Bettie."

Bettie, I thought, *simple and classic*. However, knowing the Chief, there was nothing simple about this woman. What *did* surprise me was the statement that he'd introduced himself to her. Did Bettie get *a name?* No one else I'd run across since I met the Chief had gotten *a name*. And he didn't call anyone by their given names. Was Bettie really named *Bettie?* Was Mariposa truly *Mariposa?* I began to wonder if Chief wasn't actually the Chief's Christian name.

While I was rationalizing the name game, the Chief carried on with his story.

"We went for a ride, Bettie and I," he said. "I rode the Arabian I'd pet. It was amazing. I hadn't been on horseback since I was a kid. We rode for hours and talked. I knew from that very moment that

I wanted to spend the night with her. It may have been the only chance I got.

"We rode into an adjacent town. Bettie and I had a nice supper at this little diner. We talked some more. Hell, kid, I can't even remember our conversation. I just recall looking into her eyes and thinking I was seeing my destiny. Doesn't that sound ridiculous? Yeah, it does. Well, Louie—you wanted sappy."

"No, Chief, that doesn't sound ridiculous or sappy at all," I said. "Trust me. I know what you were feeling all too well."

The Chief continued. "After we ate, we rode to a little liquor store and bought a couple of bottles and then headed back to the ranch. We got in just after dusk. No one saw us. It was a good thing too. Apparently, the ranch had rules about the ponies, and we'd violated just about every one of them. Bettie and I were worried but also had a feeling of exhilaration. 'We were outlaws!' she said. We laughed, went up into a hayloft, and celebrated our day of being banditti with our bottles and our bodies. It was—"

The Chief stopped again. His abrupt pause was reminiscent of this morning when he talked about Gretchen and how he "couldn't do it in anyway." How when he touched her he knew it was "wrong." How he'd been playing "a role," and now he was "just an old bastard who can't …" I had an idea of what he *couldn't* do, but there was more to it—and Bettie was that *more to it.*

Obviously, something more than a literal roll in the hay occurred between them, and it had affected the Chief ever since. How he'd managed to keep it under wraps until now—*until Gretchen*—I don't know.

"Chief, are you okay?" I asked. "I lost you. Do you want to stop and get out of the car? Maybe take a breather?"

"No, I'll be all right. Let's just get back to town. Let's get back and go have a drink—or several. That's what I want right now."

"Okay. That sounds good to me."

We drove back to Evansville in silence. I knew I'd have to relent on my hopes of hearing the rest of the Chief's story for now. I felt guilty for wanting more. I felt guilty for wanting him to open up about things. It seemed that every time he did, he wasn't opening old scrapbooks, he was opening old wounds. These scarred patches of his past, healed and forgotten, were being brutally torn open by my curiosity and need for betterment. It made me sick to think this way.

We pulled into the hotel parking lot, and I shut the car off. I looked at the old man and saw him in a state of thought and disrepair.

"Chief, I'm sorry if I've upset you," I said. "That was never my intention. I just love to hear your stories. You've lived such an amazing life, I ..." It sounded like I was rambling more than apologizing.

"You didn't upset me, Louie," he said. "I've done that all on my own. You've actually helped me. It may not seem like it, but you're doing me some good here."

"You're right. It doesn't seem like it."

"Kid, when you get to be my age, you'll find you've racked up a shitload of regret, that's what I'm bringing to the table now—a shitload of regret."

"I'm not following. Where was the regret with Bettie? Everything seemed to be splendid between the two of you."

"It was, Louie. It most certainly was."

"So what happened, if you don't mind me asking? And how is Bettie connected to Gretchen?"

The Chief nodded and smiled. "You know something, Louie me boy. You're pretty damn smart," he said. "Let's take ourselves over to Butch's, and I'll tell you the rest of the story. Sound good?"

"Sounds fantastic. Do you really want to go to Butch's, though?" I wondered.

"Yes. It's the best place for me," the Chief said. "If I'm facing down those demons, why not do it in a place where one of them works?"

"Is Gretchen really a demon?"

"No, she's a goddamn angel. It's how she makes me feel that's demonic."

We got out of the car and went into the lobby.

"It's still early, Chief," I said. "Let's go catch a few winks and head over to Butch's about six p.m. for a bite and a belt. Does that sound good?"

"It does, kid," he said. "It sounds damn good. I'll meet you here at seventeen forty-five."

"Um … seven … quarter to six. Got it! I'll be here."

The Chief looked at the hotel restaurant. "Damn, I wish that son of a bitchin' café was open, I'm a little hungry," he said.

"Do you want to just go to the bar now?" I asked. "We could get a late lunch and an early start."

"Nah, Louie. I do want to get a little shut-eye. I'm not feeling all too well."

"Will you be okay for later?"

"Damn straight I will. I just need to rest these old bones and this spinning head."

I patted the Chief on the shoulder.

"Very well. I'm going to my room," I said. "I'll see you in a couple of hours."

"I'll be along directly," he said.

I got to my room, and once inside, I dropped on my bed. I contemplated setting my alarm, but I knew somehow I'd be awake in plenty of time to meet the Chief at 5:45. I closed my eyes and went out almost immediately.

I was standing at the perimeter fence surrounding Hell's Half Acre. I looked around to make sure no one was watching me. I took off my clothes and climbed over the fence. The coarse chain link cut into my bare feet as I made my way over the top.

Once on the other side of the fence, I slowly moved down a small trail in the clay and ended up in the bottom of the chasm. I was naked, and the wind blowing on my skin was sharp and felt as if it was cutting my flesh.

I peered up at the towering stacks of earth, mini mesas that had been here for eons but looked as though they could topple over at any second. I heard a voice—a female voice. It was strange at first, but the more I heard it, the more familiar it was becoming.

"There's no fucking way …" I said in a whisper.

I listened some more. The voice was becoming clearer and sounded like it was getting closer.

I looked around in a panic. I darted from the open into a carved notch and tried to hide. I searched my surroundings. All of a sudden, I saw a book lying on the ground. *Where did that come from?* I wondered. I squinted to read the cover. It was a copy of *Wifey* by Judy Blume. I've only known two people in my life who've read that book. I jumped out and grabbed the book.

I opened the cover and saw the library cancellations inside. "May 10, 19…" was the only one I could read, but I could not discern the year. A green check mark had been penciled by the date. *I had checked this book back in! That was my pencil mark. That was my color.* I worked at the local library while I was in high school.

Why was it here? Oh my God! I know why it's here! She'd misplaced it. That forgetful chick—she was always putting things where they shouldn't be. Now she was here looking for the book, literally searching Hell's Half Acre for it. It was my ex. She was here with me now.

I ran into another spot. I crouched down. I rubbed sand and clay over my skin to camouflage myself. *This will work,* I thought. *She'll never see me now.*

I heard her voice again. I looked out from my hiding place and saw what appeared to be a blouse. I quickly ran out and grabbed it and moved back to my cover. I smelled the blouse. It had the faint scent of Yves Saint Laurent's Opium lingering in the fabric.

I breathed in deeply, and I felt slightly dizzy. I didn't know if it was from the fragrance or the harsh way I'd inhaled it? I recognized this blouse. This was the one she was going to wear the night we went to a friend's party. She couldn't find it. She said she'd been searching all over Hell's Half Acre to find it. Silly girl—it was in the laundry hamper!

"I liked what you wore instead," I said quietly.

I heard her call out again, and again, I hastily relocated. I was sweating. My earthen concealment was slowly oozing off of my skin. I rubbed more dirt on my skin. I was red now and easily seen amid the gray and yellowed spires and foothills. She would find me soon. I was growing more frightened by the minute.

From my new vantage point, I could see papers—loose, lined pieces of notebook paper. They flew up and softly spun in a cyclonic pattern and floated back to the ground. I dropped flat, prone and parallel to the surface of the chasm. I slithered naked to fetch the papers.

I could see her shadow on the tower to my right. My heart beat fast and loud as I scurried back to my hiding place. I rolled over a berm and lay flat on my back. She walked by. I could see the wavy hair atop her head as she made her way past me. I held my breath. Did she see me? Please, God, don't let her see me. She moved past and continued on. She did not see me. I could only see her hair. I wasn't sure if I wanted to see her face.

I slowly sat up and peered over the berm. I saw her from behind as I watched her walk away. She was naked as well. A large scar curved from her left shoulder blade to her spine. I saw her reach behind her back to scratch the scar. It was more than a scratch. She was feeling for something. She was smacking herself; trying to remove something from her back. She continued walking away, and I fell back into hiding.

I read the papers. They were the wedding vows we'd scribbled down one night. We were just having fun, that's all. Pretending. I did love her. I loved her so, but things were so wrong. The timing was all wrong. Things just went too fast. I closed my eyes to fight my tears. "I'm sorry …" I whispered. "I'm so sorry …"

I didn't know she was searching this place for these vows. She'd said new ones to another man. I was fine with that—it was a long time ago. I rubbed my eyes. The tears I'd fought were now flowing and mixing with the dirt on my face. I looked around me to make sure my ex was gone. I climbed out from behind the berm. I saw something lying in the sand. I walked over to it and dusted it off. Sand and dirt were caked and coagulated on it.

I dug down deeper and felt something wooden. I grabbed at it and pulled it up. I was holding a knife, a large, kitchen knife. I stared at the knife and began to tremble. Suddenly I heard her voice and smelled her perfume. "I've been looking all over for that," she said. I turned around in a gasp. I never saw her face.

I woke up and bolted upright in bed. I was still dressed but soaked in sweat from my scalp to my scrotum. My shirt was drenched as were my pillow and sheets. As soon as my thoughts gathered, I began to hyperventilate.

"Oh my holy God," I said in between my panting breaths. "What just happened?"

I looked around the room to make sure I was truly *in* the room. I saw the clock. I'd only been asleep for about twenty minutes. Well, at this point, twenty minutes was plenty. I shook my head and pulled myself out of bed. I stood up and stared into space. I was blank but scared.

I wandered over to my suitcase to get some dry clothes. Everything packed within was dirty, worn, or bore a light scent of BO or spray deodorant. I'd felt disgusting already.

I raised my hand to smack myself, but I did not. I closed my eyes, took a deep breath, and held it for as long as I could. When I felt my face about to explode, I exhaled slowly and listened as the air left my lungs.

I was in a state of confusion and distress because I'd had some whacked-out dream about my ex. The only certainties were as follows: I needed a shower, my clothes were nasty, and I was going to Butch's. That was all that mattered now.

I got in the shower, and the water felt good. It was refreshing and cleansing and a nice contrast to the sweat that had soaked me previously. As the salty perspiration ran down the drain with the soap residue, I began to think. I was putting another puzzle together. This one was not mine; it was the Chief's. I was trying to figure out where his story about Bettie was going next. It was too beautiful of a beginning to end so abruptly. No matter what my brain conjured, it made no sense. I couldn't assemble anything. I'd just have to wait until the Chief finished the puzzle for me.

When the elevator stopped on the first floor, I stepped out into the hall and made my way to the front desk. I looked outside the glass doors and spied a man with a small cart. He was selling T-shirts.

I picked up a brown T-shirt. It had a yellow, screen-printed silhouette of Wyoming's state symbol: the bucking horse and rider on it. Below the image in an arched, yellow, Old West font were the letters WYO; above the image in the same font and arch it read "E-VILLE." Sold! I grabbed that shirt and picked up a cheesy shot glass for the Chief as well.

I checked the clock and saw that it was not yet five thirty. I still had a few minutes. I ran up to my room to change my shirt.

Once I changed, I made my way back downstairs. I walked to the lobby, found a seat, and waited for the Chief.

I heard the bell for the elevator ring. I craned my neck to see who was getting out, and it was the Chief.

"Evening, Chief," I said.

"Evening, Louie," he said. "You ready to depart the premises?"

"Yep. I just need to call us a cab."

We got to Butch's, and the place was damn near empty. A few patrons sat and watched TV; a couple bookended the bar and that was about it.

"Where the hell is everyone?" the Chief wondered aloud.

"It's early yet," I said. "Remember, last night we got here later."

"True. Well, at least we won't have trouble getting a table."

The Chief found a decent spot and sat. I went to the bar to order drinks. Freddy was working and remembered me.

"Hey, Hemingway!" he shouted. "What'll you have tonight?"

"A pitcher of Grand Teton to start, and can we get a couple of menus for the grill?"

Freddy laughed. "I'll spare you the menus," he said. "We have three things in the kitchen: hamburgers, cheeseburgers, and chicken burgers. They all come cooked the same and with a bag of potato chips."

"Can I get a chicken burger for me and a hamburger for the old man?"

"Nope. We're out of chicken."

"Then why did you mention it as an option?"

"Cause it is an option any other time—just not tonight."

"Okay, a hamburger and a cheeseburger then."

"How do you want them cooked?"

"I thought they were cooked the same."

"They are burnt. How bad do you want them burnt?"

I shook my head.

"And what kind of chips do you want?" Freddy asked.

"You said *potato*." I noted. "There are choices?"

"Yeah. I'm not a total commie," Freddy said. "I've got Lays or Jay's."

"'Jay's'? *Here?* I thought that was a Midwest thing?"

"I'm originally from Michigan—and I know a guy."

I nodded and laughed. "Make it Jay's then," I said. "I'm sure the Chief will enjoy a taste of home."

Freddy drew the pitcher of beer and topped it perfectly. He pulled two frosted pint glasses from a cabinet and set them atop the bar.

"Your grub will be up in a few," he said.

I thanked him and went back to the table. When I got there, the Chief was gone.

Suddenly, I heard a familiar, boisterous bellow. I looked across the bar and saw the Chief standing and talking to Lefty and his pal—I guess I'll call him *Righty.* They were having a good laugh and chattering away about something. It was probably baseball.

I was just about to sit, when the Chief called me over to join him and his new bar buddies. I sloppily poured a half glass of foam and went to see what was going on.

"Louie, you remember ol' Lefty and *Rex,* right?" he asked.

Righty was now Rex, and I did remember them.

"Hey, hey, Chief Noc-a-homa!" Rex said. "Cop a squat. We're talking 'bout …"

"DA BAY-YERS!" Frighteningly, all three men said this in unison. They sounded like something from a *Saturday Night Live* skit. I began to wonder if people from the Chicagoland Area really did say *The Bears* with that inflection. Perhaps it wasn't just a go at the accent?

I sat down. Lefty looked at my beer and shook his head.

"Ya' drinkin' light tonight, Lou?" he asked.

Rex and the Chief laughed at the comment. I smiled and sipped my foam. I didn't say a word.

I listened to the guys talk football. This year's preseason was underway, and the discussion of a return to greatness and the prospects of another ring were on the table. It seemed too early to think such things, but it had been twenty years. They were certainly due.

The hated Green Bay Packers and Detroit Lions were mentioned then quickly scoffed and shoved aside as if they were mere debris on the table—just an annoyance and not worthy of further concern.

Their talk was narrowed down to the greats of the game, and when Walter Payton's name arose, the men became somber. They lowered their heads but raised their glasses in tribute. The mention of Sweetness's name invoked great reverence and emotion, strong nods of approval, and manly tears. This was it. Their discussion of all things Chicago Bears could go no further.

I found it fascinating how invested these guys were in this. They'd argued like an umpire and an angry manager kicking dirt on home plate when they talked baseball; ironically, they found common ground and peace within the confines of the gridiron. It made me realize just how disconnected from sports I truly was. I made a promise that when I went home I'd *really watch* the Braves and Falcons this year—I figured I owed it to these guys.

I got up to grab the pitcher. I figured if I wasn't sitting at the old table, then our beer shouldn't either. As I went from point to point, I noticed our burgers sitting on a counter above the bar and ready to be served. I set the pitcher down and went to get our food.

"Order's up," Freddy said.

"That's why I'm here," I responded.

He handed the two plates to me. They were hot, and I couldn't hold on to them.

"Got any mitts?" I asked. "These plates are freakin' hot."

Freddy shook his head and mumbled, "Mitts." He handed me two bar towels.

"Don't hurt yourself," he said, as he watched me pick up the plates and take them to the table.

I looked around the bar. "Hey, Freddy, where are the servers?" I asked.

"Off. It's Sunday," he said. "They don't come in on Sunday. You know the old proverb: 'The Lord helps those who help themselves'? It's every man for himself on the Lord's Day around here. Plus, that whole not working on the Sabbath thing—throw that in too."

I nodded. "I see," I said. "But that makes extra work for you."

Freddy laughed. "Not really, kid. Sundays are slow and I close up early," he said. "What you see here now is about as good as it'll get. You are—and will probably be—my biggest pain in the ass today."

"Glad to be of service," I said.

"I'm joshin' ya, man! You and the old man are *okee-doke* in my book."

"Speaking of okee-doke, have you talked to Gretchen today?"

"Yes, I have. She stopped by just after I opened today. She left something for you."

"Really? Good or bad?"

"None of my business. It was this ..."

Freddy handed me a folded note. There was a heart and a smiley face drawn on it. Below the picture, it read, "For the Chief."

"You gonna open it?" Freddy asked.

"I'm not the Chief," I said. "This is for his eyes only."

Freddy nodded. "All I can say is that when she gave this to me, she seemed happy," he said. "Probably the happiest I've seen her in a long time."

"That's good!" I said. "Hopefully what's written on this will convey that happiness."

"Don't see why not."

"You didn't have breakfast with the old man this morning."

I put the note in my pocket and returned to the table. The Chief had already devoured half of his burger and he, Lefty, and Rex had taken care of most of the chips—mine included.

I shook my head. "Good thing I didn't want any chips," I said.

Lefty laughed. "You couldn't handle this, Lou, they're Jay's," he said. "Too much spud for a Southern boy like you."

"Thanks for looking out for me," I said. "I'll leave the extreme *cholesterolics* to you Midwesterners."

Rex looked at me puzzled. "Cholesterolics? Did you make that up?" he asked.

The Chief patted Rex on the back. "Louie makes up words all the time," he said. "He's a world-class scribe. A regular Remington Rand—a writer type. In fact, you could call him a real Bookie Lou."

I rolled my eyes. "I think they got the gist, Chief," I said.

"What kind of stuff do you write about?" Lefty asked.

"Travel stuff, mostly," I said. I pointed to the Chief. "That's why I'm hanging with this guy. He's helping me write the great American road novel."

Rex and Lefty stared at the Chief.

"Is that true?" Rex asked.

"Yeah, Chief, are you gonna be a celebrity?" Lefty wondered. Both men seemed overly excited.

"No, fellas—I'm just along for the ride. Nothing more," the Chief said.

I watched the Chief's face glow as Lefty and Rex looked at him like he was some kind of god. It seemed fitting, I suppose: two friends relocate from Chicago to Wyoming—possibly to work to oil fields. They spend their days and money in this bar and hope for something better; some old bastard from their hometown blows in and regales them with tales from the glory days of Chicago baseball to the lush, tropical landscapes of Polynesian Islands, *and* he's with a guy who's allegedly writing a book. How can you not feel some sense of reverence?

"You gonna write about us, Lou?" Rex asked. His face lit up. This seemed the best news he'd ever heard

"If it's happening now, Rex, it's going in the story," I assured him.

Rex and Lefty—two grown-ass men—bounced in their chairs with glee. It reminded me of when I was seven and I'd swept a game of marbles from the eleven-year-old cul-de-sac champion. I'd won his coveted cat's eye and knocked him from his perch. Such elation. It was all over something fleeting, but in the moment, it meant every-thing. These men didn't have to say a word. They felt famous, and it made me smile.

I poured myself a proper glass of beer and sat and listened to the conversation around me. The Chief told tales I'd already heard, but it was fun to hear them again. Lefty and Rex were mesmerized, and their captivation made the Chief's stories even more interesting.

I took out a pen and jotted down a few things on a napkin—nothing much, just something to construct a scene. I felt more like a playwright: designing a visual, setting a stage. In between scrawling, I ate bites of my hamburger.

I put my hand on my pantleg and felt Gretchen's note in my pocket. I'd forgotten about it, but now my curiosity was piqued again. *What had she written?* It couldn't have been bad, right? Freddy said she was happy when she dropped it off—that was good, wasn't it? I didn't know, and I wouldn't until the Chief read it. Even then, I wasn't sure if he'd share it anyway. As Freddy said, none of my business. *Goddamn right.*

I took the plates back to the bar and ordered a round of drinks for the table. I got everyone a glass of Jack Daniels.

I returned to the table and set the glasses down. I took my seat and finished my beer. Lefty asked if he could have "a splash of suds." I gave him a look—*you have to ask?* I poured it for him. I used the Chief's glass. He hadn't touched it since we got here.

As quickly as I'd sat down, I was back up and off to the bar to refill my pitcher.

"More of the same," I told Freddy. "And two extra glasses—just in case."

Time had flown. It was almost 7:00 p.m., but it seemed as if hardly ten minutes had gone by. The quiet atmosphere usually slows things down in a bar, but the lively conversation at this table greatly sped the clock.

"Oh my God," Lefty said. "I didn't know it was so late."

"Late?" the Chief said. "How late is it?"

"Damn near seven! We're gonna have to tab out and get."

"Why so early?"

"We have to get up tomorrow, Chief. Our shifts start at 4:30 a.m."

"That's an easy one, Lefty. The kid and I will be on the road before then. Come on, stay a little longer. Have another belt with the ol' Super Chief. We'll close the place down in style."

Lefty seemed tempted, but he knew better. His livelihood depended on being at work by 4:30 a.m. I could tell he'd had a close call or two. There was no way he was going to take another chance and jeopardize that job—even for another drink with his new deity.

Rex had already squared himself away. The Chief was flabbergasted. It was as if no one had ever turned him down for a drink before.

"Chief, they've got to go," I said. "They work for a living."

"Not even one?" the Chief pondered. "Just one lousy beer?"

"Not even one. Let 'em go. We'll put a couple down in their honor."

Lefty nodded at my comment. "Yeah, Chief. You and Lou toss 'em back for us," he said. "Show the kid how we do it in the Windy City, okay?"

The Chief was distraught, but so were Lefty and Rex. The men shook hands and hugged. We watched them leave the bar, and the Chief sat and sighed.

"It's okay," I said.

"You don't understand, Louie," he lamented. "You just don't."

"I do. Honestly. Let me see here: you meet up with these two guys, you're relatively close in age—give or take twenty years—you're passionate about a lot of the same things, and you're all from the same hometown. Is that about right?"

The Chief sat and glared. He huffed. "Dammit, son, you're straight on—once again," he said. "Hell, I'm even forgiving them for being South Siders."

"It's not that difficult," I said. "I listened to you guys talking. It's like you've known each other your whole lives."

"Funny thing about Chicago, Louie: no matter where you're from in that toddlin' town, you run into another big-shouldered sucker and they've been there too. There's no other place like it. Can you say the same thing about Atlanta?"

"No. I don't think so—at least *I* can't. Then again, I haven't lived in Atlanta since I was a little kid."

"Well, I haven't lived in Chicago since the 1950s—so there you go."

"And there I go, indeed."

I poured the Chief a beer. "Okay, old man. Show me how to drink like a real Chicagoan," I said.

The Chief laughed. "Just throw it back and try not to spill it or choke," he said. "That's the trick. Oh yeah, and pretend it's Old Style."

"Why Old Style?" I asked.

"Because, Louie, if you've ever had to drink Old Dog Style, you want to get it down and out as fast as possible," he explained. "That's why Chicagoans drink like we do. It's out of necessity."

I took a Chicago-sized gulp and dropped the glass. "How's that?" I asked.

"Just like a native, kid," the Chief said. "You'd fit right in pub crawling around the Loop."

We drank ours—and Lefty and Rex' Jack. I poured another couple of pints, and the Chief and I sat watching the Colorado Rockies get thumped by the Houston Astros. The jukebox played for the first time all evening. The opening number was Hank Williams Jr.'s post-mortal duet with his father: "There's a Tear in My Beer." It seemed an appropriate song as the Chief was still lamenting the departure of his new friends, and one of the guys from the Astros belted a three-run tater to further disappoint the scant bar crowd.

I put my hand on my leg again and felt Gretchen's note. Why did I keep forgetting it? I pulled the paper out of my pocket and put it on the table. The Hank Junior song continued playing. It was not the confidence booster I needed to give the letter to the Chief. He commented on the game and then turned back toward me. He noticed the paper.

"What's that?" he asked.

"Freddy gave it to me," I said. "It's for you. It's from Gretchen."

The Chief's face was expressionless. I'd expected something, but there was absolutely nothing on the man's face.

"Did you read it?" he asked.

"No, of course not," I said. "It's for you."

"Well, I don't want to read it."

"Why not? Freddy said she was happy when she brought it by."

"Yeah, Louie. Happy. Happy to be teasing an old man. I don't want to read it."

"What do you want me to do with it?"

"You read it. If it's good, tell me. If it's not—fuck it. Just pitch it."

"Are you sure? It may be really personal."

"Then skip those parts. Just read the son of a bitch and get it over with."

"Whatever you say, Chief."

I opened the note and glanced at it quickly. I found Gretchen's penmanship to be exquisite—very feminine and inviting. Even if this woman chastised the Chief from here to eternity, the harshest words written in this script would read like poetry. I went back and read the first couple of sentences. I didn't see anything degrading or hostile.

"Well, Chief, from what I can see, there's nothing to be afraid of here," I said. "Are you really sure you don't want to read it?"

"I'm sure, Louie," he said.

"Okay. I'll read it, and I'll fill you in on the important stuff. Does that sound good?"

"That sounds fine."

I glanced over the note one more time, just to make sure there was nothing *truly* bad written within those lines. It all checked out okay, and I began to read.

Dear Chief,

Geez-a-weez it sounds weird to call you that, but I know you like the handle and I'm gonna respect it! Anyway, I want to thank you for one bodacious time. You were a most perfect gentleman to me, and I loved that! Most men in this patch don't know how to pay proper attention to a woman, let alone show her any kind of respect, but you did, and I love you for that.

There were so many things we missed in our time together. You were supposed to tell me about those islands. I would've loved to hear about them—even just one. Hell, you coulda fibbed it for me and I woulda soaked every bit of it in. You know, I'm just a simple bumpkin from Casper. I've never been much farther than Denver, and that seemed a bazillion miles from here! I've never been anywhere or done much. I just work in the bar, make a modest wage, and get the occasional decent tip or pat on the ass. By the way, thanks for not patting my ass! I liked you patting my hand much better!

I'd love to be able to see you today (Sunday), but it's my day off, and I'm gonna shoot straight with you: I don't come in to Butch's on my day off for any mother-loving reason—except for fund-raisers and benefits—and someone had to have died. Sorry, that's harsh, I know, but that's the terms of the 'tract, baby! I'm making a little bit of an exception this morning by dropping this note off for you.

I doubt I'll see you again, since you said you and that big tipping, cutey-patootie Louie (that kinda rhymes! Well, look at me, will ya?) were eastbound and down on Monday morning. It makes me sad, but I know you've got better places to be than Evansville, Wyoming, and I know Louie's got big things ahead of him too.

I'm gonna miss you, Chief. You didn't have to do anything and you made me feel like a real lady. I'd ask you to look me up, but it's better we part this way and leave the rest a mystery. I just couldn't let you leave town without saying something. Thank you for being you.

Think of me when you can, and I'll think of you too. Let's think of us together on a beach somewhere. That's even better!

Love always,
Gretchen (Gretel—hee-hee!)

I finished the letter, folded it back up, and looked at the Chief. He glanced at the paper and back to me. His curiosity was getting the better of him—he just wouldn't admit it yet.

"Do you want to know anything?" I asked.

The Chief looked around. "How bad did I screw up?" he asked.

I shook my head. "You didn't screw up at all," I said. "This was a wonderful letter."

"Did she mention—" The Chief glanced quickly at his lap and back to me.

"No. She said—and I quote—'You didn't have to do anything and you made me feel like a real lady.' That sounds like high sentimental praise for getting emotional without getting physical."

"What else did she say?"

"She said she *did* want to hear about the islands. You had her wrong."

"Why the hell would she—"

I cut him off. "Because she's never been anywhere," I said. "You were like no one she's ever met. Hell, I can attest to that. I've been all over the place and *I've* never met anyone like you. You must've blown her goddamn mind!"

"I ain't that special, Louie," the Chief said.

"The hell you aren't! You've been to all points known and unknown, and ..." I leaned in closer to him and whispered, "you worked at NORAD, for Christ's sake. I wouldn't be surprised if you knew the freakin' president personally."

The Chief smiled. "Well ..." he said.

I fell back. "Jesus! You're kidding me, right?!" I asked. At this point, I didn't know anymore.

He shook his head and winked. "Nah, kid, I'm fucking with you again."

The Chief waved his hands to me, signaling for more information.

"Anything else?" he asked.

"She thanked you for not patting her ass," I said.

"Hmmm. I thought I did," he said.

"Nope. Apparently, you just patted her hand."

"Geez. What kind of a dolt does that?"

"You. And she thought it was very gentlemanly."

"Did you see her ass, Louie?"

"Yes, I did. It was quite nice."

"*Nice* doesn't cover it. I'm sure I gave her a tap. How could I not?"

"I don't know, but she said you didn't. It's her bottom—she should know."

"You are correct in that reasoning. okay. What else?"

"Just a lot of sentiment. You really made her feel good. You didn't screw up, Chief. You did everything right."

The Chief nodded and smiled. "I'll be a goddamn mare's ass, Louie," he said. "Here I was all busted down and she put me up there in the first-class car. Damn, that's a good woman. I'm really going to miss her."

"I know you will, Chief," I said. "If you didn't, you don't have much of a soul—or a heart."

"I think we need another round," the Chief said. "I still owe you the rest of my story."

"That you do," I said.

The Chief needed to clear his conscience. There was a tie between his past and his present; between Bettie and Gretchen, and I was dying to know what it was. I'd been waiting all day. The wait was about to be over.

"I'll get the drinks," I said as I got up and went to the bar.

Freddy was waiting for my order. "Another pitcher and ..." he said, pointing to the bottles behind him.

"Gimme two Wyoming-sized snorts of Evan White, please," I said.

Freddy smiled. "I don't pour 'em like Gretchen," he said.

"I'll pay the extra," I assured him.

Freddy dropped three ice cubes into the old-fashioned glasses and poured a generous amount of Mr. Williams's 100-proof elixir in to keep them company.

"You boys are going to get destroyed, you know?" Freddy warned.

"We'll take our chances," I said as I took the tray of drinks and went back to the table.

As I walked back, I saw the Chief watching one of the TVs. He looked dejected, and I knew it had nothing to do with the game.

"You okay?" I asked, setting the drinks down.

"These boys from Colorado," the Chief said. "They're getting nuked."

I found his critique of the game to be slightly ironic. I sat down and poured a pint for myself. The Chief waved me off when I offered to refill his glass. He took his bourbon and stirred the ice with his finger, licked the booze off, and took a quick sip. He set the glass down and fell away, going back to Colorado again.

"Where did I leave off, Louie?" he asked. "Had we gotten back from town?"

"Yes, Chief," I said. "You were in the hayloft."

The Chief's face began to glow. "Ah, the hayloft," he mused. "That was something. We drank those bottles we'd bought. I can't remember what they were. I can remember everything else but not what we drank. Ain't that some shit?"

"It does surprise me," I said.

"Bettie and I were instantly connected," the Chief said. "And I mean that in every way. She and I ... we just ... we just did everything right."

I was relieved to hear him say they'd done everything "right." So far today, everything he'd done was "wrong."

"We met up as much as we could," the Chief continued. "We'd ride some days. We ate most of our meals together and we tried to spend every possible night with each other—by now, we'd moved from the hayloft to more comfortable and less itch-inducing environs, you see. It was beautiful. I was so far from home, and yet, I felt like I'd found my place to be. Does that make sense?"

"It makes perfect sense, Chief," I said.

I listened to him talk like a Bobby-Soxer listening to Sinatra: eyes twinkling, stupid adoring smile on my face—I didn't have my face cradled in my palms and my elbows resting on the table, though. I probably should have. I think I did swoon once too. God only knows.

"Yes, Louie, I had it big for this gal," the Chief said. "And she was crazy about me too. We were in love, and it was a *good* love. It was a love I hadn't known for quite some time—not since Cuba, and even then …"

He stopped talking again and looked around the room. I watched his face change from glowing to uncertainty in a second. I began to get concerned, but I said nothing. The Chief was here in this bar physically, but his heart and mind were not. It was like waking a sleepwalker—I chose to let him move between realities uninterrupted.

He took another sip of bourbon and chased it with a long draw of beer. He sighed and shook his head.

"You okay, Chief?" I asked. "You don't have to say anymore."

"No, son," he said. "I do. I have to get this out. It's been too damn long."

I kept watching his face. He didn't look like he was going to shut down, but he did look lost and forlorn. That scared me.

He started talking again. "Everything was too good, Louie," he said. "She was too good. *We* were too good. Things that good … they're destined to fail. God never lets you catch a break, does he?"

"Sometimes I wonder," I said. His question was rhetorical.

"Bettie and I … we just … *it* wasn't meant to be, dammit. It just wasn't meant to be."

"I don't understand."

"We got too close. She didn't know. How the hell could she know?"

Now I was really lost. "She didn't know what, Chief?" I asked. "You got too close to what?"

The Chief rattled. "There was just no way, you know?" he said. "Those times. They didn't want things like this to happen. It wasn't supposed to happen like that. None of it. I should've just stayed away. She got too goddamn close. Fucking stupid woman."

"Chief, bring me around," I said. "What happened that wasn't supposed to happen?"

"Bettie, Louie. *She* wasn't supposed to happen," he said. "Not for me. Not for a man with my clearance."

I had something to work with. "Chief, just because you have a 'clearance' doesn't mean you can't fall in love," I said. "That shit happens every day."

"Not in those days. Not for us. Not at that time."

"Did you say something to her? Did you think she knew something?"

The Chief gave me a death stare. "Hell no! Not a word was spoken!" he shouted. "I was dedicated to my job and to Bettie, but those two worlds existed separately. They had to. She wasn't a goddamn spy, and I wasn't a fucking traitor, if that's what you're hinting at."

I put my hands up. "No! I didn't mean anything like that at all," I said. "I understand how sensitive the situation was."

"Do you really, kid?" the Chief asked. "You could have no idea. Trust me, your books and all that—they'll never tell you the whole story. They didn't teach you the real thing in school."

I looked at the Chief and waited for him to fill in the blanks.

He took a drink and scowled at me. "What?" he asked. "What's that look for?"

I didn't want to say anything. I shook my head to indicate nothing was wrong. It was making things worse.

"Fine, Louie. I don't have to tell you any more," he said. "It's a stupid story anyway. Talking about this stuff is just a waste of time."

The Chief took a long drink of his bourbon and turned toward the TV. He feigned interest in the baseball game, cheering bad plays and arousing the ire of some of the bar patrons. I knew he was angry. Moreover, I knew he was torn apart. I had to know why.

"This game sucks," I said. "It's two teams that aren't *our* teams. Why even bother?"

"Absolutely right, son," he said. "Why even bother? With this game—or with anything?"

"Some things are worth the trouble."

"Nothing's worth that kind of trouble."

His response was cryptic but back on track. Maybe that panoramic shot of the Rocky Mountains during the game had helped him refocus.

"No," he said, almost questioning himself. "No, dammit. She *was* worth the trouble. Bettie was definitely worth the trouble."

I stuck to my silence and let to old man spill.

"Louie, I was in love. I told you that," he said. "I was one *L* short of the whole enchilada with this one. *One goddamn letter short.* I told you it was a good love—it was the best love! Hell, I could've made something out of this. It could've been something legendary, but ... as I said ... it really was just too good. And *just too good* is never good at all. It wasn't meant to be."

The Chief got up and looked around and announced he had to piss.

As I waited for him to return, I tried to figure out what happened between him and Bettie, as well as continue to tie her to Gretchen. The only connections I'd made were Colorado and horses. There was more, but it was hidden amid the words and memories the Chief was culling and sharing. I'd know the truth soon—at least I hoped I would.

The Chief returned and sat. He took a breath, a drink and another breath, and without hesitation, began speaking again.

"I could've married Bettie, kid," he said. "Yes. I could've made her my wife. I wanted to. Even after a few days, I knew I could be with her forever. I just had to get away from all the other bullshit. There were too many extenuating circumstances. Those—*those*—the extenuating circumstances are what kept me from doing the right thing. They're the very things that killed what we had, Louie. *They killed it.*"

The Chief slammed his fist on the table. Our glasses jumped and spilled slightly. The entire bar looked in our direction. I patted my hand down to signal all was well. My signal was a lie. All was definitely not well.

Freddy glanced over. "You boys all right?" he asked.

"We're good, Freddy," I said.

The Chief was still at sea, and I didn't want him to come ashore just yet. The reasons for his heartache were surfacing and ready to emerge. We only needed a few more minutes to get them out. I tried to keep myself out of his story, but the more he talked about his quick fall, the more I thought of April.

"Chief, what happened?" I asked. "There's a lot more you're holding back, and it's not getting any better. Just let it out. It'll help you, I swear."

"I don't think I can say any more, Louie," he said. "I don't think I want to …"

The Chief closed his eyes and put his head back. He took a deep breath through his nose and held it for a long time. He exhaled slowly. He dropped his head. I didn't say anything. I just watched him.

His head hung, and he slowly shook it back and forth. There was something inside he was trying to either wrangle out or stir up. When he stopped, he took another breath and then a drink. I continued to sit silent.

The Chief looked up for a second and dropped his head again. This time, he did what any man does when he's trying to fight back tears: he formed a claw with his hand and placed his fingertips where his nose meets his brow. I saw his eyes close tighter. Mine began to well. I was not going to fight my tears. I'd decide to cry for the both of us, and I wasn't even sure why yet.

"They killed it, Louie," the Chief said again. "They killed … *her.*"

I gasped and covered my mouth. Tears began to flow from my eyes. I saw two drop from the Chief's as well. They hit the table and assimilated themselves into to water rings from his glass. He sniffed and sighed.

"She went out for a ride and she never came home," he said through his tears. "Bettie was the best rider. There was no way that horse got away from her. No way in hell. But that's what they said. Said that goddamn Arabian got spooked and bucked her off into a ravine. Said she fell and hit the rocks. She didn't fall into any ravine. There were no ravines within fifty miles of where she was. I know, because we'd ridden out to there. She and that horse were put together by God—there's no way he threw her off like they said. They made it look that way."

I shook my head in disbelief. "Who, Chief? Who made it look that way? Who are 'they'?" I asked. I was frantic.

"The goddamn government. That's who *they* are," he said coldly. "They knew we were lovers. They couldn't let that happen. They shot her, Louie. The fucking sons of bitches shot my Bettie in cold blood. They shot her in the head and killed her horse. They did it because she got too close to me. *Me! I was nothing.* I was just a nerd from Chicago, plucked up for some assignment. What did I know? I didn't want to be there. Bettie made me want to be there. She made me feel alive and like a human being—not some low-rate junior *g-man* with a pocket protector and an affinity for numbers.

"She was everything to me then. My happiness. The only happiness I'd known for years. The cocksuckers took it all away when they took her away. What was she gonna do? Steal the plans for their secret base? I worked there and didn't know shit about it. Oh my God …"

The Chief broke down and sobbed. I jumped from my chair and grabbed him. He tried to push me away, but once he realized I was there to comfort him, he fell into me. The other men in the bar slowly approached our table.

"It's okay," I whispered. "I've got him."

Freddy looked worried. I looked at him and shook my head. He read my nonverbal and nodded in response. He knew the old man was having this moment. Freddy had tended bar for a long time. He knew this type of thing all too well.

The Chief sat up. He wiped his eyes and looked away.

"Goddammit," he said. "Look at me. What kind of a man am I?"

"A real man, Chief," I said. "It takes balls to shed tears."

"Bullshit, kid. I just checked myself: I've got a vagina now."

I laughed. "Check it again," I said.

Freddy patted the Chief's shoulder. "You all right, Chief?" he asked. "Can I get you anything?"

"No, 'Red', I'm gonna be all right ..." the Chief said as he pointed to me, "thanks to this little bastard's persistence."

Everyone moved from our table. They still kept a watch over the situation but from a distance.

"I'm so sorry," I said. "That must've been ripping you to shreds all these years."

"It was me boy," the Chief said. "I don't know if I'll be better now, but I hope it helps somehow."

The Chief raised his face to the ceiling. He hoisted his glass of Evan white and mouthed, "To you, my love." He sighed hard and in one swallow drained the glass. He shook his head. The booze had hit him, but it was the ghost of his lost love that rattled his body. Bettie's spirit was finally free. As I saw the Chief muster a smile, a tear streamed down his cheek. I know he was watching Bettie riding her Arabian through the clouds of heaven.

"Five, Louie," he said. "It took me this long to give her five."

"Five, Chief?" I asked.

"Yeah. *Ls.* I finally cried for Bettie."

The night was young, but for me and the Chief it was over. It was time for us to go. Our trip to Evansville had proved a little more successful than we'd imagined. The Chief had learned the truth about the Roman Nose his dad had spoken of; I'd discovered that Hell's Half Acre was more than a metaphoric place where my ex misplaced things; the Chief reunited with a long, lost love—if only in spirit—and shed heavy layers of the past—and finally tears for her. As for me, I found I could be a persistent bastard.

More than anything; however, the Chief had met Gretchen. She seemed fun and friendly but had become more than either one of us

197

could've imagined or bargained for—but in the best of ways. I was still unsure of her connections to Bettie, and now I may never know.

I paid our tab and tipped Freddy. He slid part of the money back my way. "You're cool," he said.

I smirked. "I know I am," I joked. "But I still have to pay my bill!"

Freddy chuckled and shook his head. "You're an ass, kid," he said. "Don't make me change my mind."

"I couldn't resist," I said. "Thanks for everything, Freddy."

"My pleasure. You guys swing into this part of the world again, you know where we are."

"Indeed. Please give our regards to Gretchen, okay?"

"You know I will."

I took the money and put it in my pocket and walked from the bar to call our cab.

I glanced back and noticed the cattle prod again. I just had to know what the hell it was for.

"Freddy, one last thing," I said. "The prod. You ever use it?"

Freddy laughed. "I haven't," he said. "But Gretchen is a beast with it."

"Jesus, don't tell the Chief that. I'll never get him to leave!"

We both laughed, and that signaled the end of our time at Butch's.

The Chief and I left the bar and got into the cab. It was warm outside and slightly windy. The stars were out and shining like no other night we could recall. The Chief looked out the window and surveyed them. One seemed to shine brighter than the others. He tapped his finger on the glass and smiled. I nodded. *I'll take care of him, Bettie*, I said to the star. I looked away. I didn't want the Chief to see my eyes tearing again.

* * * * *

When we returned to the hotel, I thought about asking the Chief if he wanted to stay an extra day, but I did not. I knew he was ready to go. So was I.

We went to the elevators, rode them to our floor, and headed to our rooms.

"Chief, I'm off to bed," I said.

The Chief nodded in concurrence but said nothing.

"We're leaving in the morning. Oh five hundred," I said.

The Chief finally spoke. "I'll believe that when I see it, kid. Good night."

"Good night."

My alarm went off at 4:00 a.m., and for the first time since we started this trip, I wasn't dreading the early hour. I got out of bed and took a shower. My mind was clear of worrisome bullshit for once, and I wasn't dreadfully hung over.

Last night had taken a lot out of me emotionally, and I wasn't the one telling the story. Some people have closets for their skeletons and secrets, but the Chief seemed to have enough buried bones to fill an entire cemetery. I wasn't sure how much he'd reveal, but I wanted to know it all—the good and the bad. I felt the more time I spent with the old man, the better *my* story would become. I'd already learned a few things about myself and was looking forward to discovering more.

I got out of the bathroom and started to get dressed. I looked at the clock and noticed it wasn't quite 4:30 a.m. I realized it was Monday morning. I was due back in Valdosta last Wednesday. Almost a week had passed and I hadn't called my publisher. I'd also blown off a plane ticket and failed to extend my car rental, thereby screwing my publisher even more—he was picking up the tab. *I was so dead.*

I dialed out and got long distance.

An operator came on and asked me for the number I'd like to call. I found it very nostalgic and quaint to tell someone whom and where I was calling.

"Number and city, please," the operator asked.

"Nine, one, two. Five, seven, three. Six, six, zero, four," I said. "Valdosta, Georgia."

"Thank you, sir. I'll connect your call now. And thank you for using Qwest Communications."

I smiled as the phone rang. All I could think of was a group of ladies in flowery blouses and pinned hair, wearing headsets, plugging patch cords into a huge switchboard and drinking Yuban Coffee from short porcelain mugs. *I'll bet my operator's name is Gladys*, I thought.

The line stopped ringing, and I heard a voice.

"Good morning, Southern State Publishers. This is Keith, how can I help you?"

"Keith. It's Louis DeCarlo," I said. "How are you?"

There was a hesitation. "Louis?" he asked. "Where are you?"

"Don't freak, okay?" I said. "I'm in Wyoming."

"Wyoming? No wonder I didn't recognize the number. What the hell are you doing in Wyoming?"

"It's an interesting story."

"I hope so. You're almost a week out, and your deadline on that Crater Lake story is coming up."

"Yeah, I know. I ..."

Keith interrupted me. "Is the story finished?" he asked.

"It is," I said. "But it's not any good. It's too weak."

"Too weak? What the hell does that mean?"

"It sucks, man. It's bullshit. I've been working on something much better."

"Well, where is it? Can you fax it to me?"

"No. Not yet. It's not done."

"I'm not liking this, Lou. It's not what I want to hear."

"I know, Keith. It's not like me to do you like this, I apologize."

"I appreciate the sentiment, but I'm chewing on an overdue car rental to go with the plane ticket I already ate on your behalf."

"I understand, and I'll pay you back for all of that when I get home, I promise. I just need to finish what I'm doing right now."

"Well, what *are* you doing right now—and in Wyoming nonetheless?"

"I'll keep it simple: I met an old man in Sacramento. We had some drinks, and he told me about Cuba. I was blown away by his story, and I wanted to know more. I asked him to drive back to Georgia with me. We're stopping places, and I'm writing about them."

There was a silence on the line.

"Keith? You still there?" I asked.

I heard a huff. "Yes. I don't know why, but I'm still here," Keith said.

"It sounds crazy, I know," I said. "But it'll all make sense when you read what I've written."

"Lou, it sounds *way* more than crazy," Keith stated. "You have *anything* to send me?"

"I don't. It's just scribblings in my notebook."

"Okay. I'm lost. You've got no work except for 'scribblings,' and there's some old dude. This is not good—for any of us. Do you understand?"

"I do. I just need you to trust me, Keith. Please, just give me a few days. You won't regret this. I'll give you the story of a lifetime. I just need a few more days."

There was another silence on the line.

"Your one of my best writers, Lou," Keith said. "I'd hate to have to fire you because you got stupid."

"I'm not stupid," I said. "I told you: you'll have the best damn story ever if you'll just give me the time and your trust. *You'd* be stupid to let this one go."

"Your thread is wearing thin, Lou."

"I understand. Just give me the time, okay? I'll be home next week. Two weeks was my original deadline, remember?"

"I do. I gave you that leeway. Don't make me regret it."

"You won't. I already told you that."

Keith's tone changed. "Do you need an advance?" he asked.

"No. I'm into you for enough already," I said.

"You are, but still, if you're strapped, I can help. This 'story of a lifetime' needs to be that and then some."

"You'll be floored. I guarantee it."

"Can I at least have the Crater Lake story? Whatever you've got done," Keith said. "I don't care if it sucks. It's probably better than you think."

"I'll send it tomorrow," I said.

"I'll be waiting."

"Thanks, Keith."

I hung up the phone and wiped the imaginary sweat from my brow. For the bulk of that call, my career was a sinewy string, stretched to its limit. I saw my life up to now flash by in a quick, uncomfortable blur. I had something great to hand in, but it was barely in an embryonic stage; it was just a twinkle in my eye at this point. For a second, I doubted my own words. However, the more I thought about it, the more I knew this trip would provide me with everything I'd hoped and everything I was promising to my publisher.

I heard a knock on my door and looked at the clock. It was 4:50 a.m. *Perfect timing, Chief.* I opened the door and let the old man in. He seemed surprised I was not only up and around but ready to leave as well. He placed his hand to my forehead.

"What are you doing?" I asked.

"Checking your temperature," he said. "The Louie I know would have to be mad with fever to be up and raring to go so early."

"Well, Chief, I'm not 'mad with fever,' but I am crazy to be doing this."

The Chief chuckled. "Kid, we've all got to be a little crazy," he said. "It's what keeps us from going insane."

We went to the front desk to check out. The clerk was embroiled in something on his laptop. He slammed the lid shut when I called to him.

"I'm checking out," I said. "Rooms 312 and 313."

I watched the clerk fumble as he typed.

"You okay?" I asked.

"Yeah. It's just really early," he said.

I smiled and responded: "I can dig it."

The clerk handed me my printout, and I gave him our room keys.

"Thank you," I said.

"You're welcome, sir," he replied. "And thank you for staying with us. Hope you enjoyed your visit."

"Hope you enjoy your beaver hunt," I said. "Here's to quality furs."

The clerk's face went white, and I just laughed.

* * * * *

We loaded the car and headed out of town. The streets were still empty as we drove toward Interstate 25. The Chief watched buildings go by.

"I was never much for that 'early to rise' stuff," I said, as I drove in the dark. "I never saw the point of being up when it was still halfway through the previous night."

"Louie, you never would've made it in the old days," the Chief said. "Your land wouldn't have been farmed, and your mills couldn't have competed. Back in those days, it was about making the first dollar before first light. And trust me, back then, dollars were hard to come by—at any hour of the day."

I had nothing to say. I'd found that when discussing the merits of an honest day's work with someone who'd suffered through the "good old days'" you had no chance of making your point for sleeping in. Late risers were lazy and the cause of all problems great and small.

I never gave such thinking much credence until now. It made the strangest sense, really. I thought about the world today compared to back in the Chief's heyday. We have more stuff, superior technology, and things move at a much faster pace, but people themselves have gotten sluggish. We've let the tools of betterment make us worse.

Some things are great. I'll take a four-hour plane ride over a three-day boat trip anytime, but as far as the human condition and how we operate as a whole is concerned, expedience has made us lose sight of compassion, loyalty, and pride in what we do and create. It has also made us lose sight of ourselves.

My mind continued to bounce between then and now.

"You all right?" the Chief asked. "You're awfully quiet over there."

"I'm fine," I said. "I was just thinking. I prefer a notebook to a computer, you know?"

The Chief turned and looked at me. "Yeah, I know," he said. "Why are you telling me that?"

"Because I didn't want you to think I didn't understand about work and the value of it," I said.

"I'd never think that, Louie. What brought that on?"

"Just talking about getting up early and all. I'm not against it—I just don't care much for it. I wasn't trying to be offensive or anything."

"I'm not offended. You don't like to get up early. So what? It's okay."

"I just want you to know I'm not like people of my generation, that's all. I haven't gotten caught up in all the comforts of the twenty-first century. I understand the values and methods that used to be revered …"

The Chief cut me off.

"Kid, you don't have to explain yourself," he said. "Times have changed—a lot—trust me! I've seen more than you can imagine. I wish we had some of this newfangled gadgetry back in my day. It would've made life a hell of a lot simpler."

"That's my point, Chief," I said. "Society has gotten lethargic because of all that 'newfangled gadgetry.' It's made humanity lose its vision."

"Humanity as society? Or American society in general?" he asked. "There's a lot of the world that ain't got a pot to piss in or a window to throw it out of. It's hard to have vision of any sort under those conditions."

"I guess I mean us—Americans. *We* have lost our vision."

"Bullshit, son. You're talking nonsense. If anything, our vision has gotten clearer. Sure, there's things that'll make you scratch your head, but that's the way it is. Not everything is going to be perfect, and not everyone is going to agree with it all. That's what makes this whole mess work.

"You like the *simpler* things like writing in a notebook, but that's more work. There's nothing *simple* about it. You scribble it down, but you—or someone else—will have to type it out eventually. Get a damn computer and save yourself at least one headache."

I found it ironic that the Chief was celebrating the advancements of today while chastising my embracement of the "simpler things." Here was a man who lived so vividly in the past; when he spoke about it, his words were picturesque. I envied him, the places he'd been and the things he'd seen. Then again, his past was filled with grand glimpses of the future. His work at the fledgling NORAD and his building a computer mainframe in Samoa in the 1970s put the man ahead of his time even in his past.

"Where are we going, kid?" the Chief asked.

"I don't know yet," I said. "I thought I'd let you decide."

"How am I supposed to do that?"

"By using the archaic method of opening the atlas and finding a place that begins with *E*. When we stop for gas and grub, I'll get it out."

"Why are you putting this on me today?"

"Because this journey is as much yours as it is mine, Chief. Besides, Elko and Evansville had their share of heart-wrenching moments. Maybe if you picked the next place, we might have better luck?"

"I didn't think the last two were that bad."

"It's safe to say that now—we're not there anymore."

"You make it sound like they were a total loss. I don't think so."

"Not entirely, but there were things."

"'Things' happen everywhere, kid. That's life. You roll with it and take the punches. Sometimes they hurt, other times they're just what you need to wake you up."

I smiled at the Chief's assessment of life and getting knocked around by it. The sun was up and right in our eyes as we got onto Interstate 80 to head east toward our next destination—wherever that was.

* * * * *

I pulled into a gas station outside of Cheyenne, Wyoming. The Chief gave me his list of provisions as I topped off the tank. I opened the back door of the car and grabbed the atlas.

205

"Here, Chief, keep yourself busy while I get our stuff and pay," I said as I handed him the atlas.

"What am I looking for?" he asked.

"Anything east of here. We're on I-80. Nebraska is the next state over."

"I know that, but where am I looking for?"

"Any place east of here that begins with an *E*. You know the rules."

The Chief huffed at the task. It was simple. I don't know why he didn't want to participate. All I wanted was a place that put us a good distance from Evansville. I wanted to make progress and get a little closer to home.

I went into the store and grabbed some items as well as two cups of coffee. The cashier watched as I filled the cups and paced my progress by slowly ringing up my purchase one item at a time.

"I'm on pump three as well," I said.

She squinted out at the pump as if she was trying to read the display. I followed her gaze and squinted as well.

"I can tell you how much it is," I said.

"So can I," she said. "It's $10.50."

"It is. How can you see that from here?"

"I can't. I read it on the monitor."

"What are you looking at, then?"

"Whatever your passenger is doing. He keeps spinning that book."

"Oh, him. Yeah. He's trying to find a place to go in the atlas."

The cashier crinkled her nose. "Did ya get lost?" she asked. "It's easy to do out here."

"No, we're not lost," I said. "We're just not sure."

"Not sure about what?"

"Where we're going. We're being adventurous."

"You don't look like the adventurous type."

"I wasn't until a couple of days ago. You don't look like the cashier type."

The cashier smiled and touched the bottom of her hair. "Well, thank you," she said as she blushed.

"You're welcome," I said. I wasn't trying to compliment her. *Whatever works, I guess.*

I paid for everything. The cashier thanked me again, and we bid each other a nice day. I went back to the car, and the Chief had a smile on his face that caused me concern.

"Am I going to regret this?" I asked.

"Regret what?" he responded.

"What I'm about to ask as to the look on your face."

"I found a place. It's a good one too."

"Do tell."

"Elkhorn, Nebraska."

"How far is it?"

"I don't know, but it's just outside of Omaha. Almost to Iowa."

"Well, Chief, it begins with *E*, it's across the state, and it's on our way. Elkhorn—here we come!"

We got back on the interstate and began our jaunt to the city of Elkhorn. I tried to calculate the distance from here to there. We'd already driven about two hours. I estimated we were about six hours—give or take—from Elkhorn. Regardless, it was going to be a long, flat drive. If all went well, we'd be getting into town about 1:30 or 2:00 p.m.—just in time for a late lunch.

"So why Elkhorn, Chief?" I wondered.

"It just sounded like the place to go," he said. "It sounded mighty, rugged, and adventurous. There was a pioneer spirit about the name. A locale perfect for those on the hunt—seekers like us. Anything dealing with animals and antlers has got to have something robust to offer."

We drove quietly for a while. The radio played low, and stations faded in and out. Whenever I'd tune something in it stayed strong, but the Chief would switch it out.

"How can you listen to that stuff?" he asked. "Can't understand it. Can't figure it out. *Twang, bang*—it's just a bunch of noise."

"It's not all noise, Chief," I said. "Some of it's pretty good."

"Not as good as the classics, Louie."

"Maybe not, but 'the classics' don't seem to stick around for long."

"The hell you say! That's what makes them classics. They'll be here after we're both dead and gone. They're timeless. That shit you listen to? It's a flash in the pan. No staying power whatsoever."

"No, Chief, I mean the radio signal, not the music. The classic stations don't seem to broadcast too strongly."

The Chief huffed. His music didn't last five minutes over the airwaves, where mine continued to play. These were the airwaves of a present in which he lectured me for scoffing only a couple hours ago.

I smiled as the Chief tuned another station that faded out before the current song had ended. He turned the radio off.

"Fuck it," I heard him mumble. I tried not to laugh.

* * * * *

The Chief asked where we were.

"We're right outside of North Platte," I said.

"Ah, the North Platte," the Chief said. "This river will join the South Platte and go all the way to the Missouri."

"Yep, Louie. There's a lot of history flowing in that water. Trails and trades were made along those banks over the years. It moved the early emigrants out west. I won't mention any names."

I chuckled. "Thanks," I said. "I know who you mean."

The Chief nodded. He seemed to contemplate the river as we drove along. I had to wonder if he had a personal history attached to it.

"Louie, I never finished my story," the Chief said out of the blue.

"Which story?" I asked.

"I never told you about Gretel and me."

"Yes, you did."

"No. Not the whole thing. Not why she rattled me so."

"'Rattled' you? No, you never said anything about that."

The Chief took a deep breath. "She brought back some memories for me," he said. "She took me back to a place I thought I'd never go. You know what I'm talking about."

"Are you talking about Colorado and Bettie?" I asked.

"Yes. She took me back there. She made me feel the old feelings again. And they weren't good."

"Are you sure you want to tell me this? You don't have to."

"No, son—I do. I do have to tell you. I owe you the whole story."

I nodded. "Okay, I'm listening," I said.

"It's not much, and it's probably just stuff and nonsense, really," he said. "But Gretel and Bettie—they were like the same person. I swear to God, seeing her—it was like seeing Bettie all over again."

"Did you feel that when you first met her?" I asked. "You spent time with her before you were alone. You had to have some signal."

"No, not really," he said. "I'd had a few drinks, and maybe that dulled me a bit because I didn't pick up on it right off, but things slowly came together. It was good at first. When I started to make connections, I liked where things were going. She made me happy. I haven't felt that kinda happy in a very long time."

"I can only imagine."

"The longer I spent with her, the more difficult things became. The past and the present were colliding. That's where I lost focus and forgot where I was."

"Did you see Bettie?"

"I did. Hell, kid, she even *felt* like Bettie. Figure that? How can two different women from two separate worlds feel exactly the same?"

I shook my head. "Wow. That had to be crazy," I said.

"'Crazy' don't even cover it," the Chief said. "I almost slipped up and called her the wrong name. That's when everything went wrong for me. I knew I had to leave. I couldn't be with this gal another second. It was nothing to do with her, but everything to do with someone else. My God, Bettie could've been Gretel's mother, they were so much alike. How does that sound?"

"I don't know," I said. "It does sound odd."

"Yeah it does. What was I going to say? 'Sorry, honey, I'm down for the night because you remind me of someone,'" the Chief asked rhetorically. "Or this one: 'Damn, I think I may have made love to your mother in the sixties.' What girl wants to know something like that? Jesus, Louie—she could've been Bettie's daughter, if ..."

The Chief stopped. I knew what he was going to say next, and I was glad he cut himself off. He'd reconciled his old feelings for Bettie last night and that was a major step for him. He'd just revealed why he "couldn't" with Gretchen. Everything had culminated in this moment. There was nothing more to say. The Chief had assimilated the emotions of his distant and now recent past. He could breathe easier knowing the complete truth and opening up about it. It wasn't going to disappear, but it wasn't going to haunt him like it did. There was nowhere else to go now—except to Elkhorn.

Elkhorn, Nebraska

The Chief and I arrived in Elkhorn at about 3:30 p.m. We'd made good time crossing the big state of Nebraska. The law was lenient and light on the freeway, which helped in my need to test the posted speed limits. Our stops were quick and few—in and out for fuel and food and back to the pavement. We'd lost an hour and gained a time zone along the way as well. No longer on the Cowboy Clocks of Mountain Time, we were in the heart of it all: Central Daylight Time—when TV shows are an hour behind and your late local news is in primetime.

We drove around town to find a place to stay and a place to eat. I'd decided we could use some fancy digs to park our carcasses for the next couple of days, so when I saw the Sheraton pop up, I pulled into the parking lot and told the Chief, "Welcome home."

* * * * *

As I filled out the paperwork, the desk clerk watched the Chief. "What's up with that?" he asked.

"That's just what he does," I said. "He's a *socialist.* Therefore, he's sociable."

"I thought a socialist was a political thing."

"It is. However, in this case, I'm using the term ironically."

"Oh. okay. Whatever."

I signed everything and got my key cards. The clerk was still watching the Chief work the room.

"I've got to meet that guy," he said. "He could help me with my dating skills."

I looked to see what kind of mischief the Chief had gotten into. Sure enough, he'd rounded up four very attractive females and had them in stitches: they were giggling, embarrassed, and giving him more *Oh you*s than I'd ever seen.

I looked back at the clerk. "Yeah, if you're having trouble with the ladies," I said. "That man will show you some tricks."

The clerk smiled and handed me a map of the town.

"Enjoy your stay, Mr. DeCarlo," he said.

"Thank you, I'm sure we will," I said.

"Chief!" I yelled. "I've got your key. You want to take your stuff upstairs?"

The Chief looked at me and scowled. "Louie, can't you see I'm busy?" he asked. "I'm in the middle of a very important meeting. Top negotiations. Only those of the highest order are privy."

One of the ladies burst out with the loudest, strangest laugh when the Chief said *privy.*

I laughed and covered my mouth.

I walked over and handed the Chief his key. He was so zoned in he took it without breaking focus. I looked at the ladies' faces. He had them mesmerized, like some televangelist promising heaven and a cure for menstrual cramps.

One of the women smiled at me. I nodded back and gave her a quick little finger wave. It was cutesy, and she responded with a blush. I grabbed the Chief's suitcase, and told him I was taking it. He was still working his magic and waved me off. I headed to my room with our luggage in tow. I knew I'd see him eventually.

I put our things in my room and sat at the desk. It was getting close to dinner time, and I was wondering what we'd do for our evening meal. There was a restaurant guide on the desk. I looked through it. It had room service options as well as places nearby that delivered to the hotel. *This is the freakin'* Sheraton, I said to myself. *They've got to have a boss restaurant here.*

As I contemplated food, my mind began to gather fragments of our trip so far. I'd talked to my publisher almost twelve hours ago, and I started to feel guilty about what I'd told him. I didn't lie to him.

From my paid assignment, I had the makings of a story, but not much. I was truly moving state to state with an old man and seeing things—lots of things—but I'd written very little about them. I would be home soon, and I would indeed turn in the promised story of a lifetime to be published. But for now, all I had were pictures in my head and memories in my heart—things that sound great but don't mean shit in terms of a tangible deadline. I needed to put something down, but I was still suffering from the same writer's block that had sent me on this trip in the first place.

I took the hotel pen and tapped it on the stationery. Nothing. I tapped harder. Still nothing. I smacked the pen on the desk. It was as if by beating the hell out of it, the creative dam I'd been staring at the last several days would miraculously crumble.

I hit the pen as hard as I could one last time, and something *finally* happened. *It broke.* Words did not spill, but a bit of ink did. The dark blue blotch sat on the edge of the paper and slowly oozed to a stop on the laminated phone list below. The shape of the ink resembled an abstract silhouette of the Braves' old mascot Chief Noc-a-homa. I laughed. "Wish Lefty and Rex could see this," I said, as I grabbed a tissue to clean up my mess.

As I wiped up the ending of what should have been a beginning, there was a loud knock at my door. It scared the hell out of me.

"What!" I yelled. "Give me a second." There was another knock, followed by a severe clearing of a throat.

"Chief, I'll be right there," I said.

I opened the door and let him in.

"Sorry, I had a mishap," I said, pointing to the ink-soaked tissue on the desk.

He ignored my comment. "Have you seen my bag?" he asked. "Someone took it."

"I took it, Chief," I said. "I told you I had it. You were a bit preoccupied."

The Chief walked into my room and sat on the bed. He was here, but his brain was still in the lobby.

"Did you see those dames, kid?" he asked. "Man, Louie. They were top-notch. Midwestern gals. They don't build them like that everywhere, you know."

"I know that, Chief," I said. "I've dated a couple of Midwestern girls."

The Chief continued to ponder the favorable attributes of the regional females, as I finished cleaning up my mess. His face was aglow. It was nice to see him back to his old virile self. I was still wondering which of the women he'd chatted up had been selected as my date for the night.

"Chief, what is on the agenda?" I asked. "What would you like to do tonight?"

"Well, first I'd like to get something to eat," he said. "Not sure what, though. What's here?"

"Lots of things I'm sure," I said. "We're a just outside of Omaha. That's the biggest city we've been to since Sacramento. Let's go downstairs and see what we can find."

"Sounds good to me," he said. "Let me check my bag, and we'll be on our way."

The Chief pulled his suitcase into his room and was ready to go. I had no idea where we were going, but I knew it would be *somewhere*.

* * * * *

"Macedonia, Louie," the Chief said suddenly. "That's where I'd like to go."

"That's a little off the beaten path," I said.

"Not the country—the cuisine. We should have ourselves a Macedonian feast for dinner."

I gave the Chief a confused look.

"Macedonian? Is that even a thing anymore?" I asked. "Isn't that pretty much Greek?"

The Chief shook his head. He reluctantly acquiesced to my use of the word *Greek*.

"I … suppose …" he said, trailing off.

We came upon a restaurant called Greek Islands. It looked nice and, for the most part, served the Chief's jones for "Macedonian" fare.

"Close enough?" I asked.

"It'll have to do," he said.

"We'll be fine, Chief."

We went into the restaurant and were greeted warmly by the hostess. She was a beautiful Greek woman, and her deep, brown eyes sparkled as she smiled at us. Once again, the Chief was smitten. She led us to a table and gave us drink menus to start. The Chief watched the hostess's every move as she walked away.

"Chief, don't …" I said.

He cut me off. "Relax, Louie," he said. "I don't know any Greek—if that's what you're worried about."

A waitress came to our table to take our drink orders. The Chief and I both ordered a bottle of *Vergina* lager. When the waitress brought the bottles, the labels were printed in Cyrillic. The Chief's face beamed as he read the letters.

"This is Macedonian, kid," he said. "Greeks don't use Cyrillics."

We clinked our bottles together and, in the spirit of the label's alphabet, said *Na zdorob'ye* to each other and took a big swig.

"Not bad," the Chief said. "It could be a little stronger, but we'll just have to order more, right?"

"Probably," I said. "We always do."

We looked over the menus, got two more bottles of beer, and ordered a round of *Meze* to go with our drinks.

When the waitress returned, she placed a large tray on a stand and set up the appetizers around the table. There was small bowl of figs in olive oil stuffed with feta cheese and seasoned with oregano. Another bowl had sliced tomatoes, cucumbers, and dates dressed in vinaigrette and sprinkled with parsley. A plate of seasoned *Loukaniko* Sausages and baby potatoes was centered on the table like a sun; the bowls orbiting around it. A bowl of stuffed grape leaves completed the setup. The grape leaves didn't last long, as the Chief and I devoured them as soon as they hit the table.

"This might be all we need, Chief," I said. "There's a lot of food here."

The Chief nodded as he piled his plate. "This is like the Basque place," he said. "We ate more than our share then too, remember?"

"Indeed I do," I said. I smiled and skewered a couple of stuffed figs.

I began thinking about the Basque feast and how that evening had turned out. This was good, but a big meal does not equate to a big night.

My thoughts shifted to the Five *L*s and how I'd been lagging behind on them. But I was okay. I know the Chief wanted me to dine, drink, laugh, cry, and ultimately love someone of the female persuasion through this method, but for now—I was enjoying *this*.

I was trying to find myself and my own strengths, and the Chief's stories were helping me achieve that. I didn't need anything else at the moment. Dealing with the Chief—for as nerve-racking as it could be at times—was much easier than trying to make a relationship on the road.

I'd felt the love. It was good. April was still on my mind, but she was fading a little each day. My feelings hadn't gone away, but they'd changed. I'd resigned myself to the fact that I'd never see her again, much in the same way the Chief would never see Gretchen.

These two women made us feel something wonderful and sometimes such wonderful feelings are not supposed to go beyond a certain point. My feelings were new and came on very quickly. The Chief held his in for a long time. Gretchen helped him ease the pain he carried for Bettie, and he'd finally come to terms with what he'd lost. I was dealing with April on my own. Our situations were quite different, but in the end, our results and what we felt in our hearts were almost the same.

"Louie, you okay?" the Chief asked.

"I'm all right," I said.

"You were elsewhere, kid. What's got you on the China Clipper again?"

I wanted to play it off.

"I was just thinking about—as you'd said before—'strangers in the night,'" I said. "Nothing major. Just … you know."

"I probably do, but I'm not sure," he said. "Anything I can help with?"

"No, not really. It's just *creativity*. That kind of thing."

"Ah, so you're taking notes then?"

"For the most part, yeah—I'm 'taking notes.'"

"Good for you, kid! It's about time you got those gears turning."

"Yeah. It is," I said unconvincingly.

The waitress came back to take our food order. I ordered the Around the World Plate of gyros.

"Louie, you can get those anywhere," he said. "You have to order something real in a place like this. It's like getting a pizza at an Italian restaurant. It's just too damn tourist—too American."

The waitress smiled and nodded at the Chief's assessment of my order.

We finished the Meze and got two more beers while waiting for our entrees to arrive. I watched the Chief—very stealthily, I must say—ogle the waitresses. They were all quite stunning and very well put-together. I smiled as I observed his behavior. His eyes gleamed and face lit up every time one of the women walked by.

Our beers arrived, and the Chief chatted with the waitress. She giggled, and he laid on the charm. These girls could easily be his granddaughters, but he didn't care. The old man was young again and oblivious to every trapping of being an octogenarian. I shook my head at the scene. So far, the one thing that had not rubbed off on me was the Chief's knack for flirting. I still didn't get it; I just knew he was damn good at it—sometimes to a fault.

The Chief slid down in his chair as if he were melting. It was tacky but cute.

"Easy, Chief," I said. "They're all pretty young."

"I'm just looking, kid. I ain't in the market to buy."

"You better keep it that way."

Our dinners were served, and I looked at my plate of gyros. I asked for a to-go box right away. There was no way I was going to make a more than a dent in this food.

I ate the veal gyro and was overstuffed. I watched the Chief devour his meal. I wondered where he put all that food as it quickly vanished from his plate.

"You know what a good meal is akin to, Louie?" the Chief asked.

Before I could say anything, he answered for me. "Good sex," he said. "It's satisfying, fulfilling, and relieves whatever cravings you may have had. And depending on what you ate, you may want to brush your teeth afterward."

I sat back and flashed multiple expressions at the Chief's comparison of sex and food. I pondered the whole dynamic of his words and cringed at the tooth-brushing aspect.

"Okay, Chief, I have to know," I said. "What's up with your focus on the *skin trade?* I mean, you talk about sex a lot."

"It's a beautiful subject," he said.

"It is, but we do talk about it *a hell of a lot.* I was just wondering ..."

He cut me off.

"Why the obsession?" he asked. "Why the worship of the female body and all of its grandeur and mystery? Why the ..."

I returned the favor and cut him off.

"Okay, I'm sorry, Chief," I said. "I was just curious."

The Chief patted his hand on the table. He apologized and continued to answer my question.

"Louie, next to air and water, sex is what keeps us alive," he said. "Without it, neither you nor I nor anyone else would be here. Every living creature does it in one way or another. You can't deny its significance."

This was heavy. The Chief was all in. I wanted to lighten the mood a little.

"Well, snails don't do it," I joked.

"Snails? Snails don't count," he said. "You know what a damn snail is? A snail is a side dish to a good French meal. A snail is a fucking slug with a camper shell. Snails don't need to screw—they're *self-motivators* anyway."

I didn't know what to say. Once again, the Chief had the right words to defend his point. I sat back and nodded. Another lesson learned.

After dinner, the Chief and I ordered a small bottle of ouzo to share and a couple baklavas for dessert. The ouzo was sweet, and the licorice flavor paired well with the flaky pastries. It was the perfect complement to our meal and helped to cleanse a bit of the sour residuals of our present conversation.

We toasted our time and the fine food we'd enjoyed. I apologized for riling him up about his sex kick, and he responded in kind—about cheapening the purpose of snails.

The Chief took a sip of his ouzo.

"I've noticed something," he said.

"What's that?" I wondered.

"You've been lagging a bit, you know?"

I looked around, and the Chief caught me.

"You can't get away so easily," he said. "You are supposed to be getting five *L*s a day. Since the first night in Elko, you've averaged about three."

"'Lagging,'?" I said as my voice cracked a bit. I was dreading this.

"What are you? A damn parrot? Yes. *Lagging*. You're not upholding the terms of the trip. What's wrong?"

"Nothing, really," I said. "It's just been a bit difficult. I've been focused on other things, I guess."

"I know you have, son, and that's okay. We just got to get you back in line."

"I'll do my best, Chief. It's gonna have to wait until tomorrow. Is that alright?"

"Yeah. You got three in with me today. We'll count them. But don't expect me to fall in love with you. I like ya, kid, I really do, but as for anything beyond that? Well, you're just not my type—even if I was desperate."

"Thanks, Chief … I guess. I'm not sure if I should be flattered or insulted?"

"Both. Either way you know where I stand."

I laughed. "I most certainly do," I said.

I paid the check, and we headed back to the hotel. I didn't realize the strength of my buzz until we pulled into the parking lot.

"Damn, Chief," I said. "I drank more than I thought."

"We had a few," he said. "What say we have a few more in the lounge?"

I needed a minute. The food, the drive, the booze—it had caught up to me all at once. I told the Chief I'd join him at the hotel bar in an hour. I just wanted to relax and disconnect for a bit. He nodded and went to the bar. I went to my room and lay down on the bed. I didn't want to fall asleep, but that's what I did.

* * * * *

The pounding I was hearing had an echo to it at first. It became dryer as it got louder. I opened my eyes and realized there was some-one at my door.

"Who is it?" I croaked.

"Louie? You in there?" the Chief whispered close into the jamb. "It's been over an hour. You coming down for a drink?"

I took a deep breath. I rolled over, looked at the door, and waited a second.

"Louie. It's me," he said. "Do I need to call security?"

"Chief I know it's you," I said. "I'm awake. I'm alive. And no, security is not necessary. Just give me a second."

I sat up and it felt like my head was about to fall off. My face itched and felt warm. I touched my cheek and could feel the deep lines my pillow had carved into my flesh. I looked at the clock. I'd slept for almost two hours. It was longer than I'd wanted but nowhere near long enough.

At first I thought about bidding the Chief *good night* and going back to sleep, but he began knocking on the door again. I had to put a stop to it, and the only way to do that was to get up and go have a drink with the old bastard. I got up and slid to the door. I opened it and let him in.

The Chief studied me quickly. "Jesus, Louie. You look terrible," he said. "You oughta go back to bed."

I shook my head. "I can't," I said. "I'm up now."

"Well, that's good. They're asking about you in the lounge."

I furrowed my brow. "Who's 'they'?" I asked.

"The gals," the Chief said. "I've been telling them all about you. You're the High Della-Lama."

"The what?" I asked. "What's a *Della-Lama*?" I was still groggy.

The Chief ignored my question. "Come on, kid," he said. "Let's get down there before the dames find better prospects."

"I'm not really up for a meet and greet right now," I said. "Why don't you go-ahead. Give my regards to the dames."

The Chief stepped into the room and looked disapproving.

"What's wrong now?" I asked.

He didn't acknowledge me.

I looked at his face. He countered every move I made. He was getting pouty again. It was starting to try my patience a little.

"Okay, I'm going downstairs," I said, relenting. "If you'd like to join me, then come on. If not, then I'm gonna have to ask you to leave my room."

The Chief spoke through his pout. "Gonna kick an old man out on his ear, Louie?" he asked. "You would do that, wouldn't you? Just throw the old son of a bitch to the goddamn wolves. It's okay. I'll make it."

I pulled my hair a little. I wanted to be frustrated, but I could not. This was drama at its syrupy best. I felt like I was in a bad adaptation of a Tennessee Williams play. All that was missing were the vapors and a damn parasol. *He'll fit in great back home*, I said to myself.

"Don't let the wolves bite your ass too hard," I said as I ushered the Chief out into the hall.

"What are you doing?" he asked. His desperate tone was too much to take.

"Dammit, Chief, let's go!" I demanded. "Stop this bullshit. Let's get some drinks. Let's talk about some islands. Let's—"

He held up a hand and cut me off.

"Now, you wait a goddamn minute," he seethed. "You don't know shit about the islands. You have no right to say a single word about them—you got that?"

I nodded in concurrence but said nothing.

"You've never been to the islands," he said. "You're too rooted in your own malaise of uncertainty and domestication to venture that far out of your comfortable little hole."

These were brutal words, but I wasn't fazed by his ire in the least. Ironically, the more he ranted about my audacity to speak of the islands, the quicker we moved toward the elevator and down to the bar.

The Chief raged on, and I heard him. I wasn't listening—I was just *hearing*. None of what he was spewing would be relevant after a couple of drinks. All would be forgiven, and I would be rewarded with another trip down the Chief's memory lane.

I sat at the bar and the Chief sat next to me. He was still rambling. The place was a little crowded for a Monday night, but there was also a preseason football game on the TV—that might explain it.

The bartender came to take our orders. The Chief was now sharing his disdain of me with the patron to his right. The bartender looked at him. I responded with a similar look and added a sympathetic shrug—for both him and the unlucky patron.

"I'll have a scotch and soda," I said. "Prince Charming would like a glass of Jack Daniels, and I'd also like to get a pitcher of beer—something local."

The bartender pointed to the taps. "Which one?" he asked. "I've got a few."

I perused the taps. "Whatever you think is best," I said. "You're the expert."

He smiled and said, "Coming right up."

I took a look around and noticed a great disparity in the population. The Chief had raved about "the gals." There was not a single female in the bar at this moment. Perhaps the dames had found "better prospects"? It didn't matter. It was actually a relief. I wasn't in the mood for much at this moment, especially trying to talk up a woman.

The volume was down on the TV, but several people hooted and hollered, while others groaned and criticized the action. I spotted the teams: the Dallas Cowboys and the New Orleans Saints. I didn't care about either of them but was in the minority with my lack of interest.

The bartender brought our drinks. My scotch and soda was bigger than I'd expected, as was the Chief's glass of Jack.

"Here's a pitcher of Empyrean ESB," he said. "You wanted local, and this is it. It's pretty damn good!"

"That's what we're after," I said. "It won't last long."

The bartender nodded and went to tend his other patrons.

The Chief seemed to have calmed down but was still ignoring me. His new friend looked riveted with their conversation. If he wasn't, he was damn good at mendacity.

I sipped my drink and tried to gain some interest in the football game. I was sitting next to my traveling partner and surrounded by several other people but felt very much alone. I watched the large TV screen blur as my focus waned and my mind drifted. I wasn't thinking of anything in particular, and that was good. It was nice to be free of committed thoughts for a moment.

"Louie!" the Chief shouted. "I want you meet ol' Bert here. He's from your neck of the woods."

I shifted back in my seat to get a look at this man I was being introduced to. I put my arm behind the Chief's back and offered ol' Bert a handshake.

"Nice to meet you," I said. "Name's Louis."

He gripped my hand firmly. "Barry Welsh," he said. "Your buddy here says you're from Georgia?"

"I am. You from the Peach State too?"

"No, I'm a volunteer—Tennessee. But close enough, I suppose."

"We're neighbors."

The Chief nodded. He had an expression on his face that resembled that of world leaders when they came to terms in solving a crisis.

"What's on your mind, Chief?" I asked.

"Nothing, kid," he said. "It's just a wonderful thing, isn't it, meeting new people?"

"It's not without its merits," I said.

I raised my glass to Barry, and he responded in kind. The Chief poured two glasses of beer. He slid one to Barry and took a drink from the other. He didn't even notice the Jack.

"Have a pint on us, Bert," he said as he raised his glass.

Barry seemed grateful for the drink but a bit hesitant to accept it.

"You okay with this, Louis?" he asked.

"Enjoy," I said. "We'll get more."

Barry laughed and took a drink of the beer. He commented on how good it was, and then he and the Chief resumed their conversation.

In the game, a Dallas corner almost intercepted a pass, and Barry slammed his hand on the bar in protest. Several other men had similar reactions. I couldn't tell who they were rooting for. Barry gulped down another swig.

"See, now if my Titans were playing—well …" he said. He never finished his sentence.

I finished my scotch and soda and asked the bartender for an extra glass for beer. He brought one and I poured a pint. I rested my lips to the rim of the glass and took a slow drink. I listened to the Chief regale Barry with slightly varied tales from the road, and I felt left out. These were *my* stories, and here he was sharing them with a complete stranger—*and from Tennessee, no less.*

I chuckled in to my glass. "What absurdity am I cooking up in my head?" I said quietly. I put my glass down and went back to not watching the game.

A couple hours past, and the crowd had thinned out. I was trying to figure out how many of the bar patrons were here on business and what they did. I'd seen some high-octane boozing going on among quite a few of them. I was trying to picture these guys decked in three-piece suits and sweating out a hangover in some boardroom or trudging through a big-dollar presentation with mild cotton-mouth and a burgeoning case of diarrhea.

The game was ending, and the bar was about empty. I'd only drank half of my beer, while the Chief had polished off the first pitcher and ordered another one. The bartender informed us that last call was at twelve thirty. No problem. We were set. I was craving a cigarette for some reason. The Chief still hadn't talked to me beyond introducing Barry.

I tried to get his attention. "Well, Chief," I said. "I think I'm calling it after I finish this beer."

He looked at me and raised an eyebrow. "You got somewhere to be?" he asked.

I smiled. I'd finally gotten the old man back.

"No, I was just trying to get a word in," I said. "You were pretty busy with Barry. He seemed like an okay cat."

"Yeah, but he wasn't interested in much," the Chief said. "He just wanted to watch the game. It was Dallas slaughtering *Nawlins*— and a preseason game at that. What's the point?"

I took a drink and nodded as I swallowed. *That's what I was wondering.*

We finished the pitcher and watched as the last of the patrons filed out for the night. Once again, the Chief and I were closing a place down.

After last call, we headed back to our rooms.

"All right, Chief, I'll see you at breakfast," I said. "I'll try to be up early."

"Reveille is at oh-five-thirty, Louie," he said. "The mess is open at six."

"I'll see you about seven then."

"If I'm lucky. I wouldn't expect anything less—except the fact you'll probably show up at eight."

"I can do that," I said, crinkling my face with an impish expression.

"Good night, Louie," the Chief said as he closed his door.

I stood alone in the hall and listened to the soft hum of the lights in the ceiling. I smelled the faded aroma of cigarettes and off-brand carpet cleaner. It was a strange combination but not unpleasant. I opened my door and smiled.

My mind was clear. I heard someone cough loud forcibly and wet through one of the doors. It was definitely not the sound I wanted to end my day with. I shook my head and chortled. I stepped in the room got undressed and went to sleep.

* * * * *

I woke up to the faint sound of a TV in an adjoining room. I rolled over and looked at the clock. It was 6:25 a.m.

I lay in bed and mulled over going back to sleep. No dice. I sat up, threw my feet over the edge of the bed, and got ready to face the day.

I made my way down to the hotel restaurant, and for as early as it was, quite a crowd had already gathered. I spotted the Chief and smiled and waved at him. He looked around as if I were a stranger and timidly returned a wave.

"Good morning, Chief," I said. I quoted him. "'How's the mess look?'"

He smiled and gestured for me to sit. "To what do I owe this pleasure, kid?" he asked. "I didn't expect you for another hour or so."

"I couldn't sleep," I said. "It was time to get up."

The Chief wasn't completely convinced.

"You trying to show me up?" he asked.

"No, not at all," I said. "I really could not go back to sleep."

"But you did think about going back to sleep, didn't you? You weren't just going to get up and come dine with the Big Banana. Your prompt came from elsewhere."

I shook my head. I couldn't lie to him. He'd already pegged me.

"Somebody's kid crying wake you up?" he asked. "Ankle biters and their little piercing wails will snap anyone's slumber."

"It wasn't a kid crying," I said. "It was somebody's TV."

The Chief nodded and smiled. "Thanks for giving me the straight dope, Louie," he said. "You cracked fast. You'd do great in a POW Camp."

"I would?" I asked curiously.

"Yeah … for the enemy," he said.

I rolled my eyes and got up to get some food.

The setup here was almost identical to the one in Evansville. The only real difference was the coffee vessels. Instead of large barrels with pictures, the coffee was in fat round glass pots with plastic handles: black for regular, orange for decaf, and another black one. They were not labeled. I didn't know what the second black pot was. Two of the pots sat on warmers atop a large stainless-steel coffee-making machine.

One of the black pots had just been filled. A restaurant attendant came out and switched the pots. She took the newly filled black one and replaced it with the decaf pot. She hit a button, and that pot was filling up. It made me wonder if the decaf pot actually had decaf in it or if the orange pot was merely a ruse to make sure people thought they were getting *unleaded.*

I pulled an egg and some bacon from a warmer and put them on my plate. The bacon was overly crisp. I struck a piece of it on the side of my paper plate, and it shattered.

I reached into the bread warmer and pulled out the last bagel. I got a look from a middle-aged mother. She had just scolded her son for not using the tongs to take something from the warmer.

"No manners," she mumbled to her kid while coldly glancing at me. "Filthy hands. Other people have to eat that food too."

I looked at her and then at her kid. He was embarrassed by the whole scene.

"It was the last one," I said. "It's heated. How's that filthy?"

She ignored me and yanked her son away from the awful, unsanitary bagel grabber. I picked up the tongs, pointed them in the woman's direction, and made nonsensical growling noises, while I clicked them at her. Her kid thought it was funny. She—of course— did not. *Your mom's a bitch*, I said to the kid via telepathy. He made a face as if he'd actually heard me.

I walked back to the table. I glanced back to glare at the mom and smile at the kid. She never saw my dirty looks. Her son caught them all. He laughed at each one.

"Figure out what you want to do today?" I asked the Chief.

"Nope," he said. "I'll leave that to you."

I crinkled my face. The Chief sat back. "I don't like that look," he said. Even though I don't know what it's about."

"I didn't think you would," I said. "You'll like it even less when I tell you what it's about."

"Gimme a shot, kid," he said. "I might surprise you."

"I need to go shopping," I said.

"You can't be serious. Well, Louie, go do your woman's work, and I'll stay here and drink the bar dry."

I shook my head. "Anything else you want to say?" I asked.

"No," the Chief said. "Nothing except you're a pussy."

We'd finished eating, and I got up to get more coffee. The Chief made a comment about me switching to decaf and how many sugars I took. I ignored him.

I'd seen him cast out and drop his lure into the deep waters of love. Talk about a man getting soft and weak. I'd never cheapen the emotions he'd expressed by calling him out on them. I just sat back and smiled.

"While I'm out, Chief, think of what you'd like to do," I said.

"Where are you going?" the Chief asked. "Were you just gonna leave me here?!"

"No, not really," I said. "I figured you were done eating as well."

"I am, but you were … OK, I understand. It's because I poked fun at you, isn't it?"

"What do you mean?"

"It's because I called you a pussy, isn't it?"

"No. That never bothered me to begin with."

"I'm sorry. Is that what you want to hear?"

I was confused. "You don't have to apologize," I said. "It didn't bother me."

"I know you're sensitive," he said. "The artist type. Probably a goddamn Pisces, am I right?"

I nodded and let him continue.

"I thought so," he said. "Listen, Louie, this old bastard says things … well, if I rib you, it's 'cause I like you. That's how we used to do things before the world got so delicate. Back in my day, you could give a man a hard time and not expect the waterworks to flow so hastily …"

The Chief rambled on about masculinity and how political correctness has ruined everything. After about ten seconds, I'd tuned him out.

I looked at the clock in the restaurant and saw that it was almost 8:30 a.m. We'd been taking up space in here for a while. I scanned the faces of the patrons and noticed they'd all changed. The Chief and I were the only ones left from the group who'd been seated when I came down close to ninety minutes ago.

"You ready, Chief?" I asked as I got up from the table.

"I am now," he said, sounding like I was forcing him to leave.

I huffed a bit. I had a feeling this was going to be one of *those* days. We'd had one at each stop; why would this one be any different?

We walked to the lobby, and I found a couple of brochures and event catalogs for the Chief to peruse while I was out. I glanced at a couple of them. My reaction was less than favorable—I couldn't begin to imagine what the Chief would say. Maybe the old man would surprise me.

"I'm going to go so I can get done," I said. "See if you can find anything interesting. I'll be back in an hour or so." The Chief waved me off as he sat down in the lobby to read the brochures.

* * * * *

I ended up at a Target store. Perfect. I bought a pack of T-shirts, underwear, and socks as well. I came across a couple of decent collared shirts and grabbed them too. I found a Hawaiian print shirt with pin-up girls in Martini glasses and tiki heads on it—for the Chief of course—*like he wouldn't wear this?*

I went to pay for my stuff. As the cashier rang everything up, she surveyed each item to see how they'd fit me—not size-wise, but in general.

Boxer briefs? You strike me as more of a low-rise brief guy. Why these tees? They're so drab—so not you. I see you as the more colorful, vibrant type. Now this Hawaiian shirt? Surely you must be buying this for your grandpa or something? Am I right? You're so cute . . .

She read the name on my credit card: *Louis.*

Would you like to have me for dinner tonight? Oops, did I just say that? Oh, dear, I meant to say, "Would you like to have sex with me on a dinner table tonight?" Oh, my, I'm so . . .

"Receipt in the bag or with you?" the cashier asked. Her eyes beamed at me, full of suspicion and accusation.

"Yeah. That'll work," I said.

The cashier twitched. It was that "Huh?" jolt.

"I'm sorry," I said. "In the bag please."

She stuffed the paper ticket into the bag and handed it to me. "Thank you for shopping at Target," she said. We smiled at each other awkwardly.

"You bet," I said.

I quickly made my way out of the store. *What the hell just happened?*

When I got back to the hotel, the Chief was still in the lobby and still thumbing through the brochures; however, he was no longer alone. I shouldn't have been surprised. He was chatting up three very attractive women, and there were four others who seem to be drifting in and out of the circle. For as much as I wanted to join the conversation, the humiliation of my wanton thoughts of the Target cashier were causing me refrain.

"Louie!" the Chief shouted as he waved to me. "Come sit, me boy. Come join the fun."

I smiled uneasily and walked toward the Chief and his new harem. "Morning, ladies, Chief," I said, nodding to all in the room.

"Sit, son. Comfort first, then pleasantries," the Chief said as he gestured to a chair.

I sat and looked at the women. They smiled back at me but said nothing. The Chief looked like Howard Hughes—surrounded by dames and important paperwork. I felt like out of my league just a bit. I wanted to leave, but I didn't know where I was going to go.

"I was just telling the girls about *Vet-Nam*, Louie," the Chief said. "Not the gory details of the war, just the beauty of the country."

Impressed, I nodded. I had no idea the Chief was in Vietnam, but I shouldn't have been surprised. What did get me was how he pronounced it: *Vet-Nam*.

I had no idea what he'd told the ladies about the 'Nam, but it had them captivated. They were hanging on every word. Even the casual eavesdroppers were now absorbing the conversation: asking questions and swooning at the Chief's lush verbal painting of the

Southeast Asian landscape. Had he mentioned his heroic acts yet? There had to be some of those in there.

I sat and listened. He said nothing about fighting, nor did he mention some great act of diplomacy that changed the course of the war. He just talked flora, fauna, and folks. I sank in my chair to hide—and not in a bad way. I just wanted to hear the man talk. I did not want to interfere with his story.

I'd heard a lot about Vietnam, but I'd never heard about it like the Chief was describing. I could feel the warm, thick air around me. It was a humidity worse than anything in Georgia. I patted my shirt to make sure I wasn't sweating.

He said the sun beamed through the vegetation. The palm fronds and tarot leaves lit and would glow an indescribable green. He'd befriended some people from outlying villages, and they showed him the land beyond the city.

"We'd walk the paddies and terraces where they grew rice," he said. "My friend Hung was the brother of the High Della-Lama in town. He took us on sampan rides down river. We'd venture out to the lagoons and see the huge limestone islands rising from the water. I wouldn't see anything like that again—well, not until Samoa."

I looked around at the women again. They were still riveted with the Chief's tale, but I know the writer and hopeless romantic in me was more taken by the old man's words than these dames could ever be. I'd heard him talk before—they had not. It didn't matter. The Chief spun yarns into sweaters for the soul, and this one was no exception.

Part of me was angry that he was wasting his words on a bunch of people he didn't know, but then again, that's what he did: he told his tales to anyone who'd listen. I, fortunately, heard them resonate at a much different level.

The Chief continued his story.

"We'd come into the inlets with the fishermen and they'd invite us to eat," he said. "Ah, the villagers. What can I say? They treated me like damn royalty, and I was honored to be a part of something so beautiful. The sunsets were breathtaking, and at the end of the meal, the kids in the village would come out and celebrate the day's catch and give thanks to the gods for the bounty."

He talked about Saigon—the big city—bustling with brightness and wonder amid the flash and destruction of the war. He described the crowds moving, teeming and smiling. The Vietnamese people were in a state of disconnect—brother fighting brother, a civil war that had become a global conflict, but they still smiled in the streets of Saigon.

"I'd eat lunch every day at this wonderful café," the Chief said. "I'd always sit outside so I could feel the breeze. The breeze in Vet-Nam was like nowhere else. It blew warm and wet as it shifted through the air. No matter the weather—sunny or rainy—the breeze always felt like a gentle cloth brushing easily against the skin.

"Most days, the city rested beneath perfect azure skies and the whitest of clouds, but when those skies were overcast, they held uncertainty. You never knew when it was going to rain, just that it would—and it would be torrential. The Vet-namese downpours were like none I'd ever experienced. The rain was so warm it did nothing to temper the heat and humidity. You hardly felt it on you. You were just soaked with it."

All of a sudden, I could smell the rain. I closed my eyes for a second, and I was dampened by a deluge that did not occur. It was just as the Chief had said; however, this storm showered from the skies of the Saigon in my subconscious.

I jolted in my seat. I peered around, embarrassed. I chuckled nervously and readjusted myself, hoping no one had noticed my sudden, seemingly unprovoked moves.

I tugged at my soaked shirt. It was dry. I got up, brushed the wet hair from my brow. It too was dry. I smiled and walked around the chairs. I was still listening to the Chief's story, but I was back in the hotel lobby in Elkhorn, Nebraska.

The Chief paused for a moment. It was as if he was opening the floor for questions. The women sat silent, their eyes big and beaming and still immersed in the Chief's nearly photographic, overtly sensuous account of his travels to Vietnam.

He looked at the women. I watched him as he marveled at their faces. He was so taken by their wonder and interest in his story. How could they not be? I was right there with them.

Moments ago, I had been jealous and snippy toward these ladies. I'd felt that they had no right to listen to the Chief tell his story. They were not worthy of the man's recollection because they didn't understand him. They didn't appreciate the beauty of what he was saying and how he'd said it. I was not being fair.

As I studied their faces, I realized that they *had* indeed fallen under the old man's spell. They had gotten rained on in that café in Old Saigon just as much as I had. The only difference was, I knew I'd been soaked in the deluge, but they did not.

It wasn't about a lack of appreciation; it was the simple fact they didn't know—or comprehend these stories as intimately as I had. Even the stories I hadn't heard were a feast for the five senses.

"Well, ladies, that's all the words of wisdom I have for today," the Chief said. "Anything else will cost you *two bits* a person."

The women groaned and seemed deflated by this. They wanted more, but that was not to be. One asked questions, and the Chief waved her off saying something about "tales for another time." I was relieved. I'd figured with this type of audience, he'd never leave the lobby. I wanted to get on with our day.

I glanced at the brochures surrounding the old boy. I wondered just how far into them he'd gotten before deciding to take his new-found entourage on a trip back in time. I hadn't read them at all. I walked over and picked up one of the magazines the Chief had shoved aside.

"Oh yes, that reminds me," the Chief announced. "This is me boy Louie. Louie, me boy ..." The ladies giggled at my expense.

"Louie needs a date for this evening," the Chief said. "Do we have any takers amongst this group of sparkling beauties?"

I palmed my face to hide my embarrassment. I should've known that he was going to pull something like this.

"Anyone?" the Chief asked. "He's a helluva man, a fine dancer, and rumor has it—a big spender! He's the man of your dreams, ladies."

They continued to giggle—harder this time—and I became more embarrassed. I didn't think that was possible.

My face was beyond red. It had to be purple. It throbbed and hurt. My cheeks felt like they were going to explode. My head ached, and my stomach began to growl. This was one of those instances where I did not know if I was going to shit or go blind. I was infuriated, but not to the point I wanted to kill—but give me another minute, and ...

I raised my hand and spoke. "Um ... yeah ... hi!" I said, my voice cracking like a prepubescent choir boy. "My name's Louis ... and ... yeah ... um ..." The women stared at me with pitiful eyes. "So ... like ... what is there to do here in town?"

The Chief looked at me and seemed shocked by my query. I know I was supposed to be seeking out the Five Ls, but at this moment, they were not my priority. I was looking to go somewhere and see something: a sight of some sort. A date with food, drinks, laughs, tears, and a possible roll in the feathers sounded great—but it was eleven o'clock in the morning. I was still digesting my breakfast. I didn't have time to think about anything beyond the fact that I was in Nebraska and I wanted to go and explore what this place had to offer within a fifty-mile radius.

One of the women turned to me and nodded. "You know, there are a lot of great places to see here," she said. "Do you boys like railroad stuff—trains and that kind of thing?"

The Chief's expression changed. The mention of "railroad stuff" got his attention.

"Why yes, ma'am, we're old brakemen from the Chesapeake and Ohio Line," the Chief said, tipping an invisible cap. "We've rode the rails from coast to coast and hit every whistle stop in between."

I shook my head and smiled. I was worried the Chief was going to go off on some yarn about his days riding the line, but he did not. He just listened.

"There is a great exhibit of old railcars and locomotives. The museum itself is built inside the old Union Station," the woman said. "I haven't been there since I was a little girl, but I remember it being massive and wonderful. My dad talked about how these great machines moved everything from place to place. He said without the railroad, there'd be no America."

The Chief smiled as his eyes glazed a little.

"And he was right indeed," he said. "Your father was a wise man."

That was it. We were going to the Durham Museum. We hadn't even left the hotel lobby, and I knew the Chief was already there. For me, we were going to see the history of transportation. For the Chief, he was going to be transported into his personal history. I looked at him again. He was still young.

Everyone seemed to get up simultaneously. Chat time was done, and the Chief's focus had switched from wooing the women with his travels abroad, to reconnecting with this person from his past who'd worked the big forge of coal-fed steel. He was hasty in trying to get himself together so we could leave.

"Not a moment to waste," cried the conductor. "All aboard!" The Chief could hear the whistle blowing. And by God—so could I!

* * * * *

We drove into Omaha and came upon the old Union Station. The giant terra cotta, art deco structure sat majestically along the street. Raised letters along the façade indicated that this was now the Durham Museum. The Chief studied the smooth, cream-colored face of the building and gazed at the awnings that protruded from it. He looked into the doors below them.

At one time, passengers moved through those doors waiting to be whisked by rail to varied destinations around the country. Now those who entered them were waiting to be whisked away, but on an entirely different journey.

"You ready to go in?" I asked.

The Chief nodded. "This old bastard's going in," he said. "But I can't be sure who's going to come out."

I smiled. "Isn't that why we're here and why we're doing this?" I asked. "How do we find ourselves if we don't get lost?"

"That sounds crazy," the Chief said.

"I learned it from you."

"Well then, it's sage wisdom—and it's *definitely* crazy."

We walked toward the building. The Chief stopped and peered at the engraving above the entry way awning.

"No other improvement … can equal in utility the railroad. Abraham Lincoln, March 9, 1832," he said as he nodded. "Mr. Lincoln sure had a way with words."

"That he did," I agreed.

"Dedicated by the railways of Omaha to the service, comfort, and convenience of the people," the Chief said as he read the text above the other awning.

I pulled the door open, and the Chief walked in. As soon as the soles of his shoes hit the tiles of the floor, the youth I'd seen in his face earlier had joined the rest of his body.

I watched him look around this lobby with wonder and awe. I don't know where he was in time, but I understood how he felt. He'd taken me on great journeys through his words, and I'd seen him become the person he talked about in those stories: growing young, reliving the times, returning to the places, and seeing the people he loved. This was no exception, but it was different.

He was more than merely a part of the change. This was more than metaphoric and metaphysical. It wasn't just my observation and getting wrapped up in the memory—the Chief knew where and *when* he was. However, this time, I could not go with him. It was like when he talked about fishing with his siblings. I could hear what he said, but I was not allowed into the memory. I was okay with that.

I walked with the Chief and didn't say a word. He seemed to float in the huge space of the waiting room. I craned my neck to see the ceilings above. They seemed so high—almost to heaven. I know the Chief felt that's where they leveled off. From top to bottom, the inside of the old station was decorated with touches of the past.

Railway schedules and large clocks lined the walls as bronze statues stood reading the timetables and purchasing tickets. A pair of military men discussed their imminent homecomings. They spoke of the happiness they'd see on their family's faces when they arrived at their destinations—one man heading east, the other journeying west.

A kindly porter helped a young mother and her children with their bags. No doubt they'd just arrived in Omaha and were anticipating seeing their doting grandparents, the mother hiding the grief of losing her husband in a war taking place a million miles away. She'd seen the soldiers chatting and laughing. She'd secretly—and shamefully—hated them.

Many trains—and people—had come and gone through this station at one time but no longer. The sculpted figures that existed in this space were forever locked in the moment—and forever waiting.

We ventured through the museum and found our way to the railcar exhibit. There was enough to see and keep the Chief happily frozen in his youth. He seemed quite taken by the old Union Pacific steam locomotive.

The Chief's expression suddenly changed, still young but now determined.

"Louie, I'm going in," he said. "I'm gonna grab that old Johnson Bar."

These were the first words he'd spoken since we came into the museum. I was afraid to ask what he meant. The term *Johnson Bar* sounded sexual and as enraptured as the Chief appeared to be at the moment, I'm sure there was some validity to my musing.

He climbed up the stairs into the engineer's cab on the locomotive. He leaned out the open window and stared down the big cylindrical boiler. A couple of boys watched as the Chief smacked the side of the cab. He waved to them as if he was rolling through town while they stood by the tracks.

"No pennies on the rails, kids!" he yelled to the boys.

They shook their heads simultaneously. "No, sir!" they shouted back in unison.

The boys' father pulled them back.

"He's harmless," I said of the Chief. "He's just reminiscing a little."

The father's expression went from cautious to cordial, and he let his kids go about their business.

"Hey, mister," one of them called to the Chief, "can we come up too?"

The Chief smiled and waved them up. "All aboard the …" He paused and looked at me. "Hey, Louie, what the hell time is it?"

"Twelve thirty-five," I said.

"All aboard the twelve thirty-five to …" The Chief paused again and asked the kids where they wanted to go.

One said "Wichita," the other said "Honolulu," and the Chief let out a loud laugh.

"Well, all right then—all aboard the 12:35 to *Wichalulu*," he said. The kids jumped happily and cheered.

"You want me to blow the whistle?" he asked the boys.

"Yeah!" they shouted.

The Chief made a noise with his mouth that sounded as close to an old train whistle as you could get.

He leaned out of the cab again and waved to me and the boys' father. We waved back. From where we stood, they didn't move, but as far as the Chief and those two boys were concerned, that engine was chugging out of Union Station and off to the great city of "Wichalulu."

They must've been in that locomotive for a half hour. The Chief ran the big engine while the boys pretended to shovel coal from the tenders into the firebox. They were laughing, but it sounded like real work was going on.

Other museum patrons gathered around to watch and listen as the mighty steel behemoth made its way down the rails, pistons pumping while the side rods moved the driving wheels. Thick smoke billowed from the chimney and filled the air.

"They're really going somewhere," one of the patrons commented.

"That they are," I said. "And only they know where that it is."

The boys' father laughed and nodded. I don't think he'd even seen his kids this involved in anything before—and it was pure imagination.

The Chief looked out the cab window and threw us all a salute. Everyone cheered as the locomotive finally came to a stop at the depot in "Wichalulu." The boys stepped out of the cab first. They looked sweaty. It was either quite warm in that cab or they had really gotten into their role-playing. The Chief stayed aboard a while longer. He made his last checks of the engine to make sure all was well and secure. This trip was over, and it was time to put the old girl to bed for night.

The observant crowd had dispersed. The boys and their father waited for the Chief to disembark from the locomotive. They wanted to thank the old man for the adventure.

I watched the Chief slowly step out of the engineer's cab and onto the stairs. He was in no hurry to say goodbye to that locomotive. Once he did, he'd have to say goodbye to that young man who was driving the big steam. My heart broke a little for him.

The boys ran to the Chief and hugged him. He wasn't sure how to respond. I don't think he'd been hugged by anyone like this in a long time. He looked at me and then at the kids' dad. We both nodded and let him know it was okay. The Chief dropped down and gave the boys a proper embrace.

"This was something they'll never forget," the father said. "I don't even know how to thank him for this."

I pointed to the trio of hardworking rail men.

"You see that?" I asked. "There's more than a million thank-yous going on right there."

The father smiled as he watched the kids run back to him.

"I think you're right," he said. The kids talked up a storm as the three walked away to visit other parts of the exhibit.

I stood and looked at the Chief standing alone. The youthful glow had gone from his face, and he looked lost. I moved toward him cautiously. I know how he could be when he transitioned, and I knew today was going to be especially difficult.

I walked up next to him. "You okay, Chief?" I asked.

He continued to gaze forward but acknowledged me.

"I'm doing all right, kid," he said. "I think I'm ready to go."

"Are you sure?" I asked. "There's a lot more to see here."

"Nope, Louie. I've seen as much as I need to. There's only so much this old son of a bitch can handle in one day."

I nodded. "I understand," I said. "Well, let's head on back to the hotel."

"That sounds good," he said. "I could use a little rest. This was something special."

We walked out of the museum and headed to the car. The Chief took one last look at the building. For a moment, it seemed as if he was contemplating going back inside and looking at more of the rail-car exhibit. He shook his head as if he were clearing a thought. This gesture was my cue that we were truly done at the Durham.

The Chief got in the car and sat quietly. I kept looking at him, but I chose not to bother him. I knew where he was, and I knew he wanted to stay there a little longer.

"Thank you, Louie," the Chief said. His sudden words of gratitude caught me off guard.

"For what?" I asked.

"For giving me a little bit of my past back," he said.

I smiled. "It's just part of the journey," I said. "This is the kind of thing I signed on for when we decided to do this."

"Kid, you have no idea how I feel right now," he said. "This was just ..."

"You don't have to say anything, Chief. I already know."

"Seeing things like that, it does this old heart some good."

"I can only imagine."

"Someday, Louie, you'll be old like me and you'll have these kinds of experiences. They're a bitch to go through, but they keep you young and alive."

"Chief, I don't have to be old to get the effect. I'm going through it right now. I'm making my adventures as we speak, and I owe it all to you."

The Chief waved me off. "Nah, kid, you don't owe a damn thing to me," he said. "If there's gratitude to be handed out, I owe it to you for getting my old, crusty ass off that barstool at Churchill's Joint."

I laughed. "Well, let's just say we're both indebted to each other for quite a bit," I said. "It's all pretty big when you think about it."

"That it is, me boy," the Chief said. "You know what else is pretty big?"

I was afraid to ask, but I did. "What might that be?" I wondered.

"My appetite," the Chief said. "When do we eat?"

We decided to eat at a place called Lazlo's. It was both a brewery and a restaurant: two-for-one. It was perfect.

A hostess seated us, and the Chief was his usual, charming self.

"So, miss, is Lazlo in this afternoon?" he asked. "The lad and I want to compliment him on such a fine place to quell our ravenousness."

The hostess's expression was one of abject uncertainty. Her bottom lip tightened, and her eyes got big. She wasn't sure what to say.

"Um, I really don't know," she said. "But I can get my manager if you'd like."

I put my hand up and shook my head. "No, it's quite all right," I said. "He's just trying to be funny, that's all."

The hostess stepped back, relieved. She sighed and smiled.

"Your server will be right with you," she said as she slinked away from our table.

The Chief did not ogle the hostess at all. I was surprised. Then again, I think he was still riding the rails in that locomotive. He was here: mind, body, and spirit, but his heart was still at the Durham.

Our waitress arrived, and the Chief was buried in his menu. This was a good thing for the moment.

"Good afternoon, gentlemen," she said. "My name is Jeanette, and I'll be taking your order." She was bubbling and bright, and I couldn't stop staring at her eyes. They were a remarkable sparkling violet blue. Her makeup was like nothing I'd ever seen: dark, smoky blue accents that were intense but not obnoxiously overstated. Her mascara was dark and thick and was drawn to a sharp point just beyond the corners of her eyes. It was stunning but looked heavy.

The Chief looked up from his menu and saw her eyes as well. "Well, hello, beautiful," he said. "Has anyone ever told you that you look like a young Liz Taylor?"

Jeanette blushed. "No, I don't think so," she said, as she coyly glanced away.

"Well, shame on them for overlooking your beauty," the Chief said with a nod. "Please allow me to be the first to tell you that you could be Ms. Taylor's twin sister."

I smiled. I had to agree with the Chief—she did look like a young Liz.

"What can I get for you two?" Jeanette asked. "We have some great specials for lunch, and all Empyrean drafts are half off all day."

I spoke first. "I'm not sure what I want to eat," I said. "But I would like a tall … what Empyrean do you have that's good and strong?"

Jeanette answered without hesitation. "That would be the Burning Sky Scottish Ale," she said.

"Then that's what I want," I said. "And a bottle of Perrier."

The Chief pointed at me.

"That sounds good to me too," he said. "We'll make it easy on you, honey."

Jeanette blushed again and giggled. She caught herself and dropped her guest check pad. I reached down and picked it up for her. She rolled her eyes. Her look screamed *I'm so clumsy.* It was adorable. She left to put in our drink orders.

We resumed looking over our menus. I'd decided on the spinach and artichoke *lahvosh*. The Chief was stuck between the rainbow chicken and the voodoo chicken.

"I could go either way," he commented. "And as my food goes, so do I."

I laughed at his remark. "Be careful, Chief," I said. "Go with something easy."

"To hell with 'easy'!" he yelled. "I'm living dangerously. Gimme that voodoo!"

We put our menus aside and waited for our drinks. While we sat, I looked around the restaurant. The Chief tapped his fingers on the table. I knew he was trying to get my attention. I pretended to ignore him. He didn't let that faze him.

"Louie, I read those papers in the hotel," he said. "I figured we'd have to stay in today."

"Why is that?" I asked.

"Because until you took me to that museum, I had this town pegged as one huge golf course."

"Really? How come?"

"Every one of those trade presses had nothing but golf shit in them. I was like Bobby fucking Jones thumbing through them. You know Bobby Jones, right? Georgia Boy, big-time golfer."

"Well, what we need to do is thank that woman in the lobby," I said. "She was the one who suggested the museum, remember?"

"We'll probably never see that lobby broad again," he said. "But I need to find a way to thank you for today. What can I do for you? Name it."

"Chief, I'm good," I said. "I'm just enjoying all of this."

Just as I finished my sentence, our beers arrived. The Chief looked at Jeanette and then back to me.

"I'll bet you're enjoying all of this," he said, with a sly smirk and a wink.

Jeanette apologized for the delay on our drinks, and the Chief and I both waved her off. She took our food orders. When she was done, we resumed our chat.

"You're getting soft, kid," the Chief said. "You haven't been out with—or even spent a quality moment with a woman since we were in Elko."

"I know, and I'm fine with that," I said, as I took a drink of my beer.

"No, Louie, there are rules and regulations we must adhere to," he said. "The Five Ls—we can't forget those."

"I haven't forgotten them. They've just been a bit elusive of late—well, a couple of them have."

"Okay, then we have to get you right. Set you straight. How long are we here in town?"

"Another day or so."

"All right, then. That's plenty of time to get your shit together. Let's get you a date. Let's get you back on the Five L Express, *tout de suite.*"

I gave the Chief a hesitant look. He didn't read it clearly. It was more of a desperate plea than anything. I did not want to deal with the complexities of love. The mere thought was mind-boggling.

I was content with my situation. The Five Ls were a grand concept, but were they really *that* defining? Did I need them to make me whole? Were they going to make me a better man and a better writer? Probably not. They were something cooked up by an old man who'd already seen and done everything. I was his merely his protégé—a willing pupil for him to impart wisdom upon. That was easy. The romantic aspect was not.

How can a man be expected to find a different woman for every night of the week? Not to mention one to dine, drink, laugh, cry, and possibly sleep with? It sounds shallow and whorish. The more I thought about it, the less I wanted to be a part of it. Then again, the more I thought about it and the less I wanted to be a part of it, the more I realized I'd already achieved it. I took a long drink of my beer. It was obvious I was still missing April more than I thought.

"How's the work coming?" the Chief asked, out of the blue. "Did you get all your affairs sorted out?"

"I'm still at it," I said. "I did get a reprieve from my boss, though."

The Chief nodded. "Did you tell him about this old son of a bitch?" he asked.

"I did. I told him you were the reason why I was behind my deadline."

The Chief got a sullen look on his face. "Oh, well, that can't be good," he said.

"No, it's okay," I said. "I told him I would give him the story of a lifetime when I got home."

"That's a lot to promise, Louie."

"And it's a lot to deliver, but that's what I'm determined to do."

"I know you've got the talent, kid."

"And Chief, I know *you've* got the stories. This is your tale as much as it is mine."

"What? Are you stealing from me?"

"No, not at all. We're writing this together. It's like I told Rex in Evansville, 'if it's happening now, it's going in the story.'"

"Everything?" the Chief asked. "Even …?"

"Everything," I said. "Don't worry—it'll be the best thing you've ever read."

"That's a tall order, kid. I've read a lot."

"You've read other people's words, Chief. These will be ours. It's something different entirely when you read your own words."

"That sounds a little jaded—conceited."

"It's only jaded and conceited if you're not published. Once you're published, your words kind of become someone else's. It's one big fucking circle."

"That's a lot to take in."

"It is. But it's going to happen. And it's going to be amazing."

Our food arrived, and our attention turned from the dynamic of being published. Jeanette set our plates on the table and inadvertently backed away. It was as if she saw the Chief and me as two primates—scraping at our plates, screeching out in pleasure when we finished our meal, then pouring our beer on our heads, and masturbating profusely in some ritualistic ceremony to appease our gods. It was so 2001.

Regardless of what Jeanette thought of us, we ate our food with little fanfare, and even less primitivism.

"It's been a great day, Louie," the Chief said. "I've probably mentioned that fact ten times already, but I just have to say it."

"Everything we've done so far has been extraordinary, Chief," I said. "You had some concerns, but even those things turned out great."

The Chief raised his glass. "That they have, son," he said. "Here's to many more extraordinary happenings on this journey."

I clinked my glass to his. "Cheers to that!" I said. "And I will do my best to get back on pace personally."

"It's a tough task, Louie, but trust me, it'll be worth the effort," the Chief said. He grabbed my wrist in a reassuring gesture.

We finished our meals, and Jeanette returned to the table. She asked if there was anything else she could do for us. The Chief winked at her. She blushed and smiled back at him. He studied her intently, and I had a bad feeling he was going to try and hook us up.

"Just the check," I said.

Jeanette returned with the check, and I paid it.

She returned to the table with my receipt and thanked us for coming in to the restaurant. I slipped a ten-dollar bill into the folio and got up to leave.

"Are you ready to go, Chief?" I asked. "This lady has had enough of our company for one day, I think."

Jeanette patted my arm. "Oh, you're just fine," she said. "I had fun serving you guys."

I furrowed my brow. "Really? We didn't scare you at all?" I asked.

"No, not at all," she said as patted my arm again—harder this time and with the knowledge we were leaving.

The Chief went to the restroom and left me alone with Jeanette. I looked into her violet-blue eyes again. She demurely glanced away for a second. When we made eye contact again, my heart began to beat fast and a rush of adrenaline shot through my body. I was definitely feeling something for this woman that went beyond top-notch food service.

In my head, I could hear myself formulating scenarios and constructing the dialogue for how I was going to ask her out after her shift. She cocked her head slightly as if she was reading my mind. She smiled, and I began to fall further.

I reached into my pocket and took out my wallet. What the hell was I doing? What was I looking for? At this moment in time, I was dumbfounded, and anything I did was either going to be profound or massively stupid.

I filed through the inserts in my wallet. I wanted to find a business card—something with my number on it—so when this newest woman of my dreams finished her shift, she could call me, and I could take her out and …

"This is for you," I said. I timidly handed her a ten-dollar bill.

"What's this for?" she asked.

"It's for the tip. I didn't give you a tip yet."

"You did. You already gave me ten."

She opened her folio and showed me the paid tab and the ten dollars I'd given her.

I blushed and panicked. "I'm so sorry," I said. "I'm just … here … please … I've kept you so long."

Jeanette took the extra ten. She seemed as hesitant to take it as I was insistent that she did.

"Thank you so much!" she exclaimed. "This is just too nice."

"You earned it, Jeanette," I said. "Just for putting up with me and the old man alone."

She smiled and blushed hard.

"Thank you," I said. "Have a great rest of your day."

I walked toward the door and waited for the Chief. I couldn't be in Jeanette's wonderful presence any more. The longer I stood close to her, the longer I looked into her eyes, the more I began to smell her soft, delicate perfume, the harder it was to control my feelings. I figured it best to remove myself from the situation—and further temptation.

We got in the car and headed back to the hotel. It wasn't late, but I was feeling tired. Sleeping—or at least *normal* sleeping—on this trip had been a luxury. It was either brought on by excessive alcohol consumption, late hours, long drives, or a combination of all three. I was hoping that today would be different. I was looking forward to tucking in early and getting a proper night's sleep for the first time since we left Sacramento.

The Chief watched the traffic go by as we made our way through town. He read signs and called out random street names. I knew he was heading somewhere with his abstract rambling.

"What's on your mind, Chief?" I asked.

"Oh, nothing, Louie. Just doing a little navigation," he said.

"Are you navigating or fishing?"

The Chief huffed. "Whatever do you mean?" he asked. "What could I be fishing for?"

"I don't know," I said. I didn't want to tap-dance with the old man, so I just came out with my query.

"That waitress was quite a doll, didn't you think?" I asked.

"She was, Louie," the Chief said. "She looked like Elizabeth Taylor. That's a beauty right there."

"Totally," I said. I decided to confess my feelings for Jeanette.

"You know, I wanted to ask her out," I said. "I just couldn't."

"I know you did, son, I could tell," the Chief said. "What was stopping you?"

I sighed. "Not what, more like *who* was stopping me," I said. I gave the Chief a morsel to chew on concerning April.

"I think I'm still a bit hung up on that gal I met in Elko," I said. "I wasn't sure, but I'm starting to wonder about her."

"Aha!" the Chief said. "I knew there was something there."

I tried to play my affections off as passing at best.

"Yeah, we hit it off well," I said. "I found what I needed with her, or so I thought. I covered all Five Ls, that's for sure."

The Chief got a contemplative look.

"Sure you did, but there's more to explore," the Chief said. "You can't eat one donut and think you've tried the whole dozen."

"But you encouraged my feelings for her, Chief," I said. "You told me she was closer than I thought. You said she was nearby. What did all of that mean?"

"I was just trying to comfort you, Louie," he said. "I knew the love bug bit you hard. That happens, but you have to let go. You need to find out if what you feel for her is true—and not just convenient. You can't know she's the one until you fully realize you can't live without her."

"I think I feel that way now," I said.

"I'm not sure you do, kid. I saw the way you looked at our waitress tonight. You felt something for her—you said so yourself. You're not locked in completely to anything just yet. Let yourself go, have fun, be adventurous. Let *her* go. You know the old cliché: if you love her, set her free … you can fill in the rest."

"I've been trying," I said. "It's just too hard to let go."

The Chief said nothing. And I felt I may have said too much.

This was the hardest part of this journey and the deal I'd made to go with it. If I was to open the door to this new life I'd wanted so bad, I was going to have let things go. I tried to be strong and tender my attachments, but it was tough. I've always been overly sentimental, and I fell in love too damn easily. It was a challenge to overcome my feelings.

I've always had difficulty cutting ties and resisting the need to hold on. I've spent most of my life carrying a collection of baggage I'd amassed. It ranged from doomed high school romances to bad deals and business ventures to people I'd given my trust and friendship to.

Now I'd found something I honestly wanted to hold on to and I was wrangling with whether or not I should. What was I going to do? Right now? Nothing—except free my calendar and live the next several days like I was supposed to: as a seeker on an adventure.

We arrived back at the hotel. The Chief looked at me. He knew he'd struck an artery but did not press the issue further. I had indeed bled out more than I'd planned, but in this case, it was okay. I needed to do it. I'm sure that tomorrow I'd hate myself for spilling, but I'd worry about that then. We took the elevator up to our floor and went to our rooms.

"Louie, I don't know about you, but I'm thinking about retiring at a decent time," the Chief said. "It's early yet, but it's been a hell of a day. These old bones could use a little extra shut-eye. You may have to count me out on nightcaps tonight."

I nodded in concurrence. I was surprised the Chief was cashing out on the evening, but I was not going to question his decision.

"Sounds good to me, Chief," I said. "I've been thinking the same thing."

"Kid, you made this old boy happy today," he said. "I wish I could repay the favor somehow."

"I'm sure you'll think of something," I said. "But not tonight. Sleep on it. Give it a thought or two."

"I'll do that. Hope you get some decent rest. You've earned it."

I gave the Chief a salute and opened the door to my room. I looked around. That double bed seemed bigger than before. Although it wouldn't take much, I was going to spread myself over every open inch of it.

I turned on the TV. I looked for the music channels, but there didn't seem to be any. It was probably for the best. If I was trying to clear my head of the recent past, I didn't need anything reminding me of it. I settled on the local news. All these things were happening in Omaha. We'd been within a close proximity to them but hadn't witnessed a single one. Perhaps we'd missed them? Maybe we weren't paying attention?

I tried to follow along with the newscast, but it was impossible. I didn't know where anything was, who the reporters were, or who they were talking about. The only definite seemed to be the weather: it was hot, dry, and would remain so until we left. I waited for the sportscast. I fell asleep some time before it had come on.

* * * * *

I woke up still in my clothes. I peered through my glass-filled, groggy eyes and noticed the news was still on and the same people were reporting the same story I'd just heard.

"What the hell?" I asked myself aloud, as I shook my head. "Did I just go back in time?"

I looked at the clock by the bed. It was 9:45 p.m. I'd slept for almost four hours! What I was seeing was not a flashback but lazy broadcasting: a nearly identical recap of the stories from earlier.

"I guess nothing much happens on the daily here," I said.

I sat up and stared at the wall. What was I going to do? I'd slept, and now I was awake. I didn't feel like working. It was too late for that. I didn't function well work-wise past 9:00 p.m.—even sober. I thought about reading, but I'd be reading my own notes—that's work.

"Fuck it," I said. "I'll get up and go downstairs." I got out of bed and got undressed.

I grabbed a clean pair of underwear and one of the new collared shirts I'd bought earlier today. I don't know what I was trying to prove; a T-shirt would've worked just fine. I got in the shower and woke up a bit more. After my soak and spritz, I brushed my teeth, threw on a dab of the hotel cologne for incentive, and put my clothes on.

I looked decent. If anything, I looked better than I should for someone who had no idea what they were going to do at 10:00 p.m. on a Tuesday night. I thought about seeing if the Chief wanted to grab a drink. Then I remembered him saying he was "retiring early" and to count him out on nightcaps. Maybe I wasn't going to drink? Who am I fooling? That's exactly what I was going to do.

I left my room and went across the hall. I know what he'd said before, but out of courtesy, I thought I should see if the old man wanted a toddy. I was just about to lay a rap on the door when I heard a most obnoxious sound. It was the Chief snoring—and it was brutal! *Other than the weirdness factor, now I know why we got separate rooms*, I said to myself. I heard the snorts and sawing of logs again, and I couldn't help but laugh. I whispered *good night* to the Chief as I stepped back from the door and made my way to the elevators.

I walked to the lobby, and there were a few people milling about. There was some quiet chatter between a couple of stragglers from the bar as they sat and nursed their drinks.

I peered around and checked out the bar. It was almost empty except for a few anglers bent and positioned at random spots around the bar. The bartender from last night was working again. He saw me and gave me a nod. I smiled back and took the same seat I'd occupied last night. It felt like home.

"Another ESB?" The bartender asked.

"Yeah, to start," I said. "Just a pint. I'm going a little easy tonight."

The bartender poured my beer. "So where's your buddy?" he asked.

"Oh, the old man? He's going even easier tonight. He's asleep."

"Well, that explains you flying solo, I guess."

"There's no place I'd rather be, though."

The bartender smiled. It was that smirk of uncertain gratitude.

I wasn't planning on getting hammered tonight. I just wanted enough to dull me so I could go back to sleep. Hopefully, that wouldn't take long.

I'd finished my third pint and was feeling the effects a little but not enough. I needed something more than beer. I wanted to be good. I just wanted a little drowse induction. So far, it was not working as planned. I eyed the bottles and thought about upping the octane. I let the idea fade.

I started watching TV. *The Tonight Show* was on and the volume was down. If I'd found it difficult to be interested in a football game with no sound, this was even harder to deal with. I'm sure the jokes were funny, but I'll never know.

I called the bartender over. "You know what? I'm ready for something a bit more *toxic*," I said.

He got a contemplative look. "I think that's been taken care of," he said.

"What do you mean?" I asked.

"Well, the lady over there bought this for you."

"Which lady?" I asked, peering around the room.

"Her. The short-haired brunette in green at that table," he said, pointing.

I followed his finger. I was surprised by what I saw.

"Wow! She's gorgeous," I said. "What did she think I'd drink?"

"A scotch and soda," he replied.

"Damn! Gorgeous *and* perceptive. I like those qualities," I said. My lips drew up into a sly grin.

I stared in the mystery woman's direction. Just as I was about to get up and thank her for the drink, she rose and walked to me. I stood up from the bar and gestured to the table nearby. She nodded in concurrence and as she approached, I pulled her chair out and asked her to sit down. She sat and smiled. She was radiant.

"How did you know?" I asked, as I tapped the side of my glass.

"I dunno," she said. "Somehow, you just look like a scotch and soda man."

"I am. Thank you for the drink ..." I paused for her name.

"Catherine," she said.

I tipped my glass to her.

"It's wonderful to meet you, Catherine," I said. "My name is Louis." I tried not to make it obvious I was a bit buzzed—and even more infatuated.

Catherine smiled and sipped her martini.

"Catherine," I said with a lilt. "What a beautiful name."

"I don't know about that," she said. "It's a *common* name."

"Not to me it isn't. Have you ever read Hemingway?"

"No—and please don't think me ignorant, though—I have heard of him."

I was beaming. "He has two characters named Catherine," I explained. "One is in one of his earliest novels, the other in his last."

"Splendid! I'm famous in two novels!" she joked.

"And they're two of my favorites at that," I said.

Catherine smiled. She seemed intrigued. "Well, what are they like?" she asked. "Tell me about these two Catherines."

"They're both strong characters," I said. "One is a bit fragile yet unafraid, the other amorous but fiercely independent."

"Sounds a bit like me," she said, with a smile. "Perhaps I should read these books?"

I smiled and concurred with her suggestion.

Catherine looked at me. She took another sip of her drink and leaned closer. I felt like she was interrogating me. I didn't mind at all.

"Are you from around here?" she asked.

"No. I'm just here for a couple of days," I said. "I'm doing research for a book."

Catherine seemed surprised by this.

"Research? In *this* town?" she asked.

"Yeah. Why? Is that funny?" I wondered.

"Oh, no reason, really. It's just that not much happens here. I'm sorry if I offended you."

"No. You didn't. It's quite all right."

Catherine smiled. She seemed relieved.

"So what is your book about?" she asked. "Or is it *under wraps?*"

I laughed and took a sip of my scotch and soda. Catherine's face beamed as she watched me enjoy the drink she'd bought me.

"No, I can tell you something about it," I said. "It's a travelogue of sorts. I'm writing about sights, happenings, and unique things to do in the towns I'm visiting."

"That sounds fun," Catherine said.

"It is," I said. "And it's a funny story how it started too."

Catherine leaned across the table again. She looked interested. I wasn't sure if it was genuine or for show. I sipped my drink again and waited.

"Well, tell me more, Louis," she said. "Don't leave me hanging."

I smiled and nodded. "Okay, if you insist," I said. "Well, it all began with a wicked case of writer's block. I went for a drink to clear my head."

"Where were you then?" she asked.

"Sacramento, California. That's where this all came together. It's where I lost my place and where I met my traveling companion."

"Oh, you're here with someone?" Catherine asked.

"Yeah, I am," I said. "He's a feisty old geez who likes to be called Chief. He's hard drinking and loud-mouthed, but a hell of guy who knows a lot about a lot."

"Had you known him before?"

"Nope. I met him that night. He was about to get tossed from the bar."

"So in a way—you saved him?"

"Yeah. Sort of," I said. "He introduced himself and sponged drinks off me. That was our initial meeting." I laughed at my recollection. It was as clear as if it had just happened.

"He struck up a conversation, and we talked about what I did," I said. "I showed him what I'd been writing and he liked it. Things went from there."

Catherine smiled. "That sounds too delightful," she said. "What happened next?"

"More drinks—more talk," I said. "The Chief told me about when he was in Cuba. I was blown away."

"Wow! Cuba! That sounds like something!"

"It was. The way he talked about it and the things he did there. I felt like I was there too."

"How did you decide to travel together? It seems an odd thing to do."

"Well, after talking, I felt we had something to share. I asked him if he'd like to come with me."

Catherine mused. "Where were you going?" she asked.

"Actually, nowhere. Just home. Back to Georgia," I said. "Then I got the crazy idea to go and see other places."

"Did he think your request was strange?" Catherine asked. "You just met. I'd have been weirded out a bit. No offense."

I smiled and waved her off. "Maybe at first," I said. "I mean, traveling around with strange people can be dangerous, I suppose. It was probably weirder for me. It's not often I go about picking up old, drunk codgers and asking them to drive cross-country with me."

Catherine laughed. Her laugh was beautiful and wonderfully classic. I felt like I was in an old movie. We both took sips of our drinks. The moment became even more Hollywood.

"How did you decide to come here of all places?" she asked.

"That's another interesting aspect of this," I said. "We played a game to decide our destinations."

"Was it called *Dregs*?" Catherine asked. She laughed and quickly covered her mouth. "I'm sorry, Louis. That was terrible of me."

I thought nothing of her comment.

I looked into Catherine's hazel eyes and felt my buzz intensifying slightly. I sighed quietly like a crushing schoolboy. Something was happening here, and if it had been twelve hours ago, I would've walked away. However, now, I was willing to let myself fall a little. Just a couple more drinks with this woman and I'd call it a night. I was certainly enjoying her company, but I didn't want to push things too far.

The best way to describe how I felt was *sparkly*. Little imaginary chimes rang about, and I could sense flecks of glitter radiating from my body. Catherine was glowing. There was truly a light around her, and it seemed to brighten as the night went on.

We ordered more drinks and continued talking about my adventures up to this point. I was hoping to God I was not boring her. She seemed to enjoy me sharing my tales. Whenever I'd ask about her, she'd tell me she was "nothing spectacular" or she was "just a regular girl from Elkhorn." I found that quite hard to believe, but it was all she would reveal.

This was all too good. Part of me wondered if the Chief was going to stroll down here and insert himself into this little intimate meeting between strangers. I'd finally done something on my own, yet in the back of my mind, I knew the Chief would somehow give himself the credit for putting us together.

"What are you thinking about?" Catherine asked. "I've watched your face change like ten times. It's crazy."

"I'm not thinking about anything," I said. "Well, not anything but you and me and a couple more drinks."

Catherine blushed. "You have to let me finish this one first," she said.

"No problem," I said. I raised my glass and drank the rest of my scotch and soda. I waited for her to do the same.

I went to the bar and ordered another round of drinks. I was well on my way to being drunk, but Catherine seemed okay. I chalked my low tolerance to the day's events. I looked back at Catherine's beautiful, glowing face and smiled. *I like this dame*, I said to myself. *She's first class all the way*. Jesus. I sounded like the Chief.

The bartender brought our drinks, and I took them to the table. I slipped a bit getting into my chair but was careful not to spill anything.

"Are you okay?" Catherine asked.

I got up and sat in the chair next to her. "I'm better than okay," I said as I put my hands on her cheeks and leaned in to kiss her mouth.

My actions seemed forward and sudden, but Catherine did not resist. I could feel her tongue softly probing my lips, trying to gain access to my mouth. I let my lips part, and we kissed deeply, our mouths encircling each other's tightly, while our tongues twisted and touched, passionately exploring one another.

I pulled away slowly. Catherine's lips were still parted and her eyes still closed. I could smell the gin on her breath as she exhaled softly.

"I'm sorry," I whispered. "I'm not sure ... I'm ... um. We should probably say good night, you think?"

Catherine looked down at her drink. "But I've still got the rest of this martini to finish," she said, as she touched my lips with her finger.

I chuckled. "I still have my drink too," I said.

"Maybe we should finish our drinks and then see what happens?" she said.

I wanted to kiss her again. My inhibitions had dropped, and any reservations I'd had were gone. I could feel myself getting excited; however, I was still coherent enough to keep things honest—at least for now.

I took a big gulp of my drink. It was not the type of swig one takes of a scotch and soda, but at this moment, I wasn't sure of anything. All reasoning was fleeting, and I was running the gamut of emotions. I opened my eyes wide as if to gain clarity, but it did little. I don't even know what I was trying to see. Everything in front of me was real. Everything I'd done was real. There was nothing to bring into focus. There was nothing to clarify.

I stood up and wobbled a bit. I picked my glass up and finished the drink. I sucked the remaining ice chips up with the alcohol. I crunched the ice and looked at Catherine. She peered up at me and her eyes beamed. I had to sit down. She followed me as I slowly eased into my chair. I saw her head jolt. I'd imagined a graceful motion, but I had, in actuality, dropped quite severely onto the seat.

"Pardon me," I said with a sloshy voice. "That didn't hurt a bit. Just bruised my pride a little, that's all."

Catherine laughed at my comment. She put her hand on mine and stroked it softly. Just this simple touch was driving me crazy. I kept looking at her hand and watching it move.

"You're so beautiful," I said. I closed my eyes tight. I felt foolish for what I'd said and what I'd done. "I'm sorry, Catherine. I really am."

"I hope you're not apologizing for complimenting me?" she said as she touched her chest, feigning shock.

"Oh, heavens, no! Certainly not for that," I said. "Just for everything else. I'm so drunk—and dreadfully embarrassed."

"You're fine Louis. It's perfectly all right."

I stood up again. This time, I did not wobble nor did I drop like a stone back onto my chair.

"Oh, yeah," I said. "I've got this standing thing down now."

I patted myself down and pretended to dust off. I looked back at my drink. I was hoping I'd left one last sip in it. Fortunately for me, I'd drained it down to nothing but a sleek, wet, glossy film at the bottom of the glass.

"I think you've had enough," Catherine said, as she gathered our glasses and took them to the bar.

I watched her walk away from me. It was the first time I'd seen her back. The cut of her dress plunged sharply to a point just above her hips. I could see the soft definition of her muscles and bones. My gaze dropped below the point of her dress. I was trying to see what lie beyond this perimeter. The longer I stared, the guiltier and more perverted I felt.

Catherine turned around and came back toward me. She saw my face and looked at me curiously.

"What's the matter?" she asked.

"Nothing," I said. "I'm just tipsy, that's all. I really need to go to sleep."

"That's not a bad idea," she said. "Let me help you to your room, okay?"

I was slightly puzzled by her request to assist me, but I didn't give it a lot of thought.

We walked to the elevator together. I was out of sorts but not as bad as I seemed. I didn't really need Catherine's help, but it was nice being with her a little longer.

"Listen, I want to apologize again," I said. "I shouldn't have kissed you like that. It was a total boozer move."

"Stop that," she said. "I liked it. I like you. That's all that matters."

"You like me? We just met. That's crazy talk."

"You kissed me. We just met. That's crazy *action*. So there you go."

"I suppose you're right."

We got to my room, and I dug in my pocket for my key. I had trouble finding it, as my eyes and thoughts were focused on Catherine.

"It's in there somewhere," I said. Everything I'd grabbed was not the key.

"I'll bet it is," she said.

I pulled my key out and held it up. "See! There it is!" I said, sounding like I'd just won a prize. "I hope you have better luck with your key. By the way, what floor are you on?"

Catherine looked about quickly. "I'm downstairs," she said.

"Okay, well. I guess I'm going to bed," I said. "Thank you, Catherine, for a lovely night, and for being so awesome and understanding and well … everything."

"You're very welcome, Louis," she said. "I had a splendid time with you too. You're a great guy."

"Um, I don't know what you're doing, but would you like to join me for breakfast tomorrow? You can meet the Chief. Maybe we could spend the day together. You know? Something? I'm sorry. I'm rambling here."

Catherine smiled. She touched my face. "Breakfast sounds wonderful," she said. "Listen, I'm not sure how to say this, but … I'm so stupid … I think I left my key in my room. Can you believe that?"

I wasn't fazed. "That sounds like something *I'd* do," I said. "Do you want to come in and we can call the front desk?"

"That would be great," she said.

I opened the door and ushered Catherine in. As she walked by, I gently placed my hand atop her hips.

"I'm sorry," I said. "I don't know why I did that."

Catherine waved me off. "It's okay," she said. "I needed a push anyway."

"I'll call the desk," I said. "I'm sorry I don't have anything to drink except coffee."

"Oh, I'm fine," she said. "I don't need any more to drink at all."

Catherine sat on the edge of my bed. She looked around the room and made several inquisitive facial gestures. Some I could discern; others were cryptic.

"Blame my mom," I said out of the blue.

"For?" she asked.

"The lack of dude-ish clutter. I'm a bit of an obsessive-compulsive when it comes to structure and order."

"You better never come to my apartment then," Catherine said with a laugh.

"I could fix it up for you."

Catherine laughed out loud and quickly covered her mouth in embarrassment.

"Oh, no," she said. "It's way beyond hope."

I pulled the desk chair out and eased myself into it. I nodded at Catherine. *See, I can sit properly.* I grabbed the phone and prepared to call the desk.

"Wait," Catherine said. "Don't call them yet."

"Okay, why not?" I asked.

"Well, it's late and ... you know how ..."

I was confused. "Do you want to just go down to the desk?" I asked. "I'll go with you. I feel a little straighter now. I can walk again—sort of."

Catherine laughed. "No. I'm just ..." She seemed nervous. "It's just ..."

"Are you okay?" I asked.

"Yes, Louis, I'm quite all right," she said. She stood up, walked over to the desk, and sat on the edge. "I know we just met, and this is so way forward, but ... would you mind if I stayed here tonight? I'll sleep in the spare bed. I just don't want to cause any problems. I'm such a burden right now."

I shook my head. "You're not a burden to me," I said. "If you're worried about some weird-ass front desk etiquette thing with the key, I'm sure it'll be fine."

"Oh, I'm so stupid. So dreadfully stupid," she said.

"It's fine. Take the spare bed. We'll get up in a few hours and go eat. We'll get your key. It's all good."

Catherine smiled and blushed. "Thank you so much," she said. "I'll make this all up to you somehow. I really will."

"Think nothing of it," I said. "It's not the most orthodox ending for an evening, but it's not bad. Let's get some sleep, okay?"

"That sounds good to me. Thank you again, Louis. You're an absolute gentleman."

I scowled at Catherine and then laughed. "Careful with that word," I said. "I have a rep to maintain."

She got a mischievous look on her face. "I'll bet you do," she said. "You dirty Southern boy."

Catherine got up and went into the bathroom. While she was gone, I pulled down the covers on the spare bed for her.

"Louis, may I use this robe here to sleep in?" she asked through the door.

"You may," I said. "Do you need anything else?"

"I'm perfectly fine for now," Catherine said. "I can't thank you enough for this."

She came out of the bathroom and hung her dress in the closet. She walked to the spare bed and pulled herself in and covered up.

"Lights out. You ready?" I asked.

"I am," she said. "Good night, Louis."

"Good night, Catherine," I said as I shut the lights off and climbed into bed.

I heard Catherine shuffle a little. She moaned quietly and sighed. She was quiet after that.

I rolled over and felt myself dozing. My buzz had increased. I was happy to finally be getting back to sleep.

* * * * *

My body felt oddly warm and heavy. I shifted but could not move completely. I was still in a sleep state but slowly waking up. My brain was floating amid the small lake that the earlier evening's drinking had created. The room did not spin entirely but tilted and wobbled a bit, only to return to its original point on its axis. I was in the throes of a fading bender that would not relent; however, there was more. There were other events taking place, and these were real. *What was going on?*

I began to feel soft, warm, and wet gentle suctioning on my forehead. It was sporadic in frequency and pressure. These strange sensations were accompanied by quick, hot bursts of air and clicking sounds. I rolled my eyeballs behind their sealed lids. I tried to see into my subconscious. I was obviously dreaming, but I could see nothing—I could only feel and hear the oddities occurring about my forehead—and now moving down my face.

I tried to roll over. When I did, my body turned and fell softly upon something. I touched the obstacle. It was warm, of varied shape had very little texture. I opened my eyes.

"Hello sleepyhead. I've been trying to wake you up for the last twenty minutes," a whispering feminine voice said.

It was Catherine. She was in my bed. She was in my bed and kissing me short and fast and erotically. I was aware of this, but I was confused as to why it was happening. I moved my hands. They were on Catherine's body. She was naked and wrapped around me.

"What's going on?" I asked. "Is everything okay?" My words sounded stupid and naïve, but at this moment, *I* was stupid and naïve.

"I want to make love," Catherine said between kisses. "I want you so bad. I want you to make love to me."

"What?" I said. I wasn't resisting, but I was groggy and not sure if I was hearing her correctly.

"Let's make love," she said. "I'm so hot. I want to fuck."

I was still feeling the effects of the drinks. This was not going to happen.

"Catherine, I …" I paused. "I can't. This is not good."

"No, it is," she pleaded. "It is—and you can. Come on. Fuck me."

"I can't get it up," I said. I felt like I was about to cry. I was being thrown in every direction emotionally. I was still riding a waning buzz. To quote the Chief, I "didn't know if it was drilled or punched" at this moment.

"I … we just met," I said. I sounded like an idiot. "What about—"

"Oh my God, Louis," Catherine said. Her voice sounded both angry and desperate. "I want your cock inside me. How else do you want me to say it? *Make fucking love to me!*"

I tried to sit up. Clarity had set in. I could feel myself getting hard. I looked at Catherine, and I began to realize this was real. This *was* happening. My body surged inside, and I was overcome with desire. I suddenly wanted to make love to Catherine. But I was still spinning.

"I don't have a condom," I said. "I don't want to be one of those guys, but—"

Catherine cut me off. "I have some in my purse," she said. "I'll get one for you. I'll help you put it on."

She got out of bed, and I watched her naked body move between the tight beams of light cutting through the curtains in my room. I took my shirt off as she dug through her purse.

"You can leave that on," she said. "That's not the important part."

I pushed the covers down. I lifted myself up and slid my pants down my legs. My underwear, jeans, and socks ended up balled and twisted amid the sheets at the foot of my bed. I looked down at my body in the dark. My sex was standing timidly—like a skinned prairie dog frightened from its home by an unknown noise in the dark.

Catherine came back to the bed and sat down next to me. She began kissing me again. Every touch of her lips to my skin was like a tiny, sensual shock. I flinched as her mouth and tongue dotted my neck and chest. Suddenly I felt her hand on my cock. She began slowly stroking me, and it felt incredible. Her palms were so smooth, and her grip was perfect. I don't think I could have masturbated with such prowess, and this was *my* junk.

Catherine kissed my nipples, and I couldn't hold still. "Oh my God … you can't …" I rambled. I tried to make a complete sentence, but it was impossible.

She stopped stroking me. I closed my eyes and heard her open the condom. She pulled the latex sheath over the head of my penis and slowly rolled it to the base.

I opened my eyes, and Catherine moved her leg over my waist and brought her body down onto mine. She took me into her hand again and raised herself up. She guided me to her and slowly lowered her thighs down onto mine. I felt myself penetrating her, and I was in confusion again.

I felt like a stupid teenager. I didn't know what to do. I'd had sex before, but at this moment, I was the world's worst kind of virgin. I had no idea what I was doing, who I was, who I was with, or why we were here.

Catherine leaned toward me, and suddenly I remembered how to do this. We locked our fingers together as she slowly moved her hips atop mine. I pushed up into her as she shifted back and forth. I tried to sit up straight and kiss her breasts, but she continued to arch back. She squeezed my hands as our hips waved rhythmically. She came down further and softly fell onto me.

We kissed and released our hands from each other. I needed to touch her. I wanted to feel every part of her body. I moved my hands all over her smooth flesh—seeking, learning, and discovering. I pushed down to her ass and held her tight to me. I didn't want her to move. She kissed my neck, and I pushed myself harder into her.

"That's it," she whispered. "Come for me."

I thrust a couple more times as she kissed my neck again, her lips pulling hard to my flesh.

"Come for me," she whispered again. "You're so close. You're so close."

My face grimaced, and I lost control of my body. My hips thrust hard and held close to Catherine's as I ejaculated. I kept pushing. It felt like my orgasm wasn't going to stop. My lower body had dropped back onto the bed, but it seemed to still be suspended—trying to give that last morsel of my sex to Catherine.

"See? I told you!" she said. "That was pretty intense. How do you feel?"

I couldn't say anything. I just nodded. Even without words, Catherine *knew* how I felt. She and I had just made love and it was incredible. Even with a condom, it was beyond amazing. If this was how she was repaying me for letting her stay the night, it was well worth it—if not astronomically overdoing it. *Now I owed her!*

Catherine slowly rolled off me, and I went to the bathroom to clean myself up.

"Sex is a great thing," I mumbled. "But it's too damn messy."

I came back to bed, and Catherine wrapped her legs around mine. I pulled the covers over us. I stroked her shoulders as she nestled her head to my chest. We lay quiet for several minutes, just gently kissing and touching. It seemed cliché and overly romantic, but I loved it.

"This was very, very nice," I said.

I could feel Catherine's cheeks plump against my shoulder as she smiled. Calling this *nice* sounded so tacky, but I didn't know what to say. I was—as they say in the Newport Cigarette ads: "alive with pleasure," but I didn't know what else I was feeling beyond that.

Was this supposed to be? I needed this, but was making love to Catherine a betrayal? Or was I finally over my clinging feelings? I couldn't believe I was even remotely thinking about someone else. My body was pressed to another's; we'd just passionately made love, and yet I was pining? I began to feel sick to my stomach.

"Are you okay?" Catherine asked. "You're awfully quiet for a man who's just had sex."

I chuckled. It sounded nervous. "I'm all right. Why wouldn't I be?" I asked. "Like you said: we just had sex. Maybe I'm one of those *'go to sleep'* guys?"

"No, you're not," she said. "If you were, you'd already be asleep."

"That's true, I suppose."

Catherine kissed my neck softly, and I flinched.

"Well, *I'm* ready to go to sleep," she said. "I'm still a little wavy from those martinis, not to mention—you wore me out!"

I smiled. My face warmed as I blushed. Catherine felt it.

"Did I just make you happy?" she asked, in a baby-talk voice as she wiggled her body against mine.

"Too many more times than I can count," I said. "I'm glad you forgot your key."

Catherine said nothing. She took a breath and kissed my cheek. Her head moved slightly, and I could feel her body ease. She was falling asleep. It was time for me to do the same.

* * * * *

I woke up slowly. It seemed the thing to do considering my uncertain situation. For a split second, I was confused, still not sure of anything that had taken place just mere hours before. When I tried to turn, I realized that there was indeed someone else in my bed. My head was clear, and I was not hung over. I turned my head and saw Catherine's face: eyes open and looking quite lovely for someone who'd just woken up.

"I must look atrocious," she said. Her voice sounded so Hollywood cliché.

I chuckled. I tried not to breathe in her face. "No, you look fantastic," I said. "It's my breath that's 'atrocious.'"

Catherine breathed into her hand. "Mine smells like gin," she said. "It's like an alcoholic breath mint."

I touched her arm and gently stroked her skin. "I don't want to get up," I said. "Can we just stay here all day? This is wonderful."

Catherine's demeanor changed suddenly. She tensed and slid up in bed. It was the abrupt motions of someone in trouble and needing a quick getaway.

I pulled up as well and looked at her. "Are you okay?" I asked. "Did I say something wrong?"

"Um, no, nothing's wrong," she said. "It's just time for me to go."

Suddenly, my heart sank. I'd been here before and heard this story. Once again, I was being abandoned, but this time, the circumstances were quite different.

"Where are you going?" I asked, sounding desperate. "What about …? What about breakfast and all that stuff? Don't you remember? You can't go."

I could feel myself becoming clingy and needy. I didn't want that; however, it was hard to fight such tendencies considering what had occurred between us.

Catherine got out of bed, and I watched her walk to the bathroom. She moved like nothing had happened: insouciant and nonchalant.

I heard the shower start. She was singing slightly off key as the water splashed and sprayed at varied intervals. I sat in the bed and listened to her. I tried to place the song as I wrestled with my feelings of being stupefied and vulnerable. *What the hell was she singing? What the hell was happening?*

I got out of bed and made some coffee. I didn't know what else to do. I looked at the clock, and it was just after 6:00 a.m.

"I hope you're making a cup for me." I heard Catherine say from the shower.

"Of course I am?" I said. My words sounded more interrogative than assured.

Catherine came out of the bathroom with a towel wrapped around her body and one twisted atop her head. She smiled when she saw the two coffee cups on the dresser and went about getting dressed.

"You're beautiful," I said. "I know you just got out of the shower, but I would so like to make love to you again."

She laughed, but it was more of a chortle. This made me feel like an absolute heel.

"What's the matter?" I asked. "It seems I keep fucking up this morning."

Catherine waved me off. "No, no. It's nothing like that," she said. "I've just got to go. That's all."

"Do you have to go to work or something? Do you have a plane to catch?"

"Well, yeah, kinda—yes and no."

"What does that mean?"

Catherine finished dressing and walked to me. I was still naked and looked worse for wear. She poured the coffee for us and took her cup. She placed it on the floor by the bed and sat down to put her stockings and shoes on.

"Listen, I don't know how to tell you this, but …" she paused. She tightened the straps on her shoes and stood up. She reached under her dress and pulled at the tops of her stockings. She made a couple of strange faces.

"Okay. That's good," she said capriciously.

I sipped my coffee. "But what …?" I asked, waiting for her to finish her statement.

"But …? Oh, yeah—*that!*" she said. "Well, I wasn't supposed to say anything, but your friend, the Chief—he paid me five hundred dollars to spend the night with you."

I jolted and in a move straight from a bad comedy—spit out my coffee.

"What the hell?" I asked. "Did you just say …?"

"I'm afraid so," Catherine said without hesitation. "You're not angry, are you? I hope you're not."

"No. I'm just …" I paused and shook my head. "Really? The Chief? He paid you?"

"Yes."

"Five hundred? Five times one hundred?"

"Yes."

"Dollars? The Chief? He gave you *money?"*

"He did. Please don't be upset with him. He said he wanted to give you a gift. Is it your birthday or something?"

I shook my head again, trying to piece this together.

"Yeah …" I paused. "In March."

"Well, happy belated/early birthday, Louis," Catherine said as she threw her arms out in mock surprise. "No. He really paid me to sleep with you. You seem quite upset."

"I am. But not at you or the fact we …" I said, trying to gather my thoughts. "Where'd he get the money?"

"I don't know," Catherine said, "but he paid me in cash."

I paced the room. "He never has any freakin' money," I said. "That son of a bitch never has *any* goddamn money—*never!"*

"I don't know about that," Catherine said. "He just called my service and I came here, he talked terms and paid me. You can figure out the rest."

"I can. I totally can," I said.

The romantic feelings I'd had toward Catherine had vanished. I was still quite enamored with her and still reeling from our lovemaking, but the love I thought I felt between us was gone. For as incredible as she'd made me feel, I was nothing more than a business transaction.

I wanted to be mad, but I couldn't. I'd just gotten laid. I'd just woken up next to a beautiful woman. These were not the basis for anger and resentment—at least not toward Catherine and maybe not toward the Chief either.

"What was I gonna say?" I asked. "Um. No … It's fine. It's all good."

"Are you sure?" Catherine asked. "It was a lovely time, and I just don't want you to be angry. It's not supposed to be a maddening experience."

"I'm sorry," I said. "I'm just … I don't know." I crinkled my face and looked at Catherine. "So you're a *career girl*?" I asked, trying not to sound crass.

She laughed. "Yeah, I guess that's one way of putting it," she said. "It's a decent living. The pay is—*well*. And I like the sound of that term: 'career girl.' It's a lot better than some of the other things I've been called."

I apologized and thanked her again for the wonderful time. She was gathering her things to leave, but part of me didn't want her to go. However, I knew I'd have to cut my personal ties right here.

Catherine looked around to make sure she was leaving with everything she'd arrived with. The only extra trinket she was taking was a little piece of me. I'm sure she had a file box full of such pieces from many different men.

I walked her to the door. We stood like a couple of high-schoolers after an awkward first date.

"This sounds terrible," I said, "But I hope I was worth the price."

She smiled and said, "Honey, that's supposed to be my line."

"I just have to know, What was that song you were singing?" I asked. "It sounded very familiar."

"'The Lady Is a Tramp.' It's Frank Sinatra," Catherine said. "Kinda ironic and appropriate, wouldn't you say?"

"I guess so," I said. "I thought I'd recognized it."

Catherine blushed. "Sorry, my singing sucks," she said. "But it was part of the deal."

I furrowed my brow. "How so?" I asked.

"The Chief wanted me to sing a Sinatra song," she said. "He told me once you'd heard it, you'd know 'the skinny.'"

"I'm a little slow today, I suppose," I said. "Well, it makes sense now."

Catherine kissed me quick, opened the door, and left. I did not watch her walk away. Once she left my room, we were no longer each other's concern. I was Louis DeCarlo: writer, errant traveler, and drunk, while she was off to become someone else's fantasy for hire.

I stood alone and naked in my room. I looked at the bed. I mindlessly moved to the dresser and finished the rest of my coffee. It was tepid, and I'd spit in it, but I couldn't let it go to waste.

For a moment, my mind was blank. My reality at this juncture was surreal at best. I closed my eyes tightly. I thought that by squeezing them hard and wrinkling my nose, I could see something that made sense. All it did was make my face hurt. I opened my eyes and took a few deep, cleansing breaths. I held the last one. When I exhaled, I finally had my period of clarity.

"*Fuck!*" I yelled in a whisper.

I pulled my clothes out from under the bed covers, and I jumped in the shower and cleaned up.

I got dressed and headed to the stairs. I was in a hurry. The elevator wasn't fast enough. I ran down the stairs and came into the lobby like a raving boozer. I must've looked like a man possessed, and in a way, I was.

I slid around and went into the restaurant to find the Chief. It was after 7:00 a.m., and I figured he'd still be having breakfast, or at least waiting for me to join him. I peered around the room, and there he was: caught halfway between a copy of *USA Today* and the remainder of a poached egg. I began to seethe.

I didn't know what I was going to do. I was incensed and shaking. I can't remember ever being this angry with anyone. I shot darts at the old bastard, but he never looked my way. His attention never wavered from his paper and his egg. I was wasting my anger.

I took a breath. I wanted to blow up at the old man, but I couldn't. No. I was okay! How could I not be? I reiterated to myself that I'd just had sex with an amazing woman—even though she was a high-dollar call girl. I started to realize that what the Chief did wasn't *that* bad. He'd told Catherine he wanted to give me a "gift." It sounded sincere.

I managed to pull a quarter smile from the corner of my mouth. I looked at the Chief again. This time, he saw me and waved me to his table.

I walked in his direction, and the closer I got, I could feel my ire rising again.

"Chill, man," I said, under my breath. "It's all good. Everything is fine."

I sat down across the Chief. His eyes darted from side to side, and he leaned forward.

"So, Louie, what do you hear from the boys overseas?" he asked.

"Nothing," I said. "However, I have heard a bit from *the girls on the street*. You know anything about them?"

The Chief got a perplexed look. "Girls? On the street?" he asked. "Can't say they ring a bell."

I gave the Chief a beckoning wave with my finger as I moved closer to him. "Yes, Chief, *girls on the street*," I said. "Ladies of the night. Those kinds of girls. Anything yet?"

The old man played dumb. "Nope, kid," he said. "You gotta clue me in."

I sat back quickly. "You're kidding, right?" I asked. "Does the sum of five hundred dollars jog your memory? That's a big bill to forget paying."

The Chief nodded and let out with a belly laugh. The whole restaurant turned and looked to see what was so funny.

"Oh, *those girls*," he said slyly. "Or *one of those girls* in particular."

I tapped my finger to my nose. "Okay. Talk," I said.

The Chief looked aghast. "You seem disappointed," he said. "I figured you'd come down here grinning from ear to ear, like a jackass eating stickers."

"Um, no. Not really," I said. "It was a bit overwhelming."

"Was she not high class enough?"

"Well. Yes. She was indeed 'high class.' She was incredible. Perfect. Everything I like in a woman ..."

The Chief cut me off. "So what's the damn problem then?" he asked.

"Chief. You bought me a hooker. A five-hundred-dollar hooker," I said. "Why?"

"Why not? I told you I wanted to repay you for yesterday. And she was not a 'hooker.' She was an *escort*. There's a *big* difference."

"Hooker. Escort. It's semantics. Regardless of her working title, it was excessive all around, wouldn't you say?"

The Chief thought for a second. "No. Not at all. It was a mere pittance," he said. "And actually, it was a twofold gesture."

"How so?"

"You helped me out, and since you were falling back on your assignment, I figured I'd help *you*."

"Did you think I couldn't find someone on my own? That I couldn't put the effort in?"

"You haven't been lately. Obviously, you put *some* effort in last night, though."

"I did ... It was ..." I paused and put my hands up. "You know what? I'm not gonna tell you what I did or how it was," I said. "That's between me and Catherine."

"Did you like that?" the Chief asked. "I picked a gal with a name right out of your Hemingway books."

I twitched in disbelief. "What the ...?" I asked. "Even her name was ...?"

"Yep, Louie. I bought you a girl that fulfilled your every desire," he said. "Her size, shape, skin, hair, name—I know what you like.

Hell, she even drank gin martinis. Most dames do vodka, but not this one. I know you like gin martinis too. I didn't forget Butch's.

"You've been learning things about me on this trip, but I've been learning a lot about you, too. Last evening was just another lesson—call it a one-night 'study a broad' program."

I shook my head and chuckled.

Although my earlier rage was still simmering, it had begun to subside. However, there was still one big concern that needed to be addressed. The old man was not free of my wrath just yet.

"Chief, I'll say *thank you* a thousand times for this, even though it did piss me off," I said. "But I have to know, how the fuck did you pay for her? Where'd this money come from?"

The Chief sat back. He looked as if he were on trial. His forthcoming testimony, either damning or redeeming, hinged on how I took what he said.

"First off, son, I have confidence in you," he said. "I know you can find someone—you just weren't. I'm hoping this puts the spark back in your heart a little."

"Fair enough. But we've covered that," I said. "What about this windfall of cash?"

The Chief took a quick breath and looked at the ceiling.

"I have not been completely honest about my … how should I put this?" The Chief paused to think. "Um … my … well … my finances."

"Really?" I asked. "And how *not completely honest* have you been?"

"Completely *dishonest*."

"The whole time?"

The Chief hung his head. "Even before you came along," he said. "I stiffed the fuck out of ol' Churchill. I played like a pauper for drinks. He kept me drunk, and I kept his patrons company. What I owe him—it's more than ten Catherines."

"You're kidding, right?" I asked. "You've been playing everyone? Why?"

"Kid, I don't have anything," the Chief said. "I've got no home, my family is God-knows-where, I've lost more than I've ever had, but I *do* have money—a lot of it."

I was floored. I didn't know what to say. I felt used and when I thought of everyone else the Chief, who—for lack of a better term, *scalped*—the feeling increased tenfold. However, for as upset as I was, I wasn't *angry*. I hated being duped, but I think I understood the old man's motives. I shook my head slowly and stared. I wanted to make him sweat things out for a minute or two.

"Louie? Are you gonna say anything?" he asked. "Come on, let me have it. Lower the boom on the ol' Super Chief. God knows I deserve it."

Referring to himself as the ol' Super Chief again made me smile a little. It was his moniker of sincerity, and something he only said in abject desperation. In Evansville, when his new hometown drinking buddies had to leave him, he'd used the nickname. It was the first time I'd heard it, but I'd also heard the tone in his voice when he said it. It was the tone of a broken man—a man who just wanted a second chance and was afraid he'd never get it.

I glared at him and still said nothing. In my heart, I'd already forgiven him. Why shouldn't I? So I found out the guy has a bunch of money stashed somewhere. That was not a deal breaker, nor was it something that made me hate him. It was certainly not the type of thing that would make me up and leave, abandoning him in a hotel in Nebraska. No, the only thing that really changed was the fact the Chief would be picking up the tab a hell of a lot more.

"Okay, Louie. I can take a hint," he said. "I've done you wrong, kid, and all I can do is tell you how sorry I am." He stood up and bowed his head.

"I'm ashamed of what I've done," he said. "And I'm especially ashamed of being a goddamn liar all this time. I hate liars. They're the worst kind of people."

I looked up at the Chief. His face was awash in guilt, shame, and remorse. He was—at this moment—the most honest I've seen him since we met. Through all the stories I've heard and all the shifts

I've watched him go through, this was purely and simply the look of a man who needed someone to believe in him. And I did.

"Sit down, Chief," I said, as I pointed to his chair. "You've got some more explaining to do, but you *are* forgiven."

He looked around the restaurant. "Am I dreaming?" he asked. "You're not pissed at me?"

"No, I *am* pissed at you—just not that much. It's only money for Christ's sake, but there's ..." I paused. I had to collect my thoughts. "Let's just say we've got some things to iron out later."

The Chief sat down and took a deep breath. "Thank you, Louie," he said as he took my hand. "Thank you so much for this."

"You're welcome," I said. "But from now on, just be straight— about everything, okay?"

"You bet, kid. *Honest Injun.*"

I got up from the table. The Chief got a worried expression on his face.

"Where are you going?" he asked. "I thought you said we're good?"

"We are—but my stomach isn't. I'm hungry," I said. "Spending the night with a five-hundred-dollar prostitute really works up your appetite."

The people at the adjacent tables stopped eating and stared at me in shock.

"She was not a prostitute," the Chief shouted. "She was *an escort!*"

* * * * *

I spent the rest of the morning and a good portion of the after-noon in my room. I wanted to work, but as usual, things were not going according to plan. I stared at my notebook. I sifted through what I'd already written, and although it was okay, it wasn't close to what I'd envisioned.

This trip had indeed been topsy-turvy at times—last night and this morning being high in that bracket. But even the question-able events have been treasured. All the promised adventures had been delivered, and there were definitely more to come. I had some great, almost unbelievable images and words to share with the world. Unfortunately, they were still stuck in my head and I could not get them out.

I found my Crater Lake story. I set it on the desk and got up to make a cup of coffee. The story had been sitting for a week. Once my coffee finished brewing, I let it sit and cool slightly—an extra ten minutes. The Crater Lake story had now sat for a week and ten minutes. This was surely enough time to shake off those first draft animosities.

I picked up the story and read it again. It still sucked. It was still as bad as I remembered it. It still sounded like it had been written by a liar—"the worst kind of people."

I wanted to crumple the story up and pitch it, but I did not. I hated it, but my publisher might find it print-worthy; it seemed someone always did. I had entertained the thought of reading it once more but decided to leave it alone and placed the papers into a folder. I would not read them, but I would fax them as promised. I finished my coffee and walked down to the lobby to electronically send my hated words across state lines.

I detested the sound of the fax machine. It was grating and archaic. With all the improvements in technology over the years, no one had managed to give the fax machine a more soothing or advanced-sounding voice. It railed like a victim in a low-budget horror flick—screaming while being disemboweled. The only sound worse was that of dial-up Internet, which this hotel still used.

As I watched the sheets of paper go in to the fax machine and come back out, I wondered if the text improved as it transferred from one machine to another. Would the words my publisher be receiving at this time be better than the ones I'd written?

I collected my work and replaced the papers into the folder. I was happy that I'd gotten them sent but was still lamenting the product. As I went back to my room, I began to think about the writings I'd pieced together in Evansville. That stuff was okay. It was a start, if nothing else. The fragments became cohesive once I'd arranged them. Maybe that's how I'd need to work? Put down whatever flows.

I sat down at the desk again, and instead of piecing together bits for *work* work, I began thinking of where the Chief and I would venture to next. It was still early in the day, and we were leaving in the morning. There was still time to get out and see some more of the Elkhorn/Omaha Area before we bailed.

I grabbed the little city guide from the dresser. In it was the perfect place for the Chief and I to go. How neither of us saw it, I'll never know.

I went across the hall to see the old man. I knocked on his door and could hear him shuffling about in his room.

"Who dat?" he asked.

"Dat me," I said. "It's Louis. Your neighbor and traveling companion."

"Louie? Damn it, why didn't you say so?"

"I did. And I've got plans for the day. Open up."

"I've got the TV on. It's hard to hear."

I closed my eyes and dropped my head into the door. "Why the hell do you do this to me?" I asked. "It's me. You know it's me. Open the damn door."

I heard the Chief grab the door handle, and I stepped back.

"Come on in, Louie," he said. "Just getting things around for tomorrow."

"Leave that for later," I said. "We're going out. I found a place you'll love."

"Really? Is it that grand?"

"Grand? It's better than that. It's big—as in band."

The Chief gave me an intrigued look. "Well, where are we going?" he asked.

"I'm taking you to listen to Count Basie," I said. "We're going to a classic jazz joint."

"Basie, eh?" the Chief said. "He did some messin' with Sinatra, you know."

"I do. And that's why we're gonna' go jump, jive, and wail," I said. "Well, maybe just sit, listen, and drink. You get the idea."

We went down to the lobby and I stopped at the desk for some additional information about where we were going.

"I've got a question about a place called Love's," I said. "What can you tell me about it?"

The clerk studied me and then peered at the Chief. "Well, it's not in the best part of town," he said. "There's a lot of hipsters there too."

"'Hipsters, eh? What kind of hipsters?" I asked.

"Jazz types. You know the ones. They just sit around and talk about all their records and the off-beat places they got 'em."

"Okay. How's the music?"

"Do you like jazz?"

"Not really. It's kinda meh."

I contemplated the clerk's assessment of Love's. I decided I didn't care about the crowd or the music; we were going.

"Thanks for the info," I said to the clerk.

"You're welcome," he said. "Have fun and be careful."

"I'm just worried about the hipsters."

The clerk laughed. "It's a concern," he said. He handed me a map of the city from behind the desk.

I flashed the map and nodded in thanks. I called the Chief over, and we left to go find Love's and maybe another part of the old man's past.

* * * * *

We drove into North Omaha. The clerk wasn't kidding. I should've done some research on this area of town. It was pretty rough-and-tumble. The Chief and I were definitely outsiders.

The Chief looked around. He studied building façades and murals painted on walls. There was blight but glimmers of hope as well.

I didn't know what to say. My closest connection to impoverished areas was what I saw on the news. That makes me one with the struggle. *Right.*

We arrived at Love's, and it was a diamond in the rough. Again, the desk clerk at the hotel was spot on. The establishment's main clientele were skinny, bowling-shirt-wearing, bearded, bespectacled hipsters. The race demographic was 98 percent Caucasian and wearing hats.

I gave a donation at the door as we came in.

I spied a poster for the events. Today was our lucky day: "Count Your Blessings—The Best of Basie. Impressions of a Master and His Work." The Chief was going to hear some Count Basie.

We found a table and sat. Aside from being Caucasians, we looked nothing like the rest of the crowd.

A waiter came to take our orders. We ordered two Budweiser's apiece and waited for the music to begin.

The Chief scanned the room. "Nice place," he said. "Cozy and cool."

"Is that good?" I asked.

"It's good for me. I hope the music fits the atmosphere."

"I'm sure it'll be fine. It's Count Basie stuff—you like his work, right?"

The Chief sipped his beer. "This place is named for Preston Love," he said. "He played in Basie's Orchestra. He was a local boy."

I nodded. "That's impressive, Chief," I said. "How'd you know that?"

"I saw something on the way in," he said. "However, I did know who Mr. Love was before that."

The band took the stage. There were six guys, and three of them looked like they were straight out of the audience. The trumpeter, the drummer, and one of the trombone players were black and seemed less than enthusiastic about jamming with the other dudes. The Chief and I had shared their expressions.

"They look competent for the most part," I said.

The Chief took a swig of his beer and said nothing.

The band's pianist leaned into his microphone.

"Good evening, everyone," he said. "We're the Big Band Boomers from Kansas City. It's great to be here at Love's!"

The crowd clapped and whistled. One man in the back yelled out an obligatory but oddly timed "Kay-See!" for good measure. I shook my head.

"All right, then," the pianist said. "We've got a smokin' set for you. Who's ready to get swingin'?"

The crowd clapped and whooped it up again and the band started playing. The first few bars were decent. The guys had a good energy, and it translated well with the audience. Any concerns about cohesiveness between the players began to melt away as well.

Jazz was not my type of music, but this was a decent feel. I found myself enjoying the groove and moving to the tones. A few people got up and danced. It was a tight fit but just enough room to shuffle and spin. The Chief watched the scene. He was stoic and unimpressed.

The band finished up the first couple of songs. The pianist and the bassist switched spots, while the trumpet player placed a muting cup onto his instrument. Another saxophone player joined the band.

"That's how Basie did it," the Chief said. "He had two tenor saxes in the band."

The band started playing again. The new man on piano laid a vocal down. The Chief caught a groove, and it was a sight to see. He started singing along with the band.

The pianist belted out, "Nice work if you can get it—and you can get if you try!"

"That's 'Ol' Blue Eyes,' Louie!" the Chief exclaimed.

I smiled and got into the song as well. If this was what I'd be listening to tonight, I was fine with it.

I'd come here closed-minded and expecting a band playing something akin to the sounds of the fax machine: mindless, random, and excruciatingly painful to endure. This was vibrant, joyful, and classy. It made me realize I needed to take a second look—or listen to things sometimes.

The Chief and I stayed for three of the band's sets. He was not ready to leave, but it was late and we had an early day tomorrow.

We left Love's and walked to the car.

"Louie, that was some time," the Chief said. "Those guys were cream of the crop."

"I'm glad you liked it," I said.

"What did you think?" he asked. "You weren't too enthused at first, were you?"

"Not really," I said. "But you were shaky to start too."

"Nah! Not me. I knew those boys could play."

"Really? You being straight?"

"Well, *natch*! I was just checking out the scene. Had to see some credentials."

* * * * *

The Chief looked around as we drove.

"It's funny to think about, you know?" the Chief said. "The music we heard tonight was so upbeat and symbolic of happier times, but the people who made it had to endure *this*.

"They made the best of what life threw at them and became revered and loved. And even through all of the praise and glory, they still struggled to be accepted as equals. They had to fight for everything they had. In the end, places like this is where a lot of them ended up. They're *still* fighting."

I'd never heard the Chief talk about civil rights issues. It was humbling to hear his stance, and it made me think about things I'd said and done. Again, I was speechless.

The Chief looked at me as if he was awaiting a response. "Those boys didn't play 'Honeysuckle Rose,'" he said. "Did you know that? And it's one of my favorites."

Of all the things he could have said after his brief but impactful social commentary, the fact the band didn't play a particular song was what stuck in his craw?

"I didn't notice it," I said. "Then again, I didn't know any of the songs they played."

"I know you didn't," he said. "But you put on a good front. Stick with me and I'll learn ya all the things that made the good old days great."

"My grandparents said the good old days didn't always live up to their name," I noted.

"Well, they were tough times, Louie," the Chief said. "You had a Great Depression followed by a World War—a *second* one at that. However, for as bad as shit got, it brought the country together and brought out the best in everyone."

I nodded in agreement. I had to. Listening to the Chief was like listening to a great motivator. Despite the things he'd done that drove me nuts—*and to drink*—he'd always countered a bad situation with something profound and outstanding.

We got back to the hotel, and I joined the Chief for a night cap. We sat and enjoyed our drinks. It had been another good day for us. We spent the rest of the night talking about music. The Chief did most of the talking. I knew very little about "his thing," but the more he told me, the more I wanted to be a part of it. Hearing about the old favorites made me feel good. I knew talking about them made the Chief feel young.

Everywhere we'd been so far provided an experience, but of all the places we'd stopped, Elkhorn had proved to be—at least for me—the most enlightening. Some things I'd learned opened my eyes a little wider than others, for sure. I was hoping our next destination would continue the trend we'd seem to be setting. I was ready for tomorrow. I just didn't know where we were heading.

"Louie, where to next?" the Chief asked.

"Not a clue," I said. "Do you have any ideas?"

"Nope. I just know we're heading southeast and to a place that begins with *E.*"

I nodded. That was about all I knew as well.

* * * * *

I woke up a few minutes before my alarm went off. I hated when this happened. Three or four extra minutes were so precious in the wee hours of the morning. I stared at the glowing digits and closed my eyes again. The blue numbers 4, 2, and 6 burned into my retinas and spun in circles until they disappeared.

I had done well last night with drinking. I'd promised myself I would behave and I kept my pledge. My issue was not with the previous night but the current morning. I dreaded these early hours. They weren't getting easier to tolerate.

The Chief told me I'd never make it in the military because I was not an early bird. I don't know. I guess if I have to get up because some drill instructor is yelling at me and throwing a trashcan into a wall, then I suppose I'd adjust. Why was I thinking about this? Oh, yeah—because it was 4:30 a.m., and I should still have been asleep.

I showered and felt a little better but no more alive. I gathered the things I'd unpacked and crammed them into my bag. I didn't care today. For some reason, I was not in harmony with this morning. I was hoping my mood would improve once we got on the road.

Geez, what's wrong? I asked myself. I replayed the events of the last couple days in my head: trains, jazz, and a hooker. Those were the highlights of my trip to Elkhorn. Nothing *too* out of the ordinary, right?

I heard the Chief knocking on my door. *And there's my trash can,* I thought. I opened the door and let him in.

"Morning, Louie," he said. "You ready to hit the old trail?"

"I suppose," I said. "We've got to go sometime, eh?"

"You okay, kid? You seem a little off."

"I'm fine. I'm just a bit tired, I guess."

"I understand. It's been a big trip. Lots of things going on. We're halfway through it all. Just think about that."

And that's what it was! Being halfway through this trip, I'd thought about it in passing, but to hear the Chief say it made it concrete. This was life imitating art: the dramatic structure at work. Elkhorn was the climax in our journey. Everything that occurred from this point on was falling action, leading to the end. This was what was bothering me.

I wasn't ready to be on the downside and for things to begin waning. I wasn't ready for the conclusion; unfortunately, it was inevitable. I didn't say anything to the Chief about how I felt; however, he was on to something. I figured I'd let him guess. And considering what had happened while we were here, I wisely left the word *climax* out of the conversation. I'd use *apex* instead.

We went to the front desk so I could pay for the rooms. The clerk told me they'd been taken care of. I smiled at the old man, and he gave me a strange look. I wasn't sure what to make of it. The Chief picking up the tab was something I should embrace, but it bothered me. So far, I'd been paying for everything. I'd wanted a little help; however, now that I knew the Chief had money, it made me upset. It made me feel that we were actually coming to the end of our time together. From here on out, everything would be shared equally: the stories would get cheaper as I paid less and less to hear them. The experiences wouldn't have the same value as before. I didn't want that. In all actuality, I couldn't afford to let it happen. I began to get frustrated.

We headed toward Omaha. When we got into town, I stopped to put gas in the car. The Chief got out and wandered around as I filled the tank. We'd only driven for about fifteen minutes, but it seemed like several hours. It was still dark, and the sky showed no signs of brightening any time soon. The pump clicked off, and I went inside to pay. The Chief followed me in and strolled through the aisles of the store.

I picked up a couple of candy bars and filled a foam cup with French roast coffee—some bourbon to go with it would have been nice.

The Chief scooped up a small jar of sausages in vinegar. He was eyeing a jar of pickled eggs as well. My guts churned angrily at the idea of anything soaked in vinegar—especially eggs. The jars were not opened, but I could smell their pungent aroma already. I tried not to think about it.

"Pump 4, this stuff, and whatever he's got," I said to the cashier.

The Chief threw a bag of pork rinds in with the rest of the items.

I shook my head. "Not concerned about health?" I asked.

"Not at my age," the Chief said.

The Chief grumbled. He dug into a bin and found a granola bar to add to his pile.

"Okay there, Yule Gibbons," he said. "I've addressed health concerns."

"I wasn't talking about your health, Chief," I said. "I was referring to mine."

"What's the matter, Louie? You sick?"

"No, but the idea of that stuff for breakfast is getting me there."

"You're not eating it, I am."

"It's in my space. It's vicarious."

The Chief dug into the bin again and found a protein bar. He slammed it onto the counter.

"To your goddamn health," he said. "Are we copacetic now?"

We walked out to the car. The tension around us was thick and static-riddled. It felt like we were walking in a field of high-voltage electrical towers. We'd had moments like this several times before, but today it seemed overly trivial. I was angry about something stupid like not having to pay for our rooms, and the Chief was mad because I'd criticized his choice of sustenance. My mood was still bad, but my reasons for it had changed. Now I just felt foolish.

The Chief got in the car and sat staring. I got in the backseat and took out the atlas. We had started this day off terribly. The only thing that could make it worse was not having some idea of where we were going—that and the stench of pickled sausages and pork rinds at 5:30 a.m.

I opened to the pages with Nebraska and traced a route just past Omaha. Interstate 29 was our starting route. First, we'd venture into Iowa. I followed the road into Kansas City. From there I put us onto I-70. I did not have an E location yet. I kept looking.

"Found it!" I exclaimed.

The Chief flinched. He didn't turn around, but I knew he was curious as to what I'd discovered.

We left the gas station and made our way to Interstate 29. The sun was slowly beginning to light the morning sky. There wasn't much of a brilliant dawn. It was overcast and rising grays and dark blues were filling the horizon. I glared at the road.

In no time at all, we'd crossed the state line and were in Iowa. We skirted the Missouri River, and every so often, the Chief would stare out as if he was contemplating the Big Muddy. I felt a weight lifting off me. It wasn't hard to discern what it was: the stupid gripes I'd had with the old man were floating off and making their way down the mighty river. I smiled, and the Chief saw it. He didn't say anything. I needed to initiate this conversation.

"That's a big river," I said.

"It's the longest, for sure," the Chief responded. "Even the Mississippi owes it a debt of gratitude. All those rivers we crossed—they're all children of the Mizzoo. At one time it was believed to go from coast to coast. Lewis and Clark disproved that. Hell, Lewis and Clark disproved a lot."

I nodded my head. What I knew about Lewis and Clark could fill less than a half a sheet of paper. The Chief had a little more information on the great explorers.

"Yep, those two—and their help—went from Saint Louis to the West Coast and back," the Chief said. "President Jefferson needed to find out what he'd just bought in the Louisiana Purchase and then see what was beyond it.

"You gotta realize at this time, the United States itself was from the Midwest to the East Coast. Everything else was a big mystery.

"There was still the threat of England and Europe snagging territory, not to mention the Spanish—who held a huge chunk of the West. There were also numerous Indian tribes no one knew about. We've driven through a whole lot of their land, Louie, and seen a lot of their sights, some you may not have known. Yeah, suffice it to say, Lewis and Clark turned America into the flag-planting winner-takes-all country we know today."

As interested as I was in the Chief's synopsis of the Lewis and Clark expedition, I was happier to hear him talking to me. I'd started this whole mess, but I was glad the Chief was putting an end to it.

* * * * *

When we got to Kansas City, Missouri, it was the morning rush hour. Every freeway was clogged and barely moving. It was the first time we'd hit traffic of this degree. I rolled my window down. The outside air was hot and noxious. The carbon monoxide emissions surrounding us seemed to be at fatal levels.

The overcast sky held the fumes and odors in place. There was a wave in the air from the heat. For a moment, I thought I was stuck on Interstate 405 in California. The influx of Kansas and Missouri license plates told me different.

"This sucks," I said.

The Chief opened his jar of sausages. I scowled at first, afraid of how I'd react to the smell. There was none. The only scents that filled the air were the exhaust of a million idle cars and a couple hundred thousand tractor trailers belching diesel fumes into the sky.

"May I have one of those?" I asked.

The Chief furrowed his brow. "One of these?" he asked. "You? Want one of these?"

"Yes. May I?"

"Not concerned about health?" the Chief inquired, parroting my words from earlier.

"Here? In this?" I asked. "No. Not at all. Gimme a pork rind too."

The cesspool of vehicular sludge crept along as we inched closer to Interstate 70. I didn't want to halt progress, but I couldn't bear to sit in this mire of internal combustion-based flatulence and greenhouse swelter any longer. I spotted a sign for a Cracker Barrel Restaurant at the next exit.

"Chief, let's stop up here," I said. "We can get out, have some breakfast, and let the good people of Kansas City get to where they need to be. What do you say?"

The Chief nodded in concurrence. I blinked and waved my way through the traffic lanes to get to the exit, and we were free of the jam. I drove into the parking lot of the restaurant and had to circle for several times to find a place park.

287

An elderly couple exited the restaurant and walked toward their car. The Chief was spinning his hand at them.

"Come on, you old fuckers," he said under his breath. "Get a move on. We want your spot."

"Be nice," I said. "They're old and probably full."

"Louie, I'm old too. By the time they get to their damn car, I'll be dead."

The Chief started to drum on the dash. He continued to mumble at the couple.

"Blow the horn," he said. "That'll speed 'em up. Let 'em know you're not playing around."

I was slightly appalled at the Chief's behavior.

"We'll get a spot," I said. "Don't worry."

"What? At dinnertime?" he asked. "Why the hell is everybody here? What time is it? Shouldn't these idiots be at work? Did everyone in the world suddenly end up in Kansas-Freakin'-City?"

As he continued to rant and rave, I found a parking spot. I pulled in and shut off the car. I sat smiling while the Chief was still having his conniption about the couple, whom he'd now named Pokey Joe and Hop-A-Long Hilda. I shook my head. He hadn't even noticed we'd parked—and in an even better spot than the one he'd wanted.

We went into the restaurant, and it was packed. A hostess came and took our names. We dodged bodies as we wandered the old country store, examining the wares and commenting on how much stuff could be crammed into such a small space.

The store was crowded with every type of person you could imagine. Adults of all shapes, sizes, and ages stood and blocked merchandise racks; hovered over them, unfolding, examining and ultimately tossing the items aside willy-nilly.

Kids ran through the tight aisles and around the displays. One little boy knocked over a rack of baseball caps with military insignias. He didn't seem to notice until the Chief called him out.

"Hey, Speedy," he said, "you need to square that mess away."

The kid glared at the old man. His mouth drooped to a slight pout, and he acted like he was going to cry.

"Pick up those hats, son," the Chief said. "Are you an ape?"

The boy shook his head but said nothing.

"That's right—you're not, are you?" the Chief asked. "Well, this ain't a zoo either, so stop acting like an ape and pick up that mess. I'll even help you."

The Chief and the kid raised the fallen tree of hats back to its upright position. The kid picked up the ones that had dropped off brought them back to the rack. The Chief was satisfied with the job and gave the kid a salute. The boy was still pouting.

"Why the face, Sad Sack?" he asked. "You're off the hook, and it was a job well done."

The kid's face did not change.

"What is it?" the Chief asked.

The boy pointed to a hat with an army insignia on it. The Chief took it off the rack and held it out to him.

"You want this hat?" he asked.

The boy, still pouting, nodded.

The Chief took the kid by the hand and walked with him to the register. He paid for the cap and placed it snugly on the kid's head. His pout was now a strange smile—it actually looked like the proverbial frown turned upside down.

"Where are your parents?" the Chief asked the boy.

He pointed to a young woman standing in a corner by a toy display. There were three other small children pulling at the woman's clothing and begging for this and that. A baby cried in a stroller next to her. She was disheveled and distraught.

The Chief walked the boy over to his mother. She looked at the old man, and her eyes were red and swollen. She seemed oblivious to everything except her own situation.

"This little soldier says he belongs to you," the Chief said.

"Oh my God, I'm so sorry," the woman said. "What kind of trouble is he in?"

"None. Well, not anymore. We had a moment, but we've got this barracks inspection-ready."

The woman's head shook and nodded. She didn't know what to say.

"I just wanted to make sure you got him back," the Chief said.

The woman looked at him and then and her son. "Timmy, you need to put that hat away," she said. "It's not yours. How many times …"

The Chief cut her off.

"That's a negative, ma'am. The hat is his," he said. "He earned it. We've worked out all the details. He's up to regs."

The woman began to cry. "Oh, please let me give you some money," she said. "I can't thank you enough. He's always wanted that damn hat."

"It was my pleasure," the Chief said. "Always happy to help an army man who's lost his cover."

The woman cracked an uneasy smile. "He misses his dad," she said. "He's …" She fell silent and her head dropped. She shook her hands in frustration.

The Chief rounded up the kids and told them to get whatever they wanted. He took them all to the counter and paid for their toys and candy and anything else they had. He bought all of them—including the baby—an army cap as well.

The children returned to their mother, and she broke down in tears. She fell into the Chief and gave the old man the tightest hug I'd ever seen one human give to another. She whispered something to him and he nodded. He kissed the woman on her forehead and said something else. He reached in his pocket and handed her some money. She refused it. The Chief stuffed it under one of the kids' hats, pulled the bill down tight, and waded through the crowd back toward me.

He stood tall, but his face was sullen and blank and his eyes were distant. He was somewhere else, and unlike other times that the Chief had drifted to faraway lands, I did not want to be where he was at this moment.

The hostess called our names and led us to our table. The restaurant wasn't any less crowded than the store. I was beginning to wonder if the Chief wasn't onto something about everyone in the world being here in "Kansas-Freakin'-City."

We sat down, and the Chief studied the paraphernalia adorning the walls.

"This stuff is useless hanging on the wall," he said. "What's the point?"

"It's kitsch, Chief," I said. "Just something to talk about. It got your attention."

He pointed out several items he'd had growing up, as well as how many of the advertised products he'd heard of and used. Listening to him talk about these things took away a lot of the camp value and gave them practicality.

Our waiter sauntered to the table and introduced himself.

"Good morning, I'm Carl," he said. "Can I get you waters to start?"

"I'd like coffee," I said.

"Okay, so no water, just coffee?"

"For me, yes."

The Chief looked at the kid and read the name on his apron. "What about tomato juice, Cliff?" he asked. "Can I get that too?"

Carl blinked hard as if he had to think.

"Carl," he said, rolling his eyes, "so you want tomato juice then?"

"Yes," the Chief said. He looked at Carl's apron again.

"Tell me about the stars," he said. "You've got two. Are you a major general in this outfit?"

Carl shook his head. "No, this isn't the navy, sir," he said.

"I know it's not the navy," the Chief said. "If it was, you'd be a *rear admiral.*"

He seemed insulted by this title. "I'll get those drinks right away," Carl said.

The Chief huffed. "Why the hell does everybody jump right to the navy?" he asked. "There's four other branches of the service. It's always the navy first."

"I don't know," I said. "My go-to would be the army."

"But it wasn't. You thought I was in the navy."

"That's because everyone calls you *Chief*. It made sense. I thought you might've been a fireman too."

"Nope. I was nothing of the sort, Louie."

Carl brought our drinks: a cup of coffee and a small glass of tomato juice. The Chief shook his head.

"Cliff, I wanted tomato juice *and* coffee," he said. "You weren't paying attention."

Carl's shoulders slumped. "I'm sorry," he said. "I thought you just wanted the juice."

"No. I said the word *too*—as in *in addition, as well as,* or *also,*" the Chief said.

I looked at Carl. "He did say that," I said.

Carl seemed frazzled. It was understandable. The restaurant was bustling and chaotic. I know I couldn't function properly under such circumstances, not to mention the Chief kept calling him Cliff.

"It's okay," I said. "Just bring another cup of coffee."

The Chief chimed in, "Yeah and when you do, bring a bigger glass of tomato juice as well."

Carl sighed. "Do you want two glasses of juice then?" he asked.

"Kid, I'm gonna make this easier for you," the Chief said. He downed the small glass of juice like it was shot of whiskey and slammed the empty vessel on the table. "I want another one of those—but a whole lot bigger."

Carl slid away from the table. It was obvious that after our brief time together, he'd had his fill of us. One of us would indeed get our food violated in some way.

The Chief looked at the menu. He randomly flicked his finger at the selections. Every time his nail snapped against the paper, I flinched. Others seated around us began to notice this as well. Each time he did it, it seemed to get louder.

"See something you like?" I asked, hoping he'd stop popping the menu.

"It all sounds the same," he said. "Eggs, meat, and potatoes—they just gave clever names to everything."

"I guess that makes it easier to order."

"Does it? It's confusing. Grandma and Grandpa have the same stuff. They must've been brother and sister?"

I shook my head. "Grandma's got grits," I said. "That's the difference."

"Grandpa should have grits," the Chief said.

"Is this a John Wayne, *Rooster Cogburn* thing?"

"No. It's an 'I Just Want a Regular Breakfast Menu' thing. Why does everything have to be so complicated? Why can't you just call it what it is? Why are there so many goddamn labels on everything? For Christ's sake just call it what it is …"

The Chief slammed his menu down. The utensils and tableware raised and clinked as they quickly dropped back to their places on the table top. Everyone seated around us stopped and stared at the old man. They fell silent for a few seconds, and concerned looks crossed their faces. He waved them off, and they resumed dining. The Chief was not himself. His face was red and his eyes glazed. This outburst was over something more than silly names for breakfast choices.

"Are you okay?" I asked.

"I'm fine, kid," the Chief said. "I just want a little clarity."

"It's hard to find in a place like this. There's too much going on."

"That there is."

The Chief looked at the walls again. He eyed a poster for Johnny Eagle cap guns.

"Every kid had a Johnny Eagle," he mumbled. "*Pop! Pop! Pop!* That was the sound of Christmas back in the fifties and sixties. Nowadays …"

I gave the Chief a quizzical glance. I wasn't sure what to make of his comment.

Carl returned to the table. He had a large glass of tomato juice and two cups of coffee.

"Job well done, Cliff," the Chief said. "I can see promotion to lieutenant general in your future."

Carl smiled blankly at the Chief's comment. "Have you decided on what you'd like to eat?" he asked.

"I'd like the Old Timer," I said. "Scrambled and sourdough toast."

Carl wrote my order down. "And for you, sir?" he asked the Chief without looking up from his pad.

The Chief cleared his throat loudly and snapped his fingers. "Over here, sunshine," he said. "I ain't on that paper—or the floor."

He glanced up and gave the Chief a condescending chuckle.

"Sorry," he said. "What can I get for you?"

The Chief sat straight in his chair and looked Carl up and down.

"Well, for starters, you can get me some goddamn respect," he said. "And after you muster that, you can get me your manager."

Carl stumbled back slightly at the Chief's aggressive response to his patronizing attitude. It caught me off guard as well.

A gentleman seated at an adjacent table turned and applauded the Chief's admonishment of our waiter with a nod and a thumbs-up.

"I don't need this shit from some diner dish jockey," the Chief said to the man. "What the hell happened to good manners and decency?"

The man said nothing. The look on his face was one of agreement with the Chief and his ire.

"I didn't mean any disrespect, sir," Carl said. "I was just …" He paused. His manager was already headed toward our table.

"Sir, is there anything I can do to make this right?" the manager asked the Chief.

"Yes. Free breakfast for both of us," he said. He looked at Carl. "And put a hook in this kid's ass."

I watched the exchange between the Chief, Carl, and his manager. Our waiter's approach had been less than attentive, but it was hardly worth blowing up about. I thought back on the morning to this point and realized that I'd set all this in motion. Cracker Barrel Carl's patchy people skills threw a shovelful of coal onto the fire.

"Sir, we want to make sure you have the best dining experience," the manager said.

The Chief waved him off. "Forget it," he said. "It's just one of those days. We all have them."

Carl and his manager left, and the Chief heaved a sigh. I thought about what he'd just said and was uncertain as to whom he was referring when he mentioned having "one of those days."

"I'm sorry, Chief," I said. "This is all on me."

"What do you mean?" he asked.

"I've been a prick since we left this morning. We've been a little edgy."

"That's old news, kid. This wasn't your fault. Hell, I don't even know if it was Cliff's, either."

The Chief looked up at the Johnny Eagle poster again. He shook his head. Earlier, this poster had made him reminisce. Now it seemed to make him bitter.

"What's wrong?" I asked. "It's like that poster's bothering you."

He put his head down. "That's ridiculous," he said. "Why would a damn poster bother me?"

Our breakfasts arrived. The manager and two different servers presented us plates full of food. Carl, however, was nowhere to be found. The people seated around us seemed jealous at the servings we'd received. The man who praised the Chief's lambasting of Carl nodded in approval.

"Now that's results," he said. "I'm gonna start getting upset with my waiter more often."

The Chief laughed. "Don't do that," he said. "It's not good for the blood pressure, and God knows what the hell they do to your food."

The manager huffed at the Chief's comment but maintained his bearing.

"Does everything look okay?" he asked.

"It looks fine," the Chief said. "Come back in a minute, and I'll tell you if it was edible."

The two servers gave their manager a surprised look. He smiled at them and nodded to the Chief.

"If there's anything else I can get you, please don't hesitate to ask," the manager said.

"You'll be the first number I dial," the Chief said. He cut into his ham and began to eat.

Even with all the drama that preceded it, breakfast was quite good. For me, it was nice to eat morning fare that looked real. It was like something you'd have at home. The eggs didn't look manufactured. They were cooked to order and white and yellow—the colors eggs should be.

The toast was buttered perfectly, soft in the middle and sliced into triangles when it was served. The choices of jelly were the norm, but apple butter was an option as well. Nothing had to be removed from warmers with tongs.

The pancakes were big, round, and fluffy. They'd been mixed, measured, poured, and flipped on a proper griddle by someone who knew what they were doing—not by a clueless hack using some do-it-yourself, as-seen-on-TV apparatus, spilling batter everywhere and leaving half of the cake raw.

The food was served on porcelain plates and eaten with stainless-steel utensils.

The coffee mugs matched the plates, their porcelain handles permanently affixed. They did not need to be folded out to use. The mugs required no cardboard slip sleeves for easy transport or a lid to keep the contents warm. My teeth clinked against the smooth surface of the cup, and it felt good.

The juice selections stretched beyond orange. Each variety came in glasses made of *real glass* in two different sizes and could be served over ice upon request.

When I was growing up, my folks put on a Saturday morning spread to remind us that although we lived out west, we were Southerners. And Southerners gather 'round the table for a hearty breakfast and good ol' family togetherness on Saturdays. It wasn't Saturday, but I felt closer to home than I had been for a while. *Momma and Daddy would be proud.* I smiled and felt warm and overly nostalgic.

"Louie, what's with the shit-eating grin?" the Chief asked. "Your gears are turning, kid. What are you thinking about?"

"About home," I said. "Just some old stuff from when I was younger."

The Chief nodded and continued eating. I took another bite of food as well. I started to wonder if my reminiscing was truly nostalgic or if I was just sick of eating semi-artificial, prefab, motel breakfasts.

We finished eating and had another cup of coffee. The restaurant was still busy. We'd been here for almost two hours, and I wondered if we shouldn't leave and give our table to an awaiting party. The Chief seemed content to stay on a little longer.

"We can't leave yet, Louie," he said. "We don't know where we're going."

"*You* don't know where we're going," I said. "But I do."

"You holding out on me? Disclosure: full and immediate."

"I haven't had time to say anything."

The Chief put his palms up. "You do now," he said. "Let's hear it."

"It's the perfect place," I said. "Especially after all the Lewis and Clark talk."

"You gonna clue me in?"

"In a word, it's a place of discovery—at least the name says so."

"Okay, out with it. Don't give me a big buildup, just in case I end up disappointed."

"Eureka!" I said. I flashed my hands as if I'd found something.

"What the hell?" the Chief asked.

"We're going to Eureka," I said.

"Eureka? California?"

"There's more than one Eureka, Chief. This one is by Saint Louis."

He nodded. "What's to do in Eureka?" he asked. "And when did you decide on this place?"

"I don't know what's there," I said. "But I decided on it when we stopped in Omaha earlier. The talk of the Lewis and Clark Expedition made it all the more fitting."

The Chief smiled and hummed out a tune. "Meet me in Saint Louie, Louie," he sang. "Meet-a me at-a the faaaaaaaiiiir!"

I blushed with embarrassment and looked around the restaurant, hoping no one else had paid attention to the Chief's croon.

The restaurant manager came to our table one last time and apologized again for any "inconveniences" or "misunderstandings." The Chief shook him off as if it was no big deal.

"What's done is done," he said. "It's all about lessons. We all have to learn them."

The manager seemed confused but content with the Chief's words.

"Your meals have been taken care of," he said. "We hope that you'll join us again soon at the Cracker Barrel and have a wonderful day."

"We will, my good man," the Chief said. "We're going to Eureka to visit Meriwether and his buddy Bill."

The manager smiled. "Well, have a nice visit with your friends," he said. "And don't have too much fun at Six Flags."

"They're not my ..." the Chief paused. He switched his focus and looked at me. "Six Flags?" he asked. "We're going to a damned amusement park?"

I shook my head. "No, but at least we know of *something* in Eureka now," I said.

"I hope we can find something else there," the Chief said. "I'm too old for roller coasters and have no patience for carnies."

"They don't have carnies at Six Flags, Chief."

"How do you know? You ever been there?"

"Not to this one. But there weren't any at the one in Georgia."

"This ain't Georgia, kid—it's *Missour-ah*."

I chuckled. "*Too-sha*," I said, jokingly.

The Chief and I made our way from the restaurant and through the store again. On the way to the exit, I saw a rack of newspapers. I picked up a copy of the *Kansas City Star*—for obvious reasons.

"Chief, I have to ask you something," I said. "What happened at the restaurant?"

He looked at me quizzically. "You know what happened," he said. "That waiter was an absolute cad to me."

"No, I'm talking about before that," I said. "We'd had a little beef, but that got squared away. It was after you talked to that woman."

The Chief turned away and looked out the window.

"That was nothing," he said. "I was just trying to keep her kids from ransacking the store."

I glanced at him. "There was more to it than that," I said. "You two had a moment. She stirred you. I saw it."

"It was nothing, kid," he said. "Nothing to get riled up about."

"You can tell me."

"I *am* telling you. It was nothing. *No goddamn thing.*"

I wanted to pry a little more, but I did not. Whatever it was, it weighed very heavily on him.

"I want to get a little sleep if you don't mind," he said. "This old brain … I just need to rest."

"Sure," I said. "I'll keep everything to a dull roar."

"You're a good kid, Louie," he said. "You always make sure I'm taken care of."

I smiled and thought about Catherine. *I could say the same for you.*

Eureka, Missouri

The Chief slipped in and out of slumber the entire drive. Even when I'd stopped for gas, he never completely woke up. I'd spotted a billboard for an *Econo Lodge* motel and decided that's where we'd stay.

I pulled into the parking lot, and the Chief snorted himself awake.

"Good morning, sunshine," I said. "Have a nice rest?"

The Chief looked around. "Where are we?" he asked.

"We're in Eureka. You slept the whole way."

"Oh, I'm sorry about that, Louie. It's hell being old. Gotta get your rest in, you know."

I smiled. "It was no big deal," I said. "It gave me a little time to myself and to think."

"What did you think about?" the Chief asked. "Anything good? Anything productive?"

"A whole lot of neither, I'm afraid," I said.

We went inside and checked in.

"Two rooms please," I said. "Same floor and across the hall if possible."

The clerk nodded, took my credit card, and began to type. I surveyed the lobby as he did his work. The place was empty, and that was good—it kept the Chief from socializing for the moment.

The Chief looked around the room. He stopped sporadically. He seemed to be reading signs and posters. I found myself doing the same thing.

"See anything interesting?" I asked.

"Nothing yet," he said. "But I'm still looking."

The clerk handed my card back. "So are you guys in for a convention?" he asked.

"No," I said. "Just a couple of days for some sights."

"Six Flags?"

"No. Not Six Flags."

The clerk looked shocked. "Really? Why else would you come here, then?" he asked.

I crinkled my face and asked, "Do we look like the Six Flags type?"

The clerk gave me a look and said nothing. He waited for the printer to finish spitting out the paperwork.

I heard the Chief singing. "Get your kicks … on Route Sixty-Six …"

I snickered as the desk clerk gave the old man a bewildered look.

"I think he found something," I said.

"Yeah, there's a park for the Old Road not far from here," the clerk said.

"Well, see? There is something else to do here besides Six Flags."

The clerk didn't respond. He handed me the papers to sign.

The Chief and I went to our rooms to put our luggage away. I wanted to lie down and take a short rest. I figured the Chief would be okay with that; after all, he had slept the whole ride from Kansas City.

"Chief, let's meet in the lobby in about an hour, okay?" I asked.

"You got something you want to do?" he wondered. "I'm thinking lunch."

"I'd just like to lie down," I said. "Get in a quick kip, is all."

The Chief scowled. "'Quick kip'?" he asked in a very poor British accent. "Who are you now? Churchill?"

"No, I'm not Churchill, I'm just tired," I said. "I need to get myself adjusted."

"Some food and drink will help with that."

"It's a nice thought, but I'd like to wait till later for that."

"Louie, by then it'll be dinnertime. We didn't stop for lunch. A man's gotta eat."

"That's true, but *this* man's burnt out. Go grab a bite downstairs. I'll see you in an hour, Chief," I said.

Just before I closed my door, I had an additional request for him.

"Please don't call me any hookers while I'm asleep, okay?" I asked.

* * * * *

I woke up to the sound of voices—a lot of them: loud and unintelligible. I sat up and looked around the room. I got out of bed and went to the door. I looked through the peephole and could see a group of bodies amassed in the hallway. They were wearing summer clothes and looked like total tourists. Several of them had their luggage. *Why were they milling in the hall outside of my room?* I opened the door and stared at them.

"Jesus, am I dreaming?" I mumbled out loud.

Everyone in the hallway turned their heads and began cheering. The crowd of applauding noise-makers formed an orderly line and backed against the walls. One of them stepped back into my room slightly. I moved for him. I wasn't sure if this was really happening yet.

I peered out through a gap in the line and saw the front desk clerk and another uniformed employee pushing two large and fully loaded, Bellman's Carts down the hall. It would seem that the Chief and I had some company on this floor. *Maybe I should've picked a different place?* I thought. Then I realized: it was summer and we were within a ten-mile radius of a Six Fucking Flags amusement park— *there is no different place.* I was suddenly in an episode of the *Twilight Zone.*

The crowd in the hall dispersed and went to their rooms.

The cacophony that had blared outside my door seemed as if it never happened. Nietzsche said, "Out of chaos comes order." I know he meant those words for something greater than an instantaneous scattering and quieting of a group of theme park goers in Eureka, Missouri; however, they just seemed to fit the moment.

The Chief popped out of his room. "What the hell was going on, Louie?" he asked.

"Our neighbors have arrived," I said. "Seems we picked the party suite."

"The hell you say? We can't have that sort of nonsense."

"There's nowhere else to go, Chief. We're near a huge attraction. Every place will be like this."

"Damn it. Well. I hope they keep it down. Keep their frolicking on a respectable level. Quiet talk."

"So on the QT, then?"

"*On the QT.*"

The Chief looked at his watch. "Your kip has been eighty-sixed," he said. "Any ideas on what to do?"

"How about that Route 66 Park?" I asked.

The Chief's face lit up. "Where's that?" he asked. "How'd you find out about it?"

"The clerk told me," I said. "He heard you singing the song. I've got a map to the place."

"Dammit! That's where I want to go. Let's go see a bit of the Mother Road," the Chief said.

During the entire walk to the car, the Chief sang the lyrics to 'Get Your Kicks on Route 66.' He name-dropped the towns and nailed the chorus but mumbled the rest of the song. I couldn't say anything—it was a lot more than I knew.

When we got to the park, the Chief picked our path. He chose the Inner Loop Trail because it crossed nearby railroad tracks. A train wasn't certain to pass through, but he wanted to be close, should it happen.

There was a lot of wetland scenery to view as we walked. The cattails grew tall and stood motionless in the ponds, while the reeds swayed softly in unison as they were pushed by the warm breeze. A bullfrog croaked his less-than-romantic serenade to any listening female.

A young couple rushed by us on bicycles. They gave no warning of their approach; they merely split their line two-wide as they passed. The rapid whirring of the spokes and the clank of switching gears and chains changing cogs were the only sounds they'd made.

Birds chirped, and the wind blew through the trees. In the distance, a small creek babbled as it channeled its way unseen through the park.

I stopped for a moment and took a deep breath. What I took in was clean and subtly fragranced pine and mint. What I was hearing and smelling was soothing and spiritual. Everything happening at this moment was harmonious and meditative. I was at peace.

"Louie. I've gotta piss," the Chief said. His voice sounded clandestine, as if he was talking from the side of his mouth. "All this water around here."

I closed my eyes for a second, hoping to regain the metaphysical vibe.

"Did you happen to see a pisser close by?" the Chief asked. "If I don't find one, I'm going to have to whip it out right here and water the grass. I may kill it."

"It's back the way we came, Chief," I said. "I'll wait for you."

He smacked my shoulder and walked back to where we'd come in. I shook my head. My moment of tranquility was gone. I was still here in this park and still surrounded by the same sights, sounds, and smells, but now I had the Chief's disembodied head floating in front of the scenery asking where the pisser was and singing strange songs. I heard the bullfrog croak again. Now he just sounded obnoxious.

As I awaited the Chief's return, I tried to imagine driving this old road. There was very little remaining of what surrounded it.

The town of Times Beach had been evacuated and its residents had moved to other locales years ago due to dioxin contamination. Mounds in the land, lots of weeded area, and a couple of hulls of buildings were the lasting legacy of a doomed town born of bad ideas.

My dad and my grandfathers used to talk about traveling Route 66. It had always fascinated me that a single highway could be so iconic and legendary. TV shows and movies were made, while books and songs were written about this artery of transport that no longer existed and had taken five interstates to replace it.

There was something uniquely American about the road. The stops and sights along the 2,500-mile stretch symbolized what this nation was all about: the ongoing pioneer spirit that was our birthright and the can-do attitude that brings out the best in us as a people.

Route 66 was the chosen path of seekers and adventurers. I started to envy those who'd sped down its long, straight segments and had tightly hugged its winding curves.

What I was seeing before me was only a tiny, indiscernible section—a mere paint fleck of a grand, glorious, historical masterpiece. This image could be reimagined and recreated through items from gift shops and nostalgia websites; however, only those who'd traversed the great canvas could truly see and understand the whole of the work. Only they could appreciate what it meant to be a part of it.

My head was spinning. I wanted to have a stake in this, but I could not. Standing on this broken, paved part of the road and zipping down Interstate 44 was as close as I would get to the great highway.

The Chief tapped my shoulder, and it scared the hell out of me.

"Louie, you okay?" he asked. "You about jumped out of your socks."

I shook myself. "I'm fine," I said. "I was just thinking."

"Probably doped up," the Chief said. "I'm sure there's still toxic stuff floating around here. I read about that."

"This isn't Chernobyl."

"Well, it never goes away, you know. There's always something in the wings. Always something waiting to kill you."

I wanted to see the old bridge that crossed the Meramec River, but it was on another trail and closed for the day. The Chief commented that the bridge was possibly contaminated as well.

I shook my head and sighed. I was hoping the Chief would regale me with his Sagas from 66, but alas, this place brought nothing out of him but piss and slight paranoia.

I wanted to ask him if he'd enjoyed the park, but I didn't think he did. It wasn't that big of a deal. I'd created some of my own memories here without the Chief's help. Now if I could only catch up on my Five-a-Days by myself, I'd be golden.

The thoughts I'd garnered were becoming vivid images as they built in my head. We walked to the visitor's center and wandered the gift shop. Not more than fifteen minutes ago, I had been quietly chastising this gift shop, saying how it cheapened the majesty of the great road and all it encompassed by turning it into a mere souvenir.

I bought a metal Route 66 shield for Missouri and California and a nice black polo shirt with the shield embroidered on the breast. I picked up a deck of cards and a shot glass for the Chief. *Jesus, I'm such a freakin' poser.*

The Chief was looking at the neon signs and pictures hanging on the walls around the gifts shop.

"Pretty cool, eh?" I asked.

"This is what I remember from the road," he said. "Not some wooded wetland preserve."

"That was a long time ago, Chief," I said. "A lot happened in this place over the years."

"Too true, kid, but still—the memories you have are what you know."

I thought about those words. They sounded undeniably profound.

We got into the car, and the Chief stared out the windshield. I had to imagine he was giving the park one last look—one more try at finding himself back on the old highway. He sighed, and his eyes peered down.

I was disappointed that the Chief did not find this place the wellspring of memories *I'd* hoped it would've been for him. I had to believe he was disappointed even more. This was not his memory lane to travel.

Conversely, I had gathered a set of images as vibrant and clear as the billboards and posters that touted the old road; however, this was not my memory lane to travel either. My recollections were fabricated, romanticized dreams of what I'd heard and seen from others— gleanings, basically—nothing more than mere observations.

I started the car, and it was my turn to stare into space. I held the wheel and just looked ahead.

The Chief snapped his fingers. "Louie, you're on that damn China Clipper again," he said. "What's going on in that head of yours?"

"Sorry," I said. "I was just thinking about something."

"Was it important? It looked pretty important."

"No, Chief, it was not important. It was silly. Stupid, really."

"Was it about this park? Hey, it was okay. It just wasn't what I'd hoped for. It's not your fault, kid. Hell, maybe I made more of it than I should of."

I nodded and smiled. "Maybe a little," I said. "But it still sucks that it wasn't what you thought."

"Did you enjoy it?" he asked. "Did you take something away from it?"

"I did."

"Then that's all that matters. You found something here. Sometimes we don't always dig up treasure. Sometimes we hit rock, and that's okay."

"That's my problem," I said. "I knew nothing about any of this, but I made my own stuff up."

"What's wrong with that?" he asked. "It's all a part of being nostalgic. People like us—we live for that shit."

"I understand, but it's not *my* nostalgia. I'm just borrowing it. That makes it fake."

The Chief shook his head and glared at me. "Son, don't ever think like that," he said. "You start thinking like that and you're gonna lose everything you have."

I was taken aback. "What do you mean?" I asked.

"Just because you didn't do it or live it doesn't mean it can't be part of you."

"How so?"

"We develop ourselves by doing, but we also develop ourselves by sharing in what others have done. It's called *living vicariously*. You know the term, right?"

"I do. It seems to have become my mantra lately."

"Well, we all do it. We're never satisfied completely with our lives, and there are times we need to see through someone else's eyes to find our pleasure. You ever flown an airplane?"

"No. I've been a passenger on plenty of them."

"Did you ever want to fly one? Sit up in the cockpit, take command of the big bird, be the captain?"

"Yeah, totally. I wanted to be a pilot when I was a kid."

"There you were, sitting in your coach seat, but really—you had the helm of that big 747. You pulled back on the throttle and screamed down the runway, lifting off and speeding into the sky. You did that."

My eyes watered. I felt like I was eight years old again. "Oh my God, yes! All the time!" I said.

"You still do it, don't you?" the Chief asked. "You're a grown man—and you're not a pilot—you're a hurried, cramped passenger, but secretly, you're still up front in the big chair, at the controls and flying that plane."

"Yeah! Yeah, I am."

"See that? You're borrowing from someone else's life. You'll never be Captain DeCarlo of Pan Am, but you can be a part of the experience. Maybe it's not the same as doing it, but sometimes it can be even better."

"Better? How so?"

"You get to make it your own. Re-create it the way you want it. It's only bullshit if you said you did it and you didn't. Movies, music, and literature are loaded with *adaptations* and *based-ons.*"

I nodded in concurrence but didn't necessarily feel any better.

"I know, but sometimes I want ..." I paused for a thought. "I just wish ..."

The Chief interrupted. "Louie, it's human nature to want and wish," he said. "If no one wanted and wished, we'd have gone extinct a long time ago."

"I never thought of it like that," I said.

"Dreams drive desire, and desire begets determination," he said. "It's all about doing, but it's got to start somewhere."

"Bruce Springsteen said, 'You can't start a fire without a spark,'" I said.

"Very true. Mister Springsteen sounds pretty wise."

"Yeah, but he also said he was 'sick of sitting 'round here trying to write this book.'"

"Take credence in the 'spark' part, Louie. I'm sure the defeatist attitude came later."

I chuckled. "Those lines are from the same song," I said.

"Well, obviously, he finished it, right?" the Chief asked. "He wasn't too fed up to get it down and get it out for you to hear and quote back to me."

I didn't say anything. Once again, the Chief was right.

* * * * *

We drove back toward the motel. It was nearing dinnertime, and I was finally ready to eat.

"Louie, I want to go to a sports bar," he said. "I want to go to a place with TVs and a game, with beer and food that can't possibly be healthy. A truly American place—loud, gluttonous, with five kinds of barbecue sauce. There's got to be one of those around here."

I laughed. I never expected the Chief would want to set foot in such an establishment.

"I'm sure we can find such a locale," I said. "Are you sure that's what you want?"

"I am. I want to 'live large,' as they say," the Chief said. "You said you felt amiss borrowing from others. This is the same for me. I will never be one of those wing-eating guys who take football too seriously while drinking cheap, mass-produced beer, but I can play like one for a night."

We found a place called Poor Richard's. It fit the criteria: it was a sports bar, there were multiple TVs, and there were games with games on each. The crowd was big and loud. The Chief was not happy to see the Saint Louis Cardinals' pre-games being broadcast on three different screens.

"Can we get another game?" he asked. "The freakin' Red Birds?"

"What do you expect?" I asked. "We're right outside of Saint Louis, Chief."

He grumbled. A couple of the patrons glared at him.

I overheard a man asking his waitress if there was another game on.

"There you go," he said.

Unfortunately, there were no other baseball games being shown. The Chief's face reddened.

"Just look somewhere else. Better yet, talk to me," I said.

A hostess showed us to a table. The Chief looked around the place and found that the décor did not satisfy his vision of how a sports bar should look.

"I was hoping for … I don't know …" he trailed off.

A waitress came to our table and brought our menus.

"Good evening, gentlemen, my name is Holly and I'll be taking care of you tonight," she said. "Can I start you off with anything to drink?"

"I'd like a beer," I said. "Something local. What do you recommend?

"Well, we have Schlafly pale and wheat—that's from Saint Louis. We also have a couple of varieties of Springfield, we have Stag, and of course—*the King*." Holly's eyes rolled, and she giggled.

I smiled. "Schlafly pale ale, please," I said. "And in the tallest glass you have."

She looked at the Chief. "And for you, sir?" she asked.

The Chief didn't say anything. He looked at Holly, and I could tell he was up to something.

"Holly …" he mused. "Would your surname happen to be Golightly?"

Holly shook her head. "No, sir, it's not," she said.

I glared at the Chief. "Just order a drink, Capote," I said. "The lady has more important things to do than play the *Breakfast at Tiffany's* challenge with you."

Holly grinned uneasily as the Chief looked at her and contemplated his order.

"I'll have what he's having," he said. "I'll make things simple. I wouldn't want to get ol' Louie's balls in an uproar."

Holly and I both blushed in embarrassment.

"Sorry about that," I said. "He's having a bad day."

She smiled at us and said she'd be right back with our drinks.

"Dammit, Louie, why do you have to be like that?" the Chief asked. "I'm trying to have a little fun and you go off and piss in my picnic basket."

"I'm not trying to rile you up, Chief," I said. "I just don't know why you can't just order a beer or food without some weird monologue, that's all."

"Kid, it's not a 'monologue.' It's me. It's what I do and who I am. I like people, especially women, and I like to talk to them. Back in my day, it's how we got on and how we made relationships."

"I understand, I really do. It's just … I'm just not used to it. Even after being with you a week, I'm still not sure what to make of it."

"That's why you can't get out of your rut. You're wrapped too tight and stuck in one place. You've got to branch out—expand your horizons. Spread those wings. They're back there, and you're letting them just rot away."

I sighed. "I'm trying to prevent that," I said. "I'm doing what I can, but it's just not happening."

"You're *thinking* about it," he said. "But you really aren't *doing* it. Every time you get close, you step back and ball up again. You don't think I notice it, but I do."

"If I'm aware of anything, Chief; it's that I'm aware of your read on me," I said.

"Well, what are you going to do about it?"

"About what?"

"About getting yourself to fly and getting me off your case?"

"I like having you on my case. It's keeping me honest."

"It was at first, now you're becoming dependent on it. We're journeying together, but it's okay to take separate paths while traveling in the same direction."

"It is?"

"Yes. Think of a divided road. We're both heading eastbound, but at some point, the road splits, and for a mile or two, we're on our own. When we meet back up, we'll have seen the same things, but from a different perspective."

Our beers arrived, and all I wanted to do was drink. I didn't know what to say. Every response I thought of sounded foolish or was a paraphrase of what he'd just said. I took a big drink of my beer and collected myself.

Holly saw me take my swig as soon as she'd set the beer down.

"Pretty good stuff, isn't it?" she asked.

I nodded my head. "Damn good," I said, sounding rushed but certain.

"Would you guys like to order, or do you need a little time?" she asked.

"We're going to need a little more time, honey," the Chief said. "We've been preoccupied with our own nonsense and haven't perused the fare as of yet."

"Um, okay. I'll be back in a few," Holly said. "Just take your time. No rush."

She walked away, and I took another drink.

"Slow down, Louie," the Chief said. "You're gonna' get shit-faced before we eat. That's no good."

"I'm sorry," I said. "I'm having one of those 'Come to Jesus' moments, I guess."

"What? Are you dying or something?"

"No, I'm just trying to … It's been a long damn day, you know? Lots of shit going on."

The Chief got a contemplative look. "Oh, I know," he said. "And the shit started early."

"How do you mean?" I asked.

"That damn restaurant in Kansas City," he said. "That was a fucking nightmare. Nothing but bad spirits all around."

I pulled my beer back and took another drink. I felt I needed a little charge before I continued the conversation.

"I was wondering about that," I said. "I know I asked you about it in the car and you said it was 'nothing,' but *something* happened. What did that woman say to you?"

The Chief grabbed his beer and, in one gulp, drained nearly half of it. He slammed the glass on the table. Holly had walked up behind him to take our order. She saw the Chief's actions and wisely turned away.

The old man leaned across the table and beckoned me to come closer. He stared into my eyes. It was almost intimidating. I could see a range of emotions, and they were all bad. I didn't like where this was heading.

"Are you okay?" I asked.

"Look at my face," he said. "What do you see?"

I thought about what I wanted to say. What I saw was anger—and like none I'd never seen before. I had to make sure my response was close, even though I wasn't completely sure.

"You're pissed off. That I know," I said. "But why I *don't* know. I saw you give that woman money. What did she tell you?"

The Chief sat back and looked over me. His vision was no longer trained on anything in this restaurant. He was seeing something far away, and it appeared to be very unsettling.

He closed his eyes and inhaled. He did not let the breath out. He held it and sat still. When the Chief exhaled, it was a burst—not a breath. It was as if his soul had been released from his lungs.

"These fucking wars, Louie," he said. His voice was low and hostile. "These goddamn, fucking wars we're mixed up in."

I looked at him, and things began to make sense. I didn't know the whole story yet, but I had a good starting point.

The Chief shook his head and began to ramble.

"Hell, they're not even calling them *wars*. They're what … 'Operations' now?" he asked. "Everything's a goddamn operation. Then they tack some bold name onto it to make it sound even better. It doesn't change the reality. It doesn't take the sting out, does it? There've been 'operations' in every war, but they were *missions*—part of the conflict. We didn't label the whole fuck-fest an *operation*. It was a *war*. But these … they're not wars. In a war, you're fighting an enemy. Tell me about Afghanistan. *Operation What the Fuck?* What's the point of that one? Who are we supposed to be fighting there?"

"It's the War on Terror. Because of the September 11th attacks in '01," I said. "We're fighting the Taliban and other groups that harbor and train terrorists. Trying to prevent something like that from happening again."

"Fighting terrorists is plausible," the Chief said. "Eliminate them, and you eliminate their mission, but sooner or later, another group crops up and continues the fight. It never ends. So what it really means is just fighting another war over an ideology or a concept. No one can win that fight.

"A War on Terror? You can't fight a war over something like that. We've tried. You know what the best weapon against a concept is? It's its exact opposite."

"What do you mean?" I asked. "Isn't it the concept that ultimately drives the fight? The cause you're standing up for? There has to be a reason."

"That is true. And an outright, unprovoked attack is a damn good reason, although no attack is ever, completely unprovoked," he said. "There's always something that initiated it. You don't just kick your neighbor in the nuts. You kick him in the nuts because his dog shit in your yard too many times or he's been trying to make time with your wife.

"Wars are fought between countries—between people. You can't fight a war on a concept or an ideology. Terror is fear—it's a concept. The best weapon against it is knowledge. If something is known, there's no need to fear it—unfortunately, though, another weapon is *more* fear."

"What about Vietnam?" I asked. "You were there. You know why we were there. It was to stop the spread of Communism. Same thing in Korea."

"Ah the old 'stop the spread of' … that's a classic excuse," the Chief said. "Yes, the commies were running rampant in Asia, but you may have noticed that neither of those wars got labeled as a War on Communism or a War to Stop the Spread of Red.

"I never thought about that," I said. "But wasn't that why we were there? Weren't we there to—um—*prevent the influence?*"

"To a great degree, yes. But there were other reasons as well," he said. "However, our presence and efforts did not work out how we'd hoped. Korea was a draw, and we fucking lost Vietnam. Nothing's changed either: China is still red, and so is just about every other country in Southeast Asia."

"The Soviet Union collapsed," I said. "So there was at least one victory over an ideology."

The Chief scowled. "That didn't happen because of a war. That happened because people stood up against it," he said. "They used the weapons of change, reform, the want of freedom and democracy to defeat it—the exact opposite of what the Soviet Union was built upon. Communism failed because enough people said 'No more,' and the whole system crumbled. You have lost control when you have nothing *to* control."

"The subjugated are the greatest warriors against oppression," I said.

"Write that down, kid," the Chief said. "Trademark it. Or someday you'll see it on a marble slab with someone else's name underneath it."

The Chief looked at me. I was done talking. He was not.

"Do you think putting a face on something justifies it?" the Chief asked.

"I don't understand," I said. "What do you mean?"

"We watch the news and see shit happening, right?" he asked. "But does it really mean anything if we don't have a face to connect it to?"

I shook my head. I still wasn't following.

"A man robs a bank. There's no picture. It's no big deal. No one gets hurt. It's a bank. But if someone in that robbery does get hurt and we see their face, we feel sorry for them. We feel their pain—or we think we do. Does the fact we've made that connection change things?"

"I'm not sure," I said. "I think it does to an extent."

"We have no idea what they're going through," he said. "We just automatically feel compassion because we're *seeing* them. We want to feel something. It's supposed to make us better. It's supposed to make us good and decent."

I watched the old man's eyes well with tears.

"Chief, are you okay?" I asked. "What's the matter?"

"That woman and those kids, Louie … it's not fair," he said. "If I hadn't had seen her face, I would've walked away. I saw her, and I knew before she told me. I'd seen that look a hundred times before."

"What happened? What did she tell you?" I asked.

By now, I knew the answer. It didn't make it any less difficult to handle.

The Chief's response was a confessional outpouring.

"I bought them their hats and toys, they'd wanted so much—I had to get it all for them," he said. "I told them to rip up the bill. I paid for their food. I tried to give that poor girl money. She wouldn't take it. I put it under her little rug rat's cap. That soldier will keep it safe. It wasn't enough, though. I couldn't do enough.

"She's so damn young—too young to be a widow. Those kids—they're never gonna know their father. I'll always remember their faces. He'll never see them. That little baby … oh my God …"

The Chief broke down. He put his face in his hands to hide his tears. I walked over to comfort him. I stood vigil while the restaurant patrons stared.

A man seated across from us heard enough of the conversation to feel the need to come to the Chief's aid—and mine as well. *Strength in numbers.* He ordered three beers and asked they be brought to our table. He sat opposite me and put his arm around the Chief.

"It's gonna be okay," he said quietly. "Bravery has its price, and sometimes it's too goddamn high."

The Chief nodded. "It's too goddamn high," he repeated through his tears. "*Too goddamn fucking high.*"

This guy—this kind, comforting stranger had heard much more than I had, and I was the one listening to the Chief's words. There was no doubt he'd been here before. There was a personal stake in his Samaritanism.

The restaurant, which had been a respectable boisterous when we'd arrived, was now silent. Everything seemed to stop for a moment. The TVs were muted. The only sounds that could be heard were the humming of appliance motors and the wisp of the ceiling fans, the soft *whoosh* of cars as they passed outside the building, the occasional shuffling of a body, and the Chief's sobs as they echoed into his hands.

The old man sat up. He looked at the gentleman seated beside him and grabbed his wrist. No words were spoken between them. The simultaneous head nods they gave to each other were all they needed to say.

The two men picked up their beers and clinked their glasses together. They held them lip to lip and looked at them. It was as if they were in prayer. They drank and set the glasses down on the table. There was a meticulous precision to it all, almost military-like.

The gentleman stood up and clasped the Chief's shoulder. He shook it and clapped it and held it again. He leaned in and whispered something to the Chief. He looked back and nodded. Everything was going to be all right.

The man walked back to his table and sat down. None of his party said a word as he resumed eating, as if nothing had happened. I raised my glass to him, and he responded in kind.

I stepped to his table. The man seated next to him got up and gave me his chair. I smiled and sat.

"Thank you so much for what you did," I said.

The man looked at me. "It was nothing," he said. "I apologize if I may have seemed like an eavesdropper."

"Sometimes it's a good thing to listen in. I'm glad you did."

The man straightened up in his chair. "I lost my boy last year," he said. "Iraq. He wasn't even there three months. My granddaughter is going to be a year old soon. At least my son got to spend a minute or two with her."

I didn't know what to say. Their situations were completely different; however, to this man, it didn't matter whether the Chief knew the fallen soldier for whom he'd shed tears or not. What mattered was the fact this man had given his life for his country, and the Chief saw enough to not only honor his sacrifice but help his grieving family as well.

I put my hand out to the gentleman, and he shook it. It was a tight, almost painful grip. I knew what this man felt and everything he wanted to say just by the strength of his handshake. I got up from the table and went back to the Chief.

Holly was sitting with him. She and the Chief were talking, but it was not the typical Chief/tomato conversation. There were no stories or songs, no friendly gropes or grabs, no mesmerizing or mystery. It was subtle and comforting.

"I'm sorry if I took your seat," Holly said. She started to get up.

"No, no. Please. Sit down," I said. "You are exactly what he needs right now."

Holly smiled and sat back down. She lightly rubbed the Chief's back. I watched his face. Her touch was soothing, and every stroke was absorbing his sorrow.

I leaned closer to Holly. "Listen. Will you do me a favor?" I asked. "When the bill is ready for that table, please bring it to me, okay?" She smiled and nodded.

The Chief touched Holly's hand. "You're very kind to sit with this old, blubbering man," he said. "I've been such a burden to you. I haven't even decided on my meal yet."

Holly smiled. "You just take your time," she said. "You've got a lot going on. And besides—we're open till one a.m."

The Chief laughed. It was good to hear that sound. I looked at the man at the other table. He smiled and toasted to the Chief's laugh. It sounded good to him too.

"Well, my dear Ms. Golightly, I think it's time to eat," the Chief said. He wiped the remainder of his tears and sat up.

Holly smiled and stood up from her chair. "What can I get you?" she asked.

"The biggest, most American hamburger you have," the Chief said without hesitation. "I want the works. And cheese too. And fries. I want something that says I was here in this restaurant. Can the cook whip something like that up for me?"

Holly nodded. The manager heard the Chief's order as well.

"Sir, my cook will make you proud," he said. "You have my personal guarantee."

Holly took my order as well. I got a small salad and a plate of chicken wings—with five kinds of barbecue sauce to dip them in.

Our food arrived. The plates were massive and loaded with an embarrassing amount of grub. The Chief's burger was akin to the Diner Double Deluxe April and I had shared in Elko. Jesus. Maybe it was bigger? Is that even possible?

"You got that thing, Chief?" I asked. "I think I just had a heart attack."

Holly asked if everything looked "OK."

"Ms. Golightly, I will require a knife," the Chief said. "And perhaps a to-go box."

I watched Holly move from table to table, filling glasses, taking orders, and dropping off bills. The gentleman who had talked to the Chief called her over. Holly pointed to me, and the gentleman's expression changed. He shook his head and gave me a perplexed scowl. I don't know why, but I patted my chest. He smiled, nodded, and mouthed "Thank you" to me. I gave him a thumbs-up and mouthed back, "No—thank *you*."

"Chief, are you about ready to go?" I asked. "Let's down these beers and head back to the motel. What do you think?"

"I think I'm just fine here for a bit, Louie," he said. "Let's get another round and talk—about something happy this time."

I nodded. Other than the fact we'd been here so long, I couldn't think of a good reason to leave. I liked this place, and even though I didn't know them, I liked the people here as well. The Chief had taken a shine to Holly, and that was helping him soothe his ache. The beer was good and cold and kept coming.

"What else are we going to do while we're here, Louie?" the Chief asked. "What's on the agenda?"

"Why don't you pick the place, Chief?" I said.

"Nope. I'm done with that," he said. "I got kicked in the dick on Route 66. I'm leaving the travel plans up to you from now on."

"Okay, if that's what you want," I said. "But if things suck, I don't want you to bitch at me, all right?"

"Me? Bitch at you? Come on, Louie! When have you ever known me to bitch?!"

I shook my head and rolled my eyes. The Chief saw my reaction. "Kid, you better as hell not answer that," he said.

I thought about what to do and where to go. What was something we could do that would be *Chiefly unique*?

"I smell something burning," the Chief said. "What are you thinking, Louie?"

"I'm not sure," I said. "I'm just …" I paused. I wagged my finger at the Chief as I began to think about what I was going to say to him.

"Yes …?" he asked.

"Let me ask you …" I said. "What's something you've never done?"

The Chief sat back and snorted. "Kid, I've done everything," he said. He put his palms up. "I've been here and there and seen and done it all."

"There's no way," I said. "Everything is *everything*, and that's a hell of a lot of stuff. No human being has done every single possible thing there is to do."

"I have. I've lived a damn full life. I've done it all."

"But you haven't, Chief. You told me you've never been to the places we'd just come from."

"Not before, but I've been to them now. We just left them."

His rationale was sound but frustrating. I tried to think of a few things I felt certain he'd never done.

"Skydiving? Have you ever been skydiving?" I asked.

"No. I haven't," he said.

"See? You haven't done 'everything.'"

"I haven't been skydiving, but I have been parasailing. It was in Costa Rica."

My shoulders dropped. "You're kidding, right?" I asked.

"Well, does that count?" the Chief wondered.

"I suppose it does," I said. "You were flying in the air on some kind of gliding thing, so …"

"Anything else you'd like to ask me?"

I tried to think of something else—something wild but nothing tropical *exotic*. Obviously, sex on the beach was out; one of the first things I'd learned about the old boy was his seaside *sexcapades*.

"I'll bet you've never been to Antarctica," I said. "I got you there."

The Chief hung his head. "You got me there, Louie, I have never set foot on the continent of Antarctica," he said. "I just flew over it on an air sightseeing tour."

I shook my hands in disbelief. "Oh! Christ! You're fucking kidding me, right?!" I shouted. The entire restaurant turned my way. I blushed in embarrassment.

"He's been to Antarctica!" I said. My tone was jovial but cynical.

"I went in 1979. I was on one of the last sightseeing flights to Antarctica," he said. "They shut down them down after the big crash. What a terrible disaster." The Chief sighed and looked upward.

I respected his tribute to those who'd lost their lives in the plane crash. I waited before I continued my interrogation.

"I have to know. How did you get there?" I asked. "How did you manage an air sightseeing trip of all things?"

"I was still in Samoa. I took a week trip to New Zealand with a couple of my *uo*—my Samoan friends," he said. "I know most people go to Australia, but we went to New Zealand! I wanted to see the Southern Alps, and my friends wanted to experience weather that was not hot or tropical."

I sat back. I was at a loss. I wasn't going to ask if he'd piloted an airplane or took a bathysphere to the darkest depths of the ocean. He probably had. Questions about space were out—only because my inquiries were kept to this planet; however, with his knowledge of the heavens and all things cosmic, his being on Skylab or some other space station-type thing wouldn't—*or shouldn't*—have surprised me.

"I'll figure something out. There has to be something you haven't done," I said. "I'll just have to go beyond. I'll find something. You'll see."

"I've got to admire your determination," he said. "But I've done it all. You think of it—I've done it. I'm eighty-four, Louie. I've been around. I've seen—*and made love to*—the entire world."

No. There was something. There had to be one thing the Chief hadn't done—one fantasy he hadn't fulfilled—and I was going to find out what it was. It was going to kill me, but I was going to dig it up and drop it in his lap.

Holly brought the bill and I paid it. The Chief looked at his beer. It was half full.

"Finish up, Chief," I said. "We're too long for Poor Richard's."

The Chief gave me a glare, but Holly ran interference.

"You should listen to him," she said. "How are you gonna come and see me tomorrow without a good night's sleep?"

The Chief perked up. "Well, then. I guess I'd *better* get some rest," he said.

I smiled at Holly and mouthed *thank you* to her. She smiled back and winked at me. I left her a twenty-dollar tip on the table.

When we got back to the motel, the bar was open and a very light crowd had settled in. The Chief glanced into the room and commented on the availability of chairs. As tempted as I was to have a drink, I wanted to go to sleep even more.

"Louie, I'm thinking we need a toddy to help end the day," the Chief said.

"I'm done," I said. "I'll sit with you, but I'm not drinking anything alcoholic."

The Chief looked at me and smiled. *Yeah right, kid.*

We took seats at the bar. I ordered a Perrier, and the Chief got a glass of Jack Daniels. It was the smallest pour I'd seen this whole trip.

The Chief noticed the disparity as well. "Where's the rest of this?" he asked.

I chuckled. "It would seem the days of the Wyoming-sized snort are definitely behind us," I said.

He shook his head and carefully sipped his drink, no doubt trying not to drain it on the first taste.

I could smell the Jack, and it was causing me to waver from my promise of temperance. I gulped my Perrier, but it wasn't helping to quell my urges. I flagged down the bartender.

"Scotch on the rocks, please," I said.

The Chief looked at me. "No soda?" he asked.

I held up the Perrier bottle. "Soda."

We finished our drinks, and true to our word, we called it a night. I had no idea what we'd be doing tomorrow, but I was still determined to find that one thing the Chief had never done.

"Good night, Chief," I said. "See you at breakfast in the morning."

"I will be there and ready to dine," he said. "I'll expect you around eight a.m.? As usual?"

I laughed. "You need to give me some credit," I said. "I've been getting up earlier—or at least, making an effort to."

"You're full of surprises, Louie," he said.

I smiled impishly. "I can be," I said.

* * * * *

I woke up early the next morning. I didn't care what time it was—I didn't want to be awake yet. I pulled the covers tight and curled into them. I was warm and secure but very alone. I began thinking about April again. She had been fading from my mind, and that bothered me. My feelings for her, so strong and unrelenting at first, now seemed distant and unclear. Strangely, sleeping with Catherine had caused my feelings for April to bubble up. I felt like I'd betrayed April and what we had. But really, what did we have? It was wonderful and romantic and almost perfect, but it was over as quickly as it started.

I'd pined over her longer than we were actually together. We didn't even make love. At least I'd done that with Catherine—even if it was just business. I closed my eyes tight. I could see April as plain as day standing before me. She looked so beautiful. I wanted to touch her, but I couldn't.

I confessed to her the things I'd done. She just stood smiling. I began to cry. I had so many reasons to shed tears right now, and every one of them centered on April. I had a flash of clarity amid my sorrow. It was something I'd already known, but it needed to be restated: she'd fulfilled the five—*she was* the one.

I sat up in bed. My mind was still racing, but my heart felt warm. I didn't have a clue where April was, but the Chief told me she was "closer than you think." For the first time, I was starting to believe it.

I got out of bed and went to shower. I still had no idea what time it was nor did I care. I was up.

I turned my back to the showerhead and let the water cascade over me. I looked at the surface of the tub and tried to discern the shapes the water made as it splashed and collected at my feet.

I took the motel soap out of its paper and smelled it. Its fragrance was unrecognizable. I rubbed it into a lather. The soapy film that covered me was cleansing at first but felt taut and sticky as I rinsed it off. The bathroom was filled with steam and the damp aroma of the soap. I began feeling less of the remnants of the lather on me as I stood beneath the shower a little longer.

I shut the water off and got out. I dried off and stepped from the tub to the mirror. I wiped the fog with my towel so I could see. The streak I'd made fogged up again just as I'd made it. I opened the door to let some steam out.

I wrapped the towel around my waist and walked out of the bathroom. I finally saw the clock. It was 5:00 a.m. Still an hour before breakfast service started and still too early for me to be up and thinking about it.

The Chief wanted a surprise. He was going to get one this morning when I knocked on his door prior to 6:00 a.m. Hopefully, it would be the first one of the day for him.

I got dressed and looked at the desk. For a split second, I thought about working. I certainly had things to say now, but I still didn't feel ready to put them down.

I found it ironic that the very words I was going to give to my publisher—this *story of a lifetime*—were the same ones I couldn't see fit to sit and begin writing just yet. How the hell was I going to do this? My only hope was that when I got home, the story would spill out and be everything I promised it would. It had to be. My job and my life depended on it.

I went to the lobby and sat down. I heard the low mumble of unintelligible singing. I looked up and saw the Chief enter the lobby and glance about. He shook his head when he saw me.

"I must still be asleep," he said. He looked at his watch and rubbed his eyes.

"It's a dream come true, Chief," I said.

"Kid, the eggs you'll have this morning will be the best ever," he said. "Fresh from the farm. Only the first customers get 'em. After that, they bring in the fake shit."

I knew he was being facetious, but part of me believed him. I'd never been to breakfast this early. Maybe the eggs were fresh from the farm this time of day? Maybe they squeezed the orange juice and ground the coffee as well?

I watched the restaurant staff fill the egg warmers with the same textured, two-toned disks I'd eaten at every other place we'd stayed. The juice was poured into the decanters from large jugs. The coffee was pre-ground and heaped into the filter baskets of the big stainless-steel urns. It might as well have been 8:00 a.m.

"Well, now I know how the other half lives," I said.

"You seem disappointed, Louie," the Chief said.

"No, not really. But I do know I'm not missing anything by getting up later."

"You're building character. That's important."

"Yeah, and now I can say I've eaten at the crack of dawn. That sounds disgusting in so many ways."

"Dawn might feel differently."

I rolled my eyes and shook my head. "How did I know you were going to say that?" I asked.

We ate our breakfast alone. We'd finished our second plates before any other guests had arrived. It was nice. The Chief and I chatted about random topics—nothing significant, just trivial things. All was well until he brought up our timeline so far.

"We're in the home stretch," he said. "It doesn't seem like much, kid, but we've done a hell of a lot."

"I know. Do you think we've done enough?" I asked. "There was a purpose to all of this, and sometimes I feel we might have missed it."

The Chief shook his head. "No, not at all," he said. "We've seen and done. You wanted to know about places I've been and I've told you the stories. Hell, you've brought some things out of me I haven't thought about in decades. That's saying something."

I sighed. "It's all been fantastic," I said. "I just don't know if it's helping me. I'm still stuck. I'm still right where I was back in Sacramento."

"You're thinking about it too much," he said. "Remember that day in the Rubies? You had an epiphany that day. I saw it."

"I did, but I haven't had another one since," I said. "I was expecting so much more. I was expecting to …"

The Chief cut me off.

"What? *Find yourself?*" he asked. "That's such a cop-out, Louie. You don't lose yourself. You lose your vision. That's what's happened to you. You knew that already. You haven't fully gotten it back because you haven't completed your journey."

"It doesn't feel like I will," I said. "Everything has been great up to now, but I'm losing sight of what I'd set out to do."

"Kid, I think you're closer to what you're seeking than you realize," he said. "Sometimes a man is standing in the middle of his own destiny and doesn't know it. There's nothing wrong with being blind to it. You don't really know what you're looking for. If you did, you wouldn't be struggling now. Your head will ache, and suddenly, all those pent-up ideas in your brain are gonna explode and splatter all over your notebook. All that blood and gray matter—that's what you were holding in."

"*Mind-blowing*," I said. "What a strange way of putting it."

"That's how it'll happen," he said. "It's not just gonna trickle out, it's gonna burst."

"It sounds like a stroke—or Russian Roulette. I can't help but wonder, is this a creative revelation or career suicide?"

"Depending on how you handle it, it can be either one."

"That doesn't really help, you know?"

"That's how life works, Louie. You can't predict the outcome, but you can manage the situations along the way to ensure some favorable returns."

The Chief was right: my head was starting to ache. However, it was not from any kind of creative burst. I was beginning to wonder if I'd failed myself and dragged the Chief on some soul-searching wild goose chase that ended with both of us miserable and perhaps dead.

"Are you okay, Louie? You look a little peaked," the Chief said.

"No, Chief. I can honestly say I'm not okay," I said. "I'm the most un-okay I've been in forever."

"What's the trouble, son?"

I shook my head and closed my eyes. "Everything, right now," I said. "I feel I've made a terrible mistake. I feel like this is all for nothing. I'm sorry."

The Chief grabbed my wrist. "No. Stop that nonsense right now," he said. "You're just worried about things. That's natural. We all worry. If we didn't sweat things, we'd never resolve any problems."

"Yeah, but this problem is different."

"How is it different? It sounds the same as it has been. You're just finally realizing the magnitude."

My face flushed with fear. "*Magnitude?*" I cried. "For Christ's sake, that makes it sound even worse! Like it's gotten bigger!"

"It has gotten bigger. You've got more shit to deal with. And you keep adding to it," the Chief said. "Unless you're stowing bits at a time and organizing them as you work, they're going to keep stacking up."

I stood up, and my chair slid and flew back behind me. It scraped with a low rumble before it fell. The clanging of the metal frame was flattened to a dull hum by the vinyl of the cushions as it bounced on the hard tile floor.

The guests in the restaurant all stopped what they were doing. They stared at me. They continued staring until my chair's discordant bouncing sped to a stop. I remained standing as if nothing had happened. The blush of embarrassment on my face told an opposite story.

The Chief looked around the room.

"I'd tell you to sit down, but you've got no chair," the Chief said. He gave me his Fred Flintstone laugh again. It did little to help.

I picked up my chair and sat down.

"That was only slightly embarrassing," I said under my breath.

The Chief nodded. "Reminds me of another time, not too long ago," he said.

I had to think. "Evansville?" I asked. "That was different, though."

"Was it, Louie? I was having *my* moment there. Hell, I thought you wanted to fight this old son of a bitch—remember?"

"I do remember. I remember it quite well. I didn't want to fight you."

"I know that. It was a heat-of-the-moment thing. However, *I was* looking for a fight."

I was taken aback. "You were?" I asked. "With whom?"

The Chief sipped his coffee. He sat back and stared. "The same person you are right now," he said. "With *myself*. You're picking a fight with yourself, just as I was."

"How so?" I asked. "I'm not picking a fight with myself."

"Oh, but you are. You're already in the midst of it. You're beating the dog shit out of yourself because you can't get your thoughts onto paper."

I glanced around, looking for a defense. I had none.

"It wasn't supposed to be like this," I said. "It was supposed to be easy."

"Why would you think it would be easy?" the Chief asked.

"Because I ..." I paused. I thought I had an answer, but I didn't.

"Did you think that listening to tale or two from someone else would magically lift you out of your hole?" he asked. "Kid, it doesn't work like that. You have to find your own path. I've told you that before."

I put my head down. "I feel so stupid," I said. "I feel like a fucking plagiarist right now. And a bad one at that. That makes me the worst of the worst liars."

The Chief laughed. "I wouldn't say you're a plagiarist," he reassured me. "You're just looking for some guidance. A little paraphrasing. Besides that, you haven't written anything, so you haven't stolen anything."

I laughed at his comment. "I can't argue with that," I said.

The Chief leaned toward me and stared into my eyes. "Louie, ask yourself: what exactly are you doing? What are you trying to accomplish?" he posed. "Have you figured that out yet?"

"I thought I had," I said.

"What was your goal?" he asked.

"Well, to start, I just wanted to finish my story on Crater Lake then move on to the next assignment," I said. "Then you took me on a goddamn trip to Cuba." I didn't know if I was lauding or lambasting him at the moment.

"You took that trip yourself, Louie. I just shared a memory."

"I know that. But it changed my thinking. It made me reevaluate … well … everything I've been doing. I've told you that."

"You have. And it fills my heart with joy, but did it make you reevaluate how *you* worked, or just make you want to write someone else's story?"

I thought for a second. "It's always someone else's story," I said.

"Why can't it be yours?" he asked. "Write about the places you've been as you've seen and experienced them. You weren't experiencing things before, and now you are. You cannot deny that."

I shook my head. "No, I can't. I truly have been experiencing the places we've gone," I said. "Some more than others, but each one has a story. I still don't feel I can do them justice."

"Don't cheapen yourself," he said. "Take everything you've learned and gathered and just apply it. It'll happen."

An enlightened look came across my face.

The Chief wagged his finger at me and smiled. "See, kid? You're already on your way," he said. "You just opened a huge door. Now walk through it, crack a window or two; sit at that desk, and get some work done."

I looked at the clock on the restaurant wall. "It's still too early yet," I said, trying to be funny.

The Chief glared at me. He stood up and angrily pushed his chair in. "Procrastination is what makes time an even more formidable foe," he said as he walked away.

My enlightened, "I'm golden" expression suddenly dimmed. It was now flummoxed and clearly read, "I'm fucked."

I looked the clock on the desk. It was shortly after 1:00 p.m. I'd been working for the last several hours without a break. I closed my notebook and held my hands tight to the cover. Did I recall a profound outpouring? No. At least not a literal one involving spilled ink.

I know what I wrote was relevant. It was worthwhile, and I did not have to proofread it—not yet. I'd used the pictures in my mind. I described them as I saw them. I remembered what the Chief said: "The memories you have are what you know." I took those words to heart.

I pressed my hands even tighter to the cover of my notebook, as if I was trying to absorb what I'd already written and transfer the next crop of words to come.

I stood up to stretch. I felt invigorated, even though my ass was asleep. I took a glass from the dresser. I went into the bathroom and filled it with cold tap water. It was refreshing. It felt like I hadn't had a drink of water in ages.

My stomach growled. It was lunchtime. I felt satisfied with the work I'd done. Now it was time to satisfy my hunger.

I knocked on the Chief's door. He did not answer right away. I knocked again, harder this time, and still nothing. I didn't knock again. I went to the lobby and thought about what I wanted to eat.

The Chief was seated in the lobby. He was reading a magazine and drinking a can of Schlafly wheat beer.

"Where'd you get the beer?" I asked.

"Where does anyone get beer? It's from the store," he responded.

"It seems a little early for beer, don't you think?"

"And that's precisely why I did not get one for you. You're one of those five o'clock guys."

"That's not true. I've had early beers with you on this trip. Remember Elko?"

"I do. Elko was the first and last place you seemed like an adventurer."

I scowled at his comment.

"So what have you done since breakfast?" he asked. "Did you find time to get a little more sleep in? Did you catch up on your serials? You know? Your pussy stories? Your *slop operas?*"

"I did. I did catch up on my stories," I said.

"Figures. Kid, I thought you were onto something," he said. "You get so close, then you piss it away. It makes me sad. You've got something good, you just keep ..."

I cut him off.

"Shut up for a second," I said. "Jesus, why the self-righteous stance? Give me a chance to talk."

The old man sat up and gave me a stern look. "Very well, Louie," he said. "The floor is yours."

"I did get caught up on my stories, Chief," I said as my face began to beam. "I wrote. I wrote like I haven't done in a while! It's finally happening!"

The Chief stood up. He stuck his chest out and gave me a sharp salute. "To you, kid," he said. "It's about goddamn time."

I tried to return his gesture, but it seemed weak and phony.

"Thank you," I said. "I thought you'd like to hear that."

He sat down and motioned to the chair in front of him. I walked to the chair, and just as I began to sit, he tossed a can of beer at me.

"You've earned this kid," he said. "Job well done."

"Thanks, but you haven't seen what I've done," I said. "Maybe it sucks?"

"No. It doesn't," he reassured me. "From now on, your work doesn't suck. You got that?"

I smiled. "I'll try to remember that," I said. "Anything else I should know?"

"Yeah. Don't open that can until you tap the top."

The Chief and I sat in the lobby and drank our beers. He'd been hiding a whole six-pack under the table by his chair. As one got finished, another would get opened. We drank all six in short order. They didn't seem to have time to get warm.

I sat up. I was buzzing a little.

"You know, Chief, I'd initially come down here to get lunch," I said. "But this beer was better than a soup or sandwich."

"Well, dammit, let's get some chow!" the Chief shouted. He looked toward the restaurant. "Cookie! Hop! Open the mess! The fleet's docked and hitting the town!"

His loud request fell on deaf ears. We were the only ones in the lobby besides the desk clerk, and the restaurant was closed until 6:00 p.m.

We started laughing like the drunks we were.

"Goddamn it, Louie," the Chief said. "I'm proud of you, me boy. It only took you half the trip to get off the stick."

I waved him off. "Don't get too worked up yet," I said. "It's only one day. It took this long."

"No. Don't think like that. You needed those days to get here. You've arrived. This is your destination. Now go and conquer it."

"What about everywhere else? Aren't they destinations too?"

"They are, but this is your landing point. From here you branch out—like a damn Viking!"

I laughed and pounded my chest. I made the half-assed sound of a Viking battle horn, belching midway through.

The Chief dug into the bag under the table. There were no more beers to be had.

"I think we're in for the day," I said. "What would you like to do tonight?"

The Chief thought. "Besides dinner? I'm not sure," he said. "Right now, I could use a little nap. Wake me when the dinner bell rings."

"Will do," I responded.

* * * * *

I tossed and tussled in bed as I tried to negotiate comfort with my sheets and my clothes. I wanted to sleep off a little bit of this buzz, but I did not want to go into full-on, stripped-down, *nighty-night* mode. I was beginning to sweat. I seemed to be putting too much work into a nap.

The late, great Jim Morrison mentioned waking up in the morning and getting himself a beer, while Sheryl Crow some years later noted the merits of the early beer buzz as well. I can't say I've had the pleasure. Cracking a cold one before I've brushed my teeth or eaten breakfast never crossed my mind; however, inebriation—at any level—at midday has always been bad juju for me.

I hate the clammy feeling I get from it: that not-quite-sweat-but-almost film that mists my body and puts my temperature somewhere between feverish and dead but nowhere near normal. It's disgusting.

I hate the lowered sense of awareness of the midday drunk even more. It seems that when I drink while the sun is still high in the sky, I become completely inept at everything. I can't talk. Everything I say sounds ridiculous—not just slurred but senseless. I don't think it is because no one has ever corrected me or called me out on it.

I feel like I'm moving slower too—trudging through a knee-deep puddle of semi-viscous mud while loosely-wrapped in tissue paper and trying to pierce a wall of Crisco-greased Saran Wrap.

I bump into things more often during a daylight drunk—probably because I can't see them as well. It's true. While my awareness and ability to speak is lowered, my sensitivity to light is increased, and I become blinded by an obnoxious, glowing aura of brightness. Obstacles I'm aware are suddenly hazards, and I'm constantly squinting and feeling about for whatever's around me and liable to trip me up.

I fell back onto the bed and curled up again. I moaned quietly to myself because the impact of my body on the mattress was painful. I may have even mumbled a minor prayer or two.

I wanted to be free of this state I was in. I wanted to wake up in a couple of hours and feel revived and ready to tackle the evening—and put on a proper *nighttime* buzz.

I closed my eyes and lay as still as possible. I could feel myself dozing. This was good—just don't think about it.

＊ ＊ ＊ ＊ ＊

The room seemed quite dark when I woke up. I couldn't have slept that long? I was slow to move, but felt better than I had before. Or so I thought. I sat up and the buzz had waned but was not completely gone. The room didn't spin as much as it swayed slightly.

I closed my eyes again, and when I opened them nothing changed. I looked at the clock on the desk. It was nearing 6:00 p.m., and I couldn't figure out why it was so dark out at this time on Midwestern summer day. The loud clap of thunder gave me my answer.

I pulled myself out of the bed and went to the window. I peered through the curtains and watched as the gray sheets of precipitation obscured everything beyond the glass. I thought of the song "Africa" by Toto and started singing it as I got my things around for a shower.

Africa—I'll bet the old bastard's never been there, I thought.

After showering and getting dressed, I felt better than I had earlier but was still not completely clear. I turned on the TV and caught the end of the six o'clock news. I wasn't paying much attention, but the abrupt cut from the sports wrap-up to a commercial for CDs made me take notice.

I went from half a story about the Cardinals' loss last night to suddenly hearing about the great crooners. I sat on the end of the bed and watched the song titles scroll up the screen as old, grainy, stretched black-and-white footage of the Chief's musical heroes popped in between numbers.

The voice-over celebrated the sounds and the voices, while the tunes and tones backed it all up. *You get hits like ... and who can forget? A must have for any collector ... But wait, there's more!* I thought about calling and ordering the set for the old man.

I made myself a little pot of coffee. It seemed late but sounded good. As it brewed I thought about the commercial I'd just seen. Before I met the Chief, I hadn't heard but one or two Frank Sinatra songs I could actually name, nor could I tell the difference between him, Sammy, *Dino*, or Bing. Now I was a semi-expert. I didn't know the songs, but I could differentiate the voices.

I poured a cup of Joe and sipped it. The songs from the CD ad bounced in my head and played like one of those early 1980s medleys—but without the canned handclaps and disco beat.

I laughed to myself as I thought about "Stars on 45" and how that song was my introduction to the Beatles. I thought of how when I finally heard the *actual* Beatles songs, my mind would naturally progress to the next song in the medley: *He's a real nowhere man … you're gonna love that girl.* Shit like that. Sad but true.

Now it was the Rat Pack and their contemporaries filling my head with a string of songs whose lyrics flowed together nicely but were not part of a single track.

I took another sip of coffee and was suddenly struck with an idea. I sat straight and almost spilled my drink. I knew what the Chief and I going to do tonight. I knew I'd finally stumbled upon something the Chief had not done. He'd been a fan of Sinatra, but the closest he'd ever gotten to him was listening to his music. Tonight, the Ol' Super Chief was going to become Ol' Blues Eyes. I was taking him to a karaoke bar! Now I just had to find one.

* * * * *

I went to the lobby and sought out the desk clerk. He was my only hope.

"Excuse me. I was wondering if you could help me?" I asked. "I'm trying to find a place to go do karaoke."

"I can tell you a ton of great places in town," the desk clerk said. "The better ones are in Fenton or Saint Louis, but you can stay close and have a good sing."

"Well then, set me up!" I said. "I'm looking for a place that does it all."

"That would be C-Notes. They've got a book for every genre, not just one or two with a mix. They've got one for fifties stuff, one for R & B, one for classic rock. You name it."

"Sounds like my place. How far away is it?"

"It's about five miles from here."

"Thanks a lot, man," I said to the clerk. "You've made this a breeze."

The clerk pointed at me like Isaac the Bartender from *The Love Boat.*

"No problem, sir," he said. "Maybe I'll see you out there after my shift?"

"Well, if everything goes well, I'm sure I'll still be there when you're off."

I ran to the Chief's room. I couldn't wait to tell him how I'd found something he'd never done.

"Chief, it's Louis," I said. I gave the door a good tap as I leaned into it.

The Chief opened the door and gave me a look.

"You look like you've got something to say," the Chief said. "Is it important?"

"No, it's not really important," I said. "But it's different."

"Really? Well, where are we going?"

"It's a surprise, Chief. That's all I can tell you right now."

"Can you at least tell me if there's food and drink?"

"Yes."

"Well?"

"Well what?"

"Are you going to tell me if there's food and drink?"

I looked at him and shook my head in disbelief. "Chief, it's me. It's us. We're going out," I said. "Do you think I'd take you someplace where food and drink were not served? I mean, really?"

"I dunno, kid," he said. "You've been trying to figure out things I haven't done and places I haven't been. I can tell you I've never been to a place that didn't have *chews and booze.*"

I laughed. "There will be 'chews and booze,'" I assured him. "And some things you never expected."

He scowled at me. "Nah, I don't like the sound of that," he said.

"It'll be fine, Chief, trust me," I said. "You'll like this."

We got to the lobby, and I called a cab to come and get us. While I waited for the dispatcher to connect, the Chief held court again.

The cab driver came into the lobby. "Cab for DeCarlo!" he yelled.

"Chief, we've got to go," I said. "Our ride is here."

The Chief looked at me like I'd interrupted some grand speech.

"Can't you see I'm entertaining guests?" he asked in a terribly executed Victorian Dandy accent.

"And you can continue to entertain," I said. "Tell them to join us for dinner."

He waved me off. A couple of the guests he was chatting up shot me cold looks as well.

"I'm sorry about this, man," I said to the driver.

"It's okay, but I've got other fares," he replied. "And they're ready to go."

I slumped in defeat. I was ready to tip him and tell him to forget the ride.

"Fuck it …" I said. I walked over to the Chief and grabbed his arm. "Come on, let's go."

It was easier than I thought to pull the Chief away from his audience. He argued and complained but did not resist. We walked out and got into the cab.

"Was that so difficult?" I asked.

"No, but why must you embarrass me like that?" he asked. "My friends want to hear my words of wisdom."

"If they were that taken, they'll come back. Besides we have plans."

"Yes, these 'plans' you mention. You still haven't said what they are."

"All in due time, Chief. I told you, it's a surprise."

The Chief leaned toward the driver. "So, *Leadfoot*, where are you taking us?" he asked.

The driver chuckled. "You guys are going to dinner and show," he said. "At least that's what I've been told."

We arrived at our destination, and I wasn't sure how this was all going to work. I'd never been to a place like this and had forgotten to find out if the place served food or not. All my questions were answered when I saw the sign in the window that read, "EATS, TREATS, and BEATS—SWEET!"

I paid the fare and thanked the driver. The Chief mumbled and got out of the cab. The driver looked back at me.

"Have fun with that one," he said.

I shook my head and laughed. "He'll be fine once he gets a crowd," I said.

The Chief and I walked inside the doors of C-Notes, and a hostess took us to a table and gave us menus. We ordered a pitcher of Schlafly pale ale to start and perused the fare.

"They've got a lot of food," I said. "Too many choices."

The Chief scowled at the selections. "It's like that place we went to yesterday," he said. "Burgers, fries—I feel like I'm at a bad barbecue."

"There's other stuff too," I said. "Steak, chicken, fish. Regular dinners."

The Chief looked at the stage. "Is there a band here or something?" he asked. "What's the deal with all that rigmarole?"

I shrugged my shoulders and played dumb. The Chief scanned the scene and shook his head. He seemed to be frustrated with the situation. The people that were coming into the building were not helping matters either.

"The warden know the gates got left open?" he grumbled as a group of twentysomethings walked by our table.

"Be nice," I said. "Probably on probation."

The Chief didn't acknowledge my comment. He just sized up and stared down every person who walked through the door—no matter what they looked like.

"This sucks, Louie," he said. "What the hell kinda place are they running here?"

"It's a dining establishment, Chief," I said. "It's 'chews and booze,' just like you wanted. Plus there's a little something extra too. That's for later."

A waiter brought our pitcher and two pint glasses. He asked if we were ready to order, and I said no. This gave the Chief another reason to be pissed off at me. How dare I speak on his behalf?

Our waiter came back, and we ordered dinner. The Chief put his menu to his face so I could not see him order his food. He ordered the surf and turf platter. I'd decided on the French dip sandwich and Caesar salad. I also got some potato wedges to share.

The Chief hummed strange little tunes as I was ordering, and this caused our waiter a bit of unease.

"Are you going to do this all night?" I asked.

The Chief gave me a "Who? Me?" stare. I didn't say anything. I poured myself a glass of beer and looked at the crowd building in the restaurant.

"Did you forget somebody?" I heard him say. "Where are your manners?"

I turned to the Chief and put my hands up. "Are you talking to me?" I asked. "Are we back on speaking terms?"

He slid his glass to me. "Just pour the old bastard a beer, kid," he said.

I smiled and fulfilled his request.

"Glad to have you back," I said.

The Chief nodded and took a drink. The waiter brought our appetizers and my salad just as the emcee for karaoke stepped onto the stage.

"What's this?" the Chief asked.

"Potatoes," I said. "They're for us to share."

"Not the potatoes. That guy up there. What's his deal?"

"He's running the entertainment tonight."

"So there is a band?"

"No, Chief, there's karaoke."

"*Croaky?* What the hell is that all about?"

"It's where people get up and sing songs. It's fun."

"Fun? You call listening to some dolt caterwauling *fun*? It's god-damn torture. Maybe we oughta go somewhere else."

I shook my head. "No. We're staying here," I said. "I told you I was gonna find something you've never done—and this is it."

"What? You mean suffer through someone butchering a song?" he asked. "I've done that before—a lot."

"Well, my idea was to get you up for a song," I said. "Let you be a star for a little while."

"Fuck that!" he said loudly. "Not for every dollar or drop of booze in the world. You're crazy, son. Goddamn crazy."

I sighed to myself. I should have known this was not going to work.

"I'm sorry, Chief," I said. "I just wanted to do something special for you. Something you'd never done. Let's just eat and we'll get going."

The Chief shook his head. "Nah, kid, let's stick around," he said. "I'm not gonna embarrass myself, but I don't mind watching other people do it."

I smiled at his comment. "Maybe they won't be as bad as you think?" I said.

He looked around the room. "You see this place? You see these people?" he asked. "They'll be *even worse!*"

The emcee tapped the microphone and got everyone in the place stirring.

"Good Friday night, C-Notes! I'm Marshall, your Captain of Karaoke," he said, as the crowd cheered and whistled. "Okay, who's ready to get up here and get things started? The books are out, but the slips are blank. Do I need to kick everyone in the can?"

The crowd laughed. Some people got up and cautiously grabbed books and request slips. Marshall's spiel was typical for karaoke—no one ever just gets up and does it; he was the prompt.

He opened the floor with Loverboy's "Workin' for the Weekend." Cliché but fitting, and it got everyone in the mood.

I was bobbing my head and singing along, loud-mouthing the lyric "Let's *go!*" when it came up and giving a fist pump. The Chief rolled his eyes and shook his head. The music and singing were not overly loud, which was nice. We didn't have to yell to talk.

"People do this?" the Chief asked. "They really do this?"

"Yeah, all the time," I said. "You've never seen this before?"

"In Japan but never in the States. And I gotta say, it's very different over there."

"Drunk-ass businessmen different?"

"That's the best way to put it."

We watched as one by one, people got up and sang their songs. Some had good pipes; others got by with what they could. For them, it was more of a show than a show of talent. I mumbled along with the tunes. I knew them all.

"Why don't you get up there and sing one," the Chief suggested. "You seem to be chomping at the bit."

"No, I'll pass for now," I said. "I've got to be in the right frame of mind to do this."

"Then why the hell are we here?" the Chief asked.

"Because I wanted you to …" I paused.

"What? You wanted me to what?" he asked.

"I wanted you to be Frank Sinatra for a minute," I confessed. "You've done all this shit and been all these places, but you've never got a chance to … well … stand in the shoes of your idol."

The Chief laughed out loud. It was a boisterous guffaw, the kind I'd heard him coax out of others. "Goddamn you, Louie! Why, you old Georgia pot-licker!" he said as he smacked the table. "That's the funniest—and most noble thing anyone's ever said to me."

"Well, that's why we're here, Chief."

"Kid, I appreciate the sentiment. And I appreciate your confidence in this old son of a bitch, but I can't sing— especially like Ol' Blue Eyes."

I nodded and smiled. "It was worth a shot, I suppose," I said.

"You gave it the old college try, Louie," he said. "Let's just sit here, drink, and let everyone else entertain us."

"That sounds good to me."

We'd been at C-Notes for a couple of hours and had gone through five pitchers of beer. I'd consumed of majority of the beverage while the Chief stayed moderate and focused. The restaurant had darkened considerably. The illumination from the neon beer signs, dim track lights, and faint glow of the kitchen fluorescents peeking through the cracks in the door were of little help in making objects recognizable. I squinted in the dark to see who was heading to the stage.

For most of the night, it was an all-male revue. There were plenty of women in the place, but only a couple of them got up to sing—and they did their songs together, even though they weren't duets.

I called to our waiter and ordered another pitcher of beer and glass of scotch. As we waited for our libations to arrive, the Captain of Karaoke gave a shout-out to the "birthday bunch at the back table." He got the crowd to honor them with a feisty if not intimidating version of "Birthday" by the Beatles. I belted out the song and riffed along on my air guitar. The Chief stared at me through the whole thing.

"I'm having a great time!" I yelled. "I may just have to get up and have a sing!"

"So you're finally in the right frame of mind?" the Chief asked.

"No, but I'm totally freakin' hammered," I said. "Stop! *Hamm-ah tam!*"

My Georgia drawl was becoming more pronounced even as the words I spoke were not.

Our waiter set the drinks down and stepped back from the table.

I stood up. "Where y'all goin'?" I asked. "C'mon, sit day-own. Have a bare widdus. Whadyasigh?"

The waiter looked at me and shook his head. "Thank you for the offer, sir, but I'm still on shift."

I crinkled my face and snapped my head. "Aw, hail! That shit juss ain' rat," I said.

The waiter laughed and patted my shoulder. It wasn't a hard pat, but it was enough to push me down to my seat.

I've been inebriated like this before—a couple of times on this trip as a matter of fact; however, this time was different. This time I wasn't pining or sulking, nor was I overthinking and paranoid. This time, I was having fun and I wanted to have more. I was going to sing a song. I needed to express myself and channel my star power.

"Ahm gittin' a soungbook, Chayf!" I said. "Be bake, dreckly." The Chief nodded and pointed toward the table with the books.

I got up and moved between tables, grabbing the backs of chairs every so often, saying things like "Sarry bat thay-yat" and "Skee-yooze may" as I did.

I found the book I wanted and found my song. I scribbled the tune, the call number, and my name onto the request slip and put it in the jar next to the emcee's booth. Marshall nodded to me, and I gave him a thumbs-up before I made my way back to the table.

As I approached my seat, Marshall called up the next singer.

"Holly, you're up, sweetheart," he said. "Holly's gonna take you on a trip."

The girl giggled and covered the microphone. She said something to Marshall, and he turned on a switch behind the booth. A pin light shot across the ceiling, and the room filled with slow spinning dots of light. A soft piano began to play from the speakers. The girl bowed her head and held the microphone tight in her hands. As soon as the first seven words spilled from her lips, C-Notes erupted as if it was a concert hall and this dame was Beyoncé or Kelly Clarkson.

"Hey, lady … you, lady. Cursing at your life …" she sang.

I sat straight and listened as this chanteuse delicately worked her way through the first verses of Charlene's "I've Never Been to Me." It was an amazing rendition of the song. I hadn't heard it in years, and hearing this woman soar effortlessly amid the lyrics brought a tear to my eye. Even the Chief took notice.

"This song could be about you, you know that?" I said. "Just listen to the words."

The Chief wasn't paying attention to what she was singing; he was paying attention to her face.

"Why does she look familiar?" he asked.

"Probably because you're horn-doggin', Chief," I said. My drawl had receded to normal proportions.

"No. It's not that," the Chief said. "Well … not entirely." We listened and enjoyed the serenade. I had no idea who this lady was, but I just knew she'd been all over the place—*but never to her*. I sang along and found myself getting way too animated—throwing my hands at her and getting caught up in the drama of the song.

When Holly had finished singing, the whole place gave her a standing ovation. I stood up and gave her a frat boy "Yeah" and a couple of boisterous "woos." I clapped until my palms were stinging and buzzing. I don't know if I was louder than everyone else, but she looked right at me and gave me a glare. Then she smiled and threw her head back. She pointed to me and waved and made her way to our table.

"Well, hello, strangers!" she said in a scratchy but perky voice. "Look who it is!" Her face lit up as she sat next to me and pushed me into the booth.

"Well, I'll be a goddamn mare's ass, Louie," he said. "If it ain't Ms. Golightly, our tomato from last night."

And so it was. Holly looked so different than she had last night. Her hair was down, and she was not wearing her Poor Richard's uniform and apron. Her makeup was slightly more conservative, and it made her look prettier and younger, fresher and happier.

Holly laughed. "That's me," she said. "What are you two doing here?"

The Chief pointed to me. "Genius here wanted me to get up and make an ass of myself," he said. "I'm gonna let him crash and burn first."

Holly looked at me. "What are you going to sing?" she asked.

"It's a surprise," I said. "Nobody's gonna know it. Not like your song. That was beautiful."

It was dark, but I could sense Holly blushing. "Thank you," she said. "I just love that song so much."

I smiled and poured myself another drink. "Me too," I said. I could feel my chest get heavy, and I didn't know why.

"Ms. Golightly, would you like a drink?" the Chief asked.

"I would love one," she said. "I've got another song in, but it won't be up for a while. I'd like a Cape Cod if that's okay."

"Holly, you can have whatever you want," I said. "It's on me. Order up! *Everybody Wang Chung tonight!*" Holly laughed, and the Chief shook his head.

"Glad you're in a good mood tonight, kid," the Chief said.

"Why's that?" I asked.

"Because you're gonna be hurting like a son of a bitch tomorrow," he said.

Marshall got on the mic again and called my song. "All right, C-Notes. When you're lost in the desert, what do you do?" he asked the crowd. "Well, Louie is gonna take you to a chill zone—you know what I'm talkin' about! Louie. Take these folks to the oasis!"

Holly stood up to let me out. The Chief seemed impressed that I'd referred to myself as *Louie*.

My knees buckled as I stepped from the table.

"Are you okay?" Holly asked.

"Ahm good," I said. "Mah foozjuss aslaype—s'all." My drunken drawl had returned.

I walked to the stage, retracing the path I'd taken earlier.

"S'up, Cap-in?" I asked as Marshall handed me the microphone.

He laughed. "Was that intro okay?" he asked.

"Werks fer may," I said.

Marshall set my tune up. "You know there's two vocals in this, right?" he asked.

"Sho' nuff ah do, but ah kin handle 'em, okay," I said.

The intro to Oasis's "Acquiesce" faded in, and I held the microphone above my head. I sang the mixed-down, reverbed vocal, but no one could hear me. I continued to hold the mic above my head as the guitars blasted through the monitors and back into my face. The sound of the opening riff spun in front and on both sides of me. I watched the lyric meter count down on the screen to my right—four, three, two, one ... *you're up, dude.*

I did my best Liam Gallagher impression, slurring through the first verses of the song. I put a hand out to grab some imaginary *anything*, while my other hand held the mic tightly as it rolled across my mouth. When the chorus came on, I was flat for the first three words. I modulated up and caught the key. This was the second vocal part. *Damn you, Noel*, I thought.

The crowd was blurry but in a groove. I loved it, but the swaying and fist pumping was making me nauseous. Every movement had a trailer. The lights on stage were hot and made me feel claustrophobic.

I was sweating, and as the song neared the second chorus, I felt I was either going to pass out or throw up. I maintained my composure and kept singing. I held the notes of the last chorus and moved in time with the outro as the guitar slowed to a halt at the end of the song.

As I had at the beginning, I held the mic above my head until the last note. I dropped to my knees, and everyone stood up and cheered for me. They had no idea this was not an act. I'd dropped from being drunk, for sure, but there was something else wrong with me. I was not okay. Regardless, I wasn't going to say anything.

"Thenk y'all ... SAY-NOWTS!" I bellowed. The speakers popped, and I cringed at the sound.

Marshall helped me up. "Are you okay, man?" he asked.

I nodded and handed him the mic.

"That was pretty damn good," he said, as he guided me off the stage. "C-Notes, let's hear it for Louie—the third Gallagher Brother!"

People moved me along as I struggled to get back to my seat. When I got to the table, the Chief and Holly were gone. A full pitcher of beer, two half-empty pint glasses, a fresh Cape Cod, and an empty low-ball glass sat alone on the table top. I smelled Holly's drink, moved the straw, and took a sip of it. I topped off my glass and took a swig of my beer.

The next song started playing, and at first, it didn't sound like karaoke. Maybe Marshall was on break for a few minutes? No. It *was* karaoke and this guy was way too good. The song was "Something to Believe in" by Poison—not what I wanted to hear at the moment.

My head sagged, and I tried to shake out what was building in my brain, but I could not. Between the song I'd sung and the current one, my emotions were going haywire. I began to fight back tears by taking bigger gulps of my beer. The Chief and Holly were still gone. I had no idea where they were. They'd left me alone, and I don't know if that was good for me at the moment.

Oh, and there's the line, "My best friend died a lonely man, in some Palm Springs Hotel room." I lost it.

I was in a dark booth, but I was surrounded by people, noise, and drinks, so I was not truly alone. However, I felt isolated. I was crying—sobbing heavily and lamenting a loss. How and why it all happened I don't know, but the memories of my friend's suicide came flooding back to me, vivid and clear. It was years ago, but at this moment—it had just happened.

Fuck you, Jay—why, man? Why?

Jay and I were tight from the beginning. We'd met when we were eight years old at one of those youth meet-and-greet things. We were too young to be awkward, but were we ever. I was fat, scab-riddled, and had fucked up teeth; Jay was a walking ribcage, had a bad speech impediment, and looked as though he'd never seen a comb in his life.

We shared a common interest in Japanese sci-fi/fantasy shows like *Ultraman* and anything the Toho Company had put out: *Godzilla, Rodan, Mothra* ... things like that. Jay had lived in Hawaii for a year and knew more of the characters than I did. I caught up as best I could.

The big kids in the neighborhood gave us a lot of grief. They didn't like the fact we were "making that stupid shit up" or "siding with the Japs." Yes, even California had its share of insensitivity in the mid seventies.

Our families shared ties as well: they'd transplanted to California from the south (North Carolina) and our dads worked in the same place, although they had different jobs.

Our parents' ideals were worlds apart, but their leanings seemed ironic at times—even reversed. My folks were liberal and pretty open; while Jay's were walled and slightly conservative. His parents drank daily; mine kept it to social circles.

Jay's mom made crabmeat *hors d'oeuvres* and spiced tea for us when we camped out in the backyard; my mom would bake football-shaped cookies and let us drink full jars of Gatorade after Friday football games against the neighbor kids.

Jay's folks had the premium channels HBO and ONTV, and his dad also had quite a stash of porn! My folks had legit movies but a lot of bootlegged blockbusters of the time—we were watching *Star Wars* at home long before it was commercially available. We were also the first family on the block to have a both a Betamax and a VHS player as well. Both of our households had MTV, though.

Jay and I got on well with each other's parents. We enjoyed the variants they brought to our lives, and they were always teaching us new things. Our families didn't socialize but were always abreast of what each one was doing.

Our home lives were different. I had two sisters and a tank of angelfish for pets. Jay was an only child but had a dog, a guinea pig, and a lizard he'd named Ghidorah. He'd made it sound like an iguana, but it was just a skink.

We lived for our imaginations. When our favorite characters left us with no new ideas for play, we made up our own stuff. We created books, drew pictures, and even acted out scenarios in a most grand fashion. We stuck together through everything and were practically inseparable.

The first hurdle in our friendship was a kid named Alan. Alan had moved to town from Oklahoma, and his dad was our dad's new boss. Alan tested me and Jay by pitting us against each other—we were just too naïve to realize it at the beginning. The worst time was when he made us fight over marbles.

Alan was an instigator of the highest order, and he knew how to rile me up. He told me that Jay had cheated me. Jay swore he had not, but Alan was convincing—conniving and evil. I believed him over my best friend.

Alan told me I didn't "have to put up with that" and said I needed to take what was mine. He shoved Jay and me together. We naturally pushed back, and that made things worse. Alan convinced us we were both going to attack each other. And that was it.

I jumped at Jay and knocked him to the ground. I punched him hard to the body, but Alan encouraged me to hit his face. I did. Alan yelled at me, telling me to hit his face *harder*. I heeded his demands. I was a lot bigger and stronger than Jay, and I hurt him very badly.

When the fight had finished, I stood over my friend's shaking, bloodied body and wept. I heard Alan walk behind me; suddenly, he kicked me square in the ass. I stumbled and fell over Jay before landing flat on the concrete. My face hit the ground. I chipped my top front teeth and cut my chin. Alan leaned over me, laughed, and called me a "pussy sperm faggot." I didn't know what these words meant—I was barely nine years old.

Alan jerked my shorts down and twisted them around my ankles, holding them in one hand. With the other hand, he grabbed the waistband of my semi-stained, fat-boy briefs and yanked them into the crack of my ass. He pulled so hard I could feel my testicles squeeze against my perineum. The physical pain was great, but it was nothing compared to what I'd felt emotionally. I felt humiliated—for what was happening to me and what I'd done to Jay.

Alan told me I needed to "scrub my shit." He pulled my underwear up even further—tugging hard until they could move no more. All that seemed to remain was the stretched, elastic band. The rest of the fabric had disappeared between my cheeks and was partially in my anus. By this time, Jay had rolled over and crawled to safety. A trail of blood marked his path. Alan—still holding my ankles and the waistband of my underwear—picked my fat ass up about three inches from the ground and then let go.

My body hit the solid pavement and a puff of dust burst from beneath me. All the air in my lungs expelled, and my forehead crashed onto the concrete—my nose and mouth followed. I could not breathe, nor could I feel pain at the moment, but I could taste blood and dirt. I wheezed to get air, but it wasn't coming. I heard gravel crunching and saw Alan's green Puma Clydes come into view. I thought he was going to kick me in the face, but he didn't. I watched his shoes turn and walk to the left. I saw him scoop up the marbles I'd fought with Jay for. He put them in a bag and started to walk away.

"Don't butt-fuck each other, you two cunt-sucking come eaters," Alan said as he left us to die.

I slid slowly over to Jay and held him. My underwear was still crammed in my ass, but I didn't care. We cried so hard in each other's arms. He kept asking me "Why?"

I kept saying "I'm so sorry." Jay asked if I was still his friend. I told him I was and always will be. He asked what all those things

Alan said to us meant. I told him I didn't know—I just knew they were bad.

Jay and I lay holding each other for what seemed like hours. We were broken and ashamed, stripped of our dignity—and our marbles. The sun beat down on us, and I could feel my skin burn. I didn't care. I couldn't control myself and peed. My urine soaked through the fabric of my underwear and Jay's shorts as well. I cried even harder as I apologized to my friend—for hurting him and now pissing on him. He didn't say a word, nor did he let me go.

* * * * *

Marshall announced the next singer. His words were garbled, but I recognized his voice. It was comforting. I looked up and saw I was still alone. The room was a slow centrifuge, and everything was becoming surreal. The only known absolutes were me, my drink, this booth, and the music. The sounds of a melancholy, dry, but jangly guitar filled the space I was in. I heard people cheering, but it was droning and slow and distant.

"I read the news today, oh boy …"

"A Day in the Life," I said through my tears. I raised my glass. "To John … to Jay …" I took a drink and even though I was draining a lot from the glass, I was spilling just as much down my shirt.

* * * * *

Jay and I remained close into our teenage years. The fight we'd had should've destroyed us, but it didn't. We had tussles as friends do, but nothing ever compared to the "Marble Melee."

When high school started, we separated. Jay and his family moved back to North Carolina, while mine stayed in California. We kept in touch—lots of letters and phone calls, and we split visits over the summer. While our friendship remained enduring, our interests and paths had not.

Jay was insufferably girl-crazy and had a chick all the time. He'd lost his virginity his freshman year and had gotten a girl pregnant before he'd turned sixteen—she ended up getting an abortion. I didn't start *dating* until I was sixteen and fell head over heels in love with the first girl I went out with. We didn't last too long—I guess I was too clingy?

Jay was heavily into film and television. He could cite lines verbatim and always had a quote that fit any situation. I was more focused on writing and drawing—I read the books that begat the flicks he watched. Don't ask me to give you the exact words, though. I was more of a paraphraser.

Our common art denominator was music. We loved the same bands and traded favorites when we'd discover something new.

Jay lashed out against his family's conservatism, becoming involved in community activities that defied their conventions. I didn't give a shit about sociopolitical things. My *rebellion* came via learning to play guitar and joining a band. Jay always told me how jealous he was that I could *play* the songs now.

At seventeen, I'd finally gotten into real, solid relationship with a girl. However, Jay had begun to drift. He professed himself to be bisexual and was experimenting as much as possible. He claimed he would not be held down by social labels.

I went to visit him in the summer. He came out and told me he was gay. At the time, he called himself *queer*. He told me if I was threatened by this, if it was okay. I was not. He kissed me on the mouth like a lover. I was more shocked than anything.

"You didn't run," he said. "You should have. I'm so sorry. I don't know why I did that."

"Jay, you're my best friend," I said. "Maybe you needed a test? Did you pass? Did *we* pass? I don't know what to say. I love you. You have to know that. And I don't care who you have sex with."

I smiled at him. "But please promise you'll never kiss me like that again," I said.

Jay blushed and shook his head. "I won't," he said. "And I think we both passed."

After that summer, we never saw much of each other. It had nothing to do with the kiss or anything—it just had to do with time and life. I moved back to Georgia to attend college at Valdosta

State. Jay made his way back to California and enrolled at Cal-State Fullerton.

He became involved with the fledgling AIDS awareness group ACT UP. I saw him on TV a couple of times. *My best friend—a celebrity for the greater good!*

He sent me a pin that said "SILENCE = DEATH." I wore it around campus and received a variety of looks. I thought it had something to do with music—if you hear a new band, spread the word: their livelihood depends on it! I was corrected by one group and called out by another. Both had asked me to remove the pin. I acquiesced but continued to carry it in my backpack—as a tribute to my friend and his fight.

Jay sent me pictures of him and his boyfriend. They were hanging out on the Embarcadero in San Francisco. He looked so happy and better than I'd seen him in years. In return, I sent him pictures of me and my new girl. We were happy too—until she'd cheated on me, "accidentally" got pregnant, and we split up. I'm glad he got to see the *photo* me. I was worse for wear for some time thereafter.

"He blew his mind out in a car. He didn't notice that the lights had changed ..."

Jay had so much promise. His activism—at least to me—was legendary. He made me aware of things that I'd become sheltered to, or just didn't think had an effect on me. I'd send him notes I'd written: op-ed pieces for my journalism classes, which I knew were too controversial for Valdosta State but were perfect for his cause. He'd write back and send pictures of signs he'd made and tell me of the marches he was in and the places he'd been.

I missed my friend. I checked the news constantly to see if I could catch a glimpse of Jay—standing tall and speaking out, spreading awareness and breaking that Death invoking silence. I was hoping an ACT UP March would make its way to the Valdosta State Campus. I knew Jay would be there, and even though I was an outsider, I could still join my friend and support him and this cause he believed in so strongly. Unfortunately, that would never happen.

I was in my senior year at Valdosta State and mere weeks from graduating. I'd just got back from a study circle with some classmates. For this particular group; however, it was more of a study *round*—as in round of drinks and very little studying. My roommate left me a note to call my folks.

LD,

Your mom called about seven thirty. Said it was important. Call back ASAP. Regardless of the time.

—Scootch

It was after midnight in Valdosta but just past 9:00 p.m. on the West Coast. I was half-crocked. I pulled myself together as best I could and called my parents. I tried to think one word ahead so I wouldn't sound drunk. I wondered what could be so important. The phone continued to ring.

"Hello?" I heard my mom say.

"Hi, Mom, it's Louis," I said, trying to sound sober.

There was silence. "Hi, honey. Are you sitting down?" she asked.

"Yeah, I actually am. What's wrong?" I asked. "Is everything okay?"

I heard her exhale.

"I'm afraid I've got some bad news for you," she said. "We got a call from Marla Trigg—Jay's mom ..."

"Yeah ..." I said.

"Louis. Jay ..." My mom paused. "Oh, honey ... Jay passed away yesterday." I heard her sniffle and start crying.

I was silent. I held the phone away from my ear for a second. *I didn't hear that.*

"What? What did you say?" I asked. "Mom ..."

"Jay's gone, Louis," my mom said. "He passed away yesterday. It was an accident."

Suddenly, the alcohol in my system and the attempt at feigning sobriety collided. I was not in my dorm room. I was sitting on my chair out in space. The phone was still to my ear.

Nothing was real. I closed my eyes and inhaled deeply. My face felt as if it were being pulled into my skull.

I tried to be calm. "Mom, what happened?" I asked, as my eyes began to well.

"Mrs. Trigg said Jay committed suicide," my mom said. "He was sick, Louis. He was going to the hospital, and he took his own life."

I was back in my room. I stood up in my chair and began yelling at my mom.

"He didn't 'pass away,' Mom! He fucking killed himself!"

My roommate: *Scootch*—Scott—jumped and grabbed me.

"Louis, please don't ... I know you're upset ... please don't yell ..." my mother pleaded. "Please. This is hard for all of us."

"How did he do it, Mom?" I yelled. *"How did he kill himself?"*

"He shot himself. He shot ..." My mom paused. I heard the phone drop.

"He shot himself? He didn't pass away—he blew his fucking brains out!" I asked, trying to rationalize what happened.

"He blew his fucking brains out?" I repeated, asking myself if that's what happened.

"He. Blew. His. Fucking. Brains. Out!" I stated word for word to Scott, as if he'd known Jay and I wanted him to be in as much disbelief as I was.

Scott was still holding me. I burst into tears. I threw the phone. It hit the closet door and dented it, but the handset was not damaged. The cord stretched and the handset flew back. It rolled on the desk and slid. I can only imagine the awful sounds that could be heard on the other end of the line. Scott picked up the phone and tried to give it back to me. I would not take it.

"Hello?" he said to my mom. "This is Scott. I'm Lou's roommate."

I could not hear my mother's voice.

"Uh-huh," Scott said. He listened and shook his head. "Oh my God ..." He looked at me in shock but was still talking to my mom. "I'm so sorry," he said.

I pulled away from Scott and paced the room. He kept an arm's length between us.

How did this happen? Why did this happen? I have to go home. I have to see Jay. How the fuck am I gonna see Jay? HE'S FUCKING DEAD! HE KILLED HIMSELF! I'LL NEVER SEE HIM AGAIN! I'LL NEVER SEE …

I dropped to my knees and cried and prayed and cursed and did all the things a human being does when their best friend dies—or worse—takes their own life.

I hated Jay right now. I hated him more than I'd ever hated anyone. My love for him would return, but now I needed this. I needed to lash out at him. I needed to let my best friend know how selfish he was. He had to know how much he'd taken away from so many. He had to know how much of a hole he'd left in the hearts and lives of those he'd touched.

My love had quickly returned as I knew it would, but it was still so overshadowed by my hate—which had subsided to bitter anger. I put my face in my hands and thought of how much I loved Jay and I missed him and how I'd never—*ever*—get the chance to tell him such things again.

I wanted to go to California, but I didn't. I couldn't. There was really no reason to. There was no funeral. Jay was cremated. His parents sent everyone they knew a small card commemorating Jay's life and all the wonderful things he had done. I found it ironic. The very things they praised were the ones to which they'd been so morally opposed. I guess they'd either come around or felt it best to honor their only son and his cause. I don't know. Regardless, it was nice to see.

Jacob "Jay" Trigg—my best friend—had tested HIV positive in 1988. An early chance casual sexual encounter was all it took. He'd unknowingly lived with the virus for a couple of years before getting treatments. Hell, he'd had it when he kissed me. Even after getting diagnosed, he never said a word about being infected. In 1990, his doctor determined the HIV had manifested itself into full-blown

AIDS. This disease he'd fought so strongly against had hit him hard and quick. The only person who knew he was sick was his boyfriend.

Jay's boyfriend said that when he learned of the diagnosis, he felt he'd betrayed those he loved and *the cause*—not himself or his beliefs. He said he felt like a hypocrite and could no longer fight. I thought the only hypocritical thing he did was give up. I found myself thinking back to the Chief's comment about fighting a concept with its exact opposite. The exact opposite of a disease is a cure. Unfortunately for Jay and thousands of others, that was not an option.

My best friend did not die like the Poison lyric says: "a lonely man in some Palm Springs hotel room." No, he died like the Beatles lyric: a very loved man who "blew his mind out in his car" in the parking lot of a clinic in Van Nuys, California. His boyfriend remained outside the car when he shot himself. He saw the traffic signal change as he heard the gunfire.

* * * * *

My mind cleared for a moment. I was still at C-Notes, still in the booth, still drunk and still by myself. Strangely; though, I did not feel alone anymore.

My eyes were sore from crying, and my mouth tasted of seasoned meat and salt, garlic and cheese, metal, acid, and—of all things—chalk. My tongue was coated, and the sensation made me shiver. There was an odd sweet finish to it all. I belched and got a quick burst of acid warmth. I swallowed it and cringed. I exhaled the odor through my nose.

My shirt was damp from where I'd spilled beer. I felt the spot. It wasn't as bad as it seemed, but it was uncomfortable—like I'd sweat below my collar. I touched the crotch of my pants to make sure I hadn't spilled there. I had not. I breathed a sigh of relief and chuckled out loud. No one heard me. The music was still playing.

I looked around the table, and things came together. I'd finished my beer, drank half of the Chief's glass, and polished off Holly's Cape

Cod. That explained the sweetness and the coated tongue. *Oops.* I flagged down a server.

A waitress came to the table. I was relieved it was not our regular server.

"Hey, I just wanted to say you were really good up there," she said. "What can I get for you?"

I smiled and blushed. "Thank you," I said. I tightened up to appear sober. "I'd like to get another pitcher of Schlafly pale and a Cape Cod."

"Coming right up," she said.

I was praying the waitress would return before the Chief and Holly.

I felt better for a moment. I continued to collect myself. I was still trying to figure out why I'd channeled back to Jay and his suicide. I know the music was a factor, but it still was not making complete sense. I'd deal with it later.

Marshall announced the next singer, and it was Holly again. This time, she sang a song I knew but didn't invoke any reminiscent feelings or tug at my heartstrings—it just made me smile: "Automatic" by the Pointer Sisters. I was amazed she could get her voice that deep.

The waitress returned while Holly was singing. She put the drinks down, and I made sure no one was wise to the exchange. I refilled the Chief's glass and mine as well. Holly's Cape Cod glass looked different. Would she notice? I hoped not.

I glanced around the restaurant again. I finally spied the Chief. He was watching Holly sing from a small table near the stage. He sat and listened to her—nodding and smiling; making sure she was hitting all the notes like some talent agent protecting his star. *What a cad*, I thought.

I was going to join the Chief, but my body had other plans. As soon as I took my first step, my face flushed. My forehead became clammy, and a cold film of perspiration spread across it like a headband. Everything that had sat dormant in my stomach began to churn. A spray of bile shot into my throat. It tasted like rotten garlic and bad orange juice.

I grabbed the table and rested against it. Gravity was working against the contents of my stomach, and I instinctively moved toward the men's room.

I kicked opened the bathroom door. I fell into a stall and didn't even consider cleanliness or sanitization—I dropped to the floor, grabbed the rim of the bowl, and vomited violently.

I made pleas to the Lord God as I pushed down and purged. I was loud, and the sounds I made echoed mightily around the bathroom. Tears streamed down my cheeks, and my throat burned. I pulled a goodly amount of toilet paper from the ringer and wiped my face as best I could.

I was shaking as I reached for the handle to flush the toilet. The power flush sucked the puke down to sewage oblivion, as the clean, cold water that refilled the bowl splashed and drops struck my skin.

I stood up and left the stall to clean myself up. I washed my hands like Lady Macbeth—scrubbing and grinding my palms. I dried them just as aggressively. I ran the faucet and splashed some water on my face. My mouth still tasted awful, and I looked terrible.

Along the wall was a bank of small vending machines, each machine dispensing different items for enhancing social situations. One had condoms, another had cologne, one had aspirin and antacids, while the last one had mouthwash. I crammed seventy-five cents into the mouthwash dispenser and out dropped a small liquid pack of Scope. I tore it open and squeezed it into my mouth. It didn't seem a sufficient amount to freshen my breath. I bought another one and it helped a little, but I was still self-conscious. I wished I had some gum.

Three dudes walked into the bathroom just as I was walking out. What timing! I slinked back to the table and tried to act as if nothing had happened.

The Chief and Holly were sitting down. I sat next to Holly and complimented her version of "Automatic," even though I'd only heard the first line or two. I didn't face her. I wasn't sure if my breath still smelled of puke or not.

"Did you brush your teeth?" she asked.

I jolted a bit. "Yeah, I did," I said, lying. "Garlic, you know?"

The Chief poured himself a beer, as I picked up my glass to finish mine. It was warm and didn't go well with distant bile and Scope.

"Well, Louie, you'll never believe this," the Chief said. "But Ms. Golightly convinced the old bastard to get up and sing."

I sat straight. "Really?" I asked. "How'd that happen?"

"Feminine wiles, kid. You know I can't resist 'em."

"Yes, Chief, I know that very well."

Holly giggled. "Oh, it was nothing," she said. "You just found a song you liked."

The Chief waved her off. "That is true, but you twisted my arm," he said. They both laughed.

"What are you two gonna sing?" I asked.

"It's on the QT, Louie," the Chief said.

Marshall called the Chief and Holly up to sing.

"We've got a special one for you, C-Notes," Marshall announced. "Once again, here's the wonderful Holly and the—*Chief*—of the Board! Give it up for them!"

The Chief *of the Board? You're fucking kidding me?*

The crowd stood up and welcomed Beauty and her beast to the stage. Marshall bowed to the old man as if he were Sinatra himself. I rolled my eyes. This was going to be good.

Holly swayed and stared moony-eyed at the Chief as their tune started. A Spanish guitar dotted the intro to the song, playing a sample of the chorus melody. The Chief smiled and almost started singing too soon. Holly put a quick hand up to stop him. He gave a nod. They were on.

The Chief and Holly sang "Somethin' Stupid" by Frank Sinatra and his daughter Nancy. They seemed to have switched roles. Holly sang a vibrant, outward lead vocal while the Chief mumbled and droned along with her. It was cute but a little uncomfortable to watch. I could tell the old man felt he was dishonoring his hero with this performance.

As I watched the Chief and Holly duet to the C-Notes faithful, all I could think of was how the old boy was having another moment, setting type for another page in his book—a book that I would ultimately write. It saddened me. I'd had a moment tonight as well. I'd delved into my past and culled a deep, vivid memory; however, the Chief was not there when it happened.

I'd shared in so much of his past, and when I finally "went beyond," he was gone—looking for a fucking song to sing with some broad he'd just met. I started to get angry. I stopped. My anger was unwarranted, purely selfish, and very much out of place.

Holly and the Chief finished their song to a rousing standing ovation. Holly had gotten a couple of them tonight. She was the queen of the scene. I stood as well and welcomed them back to the table.

"That was great," I said. "Chief! You were indeed the Chairman!"

The Chief waved me off. "It was bad, Louie," he said. "Flimflam at best."

Holly lightly smacked the Chief's hand. "It was exquisite!" she exclaimed. "Marvelous!"

Holly sipped her Cape Cod. She did not notice that the glass was different. I smiled as I watched her drink.

"Holly, how long have you been singing?" I asked.

"Oh, for a while," she said. "I'd always enjoyed it, but it was never anything I was good at. Karaoke makes it fun. It makes it okay to not be great."

I shook my head. "But you're really good at it," I said. "You could sing for a band."

The Chief glared at me as if I was hitting on his gal.

"Louie, here is a man of fair voice as well," the Chief interjected. "Well, you've heard him tonight. Don't you think he's got golden pipes?"

Holly smiled and put her hand on my wrist. It was cold from holding her glass but soft and delicate. Last night she'd soothed the Chief with her touch. However, her touch was giving me a chill— that went straight to my crotch.

"Oh, you're right," she said, rubbing my wrist. "He is good." She looked at me. "You are really good. You should sing another song."

"I can't. Sorry," I said. "I've already done my one for the night and—"

The Chief cut me off.

"He's lost his right frame of mind," he said. "Is that a correct presumption, Louie?"

I sipped my drink. "No. Not really," I said. "I'm just … I don't have another song in."

"Well, kid there's the books. Put one in. Show Ms. Golightly your chops."

Holly beamed. "I'd love to hear you sing another song," she said.

I glared at the Chief. I would have rather given him a confession than sing another song, but since Holly had asked, I felt I had to. Not twenty minutes ago I'd cursed this woman for taking the Chief away in my time of need, but now I felt I owed her something.

"Okay, I'll do it—*Holly*," I said, as I shot the Chief a smug look.

I walked to the book table and took a different route this time. I felt straight and almost sober. I found my song and filled out my slip. Marshall took it from me. He glanced at the song and raised an eyebrow.

"Really?" he said. "You sure?"

"Yep," I said. "Oh, and no intro this time. I've got my own."

Marshall gave me a nod as the next crop of stars made their way to the stage. The three dudes high-fived me as I passed them.

I went back to the table and sat down. The guys who'd given me accolades passed the mic between them and gave a speech to their buddy, Kevin, who was getting married. The music started, and the trio let loose on a blazer called "I Believe in a Thing Called Love" by a band called The Darkness.

"I hope I don't have to follow them," I said.

"I hope you do a better job," the Chief retorted. He was definitely not feeling the love.

We ordered another round as the guys were singing. I was feeling better, but my nerves about singing my song began to surface. I'd picked a song that was poignant and heartfelt. It was always a favorite, but until tonight, I'd never attached such a deep, personal meaning to it.

I started to think too much about it. I didn't want to suck, but I just knew I would. *I can't do this. It's too risky. It's not in my range. It's ...* I drank half of my beer in one, long swallow, just as Marshall called the next singer's name.

A couple of singers and songs went by, as did a few more large gulps of well-hopped, malted courage. I had loosened up, and by the time Marshall announced I was "on deck," I was ready to go. *Somewhat.*

I stood up, and Holly gave me a quick hug "for luck," and I made my way to the stage. Marshall handed me the mic.

All eyes were on me. Chants of "Lou-E, Lou-A" could be heard. They made me smile and eased my tension.

"I would like to dedicate this to an angel ..." I paused. "And it's a song by God."

The place fell silent. For a few seconds, the only prominent sound was the humming of the karaoke equipment. The silence was broken when the opening percussion of conga drums beat subtly through the speakers then again, before the bright, but melancholy guitar notes rolled through the introduction of Cyndi Lauper's "True Colors."

I closed my eyes and took a deep breath before I sang. I could not hit the pitch, but I found a suitable key.

"You with the sad eyes. Don't be discouraged, oh I realize—it's hard to take courage ..."

The whole place sat up and took notice. All I wanted to do was pay tribute to an old friend whom I'd failed to think of so lovingly until this moment. Part of me was apologizing for not being there. Part of me was again lamenting the loss. Whatever the case, *all of me* was expressing my feelings for Jay. Everyone in this room knew I was saying something—they just had no idea what or whom I was saying it to.

"I see your true colors and that's why I love you.
So don't be afraid to let them show. Your true
colors are beautiful—like a rainbow."

I handed the mic back to Marshall and walked off the stage before the last instrumental passage in the song had finished playing. He said nothing—neither did anyone else.

I walked back to my table and picked up my beer. I downed the rest of the glass before I sat down.

The Chief poured me another drink. "You went beyond, kid," he said. "And I want to hear all about it when you're ready."

Holly's eyes had teared. "That was so beautiful," she said. She softly kissed my cheek. "I've never heard anyone sing a song with such passion before."

I looked at her and smiled and blushed. My desire for her companionship had increased. I wanted to spend the night with her. I wanted her in my bed. I wanted to wake up with her tomorrow morning and share breakfast with her. I just wanted to be with her. I just wanted her *there*. I knew I could not go to sleep tonight unless she was beside me—holding me and making everything okay.

The Chief saw my face and the way I looked at Holly. He knew that Holly's company was the only thing that could soothe this savage beast that had taken me over tonight.

I got up to use the restroom. While I was in there pissing gallons of beer out of my body, my mind was still on Holly.

I wanted and needed her tonight, but suddenly, the circumstances just didn't seem right.

The more I thought about it, the less confident I was becoming.

"What the hell am I doing? What am I thinking?" I asked myself out loud.

A couple of guys overheard me. They must've thought I was trashing my performance. They poured compliments on me like a bucket of water. One guy noted he'd never heard a dude sing a chick song before. Another informed me that he'd hated that song, but I made him like it. I laughed and thanked them, gesturing like it was no big deal. *Yeah, I do this shit all the time.*

I looked around at the vending machines again. The thought of buying a couple of condoms crossed my mind. *Christ. That seems awfully presumptuous.* I shook my head and tried to get this half-drunken, selfish insolence out of my mind.

When I returned to the table, Holly was sitting alone. She looked so beautiful, and I felt so guilty. I sat across from her so I could see her face. Her glass was empty.

"Would you like something else, Holly?" I asked.

"I'm okay for now," she said. "How are you? You seemed so rattled earlier."

"I'm fine. I just got to thinking about some stuff. Old memories."

Holly got a contemplative look. "What did Chief mean when he said you 'went beyond'?" she asked.

"It's just our way of letting each other know we understand things," I said.

"How so? I'm confused," she said.

"Do you remember what happened at Poor Richard's last night?" I asked. "When the Chief broke down?"

Holly gasped. "Yes," she said. "How could I forget?"

"Well, that's *going beyond,*" I said. "It's when you talk about something but find there are more layers to it—you make discoveries. Does that make sense?"

"I guess in a way. But it sounds a bit complicated."

"It can be. It's kind of an art form. I'm still learning."

Holly smiled. "I'm think I'm ready for that drink now," she said.

The Chief came back to the table and sat next to Holly.

"The kid telling you any good stories?" he asked her.

"Yeah, kinda," she said. "You two seem to be a complex pair."

The Chief gave her a look then glared at me. "And just what have you told Ms. Golightly, Louie?" he asked.

"Nothing that could be considered 'on the QT,'" I said.

Marshall had announced last call. I ordered a pitcher of beer for me and the Chief and another Cape Cod for Holly. I still had yet to ask her anything of a personal or propositioning nature. I was wondering if I even would. For a time tonight, I'd needed her to placate me and my unstable situation. I was looking to her to take advantage of my vulnerability.

Suddenly, an errant jolt of courage surged through me. I reached across the table and took Holly's hands. The Chief saw it and smiled. I felt my guts tighten up. It was akin to what I'd felt with April, albeit to a lesser degree.

"Hey, I know it's really late and all, but would you like to go and get something to eat?" I asked Holly. "I just want to talk some more. Is that okay?" God, I sounded like an idiot.

Holly smiled coyly, and my insides compressed even more. This was good—I think. She gently rubbed her thumbs on my hands. I'd finally made my own way and began to feel a definite connection between us.

"Well? What do you say?" I asked, sounding junior high desperate.

Holly's face changed quickly, and she pulled her hands away. "I would love to, I really would," she said. "But my boyfriend is due to pick me up in a few minutes."

The wonderful, squishy feeling I'd experienced now felt like the onset of diarrhea. Even the Chief was shocked.

"I'm sorry, Holly," I said. "I hope I didn't offend you."

Holly put her hands up. "No please ... I'm the one who should apologize," she said.

I shook my head. "I made an assumption," I said. "I just thought ..."

Holly touched my hand again. "It's okay. How could you have known?" she asked.

I smiled. "Well, it's been famed in song and story that 'all of the good ones are taken,'" I said. "And you are definitely one of the good ones."

Holly's boyfriend walked into C-Notes, and she waved to him. She introduced us, and awkward handshakes and pleasantries ensued. The couple left the building, and my heart sank. I felt so stupid.

"You didn't know, kid," the Chief said. "She never gave you a sign."

The Chief and I left C-Notes, and I called a cab from the payphone outside. It was raining again. We took shelter beneath an awning. It seemed a fitting end to a night that had no bright conclusion.

"Louie, hold the cab," the Chief said. "I've got a little business to tend to."

I had no idea what he was talking about until I spied an all-night liquor store across the street from the restaurant.

"It's raining, Chief," I said. "Just forget whatever you're thinking about."

"Kid, this is a mere drizzle," he said. "Our concerns lay within a much bigger deluge."

It was too damn late for philosophy.

"Well, do you at least want *me* to go while you wait for the cab?" I asked.

"Nope. I've got this," he said. "Just don't leave without me."

I watched the old man awkwardly scamper across the empty street as the rain came down. It wasn't the torrent it had been earlier in the evening, but it was rain nonetheless—and much more than "a mere drizzle."

* * * * *

We got back to the motel: me, the Chief, and a twelve-pack of Springfield Bull Creek Brown Ale. I paid the driver, and the Chief pulled two beers from the box as an added tip. The driver reluctantly refused the incentive. The Chief gave him an extra twenty dollars and told him to "grab a six or two" on the way home. The driver laughed and gave us kudos on our purchase.

The Chief and I fell into chairs in the lobby. I grabbed two bottles from the pack and popped them open. We swilled down half of our first bottle without haste.

"Damn, that's good!" I exclaimed in a whisper.

"Fuckin' A, Louie!" the Chief grunted. "I can pick an ale, kid. Don't ever forget it."

I laughed out loud and quickly covered my mouth. It was 3:00 a.m., and the lobby of the Eureka, Missouri, EconoLodge was an echo chamber at this hour. The night desk clerk approached us—cautiously.

"Are you guests here?" she asked.

"We are," I said. "We're part of the Big Banana and High Della-Lama's Travelling Show. We're just in town for a couple of days."

The clerk crinkled her face. "Never heard of it," she said. "Are you guys headed to Six Flags?"

The Chief shook his head. "No, but we are heading toward *three sheets*," he said, straight-faced.

The clerk furrowed her brow. "Where's that …? Oh, geez …" She realized the Chief was having her on. "Do I need to call security?" she asked.

"No. That will not be necessary," I said. "We're not trying to cause trouble. We just want to drink and talk."

The clerk glared at me. "You can do that in your rooms, sir," she said.

"We'll behave, I promise," the Chief said. He held up three fingers and tapped them to his temple. "Scout's Honor."

"Just keep it down, guys. okay?" she asked. "I don't want any of us to get in trouble."

"Nor do we," the Chief said. "We'll keep it to a dull roar—respectable and honest. Like a couple of church mice."

The clerk shook her head and went back to the desk.

"Why the drawn-out bit, Chief?" I asked. "A simple 'We'll be quiet' will suffice."

The Chief finished his beer. "Louie, I like to give a little extra," he said. "It gives an air of sincerity and lets a person know I'm not just blowing smoke up their ass."

"Let me try," I said. "Chief, I'd like another beer. Pass me another bottle. Set me up with some more suds. Barkeep, my cup runneth under. How's that?"

The Chief pushed the box toward me. I pulled two bottles out and opened them. The Chief and I drank in silence for several minutes. I was tired and figured this was my last beer; however, the old man had a look on his face that clearly told me the night was not over—not until I told him my story.

"Rough night, son," the Chief said. "You had the best-laid plans, I know."

I sat back and sighed. I took a drink.

"You said 'When you're ready,' Chief," I informed him. "I'm not sure I'm ready right now."

"Kid, it's fresh in your head," he said. "You've had time. Just get it out."

I knew I had to spill, and I knew the Chief would not let up until I did. I took another drink. I wanted to stall a bit longer.

"I felt lost and alone," I said. "I just got upset."

"Why? Why would you feel 'lost and alone'?" the Chief asked. "I was there the whole time."

"No, you weren't. Not when everything was happening."

The Chief looked puzzled. "You were the happiest I'd seen you," he said. "At first, I thought you'd just hit the post. I had no idea things were happening."

"Neither did I to start," I said. "Things just went haywire when people were singing their songs. Every one of them was like a screwdriver being jammed into a locked box in my soul."

"Where was the key?"

"I don't know. These were memories I didn't want to relive in totality. I must've tossed the key."

"Okay, kid. What happened?"

I was about to motion for another beer. I did not. What I wanted was a bottle of scotch.

I told the Chief everything. Hell, I think I threw in a couple of details I'd missed in the initial breakdown. If I'd 'gone beyond' before, I'd left the galaxy in this retelling. I couldn't get a read on the old man's reactions. He'd hung on every word I'd said but didn't give an indication as to how deep he'd tunneled with me. One of us had to stay grounded, right? It was never me.

Whenever the Chief got lost, I was right there with him. But he knew the rules. He'd lost himself so many times but was always tied to something: anchored and ready to climb back should he get too far, hence the shutdowns.

He held the rope to pull *me* back this time. When the tug came, it was strong and jarring; as if I'd been physically yanked from an abyss and thrust into the light of the real world. It was cleansing but disorienting. I have no recollection of my birth, but I had to think that this is what it feels like to some degree.

The Chief handed me two beers. "Here," he said.

"What are these for?" I asked.

"You need them."

I do? "I'm okay, Chief, really. I just had—you know—*a moment.*"

"I'll say. And kid, let me say this too …" he said as he hung his head. "I'm sorry."

"For what?" I asked.

"For not being there. You needed the old bastard, and I was off trying to sing and worse—trying to be some goddamn Casanova."

I laughed. "I was a little upset," I said. "But hey, I was drunk. I got caught up in a memory—shit happens."

The Chief shook his head. "Louie, this wasn't some petty beef or some bullshit story about the Islands," he said. "This was real. This was something you've been carrying for a long time. If Bettie were here, she'd kick me in the nuts for being so neglectful."

"That's not fair, Chief. You had no idea."

"You didn't have any idea about Bettie either, but you stayed and you listened and you got me through it. I owed you the same courtesy."

"Yeah, but Bettie wasn't a friend, a buddy—she was your true love."

"You're wrong, kid. She *was* a friend as well as my love. You can have that, you know? A loss is a loss. They may seem different, but they all hurt the same."

I nodded. "You're right," I said.

I took a long drink of my beer. I didn't feel anything, and I wasn't sure what to think about that. This entire evening had been wrought with emotions, and now that I'd opened myself up again, I felt nothing. Did this mean I'd come to terms with Jay's death and the remorse I'd carried all these years? Or did it mean I'd hashed it over so much all at once that I'd exhausted it from my soul? I hoped not. It was difficult to relive the pain, but I didn't want to be *relieved* of it.

"Louie, you said you wanted to hear all about the things I've done and places I've been," the Chief said. "But I think it's your turn to share a little with me. You're trying to make your story better by learning from me. You've got your own tales to tell."

I gave the Chief a half-smile and started drinking my second *comfort* beer. I looked out the window and could see a deep, rich violet glow fill the sky. It resembled the luminance of a blacklight on the horizon. It had been Saturday morning for a couple of hours, but these burgeoning rays of daylight made it official. I was only a couple of sips into what would be my last beer of the night but seventh or eighth of this new day. I'd drunk myself sober and was so tired I didn't think I could sleep.

The Chief nursed his last bottle as well. Were we supposed to make plans for the day? I didn't know—nor did I care. The only certainty I had at this moment was that the Chief was going to start asking me more questions about my life. I wasn't sure what I had to say was all that grand or not. I'd just shared the most compelling drama my life had generated so far. I really had nothing more to say. At least I didn't think so.

We finished our last beers, and although there were a couple left in the box and temptation loomed, morning had indeed blown "Last call."

"I'm taking my ass to bed, kid," the Chief said.

I laughed. "Do you want to wait a few minutes?" I asked. "The restaurant is about to open."

"Nope. Not today. It's safe to say I've drank my breakfast."

"Me too. Well, go get some sleep."

The Chief picked up his bottles and put them in the box. He started toward his room. I stopped him.

"Hey, Chief," I said. "Thank you. For the beer, the talk—the everything."

He shook his head. "You don't owe me any gratitude," he said. "You just owe me some information. It's a fair trade."

"I'll have to make some shit up. I've led a pretty average life. You heard the best story."

"I don't believe that. And neither do you."

The Chief walked away before I could counter. I gathered my empties and put them in the box. I looked around the lobby.

A couple of people were making their way to the restaurant for breakfast, while others were assembling to leave the motel and enjoy the start of their day. Mine was ending for the moment.

I picked up the box and went to my room. On the way, I heard a feminine voice singing. I shook my head. *It's not Holly. She's sleeping right now—with someone else.*

* * * * *

I woke up at 10:00 a.m. Hardly enough sleep time, but apparently, it was adequate. My body felt rested and my head clear. I was not hungover. There were not even trace effects of the bender of last night or early this morning. I did feel a deep, thick pain in my chest, however, and I knew very well what was causing that. It would take some time before that ache subsided and went back to the place I'd hidden it for all those years.

As for my misstep with one Ms. Golightly, princess of platters and queen of karaoke? Well, she was indeed just another stranger in the night, and we all know it never ends well when one takes candy from a stranger.

I pulled myself out of bed and made myself a little pot of coffee. I sat at the desk and looked at my notebook. From here, there was no procrastinating, no thinking, no consideration—I opened it, and I started to write.

I don't know how long I'd been working. I hadn't checked the clock since I'd gotten out of bed. The coffee finished brewing long ago and quite certainly had passed the point of being drinkable. I had no distractions: no phone calls, no rumblings in the hall, no mental blocks, and oddly enough—no Chief.

I took a break and looked at the clock. It was 2:00 p.m. I was still in my *jammies* and still crusty and stank from the previous night. I peered at the coffee pot and decided that regardless of taste and temperature, I was going to have a cup—why not? I took the time to make it.

I poured a cup, and it was cold and sludgy. I drank it anyway. Oddly enough, it tasted like stout, and that was okay with me. I returned to the desk and thumbed back through what I'd written. There was a lot. It was hastily scrawled but legible and relevant. I knew I'd done something right.

I smiled at the possibility of having finally purged this damned writer's block, this bane that has plagued me for so long and the very reason for my extended trip.

I read. For the first time since I'd gotten on this wild, cross-country, inspiration roller coaster, I actually read what I'd written. I'd glanced at it before, but this time, I felt I needed to do the work justice; moreover, I felt I needed to make sure I'd truly done the work.

This was something I could use. It wasn't as grand as I thought, but it was *serviceable*. I'd hoped for something more, given the time I'd put into it, but it was better than I'd expected.

I could feel my self-doubt rising, and I needed to stop. I closed my notebook—no, I *slammed* it. I smacked the cover closed so hard it shook everything on the desk.

"I give up!" I said, angrily behind my teeth. I was seething. "What the hell have I just done? What the fuck? Did I really just waste four hours of my life? *On this?*"

I shoved the notebook off the desk and my cold, stout-like coffee went with it. I caught the cup in midair, but the contents had been ejected all over the cover and half of the desk.

I got up and went to take a shower. I took my clothes off and threw them into a heap. It wasn't my usual routine, but it fit with the day. I stood naked in the bathroom and—as luck would have it—heard a familiar sound: the Chief knocking and talking into my door asking if I was "alive." I ignored him and got into the shower.

I could hear the old man rapping at the door even with the shower running. Persistent cuss that he is, he did not quit. I got dressed and finished my beautification before I answered.

I opened the door, and the Chief strolled right in.

"Louie, I was worried," he said as he sat down at the desk. "You didn't answer. I wasn't sure. It's good to see you're still kicking."

"Didn't you hear the shower?" I asked.

The Chief ignored my question and looked at the mess on the desk. He didn't say anything about it.

He wiped off the cover and began leafing through my notebook.

"Hey, you've done a little work," he said. "It's a bit stained, but this is stuff you'd told me this morning."

I knew he'd remember what I told him, but I had to admire the fact that he was actually reading what I'd written.

"You can tell me if I left anything out, Chief," I said as I folded my clothes.

He continued reading and said nothing.

I wanted to ask for a review, but he seemed to be engrossed in the words before him. I did not want to mess with that. For the first time on this trip, the Chief was getting a real glimpse at what I'd done. The earlier notes weren't much, but I'd put a lot of time in today. Perhaps he'd see something I didn't in what I'd put down.

"I hate it," I said out of the blue. "I read over it and I hated it."

"Why do you hate it?" The Chief asked.

"I don't know. It just seems like a bunch of jive. It still sounds contrived. I thought I was free of my issues, but I guess not."

"It looks good to me. It's better than what you showed me in Sacramento."

I smacked my forehead. "Really? You're sure about that?" I asked. "Because it seems the same to me."

"Of course, it does," the Chief said. "You're always going to be critical. There is no guarantee of satisfaction when it comes to your own work. Nobody ever praises themselves and truly means it. If they do, they're either liars or overly confident—but even then."

He set the notebook down. "I'm not gonna read any more," he said. "I know you're on the right track. Just keep doing *this*.

Remember what I told you before: you won't fully regain your vision until you've completed your journey. You're almost there. What I've just read is proof. Do not give up."

I wanted to share the Chief's optimism—and I should. I've learned so much from the old man, but the one thing above all others has been the fact that he's never lied to me about my work. He's called me out, as well as complimented me, and it's always been genuine. No smoke has been blown up this ass. However, as sincere as he was, it wasn't enough to make me fully believe him—or myself.

My head was spinning, my chest was heavy, and my stomach began to growl. "I guess I'm hungry," I said.

"Then let's get something to eat," the Chief said.

"We are not going to Poor Richard's, just so you know," I said emphatically.

The Chief thought for a moment. He crinkled his face and nodded.

"Italian, Louie," the Chief said. "Let's dine with your folk."

I shook my head. "Are you serious?" I asked. "Or are you just tap-dancing to say you want pizza?"

"No, I want to eat *real* Italian food," he said. "Not goddamn pizza and definitely *not* the fucking *Olive Garden.*"

Very well, I thought.

We went down to the lobby and decided to ask the clerk for a recommendation.

"What is the best Italian restaurant in this area that's not pizza, or the Olive Garden?" I asked.

Her eyes twinkled as if responding to my inquiry was her most important task of the day.

"That's easy," she said. "Joe Boccardi's. It's a local classic."

"That's our place," I said. "Thank you, my dear!"

The clerk smiled and blushed. She stopped me before I could turn around. "Oh, but they do serve pizza there. I hope that's okay," she said.

"That's fine," I said. "Hell, what Italian restaurant doesn't serve pizza these days?"

"I've got a place," I said. "It's local and not the Olive Garden. One caveat: there's pizza on the premises."

The Chief mused for a second. "Ah, hell, what Italian joint doesn't serve pizza these days?"

Couldn't have said it better myself.

* * * * *

The Chief seemed pleased with the outside of Boccardi's restaurant. Renaissance-style sculpted pillars supported the beams of the façade and a canvas-covered awning arched over the front entrance. I glanced at the old man as he kept surveying the décor.

"Shall we go in and see if the menu compliments the aesthetic?" I asked.

"Andiamo!" the Chief said as he opened his door. He threw his hand up for effect. I was now dreading this decision.

We went inside, and the place was wonderful. Softly light but not too dark, small tables perfect for dining and conversation and a hostess named Bella. The only thing missing was checkered tablecloths.

"Ciao Bella," the Chief said. "Come stai mio caro?"

Bella smiled brightly and responded, "Io sto bene grazie. E tu?"

"Meraviglioso!" he said.

I listened to their exchange. *Oh, he's good—embarrassing as hell but good. At least she speaks Italian.*

Bella seated us and asked what we'd like for drinks. There was no thinking or inquiries about local favorites required; we ordered Italian beers. The Chief—a bottle of Moretti "La Rossa," and for me, a pint of Peroni—to start.

Bella brought our drinks, and the Chief held her up as he poured his beer into a glass. I watched but could not figure out why he needed an audience. Bella glanced at the libation as it transferred from vessel to vessel and seemed intrigued. Once the glass was full, the Chief sniffed at the contents and smiled.

"Mazzo," he said to Bella. He looked at me. "I said 'bouquet.' But you knew that, right?"

I shook my head. "No. I don't understand a word you're saying," I said.

The Chief chuckled. He motioned Bella closer and gestured to me. "Mio amico. Lui e Italiano—ma lui non parlo Italiano!"

Bella touched her chest and feigned a gasp. "You're Italian and you don't speak the language?" she asked.

"Yeah, I'm afraid it's true," I said. "I can't pronounce half of the items on this menu." I shot a look at the Chief. "And that's why I'm ordering pizza."

"Figlio di puttana," the Chief said, throwing his hands in the air.

Bella giggled and quickly covered her mouth. "That wasn't very nice," she said. "I'm sorry for laughing."

"Do I even want to know?" I asked.

Bella leaned toward me. "He said something bad about your mom," she whispered.

"What? Did he call me a son of a bitch?"

"He did! See? You can speak Italian."

"No, I can't. He just calls me that a lot. It was that or—"

The Chief cut me off. "Bastardo?" he quipped.

I looked at Bella. "How do you say 'exactly' in Italian?" I asked.

"Di preciso," she said.

I crinkled my face and glared at the Chief. "Di preciso, bastardo." There was silence for a second, then we all burst out in laughter.

"You guys are too much—troppo," Bella said. "Okay, what can I get for you?"

The Chief furrowed his brow. "Well, since he's gonna ruin the meal with pizza, I'll go first," he said. "I'd like to get the Cavatelli Arrabiata—molto arrabiata!"

Bella laughed. "The chef can make that happen," she said.

"And you, sir?" she asked. "Do you really want pizza?"

I shook my head. "No. I can get pizza any time," I said. "I'm here to enjoy real Italian food." I gestured to the Chief. "A taste of home, as this guy would say."

Everything sounded delicious, and that made deciding on a meal quite difficult.

"What do you recommend?" I asked Bella.

"My favorite is the Linguini Pescatore," she said. "But a close second is the Fettuccini A Mare Monte."

I glanced at each choice, and they both sounded grand. "Your favorite is my favorite," I said. "I'll have the Linguini Pescatore." I ordered a plate of garlic bread as well.

Bella put our orders in, and the Chief and I sat and enjoyed our beers. It was nice to relax and have nothing to do. It was the first time on this trip we weren't trying to figure out which local attraction or historical point of interest was most appealing.

"Louie, I'm proud of you," the Chief said, as he raised his glass.

I clinked mine to his. "For what?" I asked. "I haven't done anything."

"Kid, you've done more than you realize. And you've done it in the past twenty-four hours."

"What? Have a booze fit and lost my mind after singing a song? Writing more than one hundred fifty words in a sitting? That's hardly commendable."

"Dammit, there you go again chastising yourself. Just give the old boy his due, okay? Just take the praise for once. Have you always been so self-critical?"

I didn't have to think. "Yes. For as long as I can remember," I said.

"So naturally, you decide to venture into the creative realm?" the Chief mocked. "The one place that requires thick skin and a steel heart. The most soul-bearing venue one could travel."

"That's about it," I said.

"Why? Why would you subject yourself to such torture? You had to know that for all the sensitivities, the creative world was harsh and brutal."

"Because it was all I could do," I said. "It was all I was good at."

"Really?" the Chief asked. He leaned in attentively. "Do tell."

I sat back. I don't know why, but this topic was going to bother me. I did not want to get overly emotional; however, I felt that it was inevitable.

"I sucked at everything I'd ever tried," I said as I rubbed my face. "I went through the gamut when I was a kid. I wanted to do this and that but never had any success."

"You were a kid, Louie," the Chief said. "You were too young to be a failure yet."

"I knew it early," I said. "I was prodigious at being a letdown. I took solace in the arts. Drawing, music, and of course, writing. They instilled a sense of accomplishment in me. No one scoffed what I did."

"Well, you eventually found success doing something you love and are good at. I'd have to say you've found a happy medium: you write for a living."

"Right now, I don't feel I'm good at it. I've never struggled at something so much in my life."

"How so? You said you had difficulty with things growing up."

"I did. But when things went awry, I gave up. I just quit and moved on. I can't do that now. My sanctuary and my career—my 'happy mediums'—have caved in on me. They've become one in the same. My wish came true."

The Chief contemplated. "Well, you're correct there. And unfortunately, that's the pain of being a working artist, I suppose," he said. "At a *regular* job, you've got somebody telling you what to do and how to do it, but in your line, you've got to answer to someone while appealing to your creativity. If it doesn't measure up for you or your boss, it's a waste—of time and talent. That makes it tough. And add to the fact your confidence is shot. It's a bad mix."

"So you see my dilemma?"

"Yes and no."

"How's that?"

"Your dilemma is your own doing. You've gotten stuck, but you've also got a whole world of inspiration to draw from—you've just chosen to ignore it."

"That's not true. I've culled quite a bit from the places we've been."

"I know you have, but you're not letting yourself see beyond a certain point. Last night, you did, and it had nothing to do with this trip. You need to let yourself do that all the time."

"I couldn't handle doing *that* all the time."

The Chief held his hands up. "You don't have to go off the deep end," he said. "You can just wade in the shallow water. Either way, you've left the confines of dry land and allowed yourself some immersion."

Bella brought our garlic bread and asked if we'd like another beer.

"Yes. Please," I said. "Make it two for me."

The Chief nodded in concurrence.

The Chief picked up a piece of bread and broke it in half. He rubbed the open end in the small dish of herb-infused olive oil. I watched the tiny bits of chopped green herbs spin in the yellow oil. They gathered and stuck to the bread then slowly fell away and separated as the torn doughy appetizer was lifted from the dish.

"Have you figured out where we're going next, Louie?" the Chief asked as he bit the oily bread.

"No. I just know we're leaving tomorrow," I said, following the Chief's lead and dipped a piece of bread. "It's kinda sad really. We're almost done with this trip."

"Sad, yes, but once this ends, life begins anew," the Chief said. "And that's something worth looking forward to."

"I was hoping to do something else here in town. Both places we've gone seem to have less than favorable memories attached to them. I'd like to atone for that."

"I wouldn't say that. We were expecting something, I guess, but we both garnered a positive from the other's negative."

I closed one eye and thought about it. The Chief was right. I got lost in the Route 66 Park and taken the journey that was to be his, whereas he'd found happiness in something he'd lamented and I'd opened old wounds—and got rejected—at C-Notes. *All's fair.*

We could smell our food as it made its way to the table. If the aroma emanating from these plates was an indicator of their flavor, we were in for a grand dinner. *Delizioso!*

Bella set my plate down first.

"Does it look okay?" she asked.

"It looks fabulous," I said. "I'm not sure if I want to eat it. It's a work of art." I took a deep breath in. "And it smells absolutely divine."

Bella giggled. *"Molto bene!"* she said. "That means very good."

She set the Chief's plate in front of him. "Bavaglino?" she asked.

The Chief smiled and nodded. "Si, mi piacerebbe un bavaglino."

"Molto bene," she said.

Bella stepped behind the old man and draped a huge cloth napkin across his chest. She tied it loosely behind his neck. "É okay?" she asked.

"Si. Molto bene, mio caro," he said.

I didn't know if I was feeling cynical or just a bit jealous of the exchange between Bella and the Chief. She lauded over him, and he absolutely loved it. He was definitely in his element. The old boy impressed Bella with his semi-Americanized Italian, and she pampered him like he was the Don of the village. I just smiled and stealthily rolled my eyes.

"You two let me know if you need anything," Bella said. "I will get you some more beers for now."

We nodded simultaneously, and the Chief commenced to eating. I didn't know where to start: the calamari, a mussel, or a shrimp? I picked at the dish. I'd told Bella it was a work of art. I was not lying to her.

"You gonna eat?" the Chief asked as he waved his hand toward my food.

"I am. Just give me time," I said. "How's yours?"

The Chief sat back. "Meraviglioso!" he said. "That means 'marvelous.'"

"That one I could figure," I said. "I haven't tasted this, but I'd venture a guess that it is … mara-vee … um … what you said as well."

The Chief laughed and repeated the word *meraviglioso*.

"You'll get it, kid," he said. "When you get home, you should get in touch with your roots. Learn the language: *imparare la lingua*."

"I may have to do that," I said.

I stuck a shrimp and a ring of calamari on my fork and put them in my mouth. I could not pronounce the word, but what the Chief said—that was how this food tasted. I too fell back in my chair a little. Great beer, beautiful waitress, and divine food—it does not get any better than this.

"I have to know," I said. "What's the deal with the napkin?"

"Oh, this? It's a *bavaglino*," he said.

"Okay, so what does a bavaglino ...?" I paused for the Chief to check my pronunciation. When he nodded, I continued. "What is it?"

He repeated that stupid phrase of obviousness: "It is what it is," he said. "It's a bib."

"Why? Is it because you're ... *elderly* and she thinks you're gonna slop on yourself? I didn't get one."

"No, Louie, it's not like that. It's actually a sign of respect— *rispetto*—it's like a luxury. The elders are taken care of at meals. Their needs and accommodations are priority."

I hung my head a little. "I'm sorry, Chief," I said. "I hope I wasn't offensive."

"Nope, not offensive," he said. "Maybe a little ignorant, but how do you know, right? Obviously your family is not Old World?"

"My family is Southern," I said. "Old and New World but Southern above all else."

The Chief set his fork down and took a drink. His eyes studied my face, and I could tell he had something major to ask.

"You looking for something?" I asked.

"Yeah, kid. I'm looking for *you*," he said. "I told you you've got your own tales. I think it's time you share them with the Ol' Super Chief."

I smiled bright. I loved it when he referred to himself as *the Ol' Super Chief*. This, however, was the first time he'd said it and did not sound desperate.

I didn't know where to start. I really didn't have anything grand or glorious to tell him. The story about me and Jay was the about the best I had.

Our new beers came, and the Chief held his glass in a toast.

"To Louie DeCarlo and all he's done," he said.

I clinked my glass to his. "And here goes nothing," I said. "What do you want to know?"

"Everything you've got. Take me to Cuba, kid."

"Hell, Chief, I can't even give you a push across the street."

"Okay, I'll make it easy. Tell me about your family. How it was growing up—and why the hell you're the worst Italian that ever existed."

"Well, for starters, I'm not Italian, never have been," I said. "My biological father left my mother right after I was born. Mom remarried, and the guy's last name was DeCarlo. He was only half Italian to begin with. He adopted me and my older sister right away. We've always been DeCarlos."

"See, kid, that's a start," the Chief said. "Don't stop now. Keep going."

"We lived in Atlanta, but I don't remember much about it," I said. "We moved out to California when I was very young. It was a great place to grow up, California. You know that, though."

"I do, but my California was a lot different from yours," the Chief said. "A different part and a much different time. However, we have something else in common: we were both adopted by the men whom our mothers remarried."

"To the brotherhood of adoptees," I said, raising my glass.

We clinked glasses and drank.

"Tell me about your sisters," the Chief said.

"My older sister. Her name is Wanda," I said. "My little sister— my half-sister—her name is Camille. There's four years between each of us. We got on pretty well growing up and still see each other when we can."

The Chief nodded and smiled. "I envy you that, kid," he said. "My siblings and I were closer than brothers and sisters could be, but as for seeing each other …" He trailed off. "Go ahead, Louie. I'm sorry I interrupted."

I felt bad—as if I'd tapped a sore spot in the old man's soul. That was not my intention. I took a drink and resumed eating.

"Why'd you stop talking?" the Chief asked.

"You seemed upset," I said.

"Dammit, Louie, what did I tell you about that word?"

"Only favorites, buckets and stomachs …?"

"Right. Now continue."

I took another bite and drink and obliged the Chief's request.

"I hated school as most kids do," I said. "I did well in art-type classes, but academics and I failed in our relationship."

"Speaking of relationships, why are you a bachelor?" the Chief asked. "You ever been married?"

I shook my head emphatically. "Nope. Never," I said. "I was always a terrible boyfriend."

"What does that mean?"

"I was always too needy; too clingy, and too hapless in love."

"It's not that difficult, you know. Sounds like you were just too *spoony*."

"*Spoony* is a good word for it. I was too spoony, they didn't want to fork, hence a knife in the relationship."

"That's clever, kid—give a shout to all the utensils."

We ate and drank a little more. I wasn't sure what else to tell the Chief, but I knew he wanted more information.

"You mentioned a tomato in college—the pregnant one," he said. "That sounded serious … I mean … *until*. Any big ones after that?"

"Yeah, a couple," I said. "But none that really stayed. I was always searching for that perfect girl. If she was out there, I kept missing her or running her off."

"Kid, love is big, blind, with strong legs and a penchant for the unknown. But she's also fine as wine and fun as summertime if you catch her in a good mood."

I laughed. "That about covers it," I said. "You know, right now, I'm married to my job. My present career is not conducive to maintaining a healthy relationship."

"You need to find a girl who understands that," the Chief said. "Someone who knows you have to travel and, if they can, will go with you on your adventures."

"My life mate?" I asked.

"To make such a commitment? Yes. She would indeed be your life mate."

"I'll have to look into that when I get home."

"As I'm sure you will, kid."

We resumed eating and didn't talk anymore during our meal. We'd had some great food on this trip: the Chief made sure of that. However, this was undoubtedly the best. After eating here, I wanted to vow to never eat Italian food again. To dine elsewhere would be a betrayal of taste and an outright sacrilege to the soul.

After our supper, the Chief belched. "*Scusami!*" he bellowed, as if to make sure everyone heard him beg pardon. "The sign of a good meal, Louie. Compliments."

"I thought that was a German thing?" I wondered.

"Sure. The Germans do it. They all do it—the Europeans. They're not as uptight about bodily functions as Americans are. Over there, you can burp in a place like this, but don't you dare blow the horn in a restaurant in the Fabulous 50. No, sir. You can't even do in a burger shack like we ate in last night. And *that* food was tailor-made for the hog's mating call."

I chuckled at what the Chief said. Cultural differences and customs have long fascinated me. One thing that's baffled me is how we Americans are the first to call someone out on a manners violation, while our country is filled with some of the basest and rudest people on the planet. Double standards? Who knows? *Love it or leave it.*

Bella came around and took our plates.

"How were your meals?" she asked. "You seemed to take a while to eat them. Savoring, I hope?!"

"Absolutely," I said. "This was the best I've ever had. You may have ruined me for Italian food forever!"

Bella laughed. "Well then, I guess you'll just have to come back and eat here again," she said.

"That I will, Bella!"

She giggled and patted my shoulder.

The Chief wiped his mouth and removed his *bavaglino.* "Molto bene, Bella! Molto bene!" he said, talking with his hands. He kissed his fingertips and blew the buss toward Bella. She caught it and patted her chest. "Grazie mille."

"Bella, mio caro, we must know," the Chief said, pointing to me. "Is it possible to speak with Signore Boccardi? We want to tell him about you and his most wonderful food—*cibo meraviglioso*."

I shook my head. Oh, great—it's fucking Lazlo's all over again. I wanted to tell the Chief to stop asking to talk to the person whose name was on the front of these restaurants. Half the time there was no one with that name, the other half they were dead. I had no idea which one it would be here.

"*Impossibile*," Bella said. "Signore Boccardi is in Saint Louis tonight—at the big restaurant."

Holy shit! So there really is a Joe Boccardi? And he's still with us? Well, I'll be a figlio di puttana.

The Chief was bummed, and I was blown away.

"Well, you tell him that Louie DeCarlo and *il Capo* were here and that he has a damn fine establishment and the best waitress in the world. *Il migliore—e più bella!*"

Bella's cheeks reddened. She blushed harder than I'd ever seen a person do before. She was so grateful of the Chief's words. They were probably the most complimentary thing anyone has ever said to her; even though, I hoped that she heard such things regularly.

We ordered another round of drinks, including a small bottle of Grappa. Bella smiled at our *digestivo*; adding it was a better choice than the Chianti. The Chief inquired about the possibility of a third glass. Both Bella and I waved him off, indicating it was not a good idea.

"Forse più tardi," the Chief said as he frowned. "Maybe later?"

Bella smiled and shook her head. "No, mi dispiace," she said. "I'm so sorry. Please forgive me for turning down your invitation."

"It's quite alright, mio caro," the Chief said. "Some other time. *Un'altra volta*." He smiled and winked at Bella. She blushed again and turned away demurely.

When Bella left the table I shook my head. "Chief, I've got to hand it to you," I said. "You are a man of the people, as well as a man of the world. I'm envious."

"How so?" he asked. "Is it my people skills or my worldliness?"

"All of the above. And the fact you can speak so many languages."

"I thought that bothered you?"

The Chief caught me. "What makes you think that?" I asked.

"You roll your eyes whenever I speak the native tongue," he said. "If you're not rolling your eyes, you're just pissed off. Didn't think I'd noticed, eh?"

I crinkled my face. "No, not really," I said. "Then again, I didn't take strides to hide the obviousness either."

"No, you didn't."

"I'm sorry, Chief."

"It's okay, kid. Have you learned anything—language-wise?"

"Not really—except how to say 'son of a bitch' in Italian!"

The Chief laughed. "Well, that's a good start," he said. "Now I'll have to teach it to you in Samoan or Hawaiian—that way you can tell 'em how you feel on both sides of the globe."

Our drinks arrived. Bella poured our Grappa into small cordial glasses. The Chief seemed disappointed the vessels weren't bigger; I was surprised he didn't know the proper glasses for such libation. Chalk one up for the Southern boy.

We toasted to the day and gently clinked our glasses. The Chief downed his Grappa, and I sipped mine. He poured himself another glass, while I still had three-quarters of mine left to finish.

"Okay, Louie. You still haven't finished your story," the Chief said. "What was it like growing up? You told me about your buddy and the marbles."

I took a deep breath. I wasn't sure what to say.

"Well, there's not much to tell, really," I said. "I was kind of a punching bag when I was younger. Kids like to pick on the fat asses."

"Kids are cruel," the Chief said. "And they've gotten worse over time."

"They were horrible back then, I can attest."

"I know you can. What happened? What did you do?"

"I just toughened up, but not by fighting back. I did it by becoming friends with those who hurt me. I figured someday I'd fuck 'em all up by becoming successful while they were rotting away in prison or in a coffin at the local cemetery."

"That's grim but effective. How'd it all work out?"

"We balanced. I ended up being a half-ass journalist, and they all ended up with dead-end jobs. So it was bittersweet."

"You said you became friends with these bullies. Still in contact with any of them?"

"A couple of them. Just a Christmas card and a letter every year. The usual bullshit: 'I'm great, my kids are the best, and you're jealous.'"

"I hate that shit."

The Chief shot down his second Grappa. I was still working half a glass. He poured himself a third and left barely a swallow in the bottle.

"Louie, you're gonna get your revenge, you know," the Chief said. "You're gonna go home, write this book, and every success you've ever dreamed of is going to happen for you. I've no doubt about that."

I smiled and nodded. I liked the sound of that—even though I didn't fully believe it.

"Keep going," the Chief said. "You left California and went to college, right?"

"Yes. I moved back to Georgia and went to Valdosta State," I said. "It wasn't my first choice, but they gave me a partial scholarship. I couldn't say no, right?"

"No to free tuition? Even partial?" he asked. "If you did, you'd be a fool—or at least a half-wit."

I laughed. "So I took the gig and did my four," I said. "I tried to avoid the journalistic trappings—you know—the clichés: drinking, long hours, all that garbage, but I got caught up in it."

"As you do," the Chief interjected.

"As you do," I responded.

"What was your first job?" he asked. "Were you a cub reporter? Jimmy Olsen, type—on the beat? Or did you settle in to something softer?"

"No, I was a beat writer for the college paper at first. Then after graduation, I landed a spot at the Valdosta *Daily Times*," I said. "I hated it. I hated the choppy pace of newspaper journalism. I hated interviewing people and having to condense their words to menial blocks, only to lose the crux of the story in editing and then get tagged for misquoting.

"I liked the big story. I liked the expansion of the magazine: the gloss and glamour. So I made myself allergic to newsprint! I quit the paper and freelanced for a while until I went broke."

"What did you work on while you freelanced?" the Chief asked.

"I started a novel," I said. "A weird love story. I killed off my characters. It was a total rip-off of *Romeo and Juliet.*"

"Sure it was—most love stories are," the Chief noted. "Especially the ones where the main characters die."

"After that, I tried a couple of different genres. Nothing worked."

"What did you do then?"

"I went *even broker* and had to find a real job. That's how I ended up with Southern State Publishers. I've worked with them for the last several years."

The Chief took a sip of his Grappa. "Well, how'd you end up with the traveling show?" he asked.

"That was easy," I said. "Nobody wanted to leave home. I was the only one willing to go mobile."

"And just look at you now, kid—sitting pretty in an Italian restaurant in Eureka, Missouri, getting sloshed with the Big Banana."

I laughed and almost spit my Grappa all over the table.

"That's it!" I exclaimed.

I finished off the *digestivo*. There was just enough to make a modest swig but not enough to fill the glass.

I flagged Bella down and she gave me the bill. I paid with my credit card. It was the first meal I hadn't paid cash for. The Chief reached for his wallet as well. I was shocked.

"I got this, Chief," I said, adding jokingly, "It's on Southern State Publishers."

"Let me get the gratuity, Louie," the Chief said. "I want to do that."

"Okay. I'm all about that," I said.

The Chief took the check folio from me and thumbed through his wallet. His eyes lit up when he found the right bill. He moved so quickly I couldn't see what denomination he'd placed inside the folded leather booklet, but I knew it was good. He loved Bella, and she was phenomenal. *At least a twenty—at the* very *least*, I thought.

We left the bill and made our way out to the car. Bella was busy but smiled and waved to us as we left.

"Ciao, Bella!" We shouted over the crowd. She threw her head back and beamed.

The evening was still young, but we were heading into Tipsytown. We stopped at a liquor store and decided to go easy the rest of the way. We picked up a six-pack of Schlafly wheat and headed back to the motel.

When we got back and entered the lobby, the place was teeming with Six Flaggers heading out for the nightlight roller coaster rides and after-dark fireworks. We waded through the mob and found a couple of seats. It was as if the sound of the beer bottles divided realities. As soon as we opened them, the lobby crowd dispersed and only the Chief and I remained. It was nice and quiet.

"Chief, I have to know," I said as I passed him his beer. "Have you ever been married?"

The Chief looked at me as if I'd posed the forbidden question.

"What brought that on?" he asked.

"Well, you asked me if I'd ever been," I said. "Turnabout, fair play, and all that."

He looked at me hard with his steely-blue eyes. "What do you think?" he asked.

"I don't know. I want to say yes, but judging by—"

He cut me off.

"Nope, Louie, this old duffer has never been hitched," he said.

"Really?" I said. I wasn't sure if I sounded surprised or confused.

"Really. You said it best: I was 'married to my work.'"

"Yeah, but I'm ... I mean, in all those years. There had to be someone."

"I got close, just like you did. But for me, after Bettie—no one ever compared."

"You never fell in love again?"

"Not like that. And the love I had for Bettie was the love I needed. Not even Mariposa compared, kid—and that's saying something."

I took a swig of my beer. "So no kids then?" I asked.

"That one I can't answer," the Chief said. "I'm sure there's one or two or seven running around looking for me."

The Chief took a swig of his beer. "Louie, you're the closest thing to an offspring I have," he said. "At least that I know of for sure. How's that make you feel?"

I smiled and raised my bottle. "Pretty damn good, Chief," I said. "Pretty. Damn. Good."

The old man gave me a nod. He didn't speak a word, but I knew what he was saying in his head: 'Louie, you son of a bitch!'

* * * * *

My calendar was running out of dates. I had to get home. Where were we going next? Our schedule allowed for one more E stop before we parked our bacon in Valdosta. Since it would be our last mystery destination, I wanted the Chief to pick the place. It had to be good—and I knew he could find just the right locale. Elkhorn certainly had been a fine choice.

Morning came quick. I'd slept, but it didn't seem like I'd gotten a great eight or even a snore of a four. What time was it? I looked at the clock. It was a blurry 4:30 a.m., and it was time to get up.

I made a cup of coffee and turned on the TV. The commercial for the crooner's CD was on again, and I felt like I was reliving Friday night—at four-something Sunday morning. I shut the TV off and packed my stuff.

The early news began as I was closing my suitcase. I didn't pay much attention to the stories as they were more ambience than information at this point. However, a slug for one of the features caught my eye. It wasn't the story—it was the location: Elizabethtown,

Kentucky! There was no need to rationalize this one—that was our destination today. I had no idea how far it was, but distance didn't matter; it started with an *E*, was close to Georgia, and best of all, it was named after a woman—*trifecta!*

"Chief, do you want to know where we're going today?" I asked. "You're gonna like it, I promise."

This time I got a response: "Psh …" That'll work for me.

"Let's get on the road. We'll stop and get some breakfast in a bit, okay?" I said.

The Chief huffed. "Where are we going? Indiana?" he asked. "I told you I hate Indiana."

"Nope. No Indiana," I said. "I've got a place you'll love. It's our last before home. I made it a good one."

"I'll believe that when I see it. So where are you taking me?"

I smiled. "Someplace you're going to love," I said. "Trust me."

The Chief furrowed his brow and said nothing as we made our way to the car.

We drove out of Saint Louis on Interstate 64. The Chief was on about eating breakfast but did not want to stop at a place like "that barrel joint." Fair enough. We were into Illinois, and the Chief lightened up.

"Ah, my home state," he said. "But this is part I never saw. All I saw was Chicago."

"I'll bet this is a far cry from that," I said.

"Kid, let me tell ya 'bout the Land of Lincoln. It's one giant farm and one giant city—that's it. Most Midwestern states are like that. Except Ohio. Ohio has a lot of big towns."

"I never thought much about it. I guess Georgia is like that too."

The Chief was still on about Ohio. "Louie, you know how to tell a cat's from Ohio?" he asked.

I was hesitant to answer. "Um … no," I said. "How do you tell a cat's from Ohio?"

"Easy. He'll have an *O* under his tail," he said. "You get it?"

"Unfortunately, I do," I said. "And for the rest of the day, I'll have the picture of a cat's ass stuck in my head. Thanks."

The Chief gave me his Fred Flintstone laugh again—it sounded more devious than ever.

We drove about an hour and stopped for breakfast in a town called Mount Vernon. None of the local "greasy spoons"—as the Chief called them—were open. We ended up at a chain place. This time it was Bob Evans, and oddly enough—the Chief was okay with it.

"This place has the best biscuits and gravy," he said. "And that's what I'm getting."

He was right. I have no idea what Mr. Evans puts in his gravy besides sausage, but it *is* the best stuff I've ever had—and I'm from the South!

We were seated by Mabel. She was the quintessential old-time country restaurant hostess, an older gal—short, portly, and vivacious.

She cracked wise with the Chief and laughed loud at his comebacks. She waddled when she walked and said "Shucks" and "Sugar" more than an old Southern lady losing on a game show.

Her glasses were straight out of a librarian's collection, complete with beaded chain hanging long around the back of her neck.

Her hair was silver, streaked with white, and pulled into the most perfect, tightest bun that sat dead center atop her head. This look took a little work, but Mabel had it perfected.

"Y'all know we're famous for our biscuits and gravy, right?" Mabel asked.

The Chief smiled. "Well, shucks, sugar, we sure do," he said. "That's why I'm ordering them. And a poached egg on the side."

Mabel looked at me. "And you, sweetie pie?" she asked.

"Same for me, ma'am," I said. "But I'll have my eggs hard-fried."

"Y'all want coffee or juice?" Mabel asked.

The Chief and I said *coffee* at the same time.

"Shucks, aren't you two just the easiest li'l ol' boys I've had to deal with today?" Mabel said.

I looked at the clock. It was barely 7:00 a.m. I had to wonder how many people she'd served in the last hour. Perhaps we were setting the tone for her day?

Mabel left to put our orders in. Another server came around and brought us coffee. The Chief loaded his mug with five creamers. I watched his coffee go from black to the same tan as the head on a pint of Guinness. I started thinking about beer—and it was way too early to be thinking like that.

"Kid, I've got to know, where are we going?" the Chief asked.

His demeanor had perked up. I'm sure Mabel had something to do with it. How could she not? You could've come in here rain-soaked, heartbroken, and suicidal, and she'd have put a smile on your face. I love people like that. Unfortunately, there's very few of them left these days.

"Chief, I've got a good one for you," I said. "I told you already you're gonna like it. I had to make it good, since it's our last stop before we head to Valdosta."

"Well, don't keep me in suspense," he said. "Let's hear it. Where are we headed to?"

"Elizabethtown, Kentucky."

The Chief didn't say a word. The way his face lit up was all I needed. There was a story behind this place, and I just knew I'd be hearing it very soon.

We ate our breakfast quickly and with very little conversation. This was a first. Usually, we found ourselves engaged in riveting chatter, and at least one of us flips out. Not this time. I don't know if it was anticipation to get on the road, the fact that we were in the home stretch or—God forbid—we'd run out of things to say—or a combination of things, but we ate, we paid, and we left. *Goodbye, Mabel, aw shucks, sugar, we gotta' git!*

As we drove through southern Illinois, the Chief pointed out landmarks. When I'd ask for more information about them, he'd either give me some jive story or tell me the place was famous because it's where Lincoln stopped to take a shit. This went on until we crossed the state line—into Indiana.

"You bastard! I knew you were gonna haul my ass to goddamn Indiana!" the Chief shouted. He turned on the radio and cranked the volume. "I don't want to hear a motherfucking word you have to say, you traitor!"

I shook my head. At least he picked a good station.

"Evansville—there's the exit, right there," the Chief yelled over the music. "You see, I ..."

I turned the radio down. "We're not going to fucking Evansville, Indiana, Chief, I told you that," I said. "But we have to drive through Indiana to get to I-65."

"I don't believe you," he said.

"It's true. You'll survive. It's only like two hours. Go to sleep or something. Tell me a story to pass the time."

"I'll tell you the story about how a bum named Louie took an old man to Evansville, Indiana, and left him to die. Would you like to hear that one?"

I shook my head and laughed. "No," I said.

"Why are you laughing?" the Chief asked.

"Why are you being so crazy?"

"Because I'm in Indy-fucking-ana, and it's making me batshit."

I decided to help the Chief. I pushed to accelerator and sped up a bit. "That should get us through faster," I said.

"Yeah, get us through faster to a ticket," he said. "Slow down. Don't call attention to yourself. Hell, you've already got a strike against you with those out-of-state tags. *California*. They'll ream your asshole to a rosy red with those plates around here."

"Geez. Paranoid much?" I asked.

"Like I said, I'm in Indy-fucking-ana."

* * * * *

We got through the Hoosier State with no problem. As soon as we hit Louisville, Kentucky, the Chief was back to normal—well, back to whatever constitutes as normal for the old boy.

"You made it, Chief," I said. "See? Louisville, Kentucky."

"*Lull-ville*, kid," he said. "It's pronounced *Lull-ville*."

"Lull-ville? Really?"

"Yep."

"Then why are the bats called *Louie-ville* Sluggers and not Lull-ville?"

"They're from a different town."

"The hell you say!"

The Chief drew a quick grin across his face. "Just fucking with you, Louie," he said. "This is your town, baby: Louie-ville! The Home of Champions. Home of the big wallop."

"Really?" I asked.

"Yes sir," he said. "Birthplace of the bats and the boxer—the Greatest. Former Cassius Clay, himself: Mr. Muhammad Ali."

"I didn't know he was from here," I said, just as we passed the boulevard that bears his name. I tried to imitate the Champ: "I'm pretty—I'm a bad man."

The Chief chuckled. "That was pretty bad, man," he said. "Leave the quips and poems to Ali. That's his gig. And nobody did it better."

We cruised through Louisville. It was just after 12:00 p.m. on Sunday, and traffic was moving at a decent clip. We'd skirted the Ohio River, with seemed apropos considering our earlier conversation about the Buckeye State. That made three state rivers we'd traversed: the Missouri, the Mississippi earlier this morning, and now the Ohio. In a day or two, we'd cross the mighty Tennessee as well on our way into Georgia.

Once we got on I-65, we had less than an hour until we got to Elizabethtown. The Chief saw the town's name on a sign and began beaming again. I smiled and wondered what he was thinking about—like I didn't already know.

Elizabethtown, Kentucky

As we exited the freeway into Elizabethtown, the Chief patted his chest. At first, I thought it had something to do with being here; his excitement had gotten the better of him. However, when I looked at him, I realized something was wrong.

"Chief, are you okay?" I asked. "You don't look so good."

The old man held his hand to his chest and grimaced.

"I'm good, kid," he said. "Just a bout of heartburn. You know the old guts and all?"

"Do you need a doctor?" I asked.

"Louie, I need an Alka Seltzer," he said. "We don't need some sawbones for that. Just pull over to a gas station and get it."

I stopped at the first gas station I saw and went in to get the old man some tablet-form relief. I bought some bottles of water and a cheap plastic cup both for a souvenir and to mix his medicine in. The cup read, "Elizabethtown, Kentucky—Where Bluegrass and Beauty Come Together." I liked the saying. I knew the Chief would too. And I knew he'd find it risqué. I also put twenty dollars on pump no. 6.

The Chief mixed his elixir as I pumped the gas.

"Damn, that's nasty good," the Chief said. "I just need a minute."

He handed me the cup. "You can throw this out," he said. "I'm done."

"I'm not pitching it, Chief," I said. "It's yours. Read it."

He mumbled as he read the print. No reaction, then suddenly—
BREEE-YAAWWLLP ...

"Disgusting," the old man said as he wiped his mouth and patted his chest.

"What? The cup or—*that*?" I asked.

"Excuse the pigs in the presence of the hog," he said. "That was uncalled for."

I got back into the car, and we drove to the motel. It wasn't far from the freeway.

The motel was small, quaint, and cute.

"Great choice, kid," the Chief said.

I couldn't tell if he was being sarcastic or not.

"You want to try another place?" I asked.

"No, why?"

"You don't sound too keen on this one."

"Well, it's not our usual. It's not a chain place. It does look nice and clean. And there's a pool."

"But is it gonna work for us?"

"Louie, as long as there's a bed and a shower, that's all I care about. The liquor store across the street had me sold."

I checked us in and watched as the Chief scanned the small lobby.

"Not a big sitting area," he commented.

The clerk peered about. "There's extra chairs if you need, sir," he said.

"He's okay," I said. "We just like to sit and chill in the lobby of motels."

The clerk gave me a strange look as he handed me the keys.

"Rooms 14 and 16," he said. "They're just down around the way outside."

The E'Town Motel was the first old-style motor lodge we'd stayed at. Watching the Chief walk the corridor to his room made me think this was the type of place he would've pulled into while traversing the Mother Road back in the day. In a way, I felt like I was atoning for the Route 66 Park in Eureka. The Chief stopped and looked around. I saw his face, and the young man had returned. It made me smile.

"Feeling better, Chief?" I asked.

"Feeling like a million bucks, Louie," he said. "I got me an old bungalow in Dixie, and I'm in a town named after the love of my life—what more could I want?"

I understood the old bungalow in Dixie, but the rest wasn't as clear.

"What do you mean?" I asked.

"I'll tell you about it over lunch," he said. "Find us a place, and I'll tell you a story."

I went into my room and looked around. The walls were off-white. I'm sure they had been stark white at one time, painted over a million times. The wall behind the bed was painted plain green. It added an accent to the plainness of the room. The carpet was low pile and slightly discolored. The random stains made it look patterned and strangely—to quote *the Dude* in the *Big Lebowski*—"really tied the room together."

The accommodations were sparse, but this was not the Holiday Inn Express or the Sheraton—it was the E'Town Motel! There was a TV or course, but it was an old one with a clunky, five-button remote: power, volume up and down, channel up and down. There was a radio built into the wall—just like the old days. The alarm clock on the desk was an old electric analog Westclox Dialite. It made a low guttural buzz. *I'll bet it glows orange*, I thought.

There was no coffee pot, but there was a microwave that looked quite new. However, the air conditioner was an old wall unit. It was on low but still noisy. I heard the compressor kick on, and it sounded like it was going to fall out of the wall. The bathroom was bigger than I thought. The sink was framed by a lighted mirror that looked like something out of a Hollywood dressing room. I switched on the light and looked at my reflection and quickly preened like a Georgia debutante—in Kentucky.

The countertop was white porcelain and covered with folded towels, small bars of soap, and a bottle of shampoo. There was a plastic ice bucket embossed with the design of a horsehead. Inside the bucket were four wrapped cups. The cups looked like those you used to get on an airplane: sharp-edged and rigid but cracked easily if you squeezed them too hard.

The facilities were white, porcelain. The sink and tub spigots were chrome—shiny and freshly polished; however, the faucet valve handles were white, X-shaped, porcelain with the words hot and cold printed in the center.

The floor was tiled all white to match the toilet and tub. The walls were stark white as well. There was no discoloration or bubbling of any sort within the paint. The bathroom smelled of bleach and was so clean I felt ashamed I'd have to foul it up at some point.

Two Fredric Remington prints hung on the bathroom walls. The one behind the toilet was of *The Herd Boy*; the other, which hung over the door, was of *The Hussar*. They were both small and greatly faded. They seemed odd choices at first, but they did have horses in them, and this *was* Kentucky. It made sense.

I heard a cricket chirping. I stepped out of the bathroom and saw that I'd forgot to close the door. The Chief walked in just as I was about to shut it.

"Can't get rid of me that easily, son," he said.

"I wasn't trying to, Chief," I said. "I just forgot to close the door."

The Chief looked around my room. He spotted the differences between his room and mine. They weren't that significant, but to the old boy, they were huge.

"I've got haystacks in my shitter," he said.

To which I replied, "That sounds like a personal problem."

The Chief shook his head. "You're an ass, Louie," he said.

I laughed. "So does that malady mean you don't want to get some food?" I asked.

"Kid, I'm famished. Where are we going?"

"I have no idea, but let's see what's here and local."

We walked to the office, and I asked about local diners.

"We've got a lot of good eats 'round here," the clerk said. "My favorite place is Bub's, but they're closed now. Open tomorrow at six a.m."

"Well, that doesn't do us much good right now," I said. "What else is good?"

"If you like barbecue and good country vittles, there's Mark's Feed Store."

"That sounds interesting—if not a bit like Tractor Supply with food."

The clerk laughed. "Well, it used to be a real feed store," he said. "But Ol' Mark gave it the human touch and it's a local hotspot."

I looked at the Chief. "Y'all want some Kentucky barbecue, Colonel?" I asked, bolstering my Georgia drawl. The clerk shot me a look.

"I'm from Georgia," I said. "The accent comes and goes. I wasn't poking fun."

"Ah, heck, boy," the clerk said. "I ain't mad at ya. I just didn't notice your *twang*. You hide it well."

The Chief chimed in. "Stop hassling the good man," he said. "Let's take his advice and go get some grub at the feed store."

The clerk smiled. "You'll love Mark's," he said. "Best brisket in town. Hell—the only brisket in town—at least for some folks."

"You sold us on it, son. Thank you," the Chief said.

And I concurred. We were off to Mark's to put our snouts into the feedbag.

* * * * *

We got to Mark's and found the place to be not an old feed store but a space in a strip mall. No big deal to me, but the Chief seemed a little disappointed.

"That bastard lied to us," he said.

"Don't worry about it," I said. "Let's go eat."

I went in, and the Chief stood outside. I was waiting for him to get pouty again.

"Table for one?" the host asked. It sounded like such an odd question.

"No, there's gonna be two for lunch," I said, pointing at the Chief.

"He can come in, you know. We serve our customers tasty bites, but we don't bite our tasty customers."

I laughed. "You need to tell him that," I said.

The host walked over to the door and leaned out to talk to the Chief. The old man—in a half-mope—entered the restaurant and the host led us to our table. We ordered two mugs of Hofbräu Beer and looked over the menu.

"I think our host is a bandit," the Chief said.

"Really? Does that bother you?" I asked.

"No. Kid, I don't care what you do, just don't do it to me— unless I tell you to."

"That's a good philosophy. I'll have to remember that."

"Yeah, there's too much shit in this world to worry about who's sleeping with whom or what."

"Unfortunately, a lot of people have a different view."

"That's true, Louie. You aren't prejudiced, are you? We've never broached that subject."

I shook my head. "What are you kidding?" I asked. "I grew up in California. My best friend was a homosexual. My older sister is married to a Panamanian. I can't be prejudiced—although I am against certain types of music."

"We all are, I think," the Chief said. "But that can get you in trouble too. Just so long as you don't have a beef with Ol' Blue Eyes, we're good."

"Nope. Not anymore. You fixed that one for me."

"Glad I could help make your world a better place!"

Our waiter came to take our orders. We'd glanced at the menu but hadn't really studied them. That was fine. The Chief and I took the motel clerk's advice and ordered the brisket.

"We hear tell it's the best brisket in town," the Chief said.

"It's pretty good," the waiter said. "I get it a lot."

"But is it *the best?* I want nothing but the best."

"It is the best, sir. I guarantee it."

"Well, if you guarantee it, then … how about ol' twinkle-toes the host? Does he guarantee it as well?"

"Twinkle-toes, sir? You mean *Ronnie?*"

"Yeah, *Rodney.* Do I have his guarantee as well?"

The waiter did not hesitate. He called Ronnie over to get his opinion. I just sat and watched the exchange go from two volleys to three.

"Ronnie, do you like the brisket?" the waiter asked.

"I do. It's the best in town," Ronnie said.

The Chief furrowed his brow. "You're not pulling my leg, are you, Rod?"

Ronnie shook his head, not even noticing being called by the wrong name.

"No, sir, it is indeed the best," he said. "I guarantee it."

"Well, hot damn! Ain't that a mare's ass?" the Chief exclaimed. "Two guarantees! This must be some divine brisket. I'm sold. Whisk me up some brisket, briskly boys!"

Ronnie and the waiter left us to drink our beers and wait for our food. I was hoping this brisket met the expectations heaped upon it. The Chief was asking an awful lot from a cut of meat and even more from those who were serving him. I could tell that Ronnie and the waiter liked the old man. They certainly aimed to please as well as get a huge gratuity.

When our food arrived, it definitely looked as advertised. The Chief breathed in the aroma of the smoked meat.

"Kid, this is gonna be good," he said to the waiter. "Now wait right here until I taste it. I want you to be able to tell the High Della-Lama of this establishment that the Big Banana gave this meal the seal of approval under … what's your name …?"

The waiter answered, "Dwight, sir."

The Chief continued, "Under Dwayne and Rodney's guarantee."

Dwight smiled and did as he was told: he waited for the Chief to take a bite. Once he cut a chunk of meat off, he chewed it slowly and made the most embarrassing noises as he ate.

"Damn it, Chief, you're eating, not fucking," I whispered across the table.

The Chief's mouth was full. "*Oheeyah!*" he growled. "Ah coo mag luh tah di, Lou-ah."

I palmed my face in embarrassment. "I can't take him any-where," I said.

"Did he just say he could have sex with the food?" Dwight asked.

"I'm afraid so."

"Is that normal—I mean—does he say that a lot?"

"Nope. This is a first."

Dwight smiled so big his teeth popped from his lips and his eyes crinkled.

"That's the best compliment I've ever gotten," he said. "Or that the food's ever gotten."

I waved Dwight close to me. "Keep up the good work and he'll tip you enough to make a car payment," I whispered.

"Really?" he asked excitedly.

"No, but it'll be a lot—probably more than what you've made all day."

Dwight's eyes got big and sparkly. "Holy shit!" he said then quickly covered his mouth.

"It's okay," I said. "He makes me say a lot worse."

After the Chief was done making over his meal, he settled down, and we ate like regular folks and not Romeo and Juliet. It was some good food, I must say. I'll have to thank the clerk for the suggestion. We'd try Bub's tomorrow. He had a tough act to follow.

"Chief, I have some questions for you," I said. "Things that I've been racking my brain trying to figure out, and I feel like now's the time to ask you."

"Swing away, kid." I've got the answers.

"Okay. First of all," I said. "What is a mare's ass? Is it good or bad?"

"Both. It's like being a son of a bitch," the Chief explained. "You do something foolish and say, 'Well, I'll be a son of a bitch.' Then you hear that skirt you were chasing has the big pants for you too, and you say, 'Well, I'll be a son of a bitch.' It's all in the inflection and the situation. The mare's ass works just the same."

I nodded. "Wow. okay, next. What is a 'High Della-Lama'?" I asked.

"That's a natch, kid," he said. "The High Della-Lama is the boss. To some, he's like a god among men."

"What? Like Christ?"

"Yeah, but the Della-Lama is real—and alive."

"Oh fucking hell—*the Dalai Lama?* The Tibetan Buddhist monk?"

"Yep."

I rolled my eyes and shook my head toward the ceiling. "Seriously. How did I not figure that one out?" I asked out loud.

"Any more things you'd like to know?" the Chief asked. "That's only two things."

"I have one more," I said. "And it has to do with where we are and something you said earlier."

"What about the meat? It's damn good."

"No, it's not about the meat. It's about the love of your life—and the way your face lit up when I said Elizabethtown."

The Chief sat back. He took a long sip of his beer.

"The name Elizabeth, Louie—it just does something to me," he said. "Always has."

"How so?" I asked.

"Have you ever been with a woman named Elizabeth?"

"Hell, I don't even think I know anyone named Elizabeth."

The Chief shook his head. "Oh, Louie, you don't know what you're missing," he said.

I got a puzzled look on my face. *It's just a name*, I thought.

The Chief was beaming again. There was obviously something to this name.

"Yeah, kid … *Elizabeth,*" he said. "There's something about that name that is just so regal—so majestic."

"It's a long name, for sure," I said.

"Oh, it is that," he said. "It spans from *A* to *Z*, but not in order."

"There's a couple letters missing."

"There are. And it starts with—and has—two *E*s, but that's not the point. Do you know why there's so many nicknames for Elizabeth?"

"No. I've never thought much about it."

The Chief laughed. "Well, do you wanna know why?" he asked. I nodded and smiled.

"Because with a name that long, it's impossible to get it all out while you're having an orgasm," the Chief said. "It always gets shortened. You have to try it sometime. See if I'm wrong."

I chuckled at the Chief's comment.

"And here is another perk about women named Elizabeth," he said. "They're usually gorgeous."

"Really?" I asked.

"Yes sir. Take Ms. Taylor for example," he said. "You don't get to be the cat on the hot tin roof, nor do you get to play Cleopatra if you're not a renowned beauty."

That explained the Chief's comment to Jeanette—her makeup was quite Cleopatra-esque. Not to mention her eyes were the same violet hue as Elizabeth Taylor's.

I pondered the Chief's reasoning. It made sense, I suppose. I watched his eyes sparkle as he mused and swooned over Elizabeth Taylor.

"You always struck me as more of the Ava Gardner type," I said.

"What? The World's Most Beautiful Creature?" he asked. "Ms. Gardner was every man's desire, but she was too much for any man to handle—even me. Hell, Sinatra couldn't break her, and he was goddamn Sinatra!"

"I never thought about that," I said.

"It's the truth."

The Chief switched back to Elizabeth Taylor.

"She's still stunning, Louie," he said. "You know, only one man could truly love her: Mr. Richard Burton—and even then ..." The Chief hung his head. "Now that was a romance for the ages. No two people loved each other more, kid. It's too damn bad Hollywood ruined them.

"Ah, Hollywood ... those bastards. They can write a love story that stands the test of time, but they're quick to destroy one in real life."

The Chief drifted. He was here with me, but his heart and mind were elsewhere—young and insouciant and making love to Elizabeth Taylor.

"You still haven't answered my question completely," I said.

The Chief snapped back to reality. "What was that?" he asked, still dazed.

"Other than your crush on Elizabeth Taylor, what does being here have to do with the love of your life? I thought that was Mariposa."

"No, kid, Mariposa was my *first love*. You only get one of those as well. No, Elizabeth was the love of my life—and her last name was not Taylor."

"I'm not following," I said.

"Bettie, Louie," the Chief said matter-of-factly. "Bettie was the love of my life. Her name was actually Elizabeth."

"Oh my God, Chief," I said. "I can't believe I didn't get that. Forgive me for being so stupid."

"It's okay. You're not stupid. I told you, there are a lot of nicknames for Elizabeth."

"Apparently, I'm not aware of one of them."

"Don't worry about it. Hell, I wasn't either until I had to …"

The old man went from happy to full-on shutdown mode in a second. I didn't have to ask why—I knew. This was going to require some time and another round of beers. I knew there was nothing simple about that woman.

Dwight brought us a pitcher of beer and two freshly frosted mugs. The Chief was still locked away and had half a drink left, but I poured him a new glass anyway—he'd need it when he came back.

"Is he okay?" Dwight asked.

"No," I said, flatly. "He's not okay. He will be. But for now, no."

Dwight nodded and quietly left us alone.

"Chief," I whispered, as I tried to look into his eyes. "Where are you?"

He did not respond. He just continued to stare blankly into space. This was bad.

Ronnie, the host, came over with a manager. "Is everything all right?" the manager asked.

"No, he's just having a spell," I said.

"Oh my goodness, do we need to call an ambulance?"

"No. He just needs a moment. It's nothing physical. It's just depression."

The Chief blinked, and I knew he was on his way back.

"It ain't fucking depression, Louie," he said in a grumble.

I touched his hand. "Welcome back, you old son of a bitch," I said.

Ronnie and the manager were puzzled by our exchange, but they didn't know how we worked. I smiled at them and said everything was good. The Chief just needed another minute and he'd be fine.

It took longer than usual, but the old boy snapped out of it and it was as if nothing happened, although this time, I knew he'd received a fresh scar on his heart.

We finished our meals and our beers. There was not a lot of talking. I knew the Chief needed to recover, and I was not going to disturb him as he did. I poured us more beer, and the Chief smiled.

"You take good care of me, Louie," he said. "I just want you to know that."

"I have to Chief," I said. "I made promises to some important people."

The Chief got a perplexed look on his face but said nothing.

On the drive back to the motel, I wondered how the next couple of days were going to go. This was our last stop before home, and it seemed to already be a heady one.

"Chief, what would you like to do while were here?" I asked. "Besides eat and drink of course."

He thought for a moment and nodded. "Riding, Louie," he said. "Tomorrow, I'd like to go riding."

"Riding?"

"Yes. Horseback riding. We're in Kentucky, and they've got a billion horses here. We've talked about Bettie, and I'd like to see her again—I can only, truly do that on horseback."

The Chief's words scared me: wanting to "see" Bettie, only being able to 'truly do that on horseback." What did that mean? I wanted to find out—I just didn't have the balls to ask.

"I'll find you a place," I said. "I don't know if I can ride or not."

"You don't have to," he said. "I'd rather do it alone. Just take me someplace where I can ride. Can you do that for this old bastard? Can you do the Ol' Super Chief a solid?"

I smiled. "Yes. I most certainly can," I said. "It would be an honor."

* * * * *

I woke up at 3:45 a.m. with a violent jolt. My sheets and pillow were soaked. Even my feet were wet. The room was slightly cold; however, I had become feverish in a dream, and when this fever broke, my sweat glands opened and drenched my body relentlessly.

I got up. I could see the dampened silhouette of my body on the top sheet. I went into the bathroom and grabbed a couple of towels—one for the bed and one for me. The room was eerily quiet, except for the cricket chirping outside. I put a towel on the mattress and lay back down.

I wasn't sure if I could go back to sleep. I began to piece together the dream I'd just had. The parts that came back to me were so abstract: the horses stampeding, the storm, the color white, the ocean. They had a purpose on their own but made no sense as a whole. There were too many elements missing. The only thing I was certain of was that I began to question whether or not the Chief should go riding. What was I going to say to him? *Don't ride the pony, Chief—I had a dream.* What the hell?

I closed my eyes.

* * * * *

I woke up to the sound of bird songs and the cricket again. It was still dark, but my trusty Westclox Dialite said it was 5:50 a.m. I'd gotten a little more shut-eye in, and now I felt it was time to get up. I lay in bed and listened to the outside world. I kept waiting for one of the birds to eat the cricket.

I was dry but felt disgusting. I could smell the oniony aroma of my body odor, and it was my cue to shower.

I got up and walked into the bathroom. I glanced at the print of *The Herd Boy* over the toilet. I stared into the faded picture as I pissed, and all I could think of was the horses in my dream. This one was still. Mine were not. Mine were wild, restless, and afraid. They'd been scared by a storm perhaps?

There was a storm in my dream, but were the horses in it? What of the ocean? And what of the white—nothing but a stark flash of all the colors of the rainbow culminated. It wasn't a bright white. It was more like that of linens—fibrous but billowy.

I got in the shower. The water ran over me, and it was hot. The heat felt good. It was soothing, and I could sense my tension easing just enough. I opened the soap and lathered up. It felt like the same sticky soap I'd used in Eureka; however, this had no design pressed into it.

I stood beneath the showerhead lost in a blank thought: *No worries here.* I just let the water and the hiss of the shower hypnotize me. I pulled my hair back and listened to the excess water splash behind me. My thoughtless daze would be short-lived. I heard a muffled pounding on my door. *Be right there, Chief...*

I got out of the shower and dried off as quickly as I could. The Chief knocked again—at least I hoped it was the Chief, especially this early in the morning.

"One second, Chief," I said.

I heard a muffled voice through the door. It was not the Chief.

"Mr. DeCarlo?" the voice asked.

I stood by the door. "Yes," I said. "Who is it?"

"My name is Terry Platt. I work the front desk," he said.

"Okay, hang on," I said as I pulled on my pants.

I opened the door. "Yes, what is it?" I asked nervously.

"There's a gentleman in the lobby who—"

I cut him off.

"Requests my presence?" I asked. "Old guy? White hair? Looks like he should be in an old movie?"

"Yes, sir."

"I'll be right there."

"He asked that I escort you."

I huffed and pointed at myself. "I need to get dressed," I said. Give me a minute please."

I shut the door and put my face into my hands and sighed. *What could he be up to?* I wondered. I put on a shirt and my shoes without socks and opened the door again.

"Okay, let's go," I said.

My escort led me to the lobby, and there was the Chief, sipping coffee and looking chipper and ready for the day.

"Was this necessary, Chief?" I asked. "Where's the fire?"

"There's no fire, kid, I just wasn't feeling well," he said. "I figured you'd get here quicker if I sent for you."

"What's the matter?" I asked.

"It's that damn pain from yesterday," he said. "Maybe I do need a doctor."

"Did you take a seltzer tablet?"

"I did—at about oh three forty-five. It didn't help."

"Three forty-five?" I wondered aloud. *That was when I woke up from my dream. This is too weird.*

"Should you be drinking coffee?" I asked.

"It's okay. I put creamer in it to settle my gut," the Chief said.

I shook my head. "Wait here, okay," I said. "I need to get properly dressed, and then I'll take you to the doctor."

I asked Terry how far away the hospital was. "Down the road—not even a bit," he said.

As a Southerner, I knew how far that was: *super close.*

"I'm fine, Louie," the Chief said. "I don't want to be a bother."

"You're not a bother, Chief," I said. "I'll take you in. You should see a doc."

"No. I'm fine," he said adamantly. He threw his cup in the trash and went back toward his room.

I caught up and stopped him. "Dammit, Chief, you're scaring the shit out of me," I said. "Let's go to the hospital and make sure you're all right."

"No, Louie. I don't need a doctor," he said. "You have the answer. I just need to get the shit scared out of me, that's all."

"Well then, we need to go see the doc. He'll tell you you're dying and then say *'Psyche!'* And the shit will have been scared out of you."

"Very droll."

"What do you want me to say? You have me escorted to the lobby at 6:30 a.m., tell me you're ill. You then tell me to forget it and that you just need to take a shit."

"I think something's bothering me, kid. I just don't know what it is."

"I do, Chief. You're overwhelmed. You've got thoughts racing in a million different directions. This place is messing with your head."

"Does this mean you won't take me riding today?"

"I think you wanting to go riding is one of the reasons why you're so messed up. Maybe we should skip it and do something else?"

"No. Unacceptable. I want to go riding. I want to see Bettie."

Billy Joel once said, 'You should never argue with a crazy mind." I was going to heed his advice and leave the Chief to his own devices.

"Okay, Chief," I said. "I'll take you riding—but after breakfast."

All of a sudden, the old boy's face changed. His color was back. He looked young—and slightly hungry. We were off to Bub's Café.

We walked into the place, and I didn't care if the food was good or bad. I was blown away by all the toys and memorabilia that were perched on the walls and hanging from the ceiling: old metal pedal cars and bicycles. I haven't seen foot-powered vehicles like this and in such pristine condition since I was little—and even then! I didn't have to close my eyes and imagine. I was there. I was six years old again and pedaling my little blue police car all over the driveway, making siren noises and pulling over imaginary speeders.

Our waitress's name was Tawny. She was bubbly and fun for 7:00 a.m. She winked at the Chief whether he said anything or not. She was smitten with the old bastard, and he loved every second of it.

"Now, *Tammy*, how about those eggs," the Chief inquired. "Are they fresh?"

"Honey, they are, but not as fresh as you," she said.

"How about the potatoes? I like a little bite in my potatoes."

"Well, sugar, if they don't have a bite, then I'll give you one personally!"

And this went on and on.

I ordered the French toast and a side of ham when Tawny took a moment to stop making over the Chief.

Tawny took our guest checks to a window and yelled our orders back to the cook. This was too great. I hadn't been in a place like this since the diner in Elko. And that seemed a lifetime ago.

Our food arrived, and it was huge! Good thing we were hungry.

"Chief, you'll get that shit you were after once you finish that meal," I said.

He ignored my comment and dug in.

This was one of the best breakfasts we've had on the trip, and the first that was not from a chain restaurant or a lodging facility.

"Good chow, kid," the Chief said. "I'm glad we came."

"Me too," I said. "You feeling better?"

"Fit as a fiddle and ready for love."

"Speaking of fiddles, Chief, did you hear that cricket outside our rooms?"

"Louie, do you know what a cricket is?" he asked.

"Besides a bug? No."

"It's a cockroach with talent. They're disgusting."

"My momma says it's good luck if one gets in the house, but the roach analogy makes me think differently."

"Bugs in your house is no kinda luck. However, on Guam, having a gecko in your house *is* good luck, and if you have bugs, they'll eat them. It's a bonus."

The bill came, and the Chief paid it. He'd noticed Tawny left her phone number on the receipt. He tipped her twenty dollars.

When we got back to the motel I went to the lobby to ask about places close by to take the Chief to ride. There were several that Terry had mentioned, but the one that caught my attention was called Misty Meadow Farm. That's where we were going.

I drove out to Misty Meadow Farm on US 62. It was about fifteen minutes northeast of the motel. The place was located on a road called Fudge Lane, and suddenly I was craving thick chocolatey treats. We pulled into the parking lot, and the Chief got out of the car as if he were being pulled by a force.

The woman who ran the stables introduced herself. Her name was Hannah, and her assistant was Marilyn. I extended pleasantries and told the ladies my name and shook their hands. The Chief introduced himself as Hop-a-long Cassidy. I rolled my eyes. *Whatever.*

"Hi," I said. "We don't have an appointment, but Hop-a-long here was wondering about going on a ride. Can we do that?"

Hannah smiled. "You can," she said. "We have a quick course for inexperienced riders, then we take you out and to the meadow. If you've ridden before, we can get you saddled up and ready to go right away."

"He has experience, I don't," I said. "But I'm not riding, so it'll just be him."

"Oh, why aren't you riding?" Hannah asked.

"I'm a four-wheel and enclosed carriage guy. Riding on an animal isn't for me."

"You would've made a lousy cowboy."

"They would've made me the cook—but I'd have been lousy at that too."

Marilyn chimed in. "Then they woulda killed ya!" she said with a smirk.

"Nah, I would've got to them first with my grub," I said.

Marilyn laughed and it was magical. *Oh my God. I think I want to ask this woman out on a date.*

Hannah and the Chief discussed formalities and I listened, occasionally glancing at Marilyn with that dopey puppy-dog look I tend to get around females I've got an affinity for.

"How long has it been since you rode?" Hannah asked the Chief.

"Good God," he said. "It has to be well over forty years."

"Oh my, that's a *very* long time. But you know it's like riding a bike: you never forget."

"It's been even longer since I rode a bike!"

Hannah and the Chief shared a laugh.

"Louis, are you sure you won't be riding today?" Hannah asked me.

"As sure as ol' Hop-a-long hasn't been on horseback for over four decades," I said.

Marilyn giggled at my comment. "Are you scared?" she asked.

"No, it's just not my thing," I said. "I tried to ride my cousin's Saint Bernard when I was a kid. My aunt slapped me senseless. It was very traumatic. I never forgot."

Marilyn furrowed her brow. "You're kidding, right?" she asked.

"Yes. About my aunt. However, I did try to ride the dog, though."

Marilyn had no idea what was truth and what was not at this point.

"Actually, I'm just here for moral support," I said. "And I seemed to have found some for me as well."

Marilyn smiled coyly and lowered her eyes. I couldn't believe it—I was flirting. She didn't bolt, so I must've been doing it halfway decent?

"Well, while they're out, you can enjoy some refreshments in the lounge. We have sodas, water, and beer for sale," Marilyn said. "Sodas are two bucks, water is one. Beers are three dollars, and we have the *usual.*"

'The usual'? I like her style.

I bought a Schlitz—which was anything but usual. I drank it and watched the Chief and Hannah circle the corral before heading to the meadow for the big ride.

The Chief looked happy and in control on the saddle of that horse. Hannah had even talked him into buying a Stetson hat—black of course. I tried to imagine what was going through his mind as that big stallion trotted, carrying him back to another place and time, back to see the love of his life. It was a beautiful thought. I asked Marilyn for a pen and some paper. I had a little story to write in this moment.

> They were strangers for just a short time: this man of mystery who'd come from the city and this woman who'd ridden the range in search of someone her equal. It was he. Once they'd

mounted their steeds and rode into the glen, they were as familiar to each other as they were to the horses which carried them to their destiny. Theirs was a destiny as vast as the lands upon which they traversed but as uncertain as the days to come. They cared not for the formalities nor the trivialities; they were only concerned about the moment—only concerned about themselves and what tonight would bring. They would worry about tomorrows as they became todays. And as they became lovers ...

I stopped writing and crumpled up the paper. I did not throw it away, but I couldn't look at it anymore. It seemed cheesy and stupid. This was why I was having trouble with my work. Hell, I couldn't even write something decent about the Chief riding a horse—and considering what I knew about his last ride, it was something noteworthy.

It's not my story to tell, I said to myself. *Yeah, but isn't that the whole idea? Aren't you telling someone else's story? Isn't that what makes what you do worthwhile? You give your reader words, and they take them and make them their own? What about the Chief? Aren't you taking his stories and making them someone else's? Aren't you going to ask Marilyn out?*

I snapped out of my daze and stuffed the paper into my pocket. I swallowed hard before I could get too nervous and clam up. I walked over to Marilyn and—I froze.

"Is there anything I can do for you?" she asked.

I smiled like an idiot and said nothing. I shook my head. The gesture looked as if I was telling her *no.* Marilyn turned away and went back to her work.

"Um, yeah," I said.

"Yes?" she responded.

"There *is* something you can do for me."

"Sure. What can I help you with?"

I figured I'd keep tailoring my request in accordance to her questions.

"Um …" I paused to think. *Was this the best approach?* It didn't matter. My mouth had already decided to stick with the plan.

"Would you like to *help* me eat some dinner tonight?" I asked.

I smacked my forehead. "That was the stupidest thing I've ever said," I mumbled.

"Why'd you do that?" she asked.

"Because that was really dumb, what I meant—"

She cut me off.

"Not what you said—but why you smacked yourself," she said.

"I'm sorry," I said. "That just came out wrong. It made me sound like I wanted you to help me eat. I can feed myself, you know? I'm pretty able to …"

She cut me off again.

"I'm sure you can feed yourself," she said. "And yes—even though no one's asked me quite like that before—I'd love to help you eat some dinner tonight. I get off at six p.m."

I was speechless—but the good kind for once.

Marilyn wrote her phone number down and handed it to me. "It's my cell," she said. "I just got a new one. It's a slider with push-to-talk. Same number, though. Isn't that cool?"

I crinkled my face. "So I can pitch your old number then?" I asked. "It never worked anyway, probably because I have a BlackBerry?"

She laughed. "My goodness, you crack me up," she said. "Tonight is gonna be fun!"

"I hope so," I said, as I finished my beer.

* * * * *

On the way back to town, the Chief was quiet but content. I knew he'd 'went beyond,' but had no idea how far and I didn't want to ask. I just looked at him. His glowing face and the quarter smile on his lips were all the words I needed. However, I hated the silence. I needed some conversation. I got selfish.

"I'm going on a date, Chief," I said. "It's with Marilyn from Misty Meadow."

The Chief said nothing but gave me a slight nod.

"She's gorgeous," I said. "Don't you think so?"

Another nod.

"I did it all without your help," I said.

This time, I got a response. "I had to go on a horseback ride for you to get that date, kid," he said, still looking straight ahead. "So I helped you out again."

"Well, thank you for your assistance," I said.

The Chief continued to stare forward, but I saw him wink. That was good enough for me.

There was still a lot of time left in the day. We could take in a sight or two before needing to get back to the motel. I'd managed to grab a couple brochures from the lobby earlier this morning.

"Chief," I said. "I have some brochures in the glove box."

The Chief reached in and grabbed them. He read through them, but nothing seemed to strike his fancy.

"Well, if you find something …" I said.

The Chief let out a belly laugh. "Oh, I found something!" he exclaimed. "And it sounds like every man's—and maybe a few women's—dreams."

"What is it?" I asked.

"Louie, it's the Brown Pussy House," he said. "That's where we're going!"

I shook my head. "What?" I asked. "What kind of place is this?"

"I don't know, but it's called the Brown Pussy House and I want to go see it."

"Spell *pussy*, Chief."

"P-U-S-S-Y."

"No, on the brochure."

"P-U-S-*E*-Y."

"I think it's pronounced *pee-yoo-see*. Let me see the picture."

The Chief held up the brochure, and I quickly glanced at it. There was a picture of a two-story Georgian-style brownstone on the cover. This was certainly no house of ill repute—which was what the Chief was hoping for.

"It's a museum, Chief," I said. "Not a whorehouse."

417

"Maybe it *is* a whorehouse," he responded. "They can be historic, you know."

I dropped a barricade into this conversation. "Do you really want to go see this place?" I asked. "Your hopes will be dashed."

He glanced through the pamphlet. "I do want to go," he said. "I found some things about it that interested me."

* * * * *

We drove to the Brown-Pusey House, and on the outside, it was even more beautiful than the picture on the brochure. We got out of the car and walked the grounds. The Chief decided he did not want to go in, but there were plenty of workers and docent types outside to help us along.

The Chief seemed taken by the fact that General George Armstrong Custer and his wife, Elizabeth, had stayed here while the general did a stint in the town. Custer was fighting against people making illegal bourbon and other naughty libations, as well as keeping the KKK from spreading their influence among the people of Elizabethtown.

One of the docents talked of Jenny Lind, the *Swedish Nightingale*, singing on the steps of the house. The Chief referred to her as *the Sparrow*; mistaking her for Edith Piaf and randomly correcting the docent. The more he mentioned Edith Piaf, the more I heard her singing in my head. Suddenly my mind went askew. German Focke Wulf 190s flew overhead while Edith Piaf sang—in Swedish. I was in a World War II daydream—in occupied French Kentucky, standing outside an English manor. What the hell?

We walked around some more and explored the gardens. "Now, that's Dixie for you, kid," the Chief said as he marveled at the beautiful magnolias. "And I'm here to tell ya, it's true what they say about her."

I smiled. I knew.

We drifted down the street to the public square. It was midafternoon, and the Chief wanted to grab a bite of lunch. As we walked, we heard people talking about "the cannonball." We didn't ask about it, we just looked up and it—well—hit us. It was the damnedest thing: literally a cannonball stuck in the side of the courthouse!

"Somebody must've been pissed off about a ticket," the Chief said.

"Or really didn't want to do jury duty," I replied.

We found a little tavern to eat. It was a place called the Public House. No fanfare—just chews and booze. The Chief and I ordered pub grub and a couple of pints of Guinness.

"You have a date, Louie? Did I hear that correctly?" the Chief asked.

"That's what I've been told," I said.

"I'm proud of you, kid. You wait until you're at the end of the trip—until you're almost home—to finally get enough balls to ask a dame out."

"Are you being serious or just giving me shit?"

"A little of both. I'm just wondering what took you so long."

"A few things, really. One in particular, but that's, well, history."

"Say no more. I know it's been difficult."

"There have been ups and downs for sure."

"Especially with that one in Nebraska."

I blushed hard. "Yes," I said. "Especially with Catherine."

"You remembered her name?" the Chief asked.

"How could I forget? Her name was Catherine—that's Hemingway."

"Any other reason?"

"Yeah. She fucked my brains out."

The Chief smiled and smugly said, "You're welcome."

Our food arrived, and we snacked and chatted. I already knew the drill, but the Chief reiterated the importance of giving "full disclosure" on my date.

"Maybe she'll be with me at breakfast," I said. "And she can give you all the details."

"That would be nice," the Chief said. "A first as well. We haven't had any female companionship at breakfast yet."

"Nope, and leave it to me to wait until the last stop, right?"

"Well, kid, better late than never."

We finished our lunch and our beers and walked back to get the car. It had been a great day so far, and I was hoping to continue that feeling into tonight. The only issue seemed to be the weather. It had been a gorgeous, cloudless day, but now, storms were brewing in the west and they looked ominous and severe. I just hoped they'd stay there or move in a different direction. I was nervous enough about tonight. I didn't need inclement weather dampening things any further.

The rain poured hard and came down in sheets. It was as if the storm we'd gone through in Eureka had built back up to drench another evening. I stood and watched as the deluge obscured the buildings across the street for the motel.

I heard the Chief ask to come in, even before he knocked. I walked over and opened the door.

"Wonderful weather, isn't it?" he asked. "Remind you of anything?"

"I was just thinking that," I said. "Good thing we're not doing karaoke, eh?"

The Chief smiled and sat down. "Reminds me of the tropics," he said. "It always rained like this in the Islands, 'Nam as well."

"It seems to rain on this trip whenever I make a concerted effort to do something entertaining," I said. "Last time it happened, things turned out bad, but …"

The Chief cut me off.

"Don't do this to yourself, Louie," he said. "You're gonna' have a great night—trust me."

"I know. I just can't help but be a little … *cautious* …?"

"Natch. It's understandable. Just don't blame it on the rain."

"I won't—and besides, that's a terrible song."

"Never heard it."

"You're doing yourself a favor."

* * * * *

420

Marilyn asked if she could come to the motel and pick me up. It was perfect. She also volunteered to drive, and I thought that was fine. I was a stranger in Elizabethtown, and what better way to see the place than with a local? Plus, she knew all the places to eat that weren't Bub's or the pub in the public square.

I waited in the lobby for her. She would be driving a blue 2003 Ford Focus SE. I kept looking out the window and checking the clock. It was almost 7:30 p.m., and I tried not to get too wrapped up in logistics, but I felt she was running late.

Dude. Chill, I said to myself. *She doesn't get off until six. It's still raining like a cow pissing on a flat rock. You don't know how far she has to drive. Just stop.*

When 8:00 p.m. rolled around I began to worry—both about Marilyn's safety and the fact she may be standing me up. Suddenly April popped in my head. *Great. Let's pile that on top of everything else that is bothering me.*

At about 8:15 p.m., I saw lights swing and cast their beams through the glass of the lobby doors. They were the odd triangular shape of a Ford Focus. My date had arrived.

I walked outside to get into Marilyn's car. A lightning bolt flashed and split and lit up the sky. Thunder cracked shortly after, and it scared the hell out of me. I did what no smart person would do in a lightning/water situation—I froze. It was only for a second, but it was enough time to show my panic. Marilyn pushed the passenger's door open, and I scurried to get in.

"Oh my God, that was freaky!" I exclaimed as I tried to brush the water off my soaked skin.

"Are you okay?" she asked. "That was something else!"

"I'm good. Your seat is going to be soaked, though. I'm sorry."

"It's leather. It'll be fine." Marilyn glanced at me. "You're cute, you know that?" she asked out of the blue.

"I never thought much about it," I said. "Cute as a drowned rat."

"Oh, you! Stop that."

We drove for a few minutes and chatted about trivialities before we got on the subject of dinner.

"What sounds good?" she asked. "What do you like to eat?"

"Just about anything," I said. "I'm just not big on Chinese. I'll eat it. I'm just not a fan."

"Well, that leaves out the Green Bamboo, then. What about Italian?"

I told her I'd just had Italian a couple days ago. I did not say I'd been ruined for Italian by the fabulous fare at Boccardi's in Eureka, Missouri.

We ran the gamut of international foods. We'd also decided against anything that started with a Mc, ended with a Barrel, or was any type of major chain.

"How about a diner?" Marilyn asked. "Someplace fun, kitschy—a throwback type of place?"

I swear I heard a little glass bell ring in my head—*ding!* This was a good sign. The last time I'd had dinner at a diner with a member of the opposite sex, things went better than expected. The worst part about it was that I fell in love. That seemed like ages ago, and my loyalties and affections had faded—in less than two weeks. Absence makes the heart forget, and it would seem I'd forgotten all about ol' whatshername from that one place.

"A diner sounds great," I said.

Our destination was a place called the Main Street Deli. It was a legitimate dive! I loved it. The place in Elko had been designed to look and function like an old fifties place, but the Main Street Deli was authentic and not a mere throwback. Francine, our waitress must've been a five-pack-a-day smoker in her heyday; however, now she was just a gruff-voiced, spunky old gal serving up slop and sass to a crowded restaurant.

"What'll it be, Teen Angel?" she asked Marilyn.

Marilyn giggled and ordered the Bleu Moon Salad—basically a big bowl of greens with crumbled bleu cheese and drizzled with bleu cheese dressing.

"And what can I get for the Big Bopper?" she asked me.

I ordered the American Graff-meati platter—a six ounce steak with a loaded baked potato and a small side salad. The dressing choices for the salad were odd: French, Italian, or Russian. Ironically, ranch was available for an additional charge.

Marilyn and I both ordered root beer to drink. For her it was a splurge; for me it had the word *beer* in it. We'd have to go elsewhere for real beer. I fidgeted in my chair and tried to get comfortable. She watched as I pulled at my attire and mumbled complaints.

"What's the matter?" Marilyn asked. "You seem a little off."

"No, I'm good," I said, trying my best to look good whilst feeling awful.

"Would you like to go somewhere else?"

"No, here is fine. I could use a change, though."

Marilyn scowled in thought. "What does that mean?" she asked. "Is it me?"

I shook my head. "No, no. It was not the company at all," I said. "It's the conditions. I'm all wet, and this diner is cold."

"Oh! Do you want to leave? We could go somewhere else."

"Nope. We're here, we've ordered, and I will dry."

Marilyn smiled and winked.

"So why?" she asked.

"*Why* what?" I responded.

"Why did you ask me out?"

I swallowed hard. I knew the answer, but I wasn't expecting the question.

"Because to quote you, 'You're cute,'" I said. "And I just wanted to spend time with you. Does that sound silly?"

"No, not at all," she said. "It's very nice."

I smiled and dropped my head. I didn't want her to see me blush.

"What do you do?" she asked. "Where are you from? Why are you here with your dad in good ol' E-town?"

"Well, to start, the Chief is not my dad," I explained. "We met in California, and we've been traveling across the country."

Marilyn furrowed her brow. "That sounds a little ..."

"Strange?" I interrupted.

"Yeah. Strange," she said. "But it's all on the level?"

"As level as it gets. He's actually helping me with my work. I'm a writer."

"And another mystery solved!"

"Indeed."

"Why do you call him Chief? And why did he want to be called Hop-a-long Cassidy?"

"I have no idea. You'll have to ask him. I've been with him for almost two weeks and still don't know his real name. Nobody does. Everyone calls him Chief."

"Or Hop-a-long."

I nodded. "Or Hop-a-long," I replied.

"So where's home?" she asked. "Is it close by?"

"Sort of," I said. "I live in Valdosta, Georgia."

"Oh, like the place in *Fried Green Tomatoes*?"

"The same. I'm here in Elizabethtown for my story and as part of a plan."

"A plan? To come here? How did that work?"

"The Chief and I decided where to go by the label on a booze bottle. In this case, it was Evan Williams."

"That's from Bardstown, you know?"

"I do. It wasn't where the liquor was from. It was the name— moreover, the *E* in Evan."

Marilyn closed one eye in contemplation. "I don't get it," she said.

"We picked our places based on the letter *E*," I said. "We've been to Elko, Nevada; Evansville, Wyoming; Elkhorn, Nebraska; Eureka, Missouri; and now we're here."

"Where to next?" she asked.

"This is our last stop before home."

Marilyn looked disappointed then smiled. "Well, I guess we'll have to find a way to make this last stop the most memorable one," she said.

I blushed again, and this time she caught it.

Francine brought our food. It was quite a sight to see this small lady carrying such a huge tray. It was even more of a sight to see such a huge tray with only two plates, a bowl, two mugs, and wrapped silverware. The tray was about the same circumference as a large aircraft propeller. Marilyn and I marveled as Francine negotiated it all.

"You're a real pro, Francine," Marilyn said.

"Careful with that word, sugar," she said. "You'll give the Big Bopper here the wrong impression."

We laughed out loud. Francine scowled and then winked and went off to hassle her other customers.

The American Graff-meati platter was not what I expected. The steak was bigger than six ounces. I cut into it and could see it was cooked perfectly—medium rare, with a lean toward the rare. The top was seasoned with peppercorns, paprika, and other spices I could not discern. A fat sprig of parsley sat atop the crusted skin like a pompadour hairdo. The steak sizzled as it sat on the plate. It was too hot to eat, but the smell was so captivating.

The potato was a mess. It looked like a baked potato had exploded from its skin and spilled its innards of mashed, buttered meat, bacon, cheese, and onions all over the plate. For as disastrous as it appeared, I just had to sample it. One taste set me straight—looks are deceiving.

As for the salad—you've seen one side salad, you've seen them all. I did get the Russian dressing on it. I wanted to play upon the whole Cold War vibe. Francine said the chef called me a *commie*. Excellent!

Marilyn wasted no time digging in to her salad. She was definitely not like any woman I'd gone out with before. First date food concerns were none of hers, for sure. I was okay with that. It was refreshing and, in a way, adventurous and sexy. I watched her eat.

"Yes?" she asked.

"Nothing. Just wanted to make sure it was good," I said.

Marilyn locked her eyes onto mine, reached across the table, and picked up my steak knife. She jammed her fork into my steak and cut a piece off. She held up the pink, glistening cube of meat.

"Aren't you hungry?" she asked. "Let me feed you."

I'd done this before; however, now the favor was being returned by another. The last time was sweet and romantic. This was achingly erotic. I took the bite and watched Marilyn's eyes sparkle.

"Well? How is it?" she asked.

"Delicious," I said.

"What do you want to do after dinner?" she asked. "How about some drinks? Does that sound good?"

"It sounds great," I said. "Where do you want to go?"

"To the liquor store for a bottle and a six and then back to your room."

My eyes opened wide. "So no dessert then?" I asked. "The cheesecake looks good."

"I know where we can get something a little better," she said.

Ah, there's nothing like straightforwardness. Um, check, please.

We did finish our dinners, but there was no dessert—at least not at the Main Street Deli. The rain had stopped, and the night sky had cleared. The warm, late August breeze blew gently, and even though I was still wet, the light wind felt more refreshing than repulsive.

"Do you mind if I smoke," Marilyn asked.

Her question surprised me. She'd given off no indicators of being a smoker: no smells, no getting up to leave during dinner, no nothing.

"Have at it," I said. I think my tone sounded rude or disapproving. She put her smokes away.

"Aren't you going to have a cigarette?" I asked.

"Nah, I'll wait," she said.

"Are you sure? I know what it's like to want a smoke after a meal."

Marilyn smiled. "Thank you just the same," she said. "It can wait."

We got into her car and headed back toward the motel. During the drive, I heard K. T. Oslin's "Hey Bobby" playing faintly on the radio. I didn't even know the radio was on, any more than I knew Marilyn smoked. I stealthily sniffed about her car and detected hints of tobacco. It was also becoming obvious that I didn't hear the radio because it was raining so hard and the volume was so low. My ears and nose were perked up. I looked at Marilyn, and she seemed more beautiful than she had earlier—add my eyes to the list. This night just kept getting more and more … *sensual.*

* * * * *

When we got back to the motel, Marilyn parked, and we sat for a moment. I couldn't help but wonder if my inadvertently negative statement about her having a smoke may have ruined our evening.

"I'm sorry," I said. "If I've offended you in any way …"

I didn't even finish my sentence, and Marilyn leaned across the console and kissed me. She kissed me hard and forcefully, and her tongue was like a battering ram. I fought a little at first but tried to make it not so obvious. We kissed loud and passionately, and when she pulled away, I was breathless. *Now* I could taste her cigarettes.

"Maybe we can skip the bottle," she said.

"Oh no. We want the bottle," I said, nodding. "We really do. We can skip the six."

Marilyn giggled. "Come on, let's go," she said in a whisper. I didn't know if she meant to the liquor store—or to bed.

We got out of the car and walked across the street. Marilyn took my hand as we ventured to the store. My head was starting to spin. I'd had a couple beers earlier today, but this had nothing to do with those. No. This spinning was a result of the moment and how things were becoming familiar. I tried not to make comparisons because this night, this place and this woman were so different than ——. However, too many things seemed similar to me, and I found it hard not to link the two together.

The clerk looked at Marilyn as if he knew her, and she chatted with him in the same familiar way. It was uncomfortable. I had to wonder how close these two were—if at all. Maybe it was just a local thing? Elizabethtown was not that big. She worked at the horse farm; this was a busy part of town, and it was a liquor store in said busy part of town—*blah, blah, blah …*

"What sounds good, baby?" Marilyn asked, like I was her boyfriend.

I took a breath and looked around. "Whatever you want," I said timidly.

"Well, since you're here on behalf of Evan Williams, let's invite him to the party."

Marilyn picked up a fifth of Evan black and a pint of Jim Beam rye. She also asked for a pack of Marlboro Lights. I grabbed a twenty-four-ounce bottle of Labatt Blue and two liter of Diet Coke for us as well—for mixing.

"Think we have enough?" I asked.

"You can never have enough," she said.

We walked back to the motel, and for a brief second, I thought about inviting the Chief over for a quick drink. God knows we had enough booze. I felt I needed a buffer. I didn't know where this party was going.

I was beginning to fear my feelings. Was I betraying ———? I thought about it. If I couldn't conjure her name, I was not doing her any harm. For all I knew, she'd moved on as well and was at this moment doing the same thing I was—but if she was, was she as apprehensive as I was?

"Are you okay, Louis?" Marilyn asked. "You seem out of it. Do you want to have a quick drink and call it a night?"

I sighed fast and turned to her. "No. I'm fine," I said. "I want to have more than a quick drink with you."

Marilyn smiled. "Say it," she said. Her expression became seductive.

"I'm not sure what you mean."

"I want to spend the night with you."

She stepped toward me. "If you're good to me, we'll have the best sleepover ever," she said, as she kissed my cheek. "Good thing I've got a pack of condoms in my purse."

I opened the room, turned on the light, and pointed her in. Marilyn walked past me, entered the room, and sat on the bed. I looked around as if I was crossing a street. I stopped. I put the "Do

Not Disturb" sign on the knob, shut the door the rest of the way, and locked it. *Let the night continue.*

Marilyn cracked the Evan as I went to the bathroom to put on dry clothes. When the party commenced, we passed the bottle between us. Sometimes we'd pour a cup; other times we'd just shoot straight from the barrel. We'd chase a shot or two with the beer, but neither of us mixed the bourbon with the soda. I was feeling great and finally letting myself relax. I wasn't drunk—which was a surprise—I was just enjoying the company. However, like I'd done a time before, I'd relaxed enough to be overly inquisitive.

"So how do you know the liquor store guy?" I asked. "You guys were really chatty."

"I just like to talk to people, that's all," she said. "You seem to as well. That's why I'm here now instead of home with a bowl of popcorn and High Life and old Bob."

I furrowed my brow. "'Old Bob, is that your dog?" I asked.

"Nope. He's my boyfriend," she said.

"Oh my God, you're—"

She cut me off again.

"Don't worry, he's not the jealous type," she said. "In fact, he doesn't care about anything, even when he's turned on."

I was overly confused now. "What the hell?" I exclaimed.

"He's … this is embarrassing …" She paused. "A toy. Bob. B-O-B: Battery-Operated Boyfriend."

I blushed with embarrassment. "Oh, I'm so sorry," I said. "It's … your … it's a personal massager then …" I turned away.

"You could call it that," Marilyn said. "I don't get out much."

"You're out tonight," I said.

"Yes, I am. And I'm hoping you'll convince me to break up with Bob."

I started laughing. "I can't do that," I said.

"Oh, why not?" Marilyn asked.

"Because that's an impossible task," I said. "No man can defeat—Bob!"

We both laughed loud and long before falling into each other's arms and making out like a couple of teenagers. I felt myself getting hard.

Marilyn kissed my ear. "Do you want me?" she asked.

"I do," I said. "Can't you tell?"

"Why did you ask if I could tell?" Marilyn blurted.

"Because I've been ..." I paused. "I'm really ..."

I kissed her neck, and she moaned. We stopped for a moment. We both wanted this to happen, but it was happening too fast. We looked at each other and took another drink. We'd drained three-fourths of the bourbon and almost all the beer. The *tipsys* started to set in, but I think our swirly state had more to do with chemistry than alcohol.

I turned on the radio. Every station was barely audible except one that played pop and countrified pop—this was it. The first song was Taylor Dayne's "Love Will Lead You Back." We kissed soft and slow to the song and began to undress.

I touched Marilyn's soft, silky bra, and she led my hand beneath the underwire. I cupped and gently squeezed her breast as I rubbed her nipple with my thumb. She reached between my legs and felt my sex—firm and ready for her.

"I'm ready," she said. "So are you. *Now* I can tell."

"Sorry there's not much to work with," I joked.

"You're just fine, Louis—just fine."

We continued kissing and undressing. Our clothes fell into a heap beside the bed as we rolled out of them and over each other. When we were naked, I got up and turned the light off. At first, the room was pitch dark except for the dull, orange glow of the Dailite, the even duller green glow of the radio display, and the skinny beam of light from under the door. As we spent more time in the dark, things became easier to discern.

I started laughing.

"What's so funny?" Marilyn asked, giggling.

"I can't find the rubbers," I said. "We probably need those, eh?"

"Eh," she said, mocking me. I heard her get out of bed. She took another drink from the bottle of Evan Williams.

"No fair," I said. "Gimme that bottle."

She handed it to me, and I heard her dig into her purse. I took a long swig and moved to the bedside table to set the bottle down.

"Here," Marilyn said, as she handed me the condom.

I sat down on the bed, opened the wrapper, and rolled the contents down my shaft. I turned and saw Marilyn's naked body on the bed. She'd propped herself up on her elbows and had pushed all four pillows against the headboard.

I rolled over and kissed her cheek and stroked her body. She was soft and warm and fleshy. Her skin smelled of sweet lotion and fragrant soap. I kissed her mouth slowly. Our tongues twisted around each other, and our kiss deepened.

I kissed down her chest and belly. She drew her legs up, and I pushed them apart as I continued kissing my way down to her sex.

She moaned and shifted as I pleasured her. Her sex smelled strong and inviting. I breathed her scent in and pushed harder into her. She squealed quietly and began to shudder as she neared orgasm. When she came, she pushed her crotch hard to my face and grabbed my head.

"Oh my God ... stop ... stop ... stop!" she said in an excited whisper. "You're gonna kill me with that kind of thing."

"I don't want to do that," I whispered.

"You say that to all the girls, I'll bet."

"Only the ones who think they're gonna die by cunnilingus."

Marilyn giggled. "'Cunnilingus,'" she repeated. "What a disgusting word!"

"Every word dealing with sex sounds disgusting," I said. "Think about the parts involved to start. I mean—penis? Who the hell thought of that?"

We started naming off the sexual organs and giggling. It sounded so juvenile.

"Oh man," I said. I started laughing.

"What?" Marilyn asked. "What so funny that you're 'oh manning' about? Is it about *pee-pees* and *vee-vees*?"

"No. Well, yeah, kinda," I said. "It's really nothing."

"Then why are you laughing?" she asked. "You have to share with me."

"Earlier tonight, I got soaked before dinner," I said. "You picked me up. We came to a motel …"

Marilyn reached for the bottle and took a drink. She handed it to me. "And …" she said.

I took a drink. "And I brought the woman out of you," I said. "Any of this sound familiar?"

"No. Fill me in. Don't keep me in suspense."

"Doesn't this sound like a song to you?"

"Which one?"

"'All I Wanna Do Is Make Love to You' by Heart."

"Oh! I love that song!"

"Me, too. Doesn't tonight just fit the lyric?"

Marilyn snuggled close to me. "I guess it does," she said. "But just to ease your mind, Louis, I'm not looking to get pregnant—at least not yet."

"Now let's follow the title. Make love to me."

Marilyn and I made love four times before we could do it no more. We drank in between each time—lowering our inhibitions and increasing our stamina. She was an incredible lover; her body was magic and her touch was divine. I could feel myself falling for her. The song on the radio didn't help either: The Spinners' 'Could It Be I'm Falling in Love?' *Great. Here we go again.*

After we'd finished for the night, we cleaned up and got back into bed. We were spent, tired, and in desperate need of sleep. I was worried we'd be hung over in the morning as Mr. Williams really began to make his presence known.

For me, the room began to spin the longer we stayed awake. I planted a foot on the floor over the side of the bed. I held Marilyn tight, and every time I closed my eyes, she'd start talking to me. *Just go to sleep*, I kept saying to her in my head. But every time I'd doze—she'd talk again. This went on until the wee hours of the morning; the bottle was empty and Marilyn finally passed out.

* * * * *

I woke up, and the room was still spinning. I hadn't moved. My foot was still planted on the floor. It was cold and numb. My entire body was awake except my left leg from the knee down.

Marilyn was sacked out, snoring and sweaty. She'd tossed and turned the whole night and looked a pretty mess. I kissed her cheek. She snorted and pulled closer.

I tried to read the clock, but it was an indiscernible blur from the bed, but I knew it was still early. The sun had not come up completely yet. I could see a strip of the dawn colors behind the small slit in the curtains.

I pulled myself out of bed and hobbled to the clock: 5:30 a.m. Marilyn rolled over and yanked the covers over her head. It made me smile. I was still drunk, and I wanted to make love to her again.

"Marilyn," I whispered.

"Umhmma?" she responded.

"Let's make love again."

I could see her eyes open in the dark. "What?" she asked. "Do you really want to fuck some more?"

"Yes," I said. "I'm so horny."

She rolled onto her back. "Come on in, you insatiable animal," she said.

I looked at her lying on the bed, ready to make love, and I could not get an erection. Blame the booze or the marathon lovemaking session we'd already had, but there was no way I could do it again.

"I'm sorry, babe," I said.

It was of little consequence. She'd already fallen asleep again. I slowly climbed back into bed and snuggled close to her. I closed my eyes and I too went back to sleep.

I woke up again. This time, the sun was up and I was alone. A vacuum cleaner thumped the wall in the room next to mine. Marilyn's clothes were gone and next to the empty Evan William's bottle was a business card. Marilyn had written the letters *P*, *T*, *O* on the bottom corner. I flipped it over and read what she'd written.

> You worked up my appetite, stud. Went to get
> some food. Lobby has rolls and coffee. Meet me
> when you're ready. Love, M.

I was still feeling the drink, but not as bad. The extra sleep was just what I needed. I got up and went to shower. Once I'd cleaned up, I felt less buzzed, but still not completely clear. Sexually, I felt more satisfied than I ever had—even more than after spending the night with a five-hundred-dollar call girl. *Wow! There's something to say about Southern girls.*

I got to the lobby, and Marilyn and the Chief were eating rolls, drinking coffee, and chatting.

"Chief says we're going to Bub's," Marilyn said. "Let's saddle up!"

I looked at the old man. "Is this true?" I asked. "Are we going to Bub's again?"

The Chief glanced at me, then at Marilyn, then to me again. "It was good yesterday," he said. "Portions so big, they're guaranteed to stuff your gob for a while."

I wasn't sure what he meant, and I didn't ask. I just pointed to the door, and we made our way to our cars.

Marilyn stopped. "I'm going to have to go to work after breakfast," she said. "Will that be okay?"

"Sure," I said sadly. "You gotta work, so go."

"I really don't want to, but I didn't ask for the day off."

"I don't want you to get into trouble with Hannah."

"She's cool, but I really don't want to cause any grief, you know?"

"Oh, I know. Trust me. I'm up to my eyes in grief with my boss right now."

Marilyn kissed me quick. "You're awesome!" she said. "Let's go eat."

We got into our cars, and Marilyn left first. The Chief watched her drive out of the lot and get on to the main street.

The Chief turned to me. "Does she ever shut up?" he asked. "That dame talked my ear off." He pointed to his right ear. "See? It's gone. Talked right off."

"That's crazy," I said. "She doesn't talk all that much, really."

"Well, you must've kept her busy, because the broad can dish."

"Now that you mention it, she was kinda chatty."

"*Kinda*? She didn't shut up from the moment she saw me. How did you get a word in with her?"

I grinned. "We didn't talk all that much, Chief," I said.

The Chief looked at me. "I'd ask for full disclosure, but that said it all."

"Maybe we fell asleep?"

"Not with those glows you two have. You fucked. And you fucked *a lot*. I'll consider myself briefed."

I chuckled. "And I was debriefed," I said smugly.

I didn't have to say a word at breakfast. I couldn't. The Chief wasn't kidding. Marilyn was a talker of the utmost degree. Although she left out the graphic details, she told the Chief about our whole night together—from the moment we met until now. She even rehashed the parts he knew but told them from her point of view, so they sounded different.

The Chief and I ate and listened. In between recapping our night and bites of food, Marilyn greeted people as they came in and said goodbye as they left Bub's Café. People knew her from the farm, and when those people came in, she invited them to sit with us. Most declined, but a couple did not. They sat and chatted for a moment.

Marilyn looked up at the clock and suddenly stopped talking. She reached into her purse and took out her pocketbook. The Chief and I waved her off simultaneously.

"We've got this, honey," we said in unison.

"I have to go," Marilyn said. "Louis, will you walk me out to my car?"

I nodded, and we got up. We walked outside, and the warm breeze blowing on us felt nice and romantic. We got to her car and we kissed like lovers. I saw her eyes tear, even though I know she did not want me to.

Once she left, I'd never see her again. For as wonderful as she was—*as it was*—this was just a one-night stand and would never be anything more. I felt love for Marilyn, but it was not *true* love. It was just that fragment of love you have to feel when you've had sexual intercourse with someone—be it casual or not.

She drove away, and a tear rolled down *my* face. I'd fulfilled four of the five *L*s with Marilyn, but that fifth one—the biggest one—was not complete enough for me to run after her. She had no idea about this *L* thing, but I did know she was feeling as I did.

I walked back into the restaurant. The Chief saw my face.
"You all right, kid?" he asked.
"Nah, Chief, I'm not," I said. "I'm ready to go home."

* * * * *

We went back to the motel, and the Chief and I went to our rooms. We didn't talk. We didn't have to. We both knew where I was and, more importantly, where *we* were. This was our last stop before home, and it had been a big one for both of us. The Chief reconciled with the ghosts of his past, and I slept with someone whom I had no future with—but was haunting my present.

I opened the door to my room, and it was clean and reconstructed. The only remnants from my night with Marilyn were her business card on the bedside table and the bottle of rye on the dresser.

I opened the bottle. It was just after 10:30 a.m., and I opened a fucking bottle of rye and took a nice swig. *To you, Marilyn.* I breathed in hard to see if I could still smell her. I tried the pillows, but they'd been changed—cleaned, washed, and swapped. The room smelled as it did when we arrived two days ago—like fresh linens and bleach with an old carpet finish. *Did she even smoke a cigarette?* I wondered randomly as I tried again to track Marilyn's faded scent in the room.

I took the bottle and two wrapped cups and went to see the Chief. Surely, he'd help me drink this bottle. I didn't want to do it alone.

I knocked on his door. "Chief, it's the High Della-Lama," I said. "Let's talk about the islands."

He opened the door. "Louie? What's wrong?" he asked.

"I've got a bottle of rye that needs drinking, that's what's wrong."

"No what's wrong is that you've got a bottle of rye that needs drinking. It's not even eleven a.m. and you've got a broken heart—that's what's wrong."

"My heart ain't broken, Chief, but my spirit is—just a little."

The Chief took the bottle for me. "Come on in, kid, and let's talk," he said.

He pointed me to a chair and I sat. I unwrapped the cups, and he poured two small drinks into each one—barely a shot for both of us.

"You can do better than that," I said.

"It's all you need for now," he said. "Plus you only brought a pint."

"Blame Marilyn for that. She put it on the counter."

"Drink it slow, Louie. Savor. And tell me what's wrong."

I sipped the rye. "You already know," I said.

"I do," the Chief replied. "But I want to hear you say it."

"I fell for Marilyn, but it wasn't—"

The Chief attempted to finish my sentence: "Wasn't all there?" he asked.

"No, it wasn't 'all there,'" I said. "I felt something, but it wasn't what I was supposed to feel. Everything seemed right, though."

"Louie, she was your Mariposa, pure and simple. Just a quick one-time thing. It's hard to deal with, but it happens."

"I hate it. I went through the same shit with April and ... oh, wow ... I just said her name ..."

The Chief furrowed his brow at my comment.

I continued, "And I literally only slept with her—we *slept* in the same bed—no sex. It was all platonic."

"That's okay," the Chief said. "I told you a love mate doesn't have to be someone you've had sex with. It's that person you can wake up next to and still want to be there. You've built a trust with them. You know this already."

"It's the hardest one to deal with—especially for me."

"Why is that?"

"Because I fall in love so easily."

"Is that why you've avoided it for all this time?"

"Probably. It's easier to handle that way."

The Chief poured another drink for us. This time, he was less sparing.

"Kid, you don't fall in love easily," he said. "You just fall in love with everyone you have sex with. That's your problem."

I gave him a contemplative scowl. "But I didn't have sex with April," I said.

The Chief nodded. "Ah ha! I knew it!" he exclaimed. "You did flip for that dame in Elko!"

"Yes, I did, Chief. I flipped for her, and I fell—hard."

"I knew you did, but I also knew you had to discover what else was out there. The old saying about loving something and setting it free sounds stupid, but there's a lot of credence to it—especially if it comes back to you."

"I'm not going to worry about that. April is long gone and I've betrayed her—twice already."

The Chief shot his rye down. "How the hell did you betray her?" he asked. "What because you traded skin with a couple of other broads?"

"Um, yeah," I said. "That's kinda how it works."

"Did you make a commitment to her?"

"No, not really."

"Did you tell her anything big?"

"No. I don't think so."

"Did you say you'd see her later?"

"No."

"Then you didn't do anything wrong, Louie. You did what any man in your shoes would do: you continued on your adventure.

"Listen, kid, if this gal is *your* gal, your paths will cross again. That's how it works. What? Do you think she was sitting around pining for you? I'll bet she's been out a few times since you last saw her. Probably got a little too? Women have to have it as well, you know."

I chuckled and finished my rye. The Chief poured me another. The bottle was almost gone.

"Chief, how do you do it?" I asked. "How do you stay focused on the positives, even after seeing so many negatives?"

"Sometimes life sucks, but for every bad thing, there's a good one," he said. "You take the hits—however, there are some people who can't. Those who can live enrich lives whether they know it or not. Every day you wake up is another day of enrichment and beauty and learning.

"It's simple really—you either roll with life or let it roll over you. The former is hard sometimes. The latter is deadly. Life is heavy. It'll crush you in a second."

I cringed. "You started off good," I said. "But it got dark at the end."

"Louie, it's simple," the Chief said. "Get up, get out, and get it done. Whatever happens in between is up to you. The most important thing is *getting it done*. Completion is tantamount. You have to finish. If you don't, you spend your whole life wandering and wondering."

I got up. I'd heard enough.

"Chief," I said. "Thank you for the talk. I have some work to do."

* * * * *

I went back to my room and got out my notebook. I sat down at the desk, picked up the pen, and bled like Hemingway behind his typewriter. I finally stopped and looked at the clock. It was 6:00 p.m.

I called and ordered pizza for the old man and me. While I waited, I went across the street to get a twelve-pack for us. Our last few hours in Elizabethtown were going to be easy, cheap, and anticlimactic. That was okay with me, as I'm sure it was with the Chief as well.

"Well, you finally got your pizza, Louie," the Chief said.

"It wasn't my goal," I said. "I just didn't want to go anywhere."

"What did you do all day? I never heard a peep from you after you left."

"I wrote all day. I filled two notebooks and started another."

"That's good! That's what you want. But is what you *wrote* what you want?"

"I think it finally is—at least it's the start of what I want."

The Chief opened two beers and handed one to me. "What lit the fire under your ass?" he asked.

"Just what you said about getting things done," I said. "I've been sitting on this for too long. I've been getting up and getting out but falling short from there."

The Chief nodded. "Do you think when you've finished … all of this … it's going to be what you wanted?" he asked.

"I do," I said. "I think I've finally got it all together. It was there, I just needed to put everything in its place."

The Chief shook his head. "That's not what I mean," he said. "I mean this trip—with me—do you think when this trip is over it will be what you wanted?"

I didn't have to think.

"Most definitely," I said.

The Chief smiled. "Kid, I've told you a lot of stories about places I've been," he said. "You shared with me too. What's one place you've always wanted to go?"

I had to think. "Probably Spain," I said.

"I've been there," the Chief said. "Beautiful country."

"You mentioned being there when we ate Basque in Elko."

"You're right, I did."

"Why do you want to go to Spain, Louie?"

"Hemingway."

"Ah, I should've known."

"He was in Italy as well, but his time in Spain is well-documented and colors a lot of his work. There's just something about the place. I want to go to a fiesta and see a bull fight. I want to see the *Sargada Familia* in Barcelona. I want to eat *paella* in Valencia. I want to see the Rock of Gibraltar. I want to swim the Strait."

"That's a lot of stuff to do. That's an adventure. You'll get there."

"It's just a dream."

"Dreams are where you start. You know that. We've talked about it."

"My God, Chief, I think we've talked about *everything* on this trip! I can't tell you how much I've learned. I have grown so much. I'm finally ready to get home and get to work on this."

"On what?"

"On the story I want to write."

"And what is it about?"

"It's about everything."

The Chief shook his head. "Unfortunately, it can't be about 'everything,'" he said. "That's impossible."

"Well, I'm gonna try my damnedest," I said. "It's better than what I had before."

"Which was?"

"Nothing."

The old man got a sullen look. He tried to hide it, but I'd gotten pretty good at reading his face.

"Okay, Chief. What's the matter?" I asked.

"It's nothing, kid," he said. "I just feel like I've let you down."

I shook my head. "What the hell does that mean?" I asked. "How could you have possibly let me down? Look at everything you've told me. Look at all we've done!"

"Yeah, but still …" He paused. "I told you some things and we met some people, but I'm telling you you've got to finish your shit, and here I am—unfulfilled."

"How can you be unfulfilled? You've done it all."

"I've done a lot, but obviously there's some things this old boy ain't done."

I tried to think of something, but I knew anything I could ask, he'd had already done.

"What's something you haven't done?" I asked.

"You really want to know?" he asked. "It's pretty stupid—especially for a guy like me."

"Chief, trust me—for all that you've done," I said, "nothing that you *haven't* done could be even remotely stupid."

"I want to go to New Caledonia."

"What's stupid about that? I don't even know where it is."

"It's stupid because it's just another tiny island in the South Pacific. It's stupid because I had every chance to go there but never did. And now I'll never get the chance. It's become my locale of finality, my point of disembarkation. It's where I talk about going to when I croak."

"So it's a joke?"

"Yeah, sadly, it's become that."

I thought for a moment. "Maybe we should go," I said. "I could see if my publisher can get us a trip there. I could say it's for a—"

The Chief cut me off.

"No, kid. There's no way," he said. "That's in my past—and yesterday, my past and I squared up. Now I have only the future to look into."

I smiled at the Chief's comment. I would've been sad if I hadn't gotten what I needed from this trip and from the old man himself. I was content to tell the story now. There was no need for further adventures—at least not at the moment. We'd have one last hurrah, and that was our drive home to Valdosta. I wasn't sure what we'd do once we got there, but we'd figure it out. This trip had been all about the unknown, and we'd gotten pretty good at resolving it as we made our way.

Valdosta, Georgia

The drive home took a little over ten hours. The Chief was quiet or slept most of the way. He did not eat at all. Every time I'd ask if he was hungry, he'd say "no" or he "wasn't right." After spending two weeks with him, I knew when I should just leave him be, even though it scared me.

We got home at about 3:00 p.m., and I unloaded our stuff. The Chief seemed impressed with my place. It was a two-bedroom apartment near the university and sometimes seemed too big for me. The guest room was empty, and the Chief wasted no time claiming it.

I helped him unpack as he still was not feeling well. As soon as he put his things away, he lay down and went back to sleep.

My answering machine had eighty-three messages on it. *I don't even know eighty-three people*, I thought. I listened to the messages. Thirty of them were solicitors, twelve of them were wrong numbers, nineteen were hang-ups, six were from my family, and the rest were from work—the last one was to disregard the other fifteen.

The postbox outside my door was crammed with mail—mostly bills and flyers from stores and restaurants. There was no real correspondence to speak of. I gathered the stack and put it on the table to deal with later.

I stretched hard and could hear my bones crack and feel my muscles pull as I found myself not tired but fatigued. I'd been nonstop on this trip, and now that it was over, I finally had a chance to relax—a chance to unwind and just chill for a day.

I pulled a beer out of the fridge: a Busch. It was the first cheap beer I'd drunk in a while—at least since we had those Buds at Love's. That was a week ago, but it seemed like a year, then again, it seemed like a flash of a second. Time—what a concept.

I drank half of the beer and put the bottle back into the fridge. I was fine for now. It was too early to drink and too early to sleep, but a nap is what I needed. I lay down on the couch. Within a couple of minutes, I was out.

* * * * *

I was awakened by the flickering of the TV. I rolled over, trying to remember why it was on and, moreover, where I was. I had been in so many different rooms the past two weeks I'd forgotten I was home—in my own place and laying on my own couch.

A familiar voice whispered, "Kid? You awake?"

I opened my eyes and looked around. I was awake, but I was not *aware*.

"Chief? Is that you?" I asked.

"It's me, Louie," he said. "I think I fucked up your TV."

"No, it's just …" I paused and reached for the cable remote. "The cable box is off. See?"

Local channel WSGW was showing reruns of *Buffy the Vampire Slayer*.

"Oh, I like this show," the Chief said.

"Really?" I asked. "It doesn't seem like something you'd watch."

"Oh, no. I watch it all the time," he said. "It's got monsters and girls. It's the story of my life."

I laughed. It made sense.

"What time is it?" I asked.

"It's about nine p.m. I've been up for a while. We slept the whole day away," the Chief said. "I'm still not feeling great. Got that thing I had the other day, but it feels worse."

"Well, let me get up and go to the store," I said. "I'll get some medicine for you and some food. I've got nothing to eat."

"You mind if I stay here, kid? I won't steal anything, I promise."

I smiled and said, "I ain't got much to steal."

I drove to the Winn-Dixie and bought a few grocery items as well as a couple of different stomach remedies for the Chief. I was worried about the old man. He'd been okay the whole trip, but the last couple of days had brought about a malady. I wished I knew what it was—as I'm sure he did too. The Chief said it seemed to be getting worse. I'd hoped not it was not getting serious.

As I walked the store, I marveled at how things looked so different. I shopped here all the time but with fresh, opened, and traveled eyes—even the old Winn-Dixie had a new appeal.

I picked up items to buy and created little vignettes about them—where they'd come from, their journey to get here, and where they'd wind up next. The canned goods provided the best stories, especially the ones with pictures on the labels. People looked at me like I was crazy. Maybe I was. All those stories about the islands—hell, I just may have a coconut growing in my head.

I picked Lane 5, for the number of towns the Chief and I had stopped. Oddly enough, the cashier's name was Evelyn. *Bonus!*

Evelyn totaled me up and bagged my items. I smiled at her, and she responded in kind. What a great way to end this day. I wish the Chief could've been here to see this. When I tell him, he'll be pissed that he hadn't come along.

* * * * *

On the drive home, I pulled over to let an ambulance go by. The siren blared and the lights flashed, throwing beams of strobing red in every direction. They were almost blinding.

Any time I see an emergency vehicle, I always wonder where it came from or where it was going to. And with an ambulance, who might be in it and for what. This one was undoubtedly on its way to the Lowndes County Medical Center.

I pulled into the parking lot of my building, and it would seem that the ambulance had come from either my or the adjoining complex. A firetruck was parked in the lot, and people stood outside and chatted with the paramedics.

I parked and got out. "What's the matter?" I asked. "Is everyone okay?"

"The paramedics just took a guy to the hospital," one of my neighbors said.

"From our building?"

"Yeah. An older gentleman. Probably from round the corner—the A-Block of apartments. You live in D-Block, right?"

"No, I live in B. I wonder who it was?"

"Probably Mr. Tanner. He's sick a lot these days."

I didn't know Mr. Tanner, and I hardly knew this man I was talking to, but he seemed to know the building pretty well. Perhaps I should get out more often?

I walked to my apartment, and my heart dropped into my shoes. A paramedic was standing very close to my door. I swallowed hard.

"Everything okay?" I asked.

"Are you Louis DeCarlo?" he asked.

I swallowed hard again and dropped my groceries. The bag split, and the cans rolled out onto the pavement and one continued into the lot.

"Oh my God … Oh my God … The Chief!" I shouted.

"The Chief was just here, sir," the paramedic said. "It's your father. They've taken him to the hospital."

"What? My father? My … Oh, God no …!"

"Mr. DeCarlo, your father is in an ambulance. We're taking him to County."

My eyes began to tear. "What the hell happened?" I asked. "I just went out for groceries. I didn't even buy any beer—just food, that's all."

"Mr. DeCarlo, please calm down," the paramedic said. He softly grabbed my shoulders and looked me in the eye. "It looks like your dad may have had a heart attack."

"Oh my God … no! A heart attack?"

"Yes, but we're not sure. He was responsive but was in a lot of pain. He called 911 about forty-five minutes ago."

"Forty-five minutes? Holy shit. How long was I gone?" I asked myself aloud.

"He's going to be in the ER at County. I'll help you here, and then you can go see him. He should be prepped and admitted by then."

The paramedic and I cleaned up the groceries I'd dropped. I locked up and we walked to my car.

"He'd been complaining the last couple of days," I said. "We were traveling. He said it was just a stomach thing—indigestion."

"That may be, but it was serious enough for him to call us," the paramedic said. "The docs at the hospital will know more when you get there."

"Thank you," I said as I got in my car and headed to the hospital.

On the way, all I could think was how terrible I felt for leaving the old man alone. I talked to myself the entire drive.

He said he wasn't feeling well. Why did you leave him? Because you just had to get food. Oh no. It couldn't wait until tomorrow—you just had to go tonight. You just had to throw the old bastard to the wolves. Leave an old man to die—in Valdosta, Georgia.

I got to the hospital, parked, and ran in to the Emergency Room entrance.

The guard on duty asked for my name and that of the patient I was looking for.

"The Chief," I said.

The guard looked at me.

"Mr. DeCarlo," I said. "That's it, DeCarlo."

"*Monsignor* Louis DeCarlo?"

I chucked. "Yes, that's him."

"Sign here, sir," the guard said as he handed me a clipboard with a sign-in/out log on it. "He's in ER 125. Crazy old man, your dad. Hope he's okay."

I laughed. "Yeah. Me too," I said. "Thank you so much."

The doors opened and I went in to the ER. A nurse escorted me to room 125.

When I got to the room, the Chief was hooked up to machines. There were tubes and wires everywhere. The staff had put electrode stickers all over his skin—he looked like a life-size connect-the-dots.

He waved me over, and I started crying.

"Fucking hell, Chief," I said through my tears. "We drive all the way across the country and you ..."

The Chief patted my hand. "Kid, don't waste your tears," he said. "The reaper missed me again. I'm not doing too well, but I ain't lost my head yet, me boy. See?" He pointed to his head and nodded. "Still attached."

"I'm sorry I left you."

"Jesus Louie, if you'd have been there you would've had to drive my sick ass here. I got to ride in an ambulance. Ever rode in an ambulance?"

"No, not that I can recall."

"Me neither till tonight. See, one more thing I can say I did before I kick off."

"Ernest Hemingway drove an ambulance during WWI," I said as I broke down again.

"I don't think he drove mine," the Chief said. "If he did, then we've got problems, eh?"

I laughed. It was hard, but I mustered a snort through my sadness.

"Take a seat, Louie," the Chief said. "Tell me what you hear from the boys overseas."

"Nothing," I said. "Just that the High Della-lama is scaring the hell out of his followers."

The Chief smiled. "You've spent too much time with me," he said.

I shook my head. "Not enough," I said. "I still need a little more. Promise me you'll give me that, okay? You've a lot of life left in there, Chief."

"I don't know what the hell's wrong with me, kid. But with all this apparatus they've got me hooked up to, it must be something."

"Is there anything I can do for you?" I asked.

"Yes, there is," the Chief said. "You can go home and get some sleep. There's nothing you can do here except worry, and that ain't gonna help. Plus, there's no need—I'll be fine. I just want to get some shut-eye. It's been a long couple of weeks."

"Are you sure you don't want me to stay?"

"Nah, son. *Git.* Come back in the morning. I'll have something good to tell you then."

"You promise?"

"Cross my heart and—"

I cut him off.

"Do *not* finish that statement," I said, waving my finger at him briskly.

As I walked out of the room a doctor stopped me. "Are you Louie?" he asked.

"I am," I said proudly.

"We ran a few tests on your dad and should have the results in the morning," the doctor said.

"How is he?" I asked.

"Well, he's got a few health problems, but he's also eighty-four—that comes with the territory. He obviously drinks a lot. We detected trace amounts of alcohol in his blood, and his liver is a little beat-up."

"How's his heart?"

"He didn't have a heart attack, but there is some concern. He just needs to rest. He said you two have been on the road for a while."

"Yeah. Two weeks. We just got back earlier today."

The doctor nodded. It was that "Hmmm ... I see" gesture—the one you get when you know something's amiss but don't get any clarification.

"He's got to stay overnight," the doctor said. "We'll get him to a room in the morning."

"Okay," I said. "Do I need to stay?"

"No, it's not necessary. He just needs to sleep."

"And I'll let him do that."

I drove home on the verge of tears. I felt responsible for the old man's declining health. I felt like taking him on a two-week cross-country jaunt in search of a story was selfish and stupid and is probably going to kill him. I should've let him be. I should've left him at Churchill's and left him to his own devices, oh, but no ... no ... I had to drag him to Valdosta fucking Georgia. He's here six hours and he lands in the hospital. Welcome to my home, Chief—now die! It was a grim sentiment, but it was the way I was feeling.

I knew I needed sleep, but it would be hard to come by tonight. I drank a couple of beers and had a couple glasses of scotch to make sleep happen. I eventually passed out. The infomercial on TV helped a little as well.

* * * * *

I woke up at 7:00 a.m. I'd fallen asleep in my clothes. My alarm was the muffled ringing of my home phone. I must've fallen asleep with it on me. It was stuck between my ribs and the back of the couch. My BlackBerry beeped with a message as well—that was undoubtedly from work.

I answered without looking at the number. My voice was scratchy and hoarse, with a hint of blood and bile mixed in. I must've thrown up in my sleep. Disgusting.

"Lo," I groaned. "This is Louis."

The voice on the other end was not one I recognized.

"Mr. DeCarlo, this is Bethanny Stokes," the voice said. "I'm with County Hospital."

I sat straight and sobered up. "Yes," I said. "Is everything okay?"

"Everything is fine," Bethanny said. "I'm just calling to let you know your father has been moved from the ER to a main room in the hospital. He asked that we call you."

"I'm glad you did. When can I see him?"

"Visiting hours begin at eight a.m., so any time after that."

"Thank you," I said, making a fist-pumping gesture.

* * * * *

I walked into the Chief's room, and he was still asleep. I didn't want to bother him. I went down to the café and bought a cup of coffee.

The gift shop had just opened. I bought the Chief a small bouquet with asters, hydrangeas, hyacinths, and of course magnolias. It was tacky but pretty and screamed *Southern*. I found a card I couldn't resist. It had a picture of a donkey in a cast. The sentiment read, "I see you broke your ... Get well soon!" I paid for the items and headed back to the room to see if the Chief was awake yet. He was still out.

I arranged a few things and sat down. I tried to be as quiet as possible. I started thinking about my story: how I was going to put it all together, what I'd leave out, what I'd embellish. I knew how it was going to end—and that ending did not include a stay in the hospital. I looked around for paper and pen but found none. I did something I'd never done before: I used my BlackBerry for a notebook and chicken-pecked my way through some ideas. I also listened to my message. It was a wrong number.

My ideas seemed convoluted and random. If I was to present my story to Keith, I'd have to do better than this. What I'd written was good, but in pieces and not cohesive. I didn't think that would work for him either. I just needed time, and now was definitely not that time.

The Chief woke up and stared at me. He seemed disoriented. He was a mess.

"Louie, you steal my breakfast?" he asked.

"No, but I brought you flowers," I said. "And a card. Do you want to see them?"

"The flowers I can see. The card'll have to wait; unless you want to open it for me?"

"I can do that."

"Nah, it can wait, if that's okay. I have something for you. Better to do it now, because it might take a while to get it all done."

"That's fine. What do you want to tell me?"

"It's not what I want to tell you—it's what I want to show you."

The Chief raised the upper half of his bed and sat straight.

"I need you to get into my pants, kid," he said.

I furrowed my brow. "The hell you say!" I said.

"You filthy son of a bitch!" the Chief retorted. "You didn't let me finish. I was about to say: and get my wallet."

I walked over to the Chief's clothes and took his wallet out of his pants pocket.

"Whatever it is, I can pay for it," I said.

"No, son, you've paid enough," the Chief said. "It's time I cash in on what I owe—and this is just the start."

The Chief thumbed through his wallet and pulled out a business card. I had no idea why. He set in down on his lap and covered it.

"Louie, what I have here is the key to your future," he said.

I didn't understand. "What? Is it the access numbers to your bank account?" I joked.

"Nope. Not quite. It's the access numbers to the one person who drove you crazier than I did. It's the address and phone number for April's work."

I fell back. *Oh my God. April!*

"Kid, you flipped for this gal and through everything, you never got over her—*that's love,"* the Chief said. "She is your life mate, I just know it. You two didn't even need to make love to feel the full connection of what you shared together."

"I don't understand," I said. "I can't believe you kept that card."

"Louie, you asked me to take it and keep it and I did," he said. "It's like a 'Get out of jail free' card in *Monopoly*—you keep it until it's needed or sold. I'd never sell it and you sure as hell need it more than I do."

"Why now?" I asked.

"Because you were still exploring. You were still finding your way—even though you knew, you had to seek just a little more to know the full truth."

"What am I supposed to do? Call her and tell her … What?"

"You go *see* her. You don't even call. You just go see her. You walk into her office, and you literally sweep her off her feet and you tell her you love her.

"Kid, I'm sick and my body is falling apart. Consider this my last wish. You wouldn't deny this old bastard his last wish, would you?"

"Don't talk like that," I said, as my eyes began to well. "This is crazy."

"No, the fact that you're still here is crazy," the Chief said.

"How am I supposed to find her?" I asked. "She could be anywhere. Is that the part that's going to take a while to get done?"

"You didn't read the card, did you?"

"No. I didn't want to."

"Louie. April lives in Savannah."

I stood blank-faced.

"That's Savannah, *Georgia*," the Chief said. "I told you she was closer than you thought."

"Why didn't you tell me?" I asked.

"Because you didn't want to know at the time," he said. "And as I said, you had to explore a little more to know for sure—but you already knew. You shared all of the Five *Ls* with April. You didn't experience that with any of the other women you met, did you?"

"No," I said. "Three at best."

"Go to her, kid. Go grab your destiny and tell her you love her—fulfill that elusive sixth *L*."

"I'll go, but first ..." I paused. "Chief, did you—"

He cut me off.

"Nope. Never," he said. "You think I've done it all and seen it all—well, I've never found my life mate. It could've been Bettie, but God only knows. There was never truly anyone else after her—at least no one I ever loved like that again.

"I've always had that void. Why do you think I'm such a seeker? I'm not looking for places to go, Louie. I've been doing this for so long because I was looking for love. *You've* found it. You helped me finish my adventure—now go finish yours."

* * * * *

I drove the three hours to Savannah in record time. This rental car had literally gone from coast to coast. It was two weeks overdue and supposed to be returned in Sacramento—I'll be adding a few more Georgia miles to it before it made its way back to a lot.

April worked for a marketing company called DasherWest.

I walked into the building and took a seat in the reception office. A young woman came out and greeted me.

"Welcome to DasherWest," she said. "Do you have an appointment?"

"Um, no. I don't," I said. "I am here to see April Klein, though. Is she in?"

"Is she expecting you?" the woman asked.

I had to think. My eyes welled slightly. "I … I hope she is," I said, giving an awkward smile.

"I'll call her out."

When she said those words, my heart sank. I was here, but should I be? I was in love with this woman, but I'd been unfaithful to her—*twice*—and had even tried to forget about her more than that—I didn't even know if this was even right. I thought about walking out, then I heard a voice that melted me.

"Hi, can I help you?"

I turned around, and there was no hesitation between either of us.

"*Oh my God!*" we shouted in unison.

We ran and fell into each other's arms. We hugged tightly, and I could feel her start to cry—I was already in tears.

"I've missed you so much," she whispered into my shoulders.

"I've missed you more," I said. "I couldn't get you out of my head—no matter what I did."

"Oh, Louis, I've been bad," she said. "I went out with this guy and we …"

I cut her off.

"It's okay," I said. "I strayed too."

April looked at me. "Are you …?" she asked.

"No. You?" I asked her.

She smiled and shook her head—*no*.

I looked into her eyes for a second and did what I should've done in Elko—I kissed her like she was the love of my life. *And she was.*

I told April about the Chief: that he was here in Georgia and in the hospital. She wasted no time in tying up her affairs for the day and leaving with me to go back and see the old man. We drove straight back without further hesitation.

"I do hope he's okay," April said of the Chief. "He's such a wonderful man."

"He is," I said. "And he'll be feeling much better after he sees you, my love!"

* * * * *

We arrived at the hospital in Valdosta, and we ran into see the Chief. His room was empty.

I got scared. "They must've moved him," I said.

I went to the nurse's station and asked where the patient in room 146 had gone. No one knew at first, but a doctor approached me. The look on his face was easy to discern, and I did not want to hear what he had to say.

"Mr. DeCarlo, your father is gone," the doctor said.

April grabbed me and gasped. We both started crying.

"When?" I asked.

"This morning—about eleven a.m.," the doctor said. "It was sudden and unexpected."

April buried her face into my chest. I stroked her hair.

"Why didn't anyone call me?"

"Because we were told not to."

I shook my head. "What does that mean?" I asked angrily.

"It means your father did not want anyone to know he was leaving," the doctor said.

"Leaving? Is that some kinda—"

The doctor cut me off.

"Mr. DeCarlo, your father left the hospital," he said. "He's very much alive. Against orders, he checked himself out. He called a cab and left."

"And you let him go?" I retorted.

"We had no choice," the doctor said. "He was of sound mind and checked himself out. It's perfectly legal and ethical on our part—even though we don't recommend it and this was a very rare occasion."

"Where did he go? Did he say?"

"This sounds strange, but he said he was going to New Caledonia."

I swallowed hard. All I could think of was that he was going somewhere that was not a hospital to have one last beer and die. *That* was his New Caledonia. And I had no idea how to find him to tell him—and show him—that April was here. I had no way to thank him for all that he had done for me. Moreover, I had no way to tell him how much he meant to me and, above all, how much I loved him.

I fell to my knees. April held me as I wept.

* * * * *

It was mid-December and extremely cold for South Georgia. April and I had set our wedding date for August 7—one year to the day that I'd met the Chief. We wanted to honor him and knew of no other way. I was thinking about that day and with the weather outside being what it was, wishing I was in the islands right now.

I'd been working diligently on my book since September. My publishing company financed my manuscript based on what little I'd done. Keith, my publisher, said even my "scribblings" would've been enough to turn out a quality story. I couldn't do that. It had to be right and it had to live up to the expectations I'd put forth for it; moreover, it had to live up to the legacy of the Chief.

I missed the old bastard. Not seeing him has been killing me. April was feeling my grief too. The man who I'd only known for two weeks but gave me lifetime of memories was gone. I didn't know where he went or if he was even still alive. He was—at least to me.

He'd certainly live on in the stories I wrote and the tales I told. If April and I had kids, they would know the man and carry on his memory like an heirloom—I would make sure of that! I'd raise seekers. I'd let him know that the knowledge he'd imparted on me was well-absorbed, shared, and never forgotten. And if children were not in our future; then I'd get a dog: a hunter or a tracker—one that seeks and finds and explores. Regardless, I'd make the Chief proud. I'd make him prouder than he'd ever been—or ever imagined he could be.

* * * * *

One day I was sifting through my mail—the usual bullshit: bills, flyers, and a couple of letters from print houses wanting to know about possible titles and artwork for my book. I was still undecided.

Amid all the "official" stuff and the junk, there was a postcard. The picture was of a thatched grass hut in the middle of a coral reef. The water inside the reef was a crystal-clear teal, while outside the reef, it was a perfect blue. These were colors the likes of which I'd never seen before—except in my dreams and when I heard the Chief talk about the islands. The postmark was smudged, but it was foreign. The print on the card was in French. It was from New Caledonia! I read the tiny, handwritten script on the back:

> Louie, me boy. I finally made it. My last excursion. New Caledonia is the heaven I knew it would be. You were right, kid—I have done and seen everything—well, everything I'd ever set out to do. Take care of that filly—and yourself.
>
> Regards,
> The Ol' Super Chief.

I put the postcard on my refrigerator and smiled until I cried. "You did it," I said. "You finally made it."

The old man was half a world away, and I felt closer to him than ever. He was an inspiration to me from the moment I met him at Churchill's and here he was, *still* inspiring me. I'd been struggling to put the finishing touches on this book, but once again, the Chief had the answer—he'd sent it right to my doorstep. I used his postcard for the artwork and his words for the title, and I called my book *his* book: *Excursions with the Chief.*

About the Author

Sean Siverly began his journey into writing while he was in high school. His first works were short stories based on war, music, and fictional bands as well as an attempt at a romantic novel—a strange and broad spectrum of subject matter for sure.

In 1987, while attending college in Michigan as a commercial art student, Sean was asked by his English and Composition professor to submit a short story for a campus-wide competition. He did, and even though the story was not selected by the competition committee, it did give Sean a fresh perspective on his writing.

While in the Air Force and stationed in Okinawa, Sean took an old war story from high school and began rewriting it to novel length. At this same time, he started a new horror novel called *Overpass*. Neither work was completed, but their longhand drafts still remain to this day.

After his discharge for the Air Force, Sean pursued fine arts, receiving a BFA in painting in 2002. Even though his focus was mainly on the visual arts, writing was never far from his mind, as he continued to write short stories and essays.

In 2015, Sean decided to take up writing again as a full-time venture. Since 2015, he has written several short stories, novellas, as well as a couple of novel-length works based on a variety of subject matter.